# WORLDSHAPER

## DAW BOOKS PROUDLY PRESENTS THE NOVELS OF EDWARD WILLETT

# WORLDSHAPER

## EDWARD WILLETT

## DAW BOOKS, INC.

**DONALD A. WOLLHEIM, FOUNDER**

375 Hudson Street, New York, NY 10014

**ELIZABETH R. WOLLHEIM**
**SHEILA E. GILBERT**
**PUBLISHERS**

www.dawbooks.com

First Printing, September 2018
1  2  3  4  5  6  7  8  9

*For Robert Ursan, brilliant composer, director, teacher, and friend, who shapes today's world every day through theatre and music, and whose students will shape the world of the future.*

# ACKNOWLEDGMENTS

**IT IS SAID** that imitation is the sincerest form of flattery. Since these acknowledgements will closely imitate the acknowledgements in other of my novels published by DAW, it might seem I am flattering myself—but I hope, rather, this imitation will be seen as flattery of those who, book after book, I find myself acknowledging.

First, and always, my wonderful editor Sheila Gilbert, whose immense experience and skill invariably results in a book much, much better than the one I first submit to her: any remaining weaknesses in plot or characterization are certainly my own.

Second, all the other fine folks at DAW. We speak of the "DAW family," and that is what it feels like, to be published by this fabulous company: to be a part of a family, along with my fellow siblings . . . um, authors.

Third, my agent, Ethan Ellenberg, for the knowledge and assistance he has provided over the years.

Fourth, my family: my amazing, brilliant wife, Margaret Anne Hodges, P. Eng., my astonishing and talented daughter, Alice, and our fine furry black Siberian cat, Shadowpaw, himself a member of the DAW family (Betsy Wollheim picked Shadowpaw out of a litter for us and is herself owned by his Uncle Roscoe). While Shadowpaw cares only that he is appropriately petted and adored, for Margaret Anne and Alice it must sometimes seem a very strange thing, having a husband and father who spends his life making up stories—shaping worlds, to coin a phrase—and as a result, sometimes lives more inside his head than in the present. I am always and forever grateful for their love and support.

And fifth? That would be you, dear reader. I hope you enjoy the world I have shaped for you within this book—and will join me on the journey to many more as the series progresses.

It's going to be a fun ride.

# ONE

**KARL STUMBLED THROUGH** the door, spun, slammed it closed, then slapped his palms against the rusty steel. Blue light crackled across the metal, briefly outlining the KEEP OUT: DANGER sign, faded red paint on white, that hung at eye level.

He rested there for a moment, breathing hard, then straightened and turned to see what kind of world he had entered.

He stood in a dark, rough-hewn tunnel of stone, narrower at the top than at the bottom, shored up by beams of dark wood. A dim light bulb, hanging on a twisted pair of rubber-coated wires, glowed overhead, swaying from the gust of warmer air that had entered this world along with Karl. The swinging bulb cast shifting shadows up and down the walls and across the floor, but he could see well enough to make out two metal rails, spanned by rotting wooden ties, running along a rubble-strewn floor toward the faint outline of another door. The gray light seeping around its edges spoke to him of twilight, though whether morning or evening he did not yet know.

He turned to look at the door he had just closed. On this side, it was made of rusty steel and set in a barrier of corrugated metal. Bits of broken chain scattered the floor beneath it, and a shattered padlock lay near his feet. No lock or chain could hold against the opening of a Portal.

No light spilled from beneath the door, even though he had come through it from the common room of a torch-lit inn. No sound came through it, either, though the inn had been bustling.

The man who had been following him, who had started running through the common room, shoving people out of his way as Karl opened the Portal, had been too slow. By the time he opened the wooden door he had seen Karl pass through, he would find nothing beyond it but the inn's pantry.

That should have been the end of pursuit, but Karl had thought the same when he'd entered the world he'd just fled . . . and somehow the Adversary had followed him into that world, even though he had closed the last Portal behind him exactly as he had closed this one. Which meant, if the man who had been following him was a servant of the Adversary—as he almost certainly was—soon enough the Adversary would come to this Portal, and perhaps force it open as well.

Which meant his time was limited. He needed to find this world's Shaper, see if this one might be strong enough to do what Ygrair required, and if so, convince or coerce him or her to accompany him.

He had no reason to hesitate, and indeed, every reason to hurry, but hesitate he did. He had entered many worlds, yet this one gave him pause. Without taking so much as a second step into it, he knew from the flavor of the air, from the way its gravity tugged at him, from the faint echoes of his breath and movements back from the tunnel's stone walls, that this world was similar . . . very, very similar . . . to the First World, the one from which Ygrair had taken him . . . how long ago had it been?

An old way of thinking, that. Time flowed differently from world to world within the Labyrinth. How could you measure time when some of worlds you visited did not orbit suns, but were orbited by them, or were lit by flaming chariots drawn by fiery flying steeds, or were not lit at all, except by the moon and the strange glow of the eldritch stones that paved their roads and formed the walls of their strange, twisted buildings?

Each world in the Labyrinth was Shaped, to a greater or lesser degree, by a singular imagination. This one had been Shaped less than most, so that it closely resembled the First World—but it was *not* the First World. Just another world in the Labyrinth. Nothing special at all.

He glanced back once more at the metal door. In any event, if the Adversary were able to enter this world as he had the last, it would soon be re-Shaped . . . unless its Shaper was, at last, the one Ygrair had sent him to seek.

He turned away from the closed Portal for good, then, and strode toward the door into the outside. It opened with a push, and he stepped out into the fresh air of a mountain evening. He took a deep breath, enjoying the scent of pine, then looked up at the starry sky. The constellations were the same ones he had seen as a child, lying on his back in the yard of his father's farm, dreaming of the day he would be old enough to leave it. The Earth's great cities had seemed like different worlds to him then, and he had longed to see them all: New York, London, Paris, Berlin.

He'd done it, too, traveling to those and so many more. He'd even created his own worlds, after a fashion, on stage and with his words. But then Ygrair had literally fallen into his life . . . and he had learned just how stunted his understanding of new worlds had been.

*And she has promised,* he thought. *Someday I, too, will have a world to Shape.*

But only if he succeeded at the daunting task she had set him. *Which I had better be about.* Lowering his gaze, he strode into the darkness.

I could feel the coming storm in my bones.

"Can't you guys work any faster?" I called up to the two young men standing on the scaffolding outside my two-story shop/apartment, right in front of my bedroom window. I wondered if I'd remembered to close the blinds. I hoped so, because I'd not only failed to make my bed, I was pretty sure I'd left underwear on it.

Neither one looked at me, probably because they were trying to bolt a big capital W made of brushed steel to the century-old building's worn red bricks. "Don't worry, lady," called down the older of the two, although older in this case meant he'd been shaving for maybe six years, as opposed to three. "Should be done by lunch."

"What's it going to say?" said a voice behind me. I glanced around to see a pixie-ish college-aged girl, blond hair piled up in an oh-so-casual-yet-terminally-cute fashion, with just the right number of stray strands falling across her forehead above her bright blue eyes. She wasn't looking at me, though: she was looking up at the young men, although I wondered whether it was really the sign that had drawn her interest, or the unique view available from this angle of the fit young men in their tight blue jeans. (Not that I'd noticed . . . okay, I'm lying.) The girl held a tall, blue-and-white-checkered paper coffee cup, topped with a bright-red plastic lid, trademark of the Human Bean, half a block away and just around the corner.

"Worldshaper Pottery," I said.

"Kind of long," she said, never taking her eyes off the men. "A lot of letters!" she called up.

"Tell me about it," shouted down the younger of the two. Pretty college girl, he looked at.

"Careful!" the other man snapped, as the W slipped a notch.

The younger man turned and lifted it again. "Sorry, Al!"

"So, you do pottery?" College Girl said to me, though without expending the effort to actually turn her head. "What sorts?"

"All sorts," I said. "Anything in clay. Pots, plates, mugs, vases, cups, saucers. You name it. I have a card, if you're—"

"Cool," she said, in that absentminded tone you use when you're responding to someone whose words just went in one ear and out the other. She sipped more coffee and kept watching the workmen.

I sighed and turned my own gaze west, up the street, toward the distant line of mountains. Their snowcapped peaks, sparkling in the sun in the crisp autumn morning air, were dwarfed by the towering piles of cloud behind them: white on top, a menacing dark blue beneath. I didn't like the look of them one bit. They looked like any other line of storm clouds, but in some weird way, deep inside, they felt . . . *wrong*.

The weird thing was, over the past couple of days the forecast hadn't said a word about a possible storm. It *still* didn't. I'd checked the weather app on my HiPhone half a dozen times that morning: nothing. But then, the forecasters were based more than a hundred miles away in the state capital of Helena, and their inability to accurately predict what would happen in our little city of Eagle River was so well-known that local residents joked about planning their day's activities based on the exact *opposite* of the forecast weather.

What surprised me more than the lack of storm warnings was the fact that no one but me seemed worried. I glanced at College Girl. "Those clouds over the mountains look nasty," I said conversationally. "Don't you think?"

She finally looked at me, then at the mountains, then at me again. She shrugged. "They're just clouds. Anyway, a little rain would be nice." She turned her attention back to the young men.

*A little rain?* I frowned at the mountains. Torrential rain with damaging wind, hail, possible tornadoes, serious lightning, and flash flooding, if I were any judge. In fact, the clouds had risen visibly higher just in the short time I'd stood there, and beneath their white heads and shoulders, their hearts were black as night. *Okay, that might be bit overdramatic*, I thought. I studied the clouds some more, then shook my head. *No, it isn't.* I looked back up at the workmen. "Please hurry!" The guy who had grinned at College Girl finally looked at me, but all I got was a teenaged-boy-to-nagging-mother eye roll.

I was *not* old enough to be his mother. But if I was, I would have grounded him on the spot.

Giving up, I turned to College Girl again. "Want to come in and have a look at the shop? First day open!"

She gave me a perfunctory smile. "Nah, I'm good." She tossed back the last of her coffee, took one more appreciative look at the workmen, then walked on down the street, throwing her cup into a blue recycling bin as she went.

"Come back any time!" I called after her. She raised her left hand and wriggled her fingers, but didn't look around.

Not a great start to my first day in business, but it was early yet. While College Girl and I had been "talking," a dozen other people had hurried past without stopping to look up at the sign or its installers, or (more to the point) into the shop windows. Then again, the scaffolding wasn't doing anything to make the shop look inviting, and anyway, it wasn't even nine o'clock. The people passing weren't shoppers, they were on the way to work. Once the sign was up and the scaffolding gone, no doubt customers would *pour* into Worldshaper Pottery.

*They'd better,* I thought, thinking of the size of my lease. I yawned and rolled my head, trying to ease a kink in the back of my neck. I hadn't slept well for two nights, and the reason why made me turn and survey the people strolling, striding, or—in the case of the teenager looking at her smartphone—stumbling along the cobblestones, between spindly trees, flower planters, and decorative benches.

Worldshaper Pottery had an ideal location—I'd been incredibly lucky to get it—on Blackthorne Avenue, which was pedestrian-only for four blocks. My shop was on the north side of the street at the far west end, half a block from busy 22nd Street (which the Human Bean fronted) and only a block from one of the public parking lots where people visiting the pedestrian mall left their cars while they enjoyed a stroll over the cobblestones. The "Shoppes of Blackthorne Avenue," as the local business association styled itself (apparently there'd been a sale on pretentious silent Es) catered to the artsy foodie crowd: galleries, boutiques, restaurants, brewpubs, and coffee and tea shops. (Sorry, "shoppes.") To paraphrase Ol' Blue Eyes, if I couldn't make it here, I couldn't make it anywhere.

Normally Blackthorne Avenue was deserted in the early morning, once the last of the craft-beer drinkers had headed home. But for the last two nights, it hadn't been.

It had started Sunday night. Brent, my tall, blond, handsome and awesomely fit boyfriend (I know, I know, he sounds like something from a romance novel, but what can I say? I lucked out) had just left, after spending the day helping me set up the workshop. Normally he might have stayed over—normally I'd have *insisted* he stay over—but he'd had to work early the next morning and I was too tired to think straight, my libido as exhausted as I was.

As a result, I was alone when I clawed my way up out of sleep, only to find that I *wasn't* alone, that someone was standing at the foot of my bed, a tall figure, just a shadow barely visible in the darkness of my room, though I could tell it wore a long coat and a broad-brimmed hat. Beneath that hat glinted two cold sparks of light, reflections from the eyes staring down at me. I tried to scream, but could only manage a strangled moan; tried to sit up, but couldn't move a muscle. I could only wait, helpless, for the intruder to do whatever horrible thing he intended . . .

And then he had vanished, and I was *really* awake. I gasped, sat up in bed, and snapped on the lamp on the side table. I touched my HiPhone and it lit to show the time: 3:10 a.m.

There was no one in the room with me. There never *had* been, of course—I knew that. It was just a dream. No, *sleep paralysis*, that's what it was called, where you think you're awake but you can't move and you hallucinate someone standing by your bed—or in some cases, a monster sitting on your chest. I'd read up on it once because I'd experienced it before—not often, but often enough to recognize it.

But this one had seemed, somehow, more *real* than the other incidents I remembered, and so even though I knew it was silly, I got up, pulled on my warm, brown terry cloth bathrobe, and checked the apartment. No one there but me, of course, and the door was locked.

A cool breeze through the open window lifted the curtains. Though I was on the second story, and the window was much too high above the sidewalk for anyone to have climbed through it without a ladder, I decided I'd feel better if it were closed and locked for the rest of the night.

As I reached out to pull it shut, I saw someone standing in the middle of the cobblestoned street, in a shadowed spot ill-lit by the old-timey wrought iron streetlamps: a tall man, wearing a long black duster and a cowboy hat. While neither of those were un-usual apparel in our western town, the sight stopped me cold, hands frozen on the window frame, because I suddenly realized *the figure in my dream had been wearing the same thing.*

The man's head was tilted back. I couldn't see his eyes in the shadows beneath the brim of his hat, but knew without a doubt he was staring straight at me. It didn't feel like his gaze had just been attracted by my silhouette against the bedroom light: it felt like—in fact, I was *certain*—he had been standing there, staring at my window, a long time.

I slammed the window shut, latched it, and scrambled back into my bed, without taking off my robe or turning off the light. I felt like a frightened little girl, and I didn't like it. Questions darted through my mind: *Who is he? What's he doing out there?* And, scariest of all, *How did he get into my dream?*

I didn't believe in ghosts. I didn't believe in ESP. I didn't believe in omens. But I knew what I'd seen, in my night terror and out my window.

I lay there, hardly breathing, every sense straining, listening for—and sometimes imagining—a sound from downstairs. Finally, I couldn't stand it any longer. I got out of bed, turned off the light, crept to the window, split the curtain no more than an inch with my hand, and peered out into the street once more.

The streetlights showed nothing but cobblestones, benches, trees, and planters.

I opened the window and pushed my head out through the curtain so I could look both ways along the street. Nothing moved, except for a cab on 22nd Street, which passed the end of Blackthorne Avenue without slowing.

I closed the window again, let the curtain fall shut, and climbed back into bed. I checked the time. 4:02 a.m. I lay there staring at it, certain I'd be up until daylight . . . but as my adrenaline drained, exhaustion from the day's work flooded back in, and I soon slipped back into sleep.

I woke later than I should have, with another day of preparing the shop for Tuesday's opening ahead of me, this time without Brent's help. I also woke feeling singularly unrested, the night's unease clinging to me all day like stale cigarette smoke.

That night, Brent took me out to dinner, but since he was still on an early-morning work schedule and I was even more exhausted then the previous night, he left my place about ten. I didn't tell him about my dream, or the man in the street. After all, by morning I hadn't been entirely sure I'd really *seen* the man in the street. Maybe I hadn't been as awake as I thought, and he'd been nothing but a slow-to-fade fragment of my nightmare. By the end of the workday I'd pretty much decided I'd imagined the whole thing, and there was no point worrying Brent about a bad dream.

But that night I woke from *another* bad dream, this time one of those dreams that deeply unsettles you, but you can't remember a single detail of the moment you're awake. My HiPhone informed me it was 4:09 a.m. I went to the bathroom. As I returned to bed, I decided—I don't know why—to take another peek out the bedroom window, still closed and latched from the previous night.

The workmen had already erected the scaffolding by then, but it didn't block my view of the man in the duster and cowboy hat, standing in exactly the same dim-lit spot as the night before, once more looking up at my window. With my bedroom light off, I could even see the glint of his eyes in his shadowed face. My hand tightened on the curtain and my heart pounded in my chest.

He couldn't possibly have seen me. But he certainly gave me the impression he could. When he turned and walked away, I scurried back to bed, and this time I *did* lay awake until daylight, listening for the sound of someone at the door.

# TWO

**TWO DAYS AFTER** Karl Yatsar had passed through it, the rusty red door in the abandoned mine tunnel burst open again, with a flash of blue light and a sound like a thunderclap. Like the chain it had replaced, the new chain locking the door shattered, shiny silvery links skittering across the floor and ringing against the metal rails. The single incandescent bulb lighting the tunnel swayed, sending black shadows dancing.

From the flickering torch-lit dimness of the room beyond the door stepped an ordinary-looking young man, of medium height and medium build, his hair and eyes both the same shade of mahogany brown. Like Karl before him, the young man stood in the tunnel and looked around at the rough-hewn stone walls and ceiling, at the twin metal rails stretching to the dim outline of the door at the tunnel's exit. Unlike Karl, he did not turn and close the door through which he had come.

Twelve more people came through the door behind him, eight men and four women. They wore unmarked black military-style uniforms. They carried automatic rifles, along with pistols and knives. The young man did not turn to look at them. Instead he strode toward the tunnel's exit. The armed cadre followed.

Beyond the stone walls, thunder grumbled. A flash of lightning limned the outline of the door at the far end of the tunnel.

The young man strode to that door and pushed it open.

He had another world to conquer.

The workmen arrived far too early the next morning. While they began unloading the letters from their truck, having been given special permission to drive into the pedestrian mall for the purpose, I called my friend Policeman Phil—technically Sergeant Phil Jensen, but we were both from the same small town in Oregon, and I'd known him since junior high. "I think I have a stalker," I said into the phone.

The response was . . . underwhelming: a long silence that somehow also managed to convey disbelief, followed by a sigh. "Is this a joke, Shawna?"

"No!" I said, offended. "Would I joke about something like this?"

"Honestly? Yes. Remember that time in high school when you—"

I cut him off. "Okay, okay. No need to bring up ancient history. But I'm not joking this time. This is an official call to an official police sergeant."

I paused. Silence.

"That would be you," I prompted.

Another sigh. "All right, I'll bite. Why do you think you have a stalker?"

"Because at four o'clock this morning I looked out my bedroom window and saw someone staring up at my apartment," I said. "The same man who was also staring up at my apartment the night before."

The pause this time was shorter. I sensed frowning. You might not think that's possible over the phone, but with someone you've known as long as I've known Policeman Phil, it totally is. "And what did this person look like?"

"Tall. Thin. Wearing a duster and a cowboy hat."

"A duster and a cowboy hat."

"Yes."

"Like how many other guys in Eagle River?"

"It's not my fault my stalker is a walking Western cliché."

Another sigh. "And was he there at the same time the night before?"

"Not quite. The first night it was 3:20 a.m."

"And what made you look out of the window at 3:20 a.m.?" Phil said, a reasonable question I'd rather hoped he wouldn't ask. "Did you hear something?"

"No," I said, reluctantly. "I'd had a bad dream."

"What kind of dream?"

*Drat.* "I dreamed someone was standing at the foot of my bed."

"Someone? What did this someone look like?"

*Double drat.* "Tall. Wearing a long coat, and . . ."

"And a cowboy hat."

"Well . . . maybe."

Phil said, with studied neutrality, "Don't you think it's possible that you simply saw someone passing in the street and projected the bad dream you'd just awakened from onto him?"

"Why was *anyone* out there at 3:20 a.m.?" I countered.

"There's nothing illegal about being a night owl."

"Two nights in a row? Staring up at my room?"

"Maybe he's a bartender heading home after his shift."

"That doesn't explain him staring up at my room."

"Maybe he wasn't. He might have been looking at the stars. Or a bird. Or a plane. Or a satellite."

"Two nights in a row?" I said again, with more heat.

Another pause. Then another sigh. "All right, Shawna. Tell you what: I'll make sure someone keeps an eye on your end of Blackthorne Avenue for a couple of hours tomorrow morning. If we see someone who matches your description, we'll have a chat with him. Best I can do."

I felt a surge of relief. "Thanks, Phil."

"You're welcome. Have a great day, Shawna."

He'd hung up. I'd put down my phone and rubbed my forehead. Then I'd tried to call Brent, but I couldn't get an answer. That wasn't a big surprise. The plumbing company he worked for was involved in the construction of the big—well, big by Eagle River standards, anyway, fifteen whole stories!—office tower downtown, and he was putting in twelve-hour days.

Shortly after I'd talked to Policeman Phil, the workmen had arrived, I'd officially opened the shop for the first time (although the *grand* opening would take place in three weeks, in early November, to cash in on the pre-Christmas rush, and would include a ribbon-cutting by Mayor Fougere, for whom I'd once made a set of plates). Now I needed to do some actual clay-shaping, and standing there watching the boys installing my sign wasn't going to a) make them move any faster or b) accomplish anything else. I took another look at the gathering storm clouds, trying to ease my unease at their steady approach (with no notable success), then ducked under the scaffolding and went inside.

The shop wasn't quite decorated the way I wanted it—I still had some paintings in storage I hadn't wanted to hang while there was a chance they might be damaged, and there were two light fixtures still on order—but it didn't look bad: bright and cheery, with glass shelves artfully (I hoped) displaying a selection of my wares. An arch behind the counter gave a clear view of the workshop: people like getting a glimpse of the potter at the wheel. Lots of people like potters. Especially hairy ones. (Sorry. Although if I were more hirsute, I would *totally* have named my shop The Hairy Potter.)

The work I needed to get to was an order for two dozen coffee mugs for Carter Truman, manager of the Human Bean, of a design

I'd created just for him: fully glazed on the inside, but only glazed for an inch and a half, from the rim down, on the outside. The unglazed stoneware exterior of the mug's main body acted as an insulator, keeping hot drinks hotter longer. On each mug, I incised the smiling-coffee-bean logo of the shop. What with the move from my old rented clay studio into my spiffy new digs, I was behind, and I didn't want to let Carter down—he'd been a good customer for years.

I went into the workshop, which was unnervingly clean, since I hadn't really used it yet, though soon enough it would be covered with a homey layer of fine gray dust. I hadn't done more than slice a chunk of clay from a new slab when the bell over the front door jingled, announcing a customer.

I wiped my hands on my apron and hurried out into the shop. "Can I—" I began, then stopped. "You're not a customer!" I said accusingly.

The young man who had just entered laughed, and ran a hand through his dirty-blond hair. "I could be," he said. "I'm looking for a present for my girlfriend. What do you think she'd like?"

"Not pottery," I said. "*Anything* but pottery." I went around the counter and gave Brent a quick hug and kiss, both of which he returned enthusiastically, then leaned back, my arms around his neck. "Why aren't you at work?"

"I am," Brent said. "Sort of. Mr. Kapusianyk asked me to pick up something from the NatEx depot, and 'as long as you're down there, grab me a coffee at the Human Bean.'" He mimicked his boss's distinctive Eastern European accent perfectly. "NatEx is a block that way," Brent nodded to the right, "and the Human Bean is around the corner that way," he nodded to the left, "so I'm in transit. I parked behind NatEx, so I've already put the package in the car. Good thing, too: it weighed a ton."

"And here you are stealing from your employer's time to pay your girlfriend a visit," I said. "Naughty."

"Not as naughty as I'd like," Brent said ruefully. "I can't steal *that* much time."

I laughed.

He grinned. "Anyway," he continued, "Mr. Kapusianyk won't mind. Pretty sure he had a hunch I'd be stopping in."

"I'm glad you did," I said, the smile slipping away from my face as I remembered my early-morning visitor.

Brent clearly saw it go, because his own grin faded. "What's wrong?"

I told him what had happened, two nights in a row now, and about my phone call to Policeman Phil. His face clouded with anger, which made me oddly happy. "I'll stay here tonight," he growled. "If he shows up again . . ."

I gave him another hug. "Thanks," I said into his shoulder. Then I pulled back, reluctantly; his body was warm and inviting. "But it's not necessary. You've got the Talons game, and then you'll have to take your dad home, and you have to get up early for work. Phil said he'd have a cop keep an eye on the street. I'll be fine. Anyway, he probably won't show up with that storm coming."

Brent blinked at me. "Storm?"

I sighed. "Not you, too. Yes, storm. Huge clouds. Black underneath. Coming from the mountains."

He frowned. "I haven't heard anything about a storm on the radio. And it plays all the time while we're working."

"You know how bad their forecasts are." I untangled myself from him and tugged at his hand. "Come on, let's head to the Human Bean, and I'll show you."

"Sure."

He waited while I went back into the studio, pulled off my apron, and covered the clay I'd just cut with plastic wrap so it wouldn't dry out. I came out again, and he followed me to the front door of the shop. "By the way, I don't like the looks of those guys on the scaffolding," he said as I paused to switch the LED sign in the window from OPEN to BACK SOON. "They make a move on you?"

"I'm too old for them."

"You just turned twenty-nine."

"And they're like, twelve." I opened the door, ushered him out onto the sidewalk, closed and locked the door behind us, then led him out onto the cobblestones of the pedestrian mall so I could turn around and see how the "twelve-year-olds" were doing. They'd made it all the way to the D, although at the moment it was hanging sidewise, so it looked like a goofy grin. I looked west again. The clouds now covered a third of the sky, and the mountains had vanished in their shadow and behind a wall of rain. "See?" I said to Brent. "Storm."

He followed my pointing finger, looked for a minute, then shrugged. "If you say so. Just a few clouds. Doesn't look very threatening to me. Nothing to interfere with the big game, at least." He looked back at me. "If you're worried about this guy in the street, you could come with me. Dad would understand."

"No, he wouldn't, not really," I said. "And anyway, you know I don't like lacrosse." I took another look at the black clouds. *Just a few clouds?* Had everyone gone blind? I shook my head, and started walking again.

Brent fell in beside me. "Millions disagree with you."

"I know." Eagle River didn't quite have 80,000 people, but there would be 30,000 in the stadium that night for the hometown Talons' first-round playoff game against the Winnipeg Pooh-Bears. Millions more would watch on television. "Would you *really* give me a ticket and tell your dad to stay home?" I said. "He'd kill you."

Brent laughed. "Probably."

"Well, sweet of you to ask. But you knew I'd say no."

"Of course I did. But this way I get boyfriend points for asking, and son points for taking my dad. Win-win!"

I laughed.

Now, if Brent had offered to take me to a moonball game, it would have been different, but since there were only six teams, one each from the Indian, Chinese, Russian, British, Japanese, and American colonies, and all games took place on Luna, only the filthy rich could afford to attend the games in person. Prices on round-trip tourist excursions to the moon were falling every year, but they'd have to fall a lot farther before they landed in my price range, or Brent's.

Kite-fighting was fun, too, but we only had a college team. Still, Brent and I had taken in a few matches—his dad didn't care for the sport.

"Is your sign going to be up today?" Brent said as we walked.

"I hope so. It's a lot of letters." I didn't say anything more about the approaching storm that nobody else seemed worried about. Maybe I was overreacting. But as we reached the corner, I took another good look at the black shadows beneath those slowly approaching clouds, and saw a flicker of lightning.

No, I really didn't think so.

We turned right onto 22nd Street. Ahead of us a half dozen round metal tables, painted in primary colors, dotted the sidewalk, with folding wooden chairs in the same bright shades arranged around them. About half were occupied by guys in suits and women in business dresses, and the other half by old guys with ponytails, wearing sandals and tie-dyed shirts, and women in flowing flower-printed dresses and floppy hats. It was that kind of town. (Cowboys like my early-morning visitor didn't go in for fancy coffee shops much.)

The window to our right boasted the same goofily grinning

cartoon coffee bean I'd soon be cutting into clay, although the one in the window also had stick legs and arms, and held an oversized coffee mug. Curly tendrils of steam rose from the mug, spreading to form the words "HUMAN BEAN." Underneath the cartoon, on blackboard, was the day's coffee *bon mot*: "God is a coffee drinker— He must be, to get all that work done in six days."

I took Brent's hand again. "Can you sit for a bit?" I asked. "Once we have our coffee?"

Brent squeezed my fingers. "I wish. But I really am just in transit. Also, I'm parked in a loading zone, and you know how . . . *enthusiastic* . . . the meter readers are around here." He nodded down the street, where a guy in a bright-yellow vest was slipping a piece of paper under a pink Cornwallis PeoplePod's windshield wiper.

I laughed. "I think they work on commission." We passed under the shadow of Human Bean's striped awning. Inside were more tables, the counter, and, at the far end, a small stage where bands of . . . let's say, *diverse* levels of musical ability . . . played some evenings. In fact, there was a band due that night, something called the DNA Eruptions. Which sounded messy. But I'd probably check them out anyway, since even a band of dubious quality beat sitting in my apartment binge-watching anime on StreamPix.

Besides, there was a good chance my best friend, Aesha Tripathi, would be free: we were having lunch together (also at the Human Bean, pretty much my home away from home) and I'd ask her then if she wanted to join me that evening. She'd just broken up with her boyfriend, an aspiring actor who had discovered he was gay during rehearsals for a Fringe show. (Well, that was the way *he* told it.) And in the evening, the Human Bean served beer (Moose Drool Brown Ale—my favorite!) as well as coffee. We could get comfortably sloshed together and stagger back to my place. And *then* we'd binge-watch anime on StreamPix.

Carter Truman, the ex-professional lacrosse player who ran the Human Bean, grinned as he saw us approaching the counter, white teeth flashing in his lean black face. "Ah, my favorite couple," he said. "Don't usually see you this time of day!"

"Serendipity," Brent said. "I just happened to have business at the post office, and look who I just happened to run into when I just happened to go into her shop."

"Every day the world is full of amazing happenings," said Carter. "The usual?"

"Large triple-sweet fat mocha latte for me," Brent said. "Large skinny latte for my boss."

I had felt myself gain five pounds just listening to the name of Brent's preferred obscene concoction. "And for me," I said primly, "medium French roast. No room."

Brent and I looked at each other. "I don't know how you can drink that stuff," we said, in unison, an old joke, and Carter laughed again as he rang up the bill.

"Irreconcilable differences," he said. "Are you certain the two of you are really cut out for each other?"

I leaned my head against Brent's arm. "We'll work through it," I said.

Brent touched his cheek to my scalp. "We agree on the important things. 'Life's too short to drink bad wine.' 'A fool and his money make great drinking companions.' That sort of thing."

Carter's grin flashed across his face again, and he turned away to work on our drinks. We moved to one side to let the people behind us reach the counter, where Carter's place had been taken by Chloe, one of the endless series of interchangeable teenage baristas the Human Bean employed.

The door opened. A blast of cool air ruffled my hair and blew napkins off the cream-and-sugar counter. Startled, I glanced out the big front windows. A dust devil whirled past, bits of trash caught in the vortex . . .

. . . and beyond it, on the far side of the street, stood a man in a long black duster, face shaded by a cowboy hat, the wind whipping the hem of the coat around his high black boots.

# THREE

PUSHING THROUGH THE door at the end of the mine tunnel, the ordinary-looking young man found himself in a large compound, surrounded on three sides by a chain-link fence, with the steep slope of the mountain behind him forming the fourth side. To his right tottered the rusty remnants of an ancient minehead. Ahead, close to the fence's only gate, he saw a small house, its walls made of peeled logs. Even as he looked at it, a door opened, and an old man in a blue uniform came out, a shotgun in his hand.

The armed cadre emerged from the tunnel behind the young man. The old man saw them and stopped in his tracks. He turned to rush back into the cabin, but took only two steps before he stopped again.

The young man and his dozen followers strode forward. The young man spoke to the old man. He learned the old man was a retired policeman whose main function was to chase amorous and/or curious teenagers away from the abandoned mine site. He learned that the old man had no memory of anyone else coming out of the mine, although he did remember having to replace the chain locking the inner door. He also learned that, two days before, the old man had mysteriously misplaced an old black duster he favored, along with a cowboy hat with a rattlesnake-skin band, which his father had given him when he was a teenager. "Probably some tramp," he growled to the young man. "I try to keep the fence in repair, but the ground shifts, and sometimes a bear takes an interest in something on this side of the fence, and tears a hole right through it. Not that I saw anything like that, but still—"

"That's enough," the young man told him, and he fell silent.

Soon after, the old man was making phone calls on behalf of the young man. By early afternoon, two white panel vans and accompanying drivers had arrived. The drivers were full of questions that died away the moment the young man spoke to them. After that, they were quietly obedient.

"What do we call you, sir?" one of the drivers said to him. "What's your name? If you don't mind my asking."

"My name changes as I need it to change," the young man said. "If you must call me something, call me by . . . what I suppose you could call my title."

"Sir?"

"Call me the Adversary."

"Yes . . . Adversary."

As dusk fell, the Adversary sat in a camp chair and closed his eyes. As his cadre, the drivers, and the old man ate and found places in and around the cabin to sleep, he remained motionless.

Night came, a dark night, the stars blotted out by swirling, boiling clouds that somehow remained in one tight swirling mass above the Portal, flashes of lightning occasionally lighting their twisting shapes. Still the Adversary sat.

He did not move until long after midnight, though there were still hours to go until the dawn. His eyes flicked open. He looked up at the lightning-riven clouds. Thunder rumbled, as though in response to his gaze. Then he stood, stretched, yawned, and entered the house. In the kitchen, he found cold chili congealing in a pot on the stove, and ate it with a spoon he found in a nearby drawer. He found a can of beer in the refrigerator, and downed it.

His sleeping bag had already been spread for him by one of his cadre. He lay down in it.

He closed his eyes.

Just before sleep claimed him, a small smile played around his lips.

Ice-blue eyes stared at the Human Bean—stared at *me*, though I must have been invisible from the sunlit street—and never wavered, even as cars, a city bus, and a semi passed between us.

My heart raced, accelerated by remembered terror from my sleep paralysis of two nights before. I tugged at Brent's arm. "Brent, it's—"

But the stranger was gone. Another truck had passed, and just like that, he had vanished.

Brent looked down at me. "What?"

*I saw the man again*, I started to say. *From the middle of the night. From my dream.* But he wasn't there now, there was no sign he had ever been there, and it suddenly seemed that saying anything about what I had just seen would be more likely to make me sound crazy than anything else. "Nothing. Forget it."

Brent frowned and opened his mouth to reply, but my coffee and his mocha-bomb and his boss's latte all arrived, and the moment passed. He picked up his and his boss's cups, glanced at his watch (carefully, so he didn't spill the coffee down his shirt), and said, "Well, gotta get back. Sorry I can't sit and chat."

I pecked him on the cheek. "Later," I said. "We'll chat. Among other things."

The corner of his mouth flicked up in the half smile I loved so much. "Deal." He raised a hand, and then turned and went out into the street, where the wind had died as quickly as it had risen moments before.

I picked up my own coffee and glanced at my own watch. Lunch with Aesha was still three hours away. Still plenty of time to get some work done. Besides the mugs I owed Carter, there was a craft show coming up at the Eagle River Arts Center's Fall Fair in a month, and I had to have stock for my table. I did a lot of sales through craft shows—though not as many as I hoped to do through my shop—and I didn't have much in hand. I'd have to work like a fiend to get ready.

Not that I minded. I loved shaping . . .

The thought died as I looked up from my watch, and saw the man in the duster and cowboy hat outside the window, now on my side of the street. For some reason, I registered a detail I hadn't noticed before: the hat had a snakeskin band around it.

Our eyes met. Most strangers look away when their gaze meets yours, but not him. Of course, *I* could have looked away . . . but I didn't either, even though the eye contact felt so invasive that my hand clutched the top of my plaid flannel shirt without my even thinking about it.

Then he turned and walked out of sight.

Maybe if I'd run to the door, I could have seen where he went, but I couldn't seem to move. I tried to remember what he'd looked like, so I could tell Brent and Phil the Policeman, but all I'd really registered were those eyes: bright, piercing blue, like polished sapphire.

I felt a chill that had nothing to do with the approaching storm or the Human Bean's air conditioning, and took a sip of coffee to warm up. Except, of course, it was *too* hot, and I felt the familiar burn that meant my tongue would feel funny for the rest of the day. Annoyed, I pressed the scalded tip to the back of my teeth, gathered my wits, and headed for the door.

I looked right as I stepped into the street, the direction in which the stranger had disappeared, but he was nowhere to be seen. *Must have gone into another shop*, I thought, but it still left me with a funny feeling. Like the oncoming storm that no one else seemed worried about, something about the stranger felt *wrong*. Out of place. Like he didn't belong here.

When I got back to my own shop, the two young men on the scaffolding were just finishing the S. I looked at the clouds above the mountains. They seemed to have stalled, filling perhaps a third of the sky. Not as a good a sign as you might think: that potentially meant a slow-moving storm, building and building over the peaks before it finally rushed down over the foothills into the city, the kind of storm that wouldn't just hit and blow out in short order, but would clobber us for hours.

Another chilly gust of wind blew down the street. I looked back up at the young men. "How much longer?"

"We've got the 'hang' of them now," the older of the two said, which was a lame pun but not an answer, and also didn't fill me with confidence, since one would generally hope that the people attaching heavy metal letters to old bricks above the entrance to one's shop had the hang of it *before* they were almost halfway through the process.

I sighed again and went inside, where I wouldn't worry as much and couldn't see those disturbing clouds. I reset the LED window sign to OPEN and then headed into the studio. I pulled on my apron, uncovered the chunk of clay I'd sliced just before Brent showed up, slapped it onto my plaster slab, and kneaded it until there were no air bubbles. I filled a plastic bowl with water and set it beside the wheel. Then I tossed the clay into the center of the wheel, shaped it roughly with dry hands, started the wheel spinning, dipped my hands into the water, and set to work. As always, the feel of the clay beneath my fingers, the near-magical, sensual way it rose from an amorphous blob to become something beautiful, calmed and centered me.

When I was eight years old, our third-grade class took a field trip to a pottery. Each of us was given the opportunity to try it, and I'd been obsessed with it ever since. Every time I put a slab of clay on the table or wheel, I felt a humbling sense of awe at the infinite possibilities inherent in that pliable material, so organic to my touch. On the wheel, the clay slips endlessly, almost effortlessly, from shape to shape beneath my fingers, as though it exists in a strange quantum state, neither one thing nor another until I make the decision to collapse its infinite possibilities into a single (hopefully beautiful) reality.

Which admittedly sounds a little high-falutin' when you're making something like coffee mugs with a goofy anthropomorphized coffee bean on the side, but art is one thing, making a living is another. And anyway, I *liked* making mugs. By the time my phone chimed an alarm to remind me of my lunch appointment with Aesha, I'd thrown ten, and put them aside to set up a bit before I added the handles. The area around the wheel had already started to collect that nice layer of clay dust I was used to.

I stretched, took off my apron, went out into the store . . . and caught just a glimpse, out on the sidewalk under the scaffolding, of someone stepping out of my sight, someone in a long black duster. My breath caught, and then I felt a surge of anger. This had gone beyond creepy to frightening, and it had to *stop*. I ran to the door, threw it open, and stormed out onto the sidewalk. I looked left, but the only person in sight was a gray-haired woman with a cane, hobbling as quickly she could down the cobblestoned street, which I suddenly realized glistened with rain.

I stepped out into the drizzle to examine the sky. To the east, a band of blue still glowed, but gray soup covered the city, and to the west . . . to the west, it was almost black. Lightning flashed, and a few seconds later, thunder grumbled. The wind swirled and gusted, as though uncertain which way to blow or how hard, though I had a feeling it would make up its mind with a vengeance soon. I strode to the middle of the street, then turned and looked up at my sign.

"WORLDSHAPER POT," it read, which was likely to attract (and then peeve) a completely different set of customers than the ones I sought. It was also likely to annoy the marijuana shop five doors down, who'd think I was horning in on their business. Just four letters left to mount, and there they were, still stacked atop the scaffolding, but there was no sign of the young men or their tools. They'd clearly abandoned the task in light of the approaching storm, which *nobody* could deny now. I just hoped they'd had securely fastened the letters they *had* managed to install. My neighbors wouldn't appreciate it if they found a P or a T or an H inside their shattered front windows.

*It's just a storm*, I told myself. *It's not a hurricane. Nobody else was worried about it.*

On the other hand, nobody else had even seemed to be able to see it coming. And certainly no one else seemed to feel the strange . . . *disturbance in the Force*, to steal a phrase . . . that I did.

I felt discombobulated (a word I don't think I'd ever before had occasion to use). But between the nightmare and the multiple encounters with the weirdo in the hat and duster—it occurred to me at that moment he might be a flasher, but if he was, I wished he'd hurry up and show me whatever he was so proud of so I could laugh and move on—not to mention the approaching storm, "discombobulated" seemed to the be the only word that fit.

"Worldshaper Pot," said a voice behind me, making me jump. "You didn't tell me you were branching out."

I laughed then, and turned to face my best friend. "Anything for a buck when you're self-employed. As you should know."

Aesha was a head shorter than me, so petite—"elfin" was the word that always came to mind—that she got carded at bars, even though she'd turned thirty a year ago. A freelance writer, she'd self-published a couple of fantasy novels through Orinoco Direct, to no noticeable acclaim, but made a pretty comfortable living writing corporate histories, annual reports, and magazine articles, plus doing freelance editing for a big self-publishing firm. She'd promised to write a history of Worldshaper Pottery for its fiftieth anniversary. She'd be eighty by then, and I'd be next door to it, but I had every intention of holding her to her word.

She worked out of her apartment just a couple of blocks from my studio, another reason I'd been thrilled to find this location: we could have lunch together whenever we wanted, like today.

She looked up at the gathering storm. A flash of lightning lit her dark-skinned face, glinting off the jeweled stud in her right ear. "Might get wet if we don't get moving."

"We'll get poured on anyway once lunch is over," I pointed out. "This isn't just a thunderstorm that's going to blow over."

She looked at me. "What makes you say that? Doesn't look bad to me."

"Doesn't . . ." I bit off my retort. To me, it looked like a tornado could pop out of the clouds at any moment. *Discombobulation.* "Well, damp, at least." I felt like an evangelical vegan at a Texas barbecue, or the weirdo who demands tea—or worse, hot chocolate—when the waiter comes around with coffee. Whenever I spoke the truth as I saw it, that the storm approaching looked like a monster, people looked at me like I was crazy—even though it was clear to me that *they* were the crazy ones. Rather than insist, I pretended to fit in. *Wimp.* But I really didn't want to argue with Aesha, any more than I'd wanted to argue with Brent.

"Well, if you're scared of a little drizzle, we'll have no choice but to linger over a second glass of wine." Aesha grinned. "Or a third. Or . . ."

I laughed. "We could just stay through the evening. I was going to ask you to join me for dinner, too. We can check out the DNA Eruptions."

"The nerd-grunge band?" Aesha made a face. "I've heard them.

We'd be better off getting soaked. I don't think I can take another rendition of 'Vasopressin Depression.' The drum solo is five minutes long."

"They live up to the awfulness of their name?"

"And then some. Their other big 'hits' are 'Tess Tossed the Roan,' which *involves* a horse but isn't really about one, and 'Estrogenesis,' which is even worse."

I laughed again. "Well, we'd better get moving, either way."

Cold rain spattered our faces as we headed down the street into the teeth of the rising wind. I grimaced and glanced at Aesha—who didn't seem to be noticing. *I am not a wimp*, I thought, but I added disgruntlement to my discombobulation.

We walked to the corner. Just as we were about to turn onto 22nd Street, something caught my eye. Maybe ten blocks up Blackthorne, where the street rose to crest a small hill, a white van had just appeared. A second followed it. They were heading our way, and they were traveling fast—too fast. Cars swerved out of their way. They ran a red light, and I saw a car rear-end a pickup truck that squealed to a halt to avoid them.

"What the hell?" Aesha might be unfazed by the approaching storm, but not the approaching vans. "Police?"

"No sirens, no lights," I said. A shiver ran down my spine that had nothing to do with the rain. *Something is very, very wrong.* "Let's get into the Bean."

"I think you're right," Aesha said. She ran, and I ran after her. As we dashed under the Bean's awning I heard squealing tires behind us, and twisted my head around to see the vans rounding the corner. Aesha grabbed my hand. "Hurry!"

We burst into the Human Bean. The vans screeched to a halt on the street outside. Everyone looked up at us, lunches interrupted. I caught the wide-eyed gaze of Rinaldo Fiorante, who ran the music shop across the street and was largely responsible for booking the acts that performed in the Bean. (Even in that moment I wondered if the DNA Eruptions had been his idea.) Then his eyes flicked past me, and I spun to see the van doors sliding open. Men and women, clad in black, faces hidden, burst out. They carried automatic weapons.

The screaming began.

Some people jumped under their tables, others leaped up, sending tables and chairs tumbling. Glasses of water, cups of coffee, kale salads, and plates of fish and chips and avocado toast skittered across the hardwood floor. The baristas dove behind the counter. I threw myself behind one of the couches that faced the stage. Aesha stood frozen. I screamed her name.

The black-clad figures opened fire.

Bullets tore through the couch above my head, showering me with singed horsehair. They cut through one of the legs of the grand piano, which crashed to the stage with a sad clanging discord. They scored a bull's-eye on the dartboard on the wall by the door leading to the bathrooms. They exploded the giant brass cappuccino machine in a spray of steam and water and coffee grounds.

They tore through Aesha's tiny body.

One second she was Aesha, my best friend, standing frozen in terror. The next she was a bloody mass of meat and shattered bone splayed across the gore-stained floor.

Blood misted the air, covered me in a sticky scarlet layer. Others must have died, but Aesha was the only one I *saw* die, right in front of me.

I'd had no time to react, to feel anything but shock. I stared at what was left of my best friend. Denial welled up inside me. *This can't be happening. This can't be happening. This can't be happening . . .*

A man came around the end of the couch. He wore black, and carried a pistol: otherwise he was a very ordinary-looking man, with brown hair and brown eyes. He looked down at me. "Hello, Shawna," he said. "And good-bye." Then he reached out and touched my forehead.

I felt something like a massive static electric shock, but deeper, invasive, violating, a shock that reached deep into my mind and made my body shudder. I jerked back, scrabbling away from the man, my buttocks smearing a track across the bloody floor. The man, expressionless, raised his pistol and pointed it at me, and I knew I was about to die.

In that instant, *this can't be happening* turned to *this isn't happening.*

"This isn't happening!" I screamed it in the face of that impossible killer. "*This isn't happening!*"

The world . . . twisted. I suddenly sensed it in a way I never had before, as though it were a giant machine whose gears and pulleys and chains and wheels had been hidden from view until that moment, as though I had opened a secret door, reached inside, yanked a lever, shifted those gears, reset those pulleys, tugged on those chains, spun those wheels to a new configuration.

And then . . .

I was right where I had been, sitting on my rear end on the wooden floor of the Human Bean . . . but there was no blood on that floor, on the walls, or on me. The grand piano stood undamaged. The sofa, seedy as ever, had only its usual moth-eaten holes in it, none caused by bullets. A dart thudded into the dartboard I had seen blown apart. The cappuccino machine hissed, but only because a barista was filling an order.

Aesha had vanished.

# FOUR

**THE ADVERSARY STOOD** very still, pistol still in hand, eyes flicking around the highway rest stop. The ten men and women of his cadre who currently accompanied him (two, a married pair, remained on guard at the Portal) were settling in at the picnic tables, opening their backpacks to take out rations and canteens. The drivers of the white vans stood between the vehicles, conversing. To the west, black clouds boiled up into the sky, swelling with every minute. Lightning flickered beneath them.

After they had eaten, checked their weapons and ammunition, and gone over the plan of attack one last time, they would board the white vans again. They would race ahead of the storm, arriving in Eagle River just before it struck. He could already sense the Shaper, thanks to the creative energy that had entered this world through the Portal from the last he had been in, and that he controlled: that energy clashed with the Shaper's, creating a spark, like flint against steel. As they neared her, that spark would grow brighter in his mind, and he would be able to pinpoint her location. They would find her, and he would take from her mind her *hokhmah*, her knowledge of the making of this world. And then he would kill her. After that, this world would be his to Shape.

Everything was ready.

But they had *already* eaten, and checked their weapons, and boarded the vans, and driven ahead of the storm into the city. He had already pinpointed the location of the Shaper, in a crowded coffee shop. They had already attacked, without warning and without mercy. He had seen her, cowering on the blood-spattered floor. He had recognized her from the First World, called her by name, touched her. He had stolen her *hokhmah*. He had raised his pistol to kill her and own it forever . . .

. . . and now he was here.

He was here, and it had been noon, and now it was once again morning.

The members of his cadre had stopped digging through their packs. They stared around in amazement, voices rising in confused discussion. They were not of this world any more than he was, and their minds could not be Shaped by its Shaper. But the drivers, staring at the cadre in befuddlement, *were* of this world. They remembered nothing of what had just happened, because for them, it never had.

Captain Arneson, the cadre commander, a burly black man who towered over the Adversary, approached. "Sir? What just happened?"

"The Shaper has Shaped this world again," the Adversary said.

"But . . . you touched her."

"I did," the Adversary said. "This world's *hokhmah* now dwells within me. But she Shaped us back to this time before I could kill her. It still dwells in her, as well."

"We killed . . ."

"Those who were dead are still dead. She has not really reset time. She has merely added in three hours to make it seem as if she has reset time."

"Yes, sir," Captain Arneson said. Though he clearly did not understand, it was just as clear that he was satisfied knowing that the Adversary did. Captain Arneson was always dutiful, loyal, and trusting toward the Adversary, just as he had been Shaped to be.

"The interesting question, Captain," the Adversary said, looking at the dwindling strip of blue sky in the east, "is whether she remembers what she has done. Has she somehow Shaped her own memories? Although I would have thought that impossible . . . in any event, I do not think she did this consciously. I think it was a reflex." He frowned. "A powerful one, though. She clearly has a vast amount of energy still remaining—far more than the Shaper in the last world. She is almost as powerful as I was in my . . . our . . . world."

"Surely not, sir," Captain Arneson said.

A brief smile flickered across the Adversary's face. "You're right, Captain. Surely not." The smile disappeared. "Karl Yatsar will not have been fooled by this time-skip, but he will surely be as impressed by its power as I am. We must act quickly."

"Yes, sir," Captain Arneson said. "Orders?"

"Mount up. We're heading in again."

"Yes, sir." Arneson snapped a salute, then turned and started shouting at the other members of the cadre. They stuffed their rations back into their packs, snatched up their weapons, and headed for the vans. The confused drivers climbed in behind the wheels and started the engines.

The Adversary boarded last, climbing into the passenger seat of the lead van, the pistol once more in the holster on his belt. He gave the driver a brisk nod, and they rolled smoothly away.

Lightning flashed, and rain sluiced across the van's windshield and spattered on the road as the leading edge of the storm caught them. The driver turned on the windshield wipers. Aside from their rhythmic swish and slap, the hum of the tires and the roar of the wind, the only sound within the van was the metallic click of weapons being locked and loaded.

"Are you all right?" Brent hurried around the end of the couch and dropped to his knees beside me. He looked frightened. He touched my forehead, just as the black-clad assassin had, and I jerked back from him. His eyes widened. "Shawna?"

I stared at him. I couldn't understand how he could be there. "What . . . ?"

"You fell. Did you faint? Did you hit your head?"

"I . . ." My voice trailed off. I didn't know what to say. I felt . . . exhausted, physically drained, as if I had just run a marathon (not that I would ever do anything that silly). Had I had a stroke? "What . . ." That word died, too. "What are you doing here?" I managed at last.

"Don't you remember?" He took my face in his hands, looking at my eyes, gaze flicking from one to the other. "Your pupils look normal . . ."

I grabbed his wrists and jerked his arms down. "*What are you doing here?*" I cried. Other people in the coffee shop turned to look at us. I didn't care.

"Shawna . . ." Brent sat back on his heels. "Don't you remember? My boss sent me downtown to pick up something from NatEx, and to get him a cup of coffee. I came by your shop, we walked here, ordered. While we were waiting for my drink, you walked this way—I thought you were going to the bathroom—and then you just . . . fell over."

"But . . . but . . . but that was hours ago," I spluttered. "This *morning*. It's lunchtime. What are you doing here *now*?"

"Shawna," Brent said slowly, "It's only a little after nine."

"What?" I stared at him. "No. It's lunchtime. I came here for lunch, with Aesha . . ."

*Aesha.*

"Have you seen her?" I struggled to my feet, my strange weariness dragging at me. Brent tried to help, but I pushed his hands away. I stared around the Human Bean. "Where did she go?"

"Aesha? Was that the name?" Brent looked around. "I don't know her. What does she look like?"

I spun on him, suddenly angry. "I'm in no mood for jokes! Have you seen her or not?"

Brent looked genuinely confused. It only made me angrier. "Shawna, I'm not joking. Why would I be? I don't know an Aesha. Is she a friend of yours?"

My anger suddenly crumbled into the beginning of fear. "Aesha," I said, carefully, clearly, as though speaking to someone hard of hearing. "Aesha Tripathi. My best friend. Tiny. Beautiful. East Indian. We had dinner together last Friday at the Canard Noir. You ordered salmon, she ordered vegetarian linguini, I had steak. Remember?"

"We had dinner at the Canard Noir on Friday," Brent said, just as carefully. "I had salmon, you ordered steak. Nobody ordered linguini, vegetarian or otherwise. It was just you and me. No one else."

I stared at him. He looked back at me, his face gently puzzled, warmly concerned. Fear and bewilderment twisted back to anger. "Are you telling me," I said, and I could hear my voice going high and tight, and knew I was getting looks from other patrons again (and still didn't care), "that you don't know who Aesha Tripathi is?"

"Shawna . . ." he said pleadingly.

*"Is that what you're saying?"*

Brent took a deep breath. "Shawna, I don't know what this is all about, but no, I've never met, or even *heard* of, anyone named Aesha Tripathi." He took my hand in his. "Let's go back to your shop and . . ."

I snatched my hand free. I turned toward the counter. Carter Truman was watching us closely, clearly as concerned by my apparently unprovoked collapse as Brent had been. I strode around the end of the sofa. "Shawna, are you all right?" Carter said as I approached. "That was frightening."

"I'm fine," I said impatiently. "Carter, did you see where Aesha went?" *Did you see a bunch of masked terrorists burst in here and start gunning people down?* was what I wanted to ask, but I still had *some* sense of self-preservation, and even more sense that something had gone horribly, horribly wrong with my world.

Carter blinked, his face bearing the same look of confusion and concern as Brent's. "Who?"

"She comes in here every day," I said, trying to keep my voice calm and level . . . and not quite succeeding: it shook. "Usually with me." In fact, she was such a regular she didn't even have to order: her coffee just appeared in front of her, strong and black, the way she liked it—the same way *I* liked it—two seconds after she walked through the door.

In fact, now that I thought about it, Aesha had been coming to the Human Bean longer than *Carter,* since she had already been a regular way back when it was called The Caffeine Castle, its walls were painted to look like brick, it was lit by fake torches and candles, and it offered drinks like Crenellation Cappuccino, Trebuchet Tea, and, in the evening, the ever-popular Motte & Bailey Mocha, a chocolate-flavored concoction which, the locals joked (which I knew because *Aesha had told me*), contained so much Bailey's it could induce anyone to lower their "drawers-bridge."

Carter looked bemused. "Doesn't ring a bell . . ."

"That's insane." *Or I am.* I spun, eyes flicking here and there around the familiar space. The Bean looked the same as always, except . . .

Except it had been full of people eating lunch, and now it was full of people on their morning coffee break. And the clock behind the counter . . . showed 9:06. The same time it had been when I had come in with Brent for coffee . . . *three hours ago.*

I looked for other differences besides the obvious one that the Human Bean was no longer splattered with blood, or filled with smoke and screams and corpses. Two of the college-age kids behind the counter were completely different from the familiar ones who had been there five minutes before. "New staff?" I said, pointing.

Carter looked even more puzzled. "No—they've worked here for months."

*That's it,* I thought. *I've gone insane.*

But I couldn't have imagined Aesha.

*Wait . . .*

My HiPhone had to have a hundred photos of Aesha on it. I dug it out of the front left pocket of my jeans ("Don't carry it so close to your ovaries," I could hear my mother saying as I did so, but where else was I going to carry it?). I turned it on, gave it my thumbprint, opened the Pictures app, scrolled through them . . .

My heart pounded in my chest as I stared at the impossible. The photos I remembered taking of Aesha were there—from the seawall in Seattle, on top of Tunnel Mountain in Banff—but Aesha *wasn't.* In every picture, where Aesha used to stand, another woman had taken her place. I recognized her as Polly Anderson, a friend from art school I hadn't seen in six years.

Except, clearly, I had. Not only seen her, but traveled with her, to all the places I remembered traveling to with Aesha. Taken selfies with her . . . the same selfies I remembered taking with Aesha. The proof was in my hand.

It just wasn't in my brain.

*This can't be happening,* I thought . . . but this time, the world did not change around me.

"Shawna," Brent said from behind me. "I really think I should take you to the hospital . . ."

"No." I didn't turn around, just kept staring at the phone, furious with it, with him, with all of them. "Just . . . go back to work. Take your stupid boss his stupid coffee. Leave me alone."

"I can't leave you when you're . . ."

*That* made me spin around. "When I'm what? Crazy?"

He took a step back, hands raised, palms out. "No, Shawna. Never. Not crazy. Just . . . confused. Are you *sure* you didn't hit your head?"

I took a deep breath, held it for a long moment, let it out with a whoosh. "I didn't hit my head," I said, my voice calmer, even if I wasn't. "I'm fine." I fought down my unreasoning rage. "I'm fine," I repeated, as if saying it twice would make it true. "Really. Just tired from working so hard trying to get the shop ready. I'll go home and rest."

"Shawna . . ."

"I'm *fine*," I snapped. "*Believe* me, damn it!"

As I said it, I felt a momentary dizziness, and put my hand on the counter for support. At the same moment, Brent's expression cleared. "Well, if you're sure," he said. "I really do need to get back."

I blinked at his sudden capitulation. "Uh . . . yeah. I'm sure."

"Great." He kissed me on the forehead. "I'll check in at the end of the day. Call if you need anything."

I opened my mouth to say . . . something . . . but Brent had already turned away to pick up the coffees he'd ordered. Leaving mine waiting for me on the counter, he walked out, whistling, as if nothing strange had just happened at all.

I stared after him, almost as shaken by *that* performance as by what had happened . . . and then *hadn't* happened . . . a few minutes before. I couldn't believe he'd given in that easily. He'd always been so solicitous of me, so concerned whenever I seemed sick, or just a little depressed. A minute ago he'd been sure I'd hit my head, must have been wondering how he could convince me to go to the ER . . . and then, suddenly, he'd just accepted that I was fine, as though whatever I said was so, and that was all there was to it.

What the *hell*?

Carter, at least, still looked concerned. "You're sure you're all right, Shawna?"

I looked into his eyes. "I'm *fine*," I said, trying to put the same conviction into it as I had with Brent. I felt another instant of vertigo, and leaned harder against the counter: and just like Brent, Carter turned away, as though he'd forgotten anything strange had happened.

Just like he'd forgotten the murderous attack on his shop not ten minutes ago.

Just like the whole *world* had forgotten it.

I took a deep breath. My dizziness had faded, but I still felt deeply tired. I shoved my phone back into my pocket, picked up my coffee (even though I'd already drunk it, *three hours ago*, I felt like I needed it again), and pushed through the door onto the sidewalk. I stepped out from under the striped awning and looked up, into clear blue sky. I looked both ways at the normal amount of traffic, moving normally: no careening white vans loaded with killers.

Across the street, a huge poster of Johann Sebastian Bach wearing sharp-looking mirrorshades stared at me from a shop window. ROCK 'N' BACH, read the sign above his head. *Rinaldo*, I thought. *I saw him in here as the attack started. Maybe he remembers something.*

I was so focused on that idea I walked out into traffic. Tires squealed to my left. My heart leaped, and I spun, expecting to see one of the killers' vans . . . but it was nothing but a beat-up blue Mojita four-by-four. The bearded young man driving it leaned out of his window and yelled at me, but whatever he said didn't register through the pounding of my pulse. Behind him, someone honked.

I checked the other way, saw an opening in the traffic, and hurried across the other lane and between the cars parked against the curb. The Mojita's tires squealed as the irritated driver sped away.

I glanced back in time to see the woman driving the electric Avro minicar who had honked at the pickup driver give me a dirty look, but she didn't have enough horsepower in her suitcase-sized motor to allow her to do anything but ooze on down the road in huffy silence.

Feeling less tired after that fresh surge of adrenaline, I pushed through the door into Rock 'n' Bach. The store was empty of customers; it usually was, which always made me wonder how Rinaldo stayed in business. There were eight rows of CDs (obscure jazz titles, forgotten Broadway shows, complete sets of symphonies by classical composers I'd never heard of), one row of used (and a few new) vinyl records, and one row of DVDs, mostly of concerts and musicals, although there was a whole bin (the "Caligari Collection") devoted to German Expressionist films, a peculiar passion of Rinaldo's.

The counter, just to the left of the entrance, was occupied by Sara, Rinaldo's clerk, who'd worked there for as long as I'd been coming in. Late-middle-aged and sour-faced, she exuded all the warmth of a frozen pickle (see above, me wondering how Rinaldo stayed in business). I gave her a smile, which she did not return, perhaps for fear her face would crack. "Hi," I said. "Is Rinaldo in?"

She pointed. "Fourth row, third bin."

I blinked. "What?"

"*Rinaldo*. First Italian-language opera written for the London stage. Composed by George Frideric Handel in 1711. We have two recordings and a DVD of the Glyndebourne production."

I laughed, though I wasn't feeling amused. "No, Rinaldo. Your owner."

Her frown deepened further, approaching scowl territory. "Is that a joke? I'm the owner."

"What?"

"Since I opened the store twenty-two years ago."

"But . . ." I didn't have anything to say after "but," so I stopped. We stared at each other. "Then who . . . books the acts at the Human Bean?"

"I do. Always have."

"Even the DNA Eruptions?"

She pointed again. "Second row, second bin, under 'Nerd Grunge.' Although I personally prefer the Naked Singularities. Physics puns are funnier than biology puns."

We stared at each other again. "Did you see anything strange happen outside this morning?" I said finally, remarkably calmly, I thought, since inside my head I was running and screaming, in ever-diminishing circles. "Wind? Rain? White vans filled with terrorists?"

No question: I'd driven her into full scowl mode now. "Are you drunk?" she said coldly. "I don't allow drunk people in my store. I think you should leave before you alarm the other customers."

I looked around. Nope, still no other customers. But I didn't want to say that, in case there actually *were*, and I just couldn't see them. Clearly Sara and I had very different ideas of what constituted reality at that moment. "I *wish* I was drunk," I muttered, then walked out.

Everything looked perfectly normal outside. Except I knew it wasn't. I'd seen my best friend murdered. I'd seen the Human Bean ravaged by gunfire, the windows broken. I'd seen it start to rain as a terrifying storm broke over the city.

The sun shone from a clear blue sky. The Human Bean remained unravaged. My best friend had apparently never existed. Neither had Rinaldo, a man I'd spoken to weekly.

Maybe I *should* go to the ER, see a doctor, tell her I was hallucinating. Maybe I *had* somehow fallen over the couch in the

Human Bean and hit my head. But they'd lock me up for observation, and I didn't feel crazy. I felt confused. I felt conflicted. I felt tired. But not crazy.

Of course, I wouldn't, would I?

My hands were trembling. I clenched them into fists, then set off for the studio. Somewhere familiar. Somewhere safe. Somewhere I could think.

At the corner, I turned and looked toward the mountains, and felt a chill. The storm clouds were still there, swelling in the sky, rushing toward us, closer than they had been when I'd walked to the Human Bean with Brent, as black as ever beneath their deceptively snow-white front. But I had already seen them pour over the city, had been caught with Aesha in the swirling wind and first drops of rain . . . in fact, my clothes were still a little damp.

*My clothes were damp.* How had I not noticed that before? My clothes were *damp*. I *had* been caught in the rain with Aesha. I *had*. And yet . . .

Swallowing hard, I turned my back on the mountains and hurried down the pedestrian mall toward my shop. I looked up.

WORLDS read the sign that I had last seen reading WORLD-SHAPER POT. The workmen were struggling with the H. I fumbled my keys from my pocket with a shaking hand, hurried under the scaffolding to the front door, opened it, slipped inside, closed it, and leaned back against it. I left my sign saying I was CLOSED. I stared around the shop. It looked the same . . .

But the studio didn't.

I hurried past the counter into the back. The mugs I had thrown after I had gone for coffee with Brent, and before I had met Aesha, weren't there. The studio remained pristine: no clay dust surrounded the wheel. The slab of clay I had cut still sat on the workbench inside its plastic wrap. Once again, it was as if the past three hours had never happened.

*It happened*, I told myself fiercely. The images were burned in my mind: Aesha's slight body ripped apart by gunfire, the blood, the smell, the . . .

It all came rushing back with such force I had to turn and dash for the bathroom, where I retched into the toilet, though there was little in my stomach: I had never had my lunch, after all, and for me, the muffin I'd eaten for breakfast was four hours ago.

*If I* had *eaten lunch at the Human Bean, what would I be bringing up?* I thought, as I clung to the porcelain bowl until I was certain the spasms had passed. *Food I ate in a past no one but me remembers?*

Shivering violently, partly from the bout of vomiting, more from the cascading feeling of normality overturned, with no hope it would suddenly be righted, I pulled myself to my feet with a hand on the sink, then turned on the tap and scooped some cold water into my mouth, rinsing it of the foul taste of bile. I spat, and then raised my eyes to the mirror. They looked red, and my face was deathly pale, but otherwise I looked the same as I had when I'd gotten up that morning. How could everything have changed so suddenly?

Something had happened, either to me, or to the world. But I looked the same. Except for the strange fatigue, I felt the same. I had unbroken memories stretching back to that morning . . . *this* morning. So, unless I was hallucinating, something had to have happened to the world.

But what power could change the world like that, rewrite the past, reset the present?

*Alternate worlds*, I thought. *Schrödinger's cat. Different timelines.*

I'd read science fiction novels, watched movies, read articles, seen science programs on TV. I knew about the many-worlds hypothesis. But outside of science fiction, nobody had ever suggested you could *really* move from one world to another.

Yet what other explanation could there be?

*Hallucination. Drugs. Stroke.* The same old possibilities ran through my brain, but I shook my head violently. No. I was myself. I was sure of it. It wasn't me that had changed, it was the world.

But how? And why?

I pulled a paper cup from the dispenser by the sink and took a long drink of cold water, filling and refilling the cup five times. Then I crumpled it and tossed it into the wastepaper basket. I looked at myself in the mirror again.

"Now what?" I asked my reflection, my voice shaking. "What happens next?"

As if in answer, the bell at the front of the shop jingled. The sign said CLOSED, but I hadn't locked the door.

Brent? I hoped so. I regretted sending him away, wished I'd told him to stay with me, wished I'd let him take me to the hospital. Even if he didn't remember Aesha, he remembered *me*, he remembered he loved me, he remembered I loved him. Suddenly I was desperate to see him. I jerked the door open. "Brent, I'm sorry—"

But it wasn't Brent.

A stranger stood just outside the bathroom: the man in the cowboy hat and the long black duster.

## FIVE

**INSTINCTIVELY, I REACHED** for a weapon: unfortunately, the only thing that came to hand was the soap dispenser, and its defensive possibilities seemed limited, unless I managed to squirt soap in his eyes.

"Shawna Keys, I presume?" the stranger said. He had a deep voice, otherwise unremarkable—no discernible accent.

I didn't let go of the soap dispenser. "Maybe. Who are you?"

He took off the hat. Without its shadow, I got my first good look at his face.

He was older than me, maybe early fifties. He had a tanned, lean face, with high cheekbones. His long black hair, drawn back in a ponytail, was beginning to develop Doctor Strange-like wings of white at the temples. Beneath the sapphire-blue eyes I had glimpsed before, and a blade-sharp nose, sprouted a pencil-thin mustache. "My name is Karl Yatsar. I have come from Ygrair."

*Ygrair?* "Never heard of it," I said.

He blinked. "Is that a joke? Ygrair is not an it. *She* is the Mistress of the Labyrinth. Your teacher. Your benefactor, who gave you this world." He frowned. "As you well know."

I took a step back into the bathroom, and raised the soap dispenser higher. "You," I said, "are a crazy person."

He stared at me. "Are you telling me," he said, carefully enunciating each word, "that you do not remember Ygrair?"

"I think," I said, enunciating right back at him, "that I just made that rather clear."

Silence, then, for a long moment. "That is . . . unexpected," he said. "Unprecedented, in fact." He frowned. "Verging on the terrifying."

"It's been that kind of day," I said. "Now. Are you going to tell me what the *hell* you're talking about?"

His frown deepened. "There is a lot to tell."

"I've got time."

"I am not so sure." He glanced toward the shop's front window, then back at me. "If you truly do not remember where you came from, you will find what I tell you very hard to believe."

"Try me."

"But if you have no memory of Ygrair, can you really . . . ?" He cut off the end of that question, which he must have intended for himself, anyway, since I found it meaningless. Then he nodded once, sharply. "Very well. May we at least converse somewhere other than in the doorway to the lavatory?"

*Lavatory? Who calls it that?* "I don't know," I said. "Standing in the doorway of the 'lavatory,' I can always jump back inside, lock the door, and call the cops." *And rub Policeman Phil's nose in the fact I wasn't making up my predawn stalker-voyeur.*

"That would not be wise."

"Sounds pretty wise to me."

He sighed, and ran a hand over the top of his ponytailed head in a very ordinary gesture of exasperation. "Miss Keys. Please. I have no intention of harming you. Quite the contrary. You are the most important person in this world to me. Possibly in *any* world. I mean that utterly and literally."

"*Any* world," I repeated. "This tendency of yours to sound insane is *not* making me any more inclined to sit and have a quiet, noncrazy conversation with you."

"I am *not* insane." For the first time, a little annoyance crept into his voice. "Nor are you, though if you truly do not remember your origins, you may well *think* you are, after what has happened today."

"I remember my origins," I said. "I grew up in Appleville, Oregon. My mother still lives there." But as I said it, I felt a cold tingle down my back, as though a spider with eight tiny shoes of ice had been hiding in my hair and had just made a break for freedom. "Wait. What do *you* know about what happened today?"

"I saw it happen," Yatsar said. "Then I saw it unhappen. I saw the attack on the coffee shop. I saw people murdered, including the friend who accompanied you. *I remember them.* Does anyone else?"

The ice-shod spider ran back up my spine to cower in my hair once more. "No," I said. "Explain that to me, if you can."

"I would be happy to. Shall I come in, or will you come out?"

I sighed. "Fine." I finally let go of the soap dispenser, edged out of the bathroom, giving him a wide berth, and pointed him toward the front left-hand corner of the shop. In that often-sunny spot (though not today, with the scaffolding out front), I'd artfully placed three chairs, upholstered in green vinyl, around a low, round, glass-topped coffee table, upon which I had equally artfully placed the latest copies of *Ceramics Illustrated*, *Glazes and Greenware*, and my favorite, *The Compleat Potter*. I sat in the chair on the left, precariously perched on the edge in case I had to make a break for it. Outside, beyond the spindly metal framework of the scaffolding, pedestrians strode along the still-sunlit cobblestones, for all the world as if nothing strange had happened today, unaware they were reliving the morning. Distantly, filtered by glass and brick, I heard one of the young men once again hanging my sign swearing about something. But no metal letters crashed to the street, so I decided I could ignore it.

Yatsar put his hat on the table, covering the magazines, then unbuttoned the duster, took it off, and threw it over the back of the third chair. I immediately understood why he'd been wearing it. "Are you an actor?"

"I have been," he said. "Though I was a better playwright than thespian. Why?"

I raised an eyebrow. "The tights, the . . . um . . . doublet, is that the word? The puffy pantaloons. The belt with the big buckle. The knife. Or sword. Is that thing legal, by the way?"

He looked down at himself. "It is a dagger, and it was not only legal, but necessary, in the last world. The clothing was also typical of the last world, which seemed to have been Shaped by a great fan of the Bard. The hat and coat," he indicated them, "were merely what came readily to hand when I arrived in this world, and served well to hide the rest."

*The last world . . . Shaped by a great fan of the Bard? This world?* I closed my eyes briefly. Just talking to this guy would have been enough to give me a headache, if I hadn't already had one, following hard on the heels of my earlier feeling of fatigue. I opened my eyes again. "Very well, Mr. Yatsar . . ."

"Call me Karl."

*Hell, why not?* "Fine. Karl. Call me Shawna. Now talk. From the beginning."

Karl Yatsar frowned at the girl . . . no, woman; she must have been at least nineteen when given this world to Shape, and that had been ten years ago, in the First World. Still, she looked half a child from *his* increasingly ancient viewpoint. He had not been prepared for this eventuality; had not even though it possible, that a Shaper could forget she was the Shaper. Yet here she was, and here he was, and the Adversary . . .

*Is too close. And coming closer every minute.* He took a deep breath. "Very well," he said. "In the beginning, God created the heavens and the earth."

Shawna Keys scowled. "Very funny."

"It is not meant to be," Karl said, though not with complete honesty. The instincts of the playwright he had once been still remained, when it came to conversation: subtlety, misdirection, sly humor, the occasional pun. It was perhaps a failing. Still, Ygrair seemed to find it amusing, and so he had never tried very hard to break himself of the habit of attempted wittiness. "Aside from the reference to God, whom you may or may not believe in . . . ?"

"I'm agnostic."

*Neither fish nor fowl.* Karl inclined his head in acknowledgment. "Very well. All the same, the biblical verse is a useful place to begin. No matter how the original universe came about, it exists. Within it, by means natural or divine, rose intelligence. Within intelligence rose creativity, and eventually, an understanding of the process of creation. That, in turn, allowed for sub-creation."

"Wait, I know this," Shawna said. "Tolkien, right? 'Mythopoeia'?"

The names meant nothing to Karl. *After my time*, he thought. "I do not understand the reference."

Shawna seemed shocked. "J.R.R. Tolkien?"

Karl shrugged irritably. "I do not know the man."

"Um . . . he was a great writer of fantastic tales."

"Ah." Karl tucked that information away, in case it every came up again, then plunged on. "Irrelevant. I am not talking about making up *stories*, though by that craft I once made my living. I am talking about the sub-creation of entire universes." He paused. That wasn't quite right. *Damn it all, the girl should already* know *all this!* "Pocket universes, at least," he amended. "According to Ygrair, the apparent size of each is an illusion: the stars and planets in the night sky, in those worlds in which they appear, are mere set dressing—flimsily painted flats, in theatrical terms."

"You have yet to say anything to convince me you are not a crazy person," Shawna said.

Karl felt another surge of irritation. "My apologies. I am not used to having to explain this . . . most Shapers already know." *Why don't you?* He paused to collect his thoughts, then continued. "Within the original universe were born certain individuals with the innate ability to create these new worlds. All they lacked was knowledge of that ability—and, of course, the raw material."

He stopped again. Shawna was staring at him in clear disbelief. "'Original universe'? That's this one."

Karl sighed. "No. It is not."

A shadow fell across her face—literally, not metaphorically. Karl turned his head to look out the window. The bright morning sunlight in the street outside had suddenly dimmed. *Time is running short*, he thought.

He returned his gaze to the young woman, and tried to put all the urgency he felt into his voice. "The storm that came before is coming again, and so are those who rode it. We must be gone before they arrive."

Karl's ominous statement hung in the air like an unpleasant smell. I had followed his glance at the window, and realized the clouds had moved in, just as they had before . . . whatever had happened had happened. *He's trying to hurry me*, I thought. *So I can't think this through.*

But I was in no mood to be hurried, not by someone who still sounded like he was spouting bad science fiction. Even *if* the attackers came again, based on their last appearance they wouldn't be here until noon. I looked back to him, folded my arms stubbornly, and sat back in my chair. "So, let me guess. You want me to believe that *you're* one of these . . . sub-creators? That you can actually create your own universe?"

For some reason, the question seemed to annoy him. "It does not matter whether *I* am one of them. What matters is that *you* are one of them. And a very powerful one, at that. You made this world, and this morning, when you were attacked, you remade it."

It's not everyday someone tells you you're the Creator, so it's not surprising the conversation lagged for a few seconds while I stared at him, he stared back, and I tried to a) absorb what he was saying, and b) figure out how to respond. It was crazy, of course, absolutely nuts, and he was clearly just another delusional mutterer-to-himself like a dozen others I'd seen on the streets (although to be fair, some of them were business types wearing Greentooth headsets), except . . .

Except something had happened to me that I couldn't explain. Except I had seen my favorite coffee shop shot up by terrorists—one of whom had called me by name!—and my best friend murdered in front of me, and no one remembered it happening—no one but the crazy man in the crazy clothes now sitting, crazily enough, in my quiet pottery shop.

Not only that, no one but Karl Yatsar remembered the dead had ever even *existed*. As far as people who had known her for years were concerned, as far as the selfies on my own phone were concerned, Aesha Tripathi, my best friend, had never lived. Even the man I thought I loved, who'd visited her home with me, had dinner and drinks with me and her, had no recollection of her at all.

If I discounted Karl's explanation, I could only see two possibilities: either I had gone crazy, or everyone else in the world had gone crazy. I didn't like either of those. (I had no problem thinking *Karl* was crazy . . . but if he was, then either I or my friends had to be, too.)

I needed a third possibility, one that did not require mental breakdowns, either mine or everyone else's, to explain things. And Shakespearean Cowboy dude, crazy (I winced; there was that word again) as it seemed, was offering one.

*So . . . run with it and see where it takes you.* "Then . . . what happened . . . you're saying *I* did that."

He nodded.

"How?"

"You altered the world so that it appears to have moved backward three hours in time."

"Sure," I said. "Let's go with that." *Why not? Once you start believing the impossible, where do you stop?* "But things are different. What's happening now didn't happen the first time."

"I said you have altered the world so it *appears* to have moved backward three hours in time. No one can truly reverse the flow of time. Not even Ygrair, in the world she has Shaped for herself. You did everything in your power to make what happened unhappen, but it *did* happen."

I rubbed my right temple. The headache was worsening. "I don't understand."

Karl looked out the window. The sunshine had not returned. He turned back to me. "Tell me this. Just before the world rewrote itself, what were you thinking? What were you feeling?"

I thought back. "Terror. Anger. Disbelief." I saw Aesha dying in front of me again, and swallowed hard. "I couldn't believe it was happening. I said it out loud: 'This isn't happening. This isn't happening!'"

"And then it wasn't?"

I nodded. "And then it wasn't."

Karl spread his hands. "There you are. Through your power, fueled by your terror and anger and disbelief, you rewrote reality with your words."

"You're telling me I'm God."

He shook his head. "No. As I told you, there is a greater reality within which this world exists—the original universe, the real reality, what Ygrair calls the First World. If there is a God, then that is the world He created." He paused. "Well," he added, thoughtfully, "I suppose it is possible that what we think is the First World is itself only a sub-reality of an even greater reality. Though Ygrair says not."

"Turtles all the way down," I muttered.

Yatsar actually smiled at that. "Well put."

I chewed my lip for a moment. "If this is true," I said at last, "and I'm *not* saying I believe you, but for the sake of argument . . . if I made what happened unhappen, can I make it . . . un-unhappen? Change the world again, only this time make it so that everyone remembers Aesha? Everything goes back to the way it was?"

Yatsar's momentary amusement faded. "I'm sorry, but no."

I glared at him, anger bubbling up again. "Why? Why is *that* impossible? If I'm God . . ."

"You are *not* God," he snapped. "I just *said* you are not God. Even Creator is too strong a word." Behind him, in the street, I saw pedestrians walking faster, heads down, the wind whipping their clothes. "Ygrair's word for you and those like you is 'Worldshaper'—Shaper, for short."

"Worldshaper." *Oh, for God's sake.* "*World*shaper." And just when I was *almost* ready to believe him. "You know that's the name of my shop. Couldn't you have been at least a *little* bit original?"

He raised an eyebrow. "You think I got it from your shop? Tell me, how did that name come to you?"

I blinked. "Well . . . it . . . it just did."

"Out of nowhere. Out of nothing."

"Yeah . . ."

"*Ex nihilo*, you might say."

"Look—"

"That name is not a coincidence. Even the fact you are a potter is not a coincidence. A part of you knows, has *always* known, the truth. Even though in the act of Shaping this world you seem to have somehow Shaped yourself, overwriting your memories so that you forgot you were the Shaper . . . which should *not* have happened, and I do not know why it did . . . a part of you knows."

"I overwrote my . . . ?" I shook my head violently. "That's nonsense. I told you, I know where I was born. I remember growing up there. I have a mother . . ."

"You do," Karl said. "And she is a real person, just like your friend Aesha was a real person. But she did not exist until you Shaped this world and called her into existence from the sea of possibility."

*Mom . . . ? No!* I shook my head stubbornly. "The world has been around for billions of years."

"It only appears that way because you Shaped it to *look* that way. Most of its long history is . . . borrowed, you might say, from the original universe, the First World." He sighed. "Time is a difficult concept when it comes to Shaped worlds, but in reality—Reality with a capital R, if you like—this world is only about ten years old."

"Ten . . ." I tried to take hold of my own reality—*this* reality—with both hands. "Ten years ago," I said, my voice trembling a little despite my best efforts, "I entered art school. Six years ago, I graduated and moved to Eagle River. I worked in a clothing store during the day and threw pots evenings and weekends. I started selling at craft shows. I saved every penny, and borrowed more than I should. I leased this building. I moved into it. I'm about to open my new business, my *own* business, Worldshaper Pottery, something I've dreamed about since I was in high school.

"I visit my Mom in Appleville several times a year," I went on, my voice rising. "I have friends." *One fewer than I did this morning.* "I have a boyfriend." *Or I did* . . . I pushed both thoughts away. "I took a trip to Europe. I saw *The Da Vinci Code: The Musical* on Broadway. Hugh Jackman did his best in the Robert Langdon role, but the show was terrible." I glared at him. "I didn't imagine *any* of that."

"In a way you did," Karl said. "You imagined the kind of world you wanted to live in."

"I wanted to live in a world with a bad *Da Vinci Code* musical?"

"Not that detail," Karl said impatiently. "Or many others. This world you have imagined . . . Shaped . . . is a lot like the First World, but not identical. Some of the changes were conscious choices on your part. Others—like, presumably, this 'musical' you speak of— were random, the world ordering itself, evolving, in the absence of specific instructions from you.

"Perhaps in the First World you dreamed of having a pottery shop of your own, a few good friends, a handsome boyfriend, a favorite coffee shop. Because you are a Shaper, when Ygrair gave you this space, this . . . sandbox . . . you Shaped a world like the one you had always imagined, and made it real." He sighed. "And then, somehow, forgot you had done so."

"You're not making sense," I snapped. "This 'space'? This 'sandbox'? *What* 'space'? What 'sandbox'?"

"Ygrair calls it the Labyrinth," Karl said. "Possibly infinite in size, apparently infinite in possibilities . . . for those with the ability to take advantage of them."

"Worldshapers."

"Yes."

"Like me."

He nodded. "Yes."

I looked out the window again. A dust devil swept down the street, paper swirling in its grip. The light had dimmed further and had an ominous greenish tinge. The storm hadn't hit this early before. Things weren't happening exactly the same. Well, obviously they weren't, since Karl Yatsar had not shown up in my shop the last time I had lived these morning hours. "Assuming—again, for the sake of argument—that I believe you—I don't, but pretend I do—then how did I find my way into this 'Labyrinth'? Did I open some sort of trans-dimensional Portal?"

"*You* didn't," Karl said. "Ygrair did."

"Ygrair."

"Yes."

I sighed. "How do you spell that, anyway?"

He frowned. "Y . . . g . . . r . . . a . . . i . . . r. What does it matter?"

"I thought it would be something like that." Yatsar? And now Ygrair? Two names beginning with Y? This guy spun a great line of bull, but he wasn't too good on the details. No decent fantasy author would create two names that similar for main characters. "Weird name."

"I suppose."

"A lot like your own."

"Is it?" He blinked. "I don't see it."

*Well, obviously, or you wouldn't have made it that way.* "And she's . . . ?"

"The discoverer of the possibilities of the Labyrinth."

"You know her?"

"Very well. She is the one who sent me on the mission that has brought me here." He looked out the window, and frowned. "The storm is almost here. Ahead of schedule."

"Never mind the weather," I snapped. My patience was wearing thin again. "Go on. Tell me more about this 'Ygrair.'"

He looked back at me. "Ygrair . . . rules the Labyrinth. But I met her in the First World, long ago. She was injured and alone, and I helped her. I have helped her ever since.

"Over the years, in the First World, she found those with the Talent, like you, and trained them—trained *you*, though you do not remember it—until they were ready to Shape their worlds. Then she opened the Labyrinth to them, and left them free to create what they would.

"But she has powerful enemies, and though she had thought herself safe from them, they found her. They attacked, and almost killed her. Badly hurt, she fled into her own Shaped world, where I resided as her deputy. And there she told me something she had never before confided to me." He took a deep breath. "The Labyrinth cannot exist without Ygrair. All the worlds are connected to each other, and all the worlds are connected to her. But she is now so badly hurt that her connection to the Shaped Worlds, to the Labyrinth itself, is weakening. Ygrair likens herself to the keystone of an arch. If she were to die, or weaken so much that she lost the thread of power that binds her to the Labyrinth and its many worlds, the whole thing would come tumbling down. If that happens, all the Shaped Worlds, the billions of individuals who live in them, and the Shapers who have Shaped them, will vanish as if they never existed, dissolving into the Labyrinth."

"Quite the apocalyptic vision," I said. "So where do I come in?"

"Ygrair needs to weave anew the thread of power that links her to the Shaped Worlds," Karl said. "She sent me to find a Shaper Talented and powerful enough to obtain, and then hold within him or her, the knowledge . . . Ygrair calls it the *hokhmah*, an ancient word meaning 'wisdom' . . . of as many of the Shaped Worlds as possible. That Shaper must travel from world to world to world, and then to Ygrair, to pass that collected *hokhmah* on to her. That transfer, Ygrair says, will save her, the Labyrinth, and the Shaped Worlds within it."

"And you think I could be that person."

"With the power you displayed, in resetting the clock of your world—which is even more impressive now that I know you remember nothing of your role as Shaper of this reality—yes, I believe you could be."

I sighed. "So I'm the special snowflake who has to save the universe. Are you sure you didn't copy all this from a bad fantasy novel?"

Karl frowned. "What?"

"Never mind. Next question. Who are these enemies of Ygrair?"

Karl shot a glance out the window. "Time is growing short . . ."

"So is my temper. Tell me."

He looked back at me again. "I am the only one Ygrair has told the truth of her origin to," he said slowly. "She has never shared it with the Shapers, over all the years she trained them."

"If you believe your own story," I said, "then these are extraordinary circumstances. I'm sure she'd want you to tell me."

He looked down. His hands, folded together on his lap, worked for a moment. Finally he looked up again. "Very well," he said. "The truth is, Ygrair . . . is not from Earth."

*Oh, good grief,* I thought. *Bad science fiction, not fantasy.* "You're telling me she's an alien."

"If you like."

"I don't like any of this. But carry on with your story."

"It is not a 'story,'" he said stiffly. "It is the truth. Ygrair is not from Earth. She comes from a race called the Shurak. She fled tyranny and oppression on her home world, seeking only to be free. In her flight, she came to Earth, injured. As I said, I found her. The Shurak knew of the Labyrinth, but they used it only as a means to span the vast distances between the stars. Once, they used it to enslave many other worlds.

"But it was Ygrair alone who discovered that those with Talent, of any race, can Shape new worlds within the Labyrinth. Every race produces those with this Talent. Trapped on Earth, Ygrair set out to find those Earth people who had it, to train them to use it . . . and then to open the Labyrinth so they could freely create whatever worlds they chose. Freedom, in opposition to the cruel tyranny of her own world—that is Ygrair's driving passion. She set up a school for Shapers . . . people like you. Upon graduation, she opened the Labyrinth for them . . . for *you*.

"But her own kind never stopped searching for her, and eventually they found her. They attacked her in the First World, destroying the school. Ygrair barely escaped with her life. She fled into the Labyrinth with her few remaining students, set them free to Shape their worlds, and closed the Portal into the First World behind them. She thought she would be safe from the Shurak in here, while she regained her strength . . . but as I have said, she is not regaining her strength, but weakening." He sighed. "And worse . . . somehow, one of the Shurak, a Shaper himself, has found his way into the Labyrinth. I stumbled upon him, two worlds ago."

Despite myself, I was intrigued by this bizarre tale. Maybe Karl really had been a playwright. "How did that happen?"

"Clearly he infiltrated the school, posing as a student. Ygrair herself must have placed him in the Labyrinth, unaware of his true nature. She did not warn me of the possibility, so I do not believe she knew."

"What does he want?"

"Based on what he did in the last world, he intends to steal the *hokhmah* of every world he can reach, stripping it from the Shaper, and then killing him or her and Shaping the world to serve his own ends. Each world he seizes is another denied to Ygrair, and as long as the Portals between them remain open, feeds more power to him. I can only believe that he means to eventually find and kill Ygrair, and take her place . . . but unlike Ygrair, who values freedom and creativity above all, and opened the Labyrinth to the Shapers to enable them to create a myriad of diverse worlds, he will make all worlds copies of his own, and set himself up as absolute ruler of all."

"Scary guy," I said. *There's always an Evil Overlord . . .*

"He is," Karl said. "And you have met him."

I blinked. "Wait. You mean the leader of the terrorists was . . . ?"

"He calls himself the Adversary."

*Well, that's* slightly *better than Dark Lord*, I thought. "He knew my name."

"You were both students of Ygrair. A fact he remembers, though you do not."

"And he's . . . an alien."

"Your word for it, yes."

I remembered the man standing over me in the coffee shop. I remembered thinking he was going to kill me. I remembered the shock of hearing my name. What I didn't remember was green skin, bug eyes, funny ears, or a bumpy forehead. "He looked human to me."

"So does Ygrair. She says the form is imposed by the planet."

*Convenient.* "And you just . . . stumbled on him?"

"Yes, in the world before last, a world he had Shaped: tightly controlled, authoritarian, with himself as the supreme and un-questioned ruler. The amount of Shaping power he retained im-pressed me—at first, I thought he might even be the one I sought. But when I approached him, I . . . discovered the truth. I fled."

"And he followed you."

Karl looked down again, and I saw that now his fists were clenched. "Yes. I did not think he could. But he did. To the last world, and then . . ."

"To this one."

He nodded.

"To *mine*."

He nodded again.

I felt cold. "If this is true—"

"Every word," Karl said.

"—then you led him here."

"I did not mean to. I knew he had followed me into the last world, but I did not think he could follow me into this one."

"You led him here, and he *killed my best friend*." My own fists had clenched: I could feel my nails digging into my palms. I stood up, for no reason except I could no longer bear to be sitting down.

He lifted his chin, met my gaze squarely. "Yes. But you Shaped your world anew in the face of that attack, even though—as I have just discovered—you did not know you had the ability to do so." He got to his feet, too, faced me across the table. "You have more power remaining to you than any Shaper I have ever seen in any other world. You have the power Ygrair needs. You are strong enough to hold the *hokhmah* of many worlds and deliver them to Ygrair. *You are the one I was sent to find.*"

Right on cue, lightning flashed—but it wasn't distant lightning, the first warning shots of an approaching storm. It lit the street like God's own camera flash, and the thunder that followed sounded like a battleship's broadside. An instant later torrential rain swept the cobblestones, a downpour so heavy it reduced the lights on the far side of Blackthorne Avenue to a faint glow in an instant.

Then came the wind. If the lightning and thunder had been an exploding bomb, the wind was the shockwave. It slammed into the scaffolding at the front of the shop, and blew it apart as though it were made of matchsticks. I glimpsed one of the young men whirling through the air, head over heels, out of my sight. I screamed, flinging up my arms to protect my face, as my beautiful display window shattered and a steel rod exploded the glass tabletop, slamming into the floor not five feet from where we sat, splintering the hardwood and impaling the latest issue of *Glazes and Greenware*. Yatsar stared at the rod, then his head shot up. "Were you touched?" he shouted above the roar of wind and rain.

I lowered my arms. "No, it missed me, but . . ." I stared at the broken glass, the water pooling on my once-beautiful, now horribly scarred floor, the metal rod still vibrating in it. "I can't believe this is happening." A wild hope leaped up in me. "This isn't happening!" I shouted at the storm, but the window remained broken, the rain kept pouring in, and as if to mock me, lightning and thunder exploded above us again.

"That won't work," Karl said grimly. "Not if you were touched by the Adversary."

"I told you—"

"Not now," he snapped. "Not by glass or metal. During the attack on the coffee shop. *Did someone touch you?*"

I remembered the brown-haired young man reaching down to me, the shock as his hand touched my forehead, just before I made him and everything else vanish. "Yes, but only for an—*ow!*"

Karl's hand had shot out and grabbed my hand so hard it hurt. "Is there a back door?"

"What?" I tried to focus. "Through the studio . . . why?"

"Because we need to run." He jerked me to my feet, almost pulling my arm out of its socket. "Now!"

Another blast of lightning—and the lights went out.

"My shop—"

"Forget your shop," Karl snarled. "If you stay here, you will die. Come on!" He grabbed the cowboy hat and duster. "Which way?"

I led him toward the back room, into my studio, through it, the studio I'd wanted all my life . . .

Or had I? If Karl were telling the truth . . . ?

He couldn't be! It was all insane gibberish, cooked up by some fruitcake who'd read so many fantasy novels he was starting to dress like a character in one, a delusion cobbled together from bits of myth (the Minotaur), science fiction (alternate dimensions), and a healthy dose of . . . what was the term? Mary Sue? . . . wish fulfillment. He wanted me to believe I was the special anointed one, the only one who could save the multiverse from the nefarious doings of the Evil Overlord. It was crazy, it was impossible, it couldn't be real . . .

And yet Aesha had died, and Brent had forgotten her. Everyone had forgotten her. Even my HiPhone had forgotten her. Rinaldo had disappeared. My clothes had been damp from a storm that hadn't broken yet. Three hours had vanished from my life.

Now the storm that had already struck once had struck again—and this time, it had arrived much sooner, much more powerfully, and seemed to be *targeting* my shop. Only Karl knew what I had seen, only Karl offered an explanation, however crazy it sounded.

And so I fled with him.

We reached the gray metal back door, slamming it open and bursting out it into the alley. My car, a brand-new silver Fjord Model Z, was parked there, underneath an overhanging tin roof that, miraculously, hadn't blown away, and at least sheltered us from the rain—now mixed with hail, judging by the machine-gun rattle overhead—as we dashed to the vehicle. I climbed in and pressed the start button as Karl scrambled into the passenger seat, though it occurred to me if I'd been a little faster I could have driven off and left him behind.

As I backed into the alley, turning the nose of the car toward 22nd Street, another almighty gust lifted the tin roof of the carport like a piece of paper and twirled it away into the rain. It smashed into a second-floor window in the back of the building across the alley, sending a glittering shower of shards to the pavement below.

At the same instant, a white van skidded to a halt at the end of the alley, blocking it. *How did they get here so fast?* I thought, even as I slammed the car into reverse and backed full-speed toward the other end of the alley, which opened onto an access road inaccessible from the pedestrian mall. Even as the van dwindled in front of me its doors opened. Flames spat from gun barrels, but whether by luck or because the wind and rain defeated their aim, no bullets struck us.

Then we reached the access road, and I jerked the wheel right, swinging the car around the corner. Gunfire blew the bricks in the wall above us into dust. I shoved the car into drive, and we roared off into the storm as if our lives depended on it.

Apparently, they did.

# SIX

**IT'S AMAZING HOW** quickly my doubts about whether Karl was telling me the truth vanished once people started shooting at me.

I'd never been in a car chase before, but television had taught me to zigzag to throw off pursuers. Which I did: I knew the neighborhood well enough not to get myself trapped in any blind alleys, and I even drove the wrong way down a couple of one-way streets, although why I thought the men who had just tried to kill me—again—would hesitate to break traffic laws, I'm not quite sure. My windshield wipers made little progress against the pouring rain, driven sideways by the screaming wind, so visibility was less than ideal, but I didn't hit anyone or anything.

Considering no one else had seemed to be able to see just how bad the approaching storm would be, they'd reacted quickly enough when it hit. There were still cars on the road, but most people seemed to have headed for shelter. I wished we could. I dodged fallen trees and fallen power lines, drove through intersections where the streetlights had failed, and once passed a car flipped onto its side. My own car shuddered in outrage at the onslaught of the storm, but remained steadfastly on all four wheels.

I pushed the radio button. Static crackled through the speakers instead of the soft jazz of my favorite station. I ran through all the other stations using the buttons on the steering wheel, never taking my eyes off the road, which—I swerved around an enormous branch skittering across the road as though alive—might have been suicidal. *All* local stations were off the air, although stations from the next city down the Interstate remained active. None of them were talking about the storm destroying Eagle River, but then, it had only struck a few minutes ago.

I flicked off the radio. We passed a collapsed building, flames flickering in the wreckage despite the rain, people digging in the rubble. I slowed, thinking I should help, but Karl snapped, "Keep driving!"

I gulped, swerved around a chunk of roof, and accelerated down the strangely empty road beyond. Two minutes later, the wind fell away to almost nothing. Ahead, light beyond the veil of rain promised an edge to the clouds, but the sky in the rearview mirror remained pitch-black, dust and debris swirling and twirling within it.

"The Adversary has lost track of us," Karl said. "For the moment."

"But if he can create a storm like *that* . . ." Seeing my knuckles white on the steering wheel, I forced myself to relax my fingers a little. "Where do I go? How can I escape him?"

"He did not create the storm," Karl said. "It arose naturally . . . well, unnaturally . . . because of the leakage of creative energy from the last world into this one, through the Portal."

"But he used it . . ."

"Using something is not the same as creating it. He controls the last world, so he was able to Shape the energy that leaked into this one to a certain extent. But the storm will dissipate quickly now that he has unleashed it, and he cannot Shape its equal . . . not as long as you are alive."

"Then let's keep me that way," I said. I took a deep, shaking breath. "How do get away from him . . . from his killers? How do I get my old life back?"

Karl had twisted around to look out the back window; now he turned forward again, and frowned at me. "You get away by flee-ing," he said. "Which we are now doing. As for how you get your old life back . . . I would have thought you grasped the truth by now. You do not."

I shook my head violently. "No! I won't accept that. I *have* to. I just opened my shop. I have a boyfriend. My Mom . . ."

"Have you listened to nothing I've said?" Karl snapped. "I *told* you—those things are Shaped. Real in this world while you are in this world, but lost to you now that the Adversary has entered it and stolen its *hokhmah* from you. This whole world is lost to you now. As your life will be if the Adversary catches you." He peered ahead through the rain, now little more than a drizzle. "The faster and farther we get away from the city, the better."

"The freeway is just a few blocks—"

He shook his head. "No. Back roads only." He opened the glove compartment and peered inside. "Map?"

"Not in there." *Who carries maps in the glove compartment these days?* I pressed the NAV button on the steering wheel instead. A screen popped up out of the dashboard and lit with a map, the triangle marking our location crawling across it. Karl closed the glove compartment, and leaned forward to examine the screen. "Left, next intersection," he said after a moment. "Three blocks, then right for four, then left again. Then straight out of town. Once we are in the country, we will pause long enough to consider our next action."

I felt like my next action should be screaming, but instead I drove, the storm falling ever farther behind us. Even after we ran out from under the rain, though, the streets remained empty, as if everyone were cowering inside . . . as if I'd fallen into some post-apocalyptic science fiction novel where plague or nuclear war had wiped out most of the population.

I tried the radio again. Still nothing about the storm on the out-of-town stations, but my jazz station had come back to life, though it wasn't playing Charlie Parker. ". . . mayor has declared a state of emergency," said a female announcer, whose ordinarily sultry voice I barely recognized in the shaken tones coming over the speakers. "Everyone is asked to shelter in place. Chief of Police Darrel Stimpson issued a statement a few minutes ago warning residents that a known terrorist has been seen in the city and may be using the storm to cover preparations for a major attack. Citizens are asked to keep a lookout for a 2017 Fjord Model Z, license plate reading POTTER, last seen . . ."

I stabbed the OFF button, so violently I almost swerved off the road. "Terrorist!" I cried. "Is that you?"

"No," Karl said. "It is you."

"Me?" I shot him a look. He certainly *looked* serious. "But that's crazy! I have a friend who's a cop. The Chief of Police *knows* me. I went to school with one of his sergeants! I called the police just yesterday . . . about *you*! I've been to a barbecue in the Chief's backyard!"

"I doubt," Karl said, "that the Chief of Police remembers that. For him, it never happened."

I felt a chill. "The Adversary?"

He nodded.

"But . . . how?"

"He has your *hokhmah*. Though he cannot Shape this world to the extent he wishes, while you live, he *can* Shape it in small ways—and the easiest Shaping of all is to alter the perceptions of one of the denizens of this world, who, after all, are *already* Shaped beings. He can do it merely by speaking to them, in person, or by radio or telephone."

I remembered how, after I told Brent to *believe* me, he had suddenly stopped worrying about me and gone about his day. I remembered telling Carter Truman I was *fine*, and how he'd instantly accepted that. I had manipulated them both, as though they were nothing more than puppets . . . animated mannequins.

"No doubt police responded to the shots fired in the alley," Karl was continuing. "It would have been an easy matter for the Adversary to Shape them, to convince them to contact the Chief of Police, and then convince him to put the Adversary in touch with the Mayor."

"And he told them I'm a terrorist?" I said.

"Apparently."

I shot an uneasy glance at the buildings lining the road. They looked deserted, but I felt like every window hid a spy, someone already reaching for the phone. My foot pressed harder against the pedal, but Karl said, sharply, "Don't speed. It is suspicious enough that we are on the road at all when so few are. Our vehicle's description and identification number have been made public. We must avoid drawing attention to ourselves."

So I lifted my foot again, and we crawled along at the speed limit, so slowly I wanted to scream (again). I came to a complete stop at every stop sign, waited patiently at every red light. We saw no more than half a dozen other vehicles on the road—none of them white vans, thank God—before we rolled past some run-down warehouses and a few empty lots surrounded by chain-link fences, and into the countryside at last, on a gravel road between stubble-covered farmers' fields. A dark pine forest rose maybe half a mile to our left, broken here and there by the bright yellow of aspen.

Though we'd run out from under the edge of the wind and rain, the sky remained clouded, hiding the mountains that lay somewhere ahead of us. Driving through open fields in my bright, white, supposedly terrorist-containing car, I felt horribly exposed.

Apparently, so did Karl. "We need some place to hide until dark," he said. "We need to get in among the trees."

*What we need*, I thought, *is a road that leads into the woods, something nobody uses.*

We crested a low rise, and there it was: a road, a track, really, leading to our left, between two fields and into the forest. "There!" I said, and winced, feeling a twinge of my former headache

Karl shot me a sharp look. "Fortunate indeed," he said. "Take it." He twisted left and right in his seat, scanning the surroundings, looking behind us. "No one in sight."

I turned off onto the track. It hadn't rained here, so it wasn't muddy, but it *was* weed-grown, so we didn't raise a cloud of dust, which might have hung in the air for several betraying minutes. A minute later we rolled into the forest, and dipped down into a shallow valley with a stream meandering along it. The trail petered out in a flat, bare spot, where blackened rocks in the center and low split log benches surrounding them spoke of campfires past.

I stopped the car, turned off the engine, and just sat, holding on to the wheel. I felt shuddery and shaken and very, very scared.

Karl put his hand on my shoulder, and I jumped. He pulled it back again. "My apologies," he said. "I did not mean to startle you. We will wait here until nightfall, then move on under cover of darkness." He nodded at the dashboard. "You should check the radio again. We need to know what is happening."

Reluctantly, I turned it back on. ". . . Mayor has expressed his thanks to the concerned citizen who came forward, Mr. Sucherl Gegner, who recognized the suspected terrorist from online images . . ."

"Gegner?" I said.

"German for 'adversary' or 'opponent,'" Karl said. "I believe it his idea of a joke."

I'd missed a few words. ". . . described as having dark hair, shoulder-length, brown eyes, five feet nine inches in height, weight 135 pounds . . ." I felt sick to my stomach as I realized who that description fit, a sense of nausea that swelled to choke me as the voice concluded, ". . . current alias Shawna Keys, owner of

Worldshaper Pottery, located at 2333 Blackthorne Avenue, where she also resides. She is accompanied by a man, approximately six feet tall, thin, dark-complexioned, long graying hair pulled back in a ponytail, mustache, blue eyes. May be driving a 2017 white Fjord Model Z, license plate . . ."

I stabbed the radio button and the maddening voice fell silent. "This is insane!"

"But at least you are no longer wondering if *you* are," Karl said.

"Aren't I?" I ran a shaking hand over my forehead. "Now I'm thinking the attack on the coffee shop happened, I'm in the ICU on life support, and this is a morphine-induced hallucination."

"There is an easy way to find out," Karl said. "Turn around, drive back into town, and surrender to the authorities. Perhaps you will wake up."

I glared at him, then returned both hands to the wheel. "No," I said. Because everything around me was *real*, dammit—the familiar pebbled surface of the leather-covered wheel, the slightly sore spot on my right knee where it pressed up against the center console, the blast of air from the vent to my left, the faint smell of the InvisiShield leather protectant I'd used on the interior a week before. This was my car, and this was the real world . . .

. . . or, at least, *a* real world. Because it clearly wasn't *my* world anymore.

My world. Literally. If Karl was telling the truth, I had made the whole thing: copied most of it from the *real* real world, maybe, but then tweaked it to be the world I wanted to live in. And now someone else had the keys to it . . . the "*hokhmah*" (that word alone seemed proof I wasn't hallucinating this, because I'd never have invented it) . . . and was trying to steal it, just like someone had tried to steal my car three weeks ago.

*That* theft had failed only because my car, which I'd only had for a couple of months (and absolutely adored), boasted the new

Fjord biometric theft-prevention system, and while the thief had had my keys (which he'd lifted from my coat, hung over a chair in the Human Bean, while I was getting a coffee refill), he didn't have my retinas, scanned automatically every time I climbed into the driver's seat.

You'd think my *world* would be at least as well protected as my *car* had been. Apparently not.

Just a few hours ago my biggest worry had been that the young guys hanging the Worldshaper Pottery sign wouldn't get it done before it rained. Now . . . my shop was ruined, my best friend was not just dead, but *had never existed*, and I was fleeing for my life, with a stranger from another dimension riding shotgun.

Shotgun. For the first time in my life, I wished that wasn't a metaphor. I used to shoot when I was a girl. (Or had I? Was that more fakery? I groaned—I couldn't keep thinking things like that, or I really would go crazy.) I'd won trophies in marksmanship at the local fair, and had gone hunting with my Mom more than once (*unless . . . no.* I wouldn't think that.) I'd left my guns at home, though, when I'd moved to Eagle River. There was so little crime in our city even Policeman Phil had joked with me and Brent the last time we went bar-hopping together about how easy the cops' jobs were . . .

Brent. Where was he in all this?

I stabbed the phone button on the steering wheel. Karl, staring out the window, turned sharply toward me as the car beeped. "Call Brent," I said.

"Shawna, no—" Karl started, but I gave him my coldest glare.

"Shut up," I said.

The phone rang. Once, twice. The third was cut off. "Hello?" said Brent's voice. He sounded perfectly normal.

"Brent, it's me, Shawna."

A pause. "Who?"

My heart skipped a beat. I felt as if cold hands had seized me by the throat. "Shawna!" I cried. "Your girlfriend! I want you to know I'm all right. I want you to know everything you're hearing about me is lies. I want—"

"Lady," Brent said, "I think you've got a wrong number. I don't have a girlfriend. And I don't know any Shawna. Sorry."

And he hung up.

I stared at the speaker, sick horror welling up in me. Then I stabbed the phone button on the wheel again, but Karl reached out and jabbed the EXIT button to cancel the call. "No," he said. "Shawna. *Think.* Either the Adversary has spoken to your boyfriend and he really does not remember you, or he believes the authorities may be listening in, and he is pretending not to know you to protect both himself and you. Whichever is the truth, you cannot talk to him. Because even if the Adversary *has* wiped his memory . . . is it not possible, in your world, to trace this form of communication?"

Trace . . . crap, I hadn't thought of that!

I jerked open the car door, stumbled out into the clearing, and ran for the circle of fire-blackened rocks. I heard the passenger door open and close behind me, but I didn't look around. I slammed my HiPhone down on one rock, then picked up another and brought it down hard, pounding the phone over and over until it was reduced to shards of glass and bits of twisted metal and shattered circuit boards.

Then I scrambled back to my feet and turned to find Karl behind me. "Problem?" he said.

"The problem is I'm an idiot," I snarled. "The authorities don't *need* to trace a call to locate a cellphone. They send out signals all the time. Even in airplane mode." I probably shouldn't have been surprised that a guy in Shakespeare-wear didn't know much about cellphones, but his puzzled frown still brought me up short. He had clearly heard of "this form of communication," and yet just as clearly didn't really grasp how it worked. So many strange gaps in his knowledge, such a strange way of talking . . . where was *he* from, really? How could he be from "Reality with a capital R" without knowing much about cellphones? They *had* to be something I'd copied from the First World, because I certainly hadn't invented the technology.

"Airplane mode?" Karl said. "I don't understand."

"It doesn't matter. What matters is . . . we can't stay here until dark. In case they've *already* located my phone." I looked up at the sky. If that were the case, a helicopter would be the next thing we saw, but the leaden sky contained nothing but clouds, and the only sound was the rush of wind through the trees, a whispering breeze compared to the furious, destructive gales the Adversary's storm had hurled at the city's heart.

"Then we must find a new place to hide," Karl said. "And we must go back to the main road." He gestured at the clearing. "There is no other path through the woods, and no bridge over that stream. If they come here, we will be trapped."

"We could just dump the car here," I said. "Flee on foot." And *that* was a sure sign of just how seriously I was beginning to buy into Karl's crazy explanation of what was going on, because I loved that car almost as much as I loved Brent.

*Had* loved Brent. I felt another surge of near-nausea, and swallowed hard.

"It's too soon for that," Karl said. "We are too close to the city, and we have no supplies, nor any means of making a fire. You do not even have a coat. We would die of exposure."

I wrapped my arms around myself. The air *was* cool, the storm having brought a surge of cold mountain air with it. "But where do we go?"

"We must find a place to hide, and quickly," Karl said.

"And after that?"

"Eventually, we leave this world entirely."

"How, and where?"

"I will explain everything, but not now. We must go." He looked pointedly toward the car.

"Fine." I strode . . . yes, let's go with "strode," rather than "flounced" . . . toward the car. "Fine. We'll find a place to hide, then you'll tell me everything. *If* we can find a place to hide."

"I am confident we will," Karl said, following me. "Perhaps even another mode of transportation." He sounded so certain I glanced back at him, a little surprised. But the expression he gave me was carefully blank.

We climbed into the Fjord. I started it, spun it around, and headed back up the track toward the gravel road. As we drove through the trees, raindrops spattered the windshield. If it really came on, the clearing we'd been in would turn into a quagmire— another reason not to linger there.

Just as we emerged from the trees, a red pickup—not a white van or a police car, thank God—zipped past on the gravel road, heading toward the city, raising a rooster-tail of dust the just-begun rain had little effect on. If the driver saw us he or she made no sign.

We turned the other way, toward the mountains, and this time I floored it. The risk of encountering a radar trap on this back road, and the inherent risk of driving fast on a gravel road—I'd always hated the juddering, not-quite-gripping-the-ground feel—both seemed less than the risk of getting caught by whatever forces the authorities had mustered to search for a "dangerous terrorist."

At some point I was going to have to sit down and have a nice quiet nervous breakdown, but for now I had to drive—and keep my eyes peeled for another hiding place. A better hiding place than the last one, which would have been a trap if we'd been discovered. I didn't have a clear idea what kind of hiding place would be ideal. I just hoped I'd recognize it if I saw it.

Nothing presented itself for the next half hour, during which the rain intensified—though to nothing like it had been when the storm first hit—and the gravel road, concomitantly, became slipperier. Since I was white-knuckling the driving, I didn't pester Karl further. He'd said he'd explain once we found a place to hide. I'd wait . . . but then I'd hold him to that promise.

The land of course rose as we headed toward the mountains, the fairly flat terrain where Eagle River was located beginning to swell and roll into the foothills. As we flew over a low rise, I glanced at the dashboard clock. It had just turned noon—the same time it had been when the white vans had screeched to a halt outside the Human Bean and the shooting had begun.

The same time Aesha had died.

I half-expected to feel something, some . . . bump . . . in the smooth flow of time, as we caught up to where we were supposed to be, but the only bump I felt was one from a hole in the increasingly decrepit road that jerked us sideways and forced me to yank the wheel the other way in response, heart in my throat. Although for all I knew, that *was* some kind of sign from the world, a message to its Shaper, that time was back in sync.

We topped another ridge and drove down into the valley below, toward a wooden bridge that crossed a swift-flowing creek. Just past the bridge a small billboard marked the beginning of a side road that led off to the right. I slowed as we approached the bridge, the kind of narrow backwoods bridge that's only wide enough for one car and only one flash flood away from vanishing forever. The barely legible sign, streaked with rain, showed cartoon cabins, once presumably red but now faded to dusty pink, nestled beneath equally faded representations of evergreens. Across the pale blue sky, I could just make out white letters: CANDLE LAKE RESORT.

What interested me more, though, was the much more recently painted sign hung on hooks and two chains from the bottom of the billboard. It read, in black letters on a white background, CLOSED FOR THE SEASON.

"That's it!" I said, braking to a halt at the turnoff.

"What's it?" Karl said.

"Our hiding place." I nodded at the sign.

"A resort?" he said doubtfully.

"A *closed* resort," I said. "Empty cabins. Maybe a shed we can hide the car in. Maybe *food*, if we're lucky. Beds, at least."

Karl looked in the direction the sign pointed. "Have you ever been to this resort?"

I shook my head. "I've never even heard of it. But it sounds like the perfect hiding place."

"Then it probably is," he said. "Very well."

I turned onto the rutted road. It was muddy, but gravelled enough I didn't *think* we'd get stuck. This had to be a back way into Candle Lake Resort, or it never could have survived. (I might have doubted it *had* survived, based on the worn-out billboard, if not for the very new CLOSED sign.) The main approach would be from the interstate, which couldn't be more than a few miles to the north of us.

We drove in among the trees, windshield wipers slapping away the still-falling rain. The road, following the river, curved left, then right. It continued on, but we didn't, because we suddenly found our way blocked by a padlocked metal gate, set in a barbed-wire fence above a cattle guard. I stopped the car. "Do you have any tools?" Karl said.

"In the trunk."

"Open it for me, please."

"It's not locked," I said. "There's a button above the license plate. Press and lift."

He nodded and got out, closing the passenger door behind him. In the rearview mirror, I saw the trunk lid open, heard the clank of metal, and then saw it close. Karl walked past again with my tire iron in one hand. He shoved it into the chain holding the padlock and twisted. The chain broke with a pinging sound. Karl pushed open the gate, then motioned me through. I rolled past him, tires rumbling on the cattle guard's metal slats, and in the mirror, saw him close the gate again and drape the chain through the mesh so that it wasn't immediately apparent—at least from this far away—that it had been forced. Then he trudged back to the car, tossed the tire iron into the back seat, and climbed into his own.

"All right," he said. He ran a hand over his wet hair. "Let's see what this resort has to offer."

"Food, I hope," I said. My morning muffin was now more than six hours in the past (my past, anyway), and a lot had happened since then. My stomach had been growling off and on for an hour.

"Then it would not surprise me if we find some," Karl said.

The resort was much farther from the gate than I expected. The road curved west again as we continued to follow the river. The tree trunks closed in around us like the bars of a prison, and the bumpiness and muddiness of the road kept me gripping the wheel and creeping along the path.

I had plenty of time before we reached road's end, maybe two miles from where we had turned in, to conjure up an image of what I thought the place would look like. I turned out to be pretty much dead-on: a gravel parking lot, separated from maybe a dozen cabins and a larger central building by a split-log fence painted in peeling brown; boardwalks instead of sidewalks; and out past the buildings, pewter-gray and indistinct in the rain, a lake. Upside-down canoes were stacked beside a boathouse, and a long wooden pier, floating on tractor-tire tubes, extended like a tongue into the water.

In the middle of the parking lot a huge oak tree stood alone, its leaves at the height of their golden autumn glory, tossing in the wind and rain, but still firmly enough attached that only a few fluttered down as I drove over to it and beneath its canopy. An acorn bounced off the hood, and by long-honed reflex I winced at the possibility of a ding. I turned off the engine, released the wheel, and massaged my temples. My headache was back, and the fatigue I'd felt just after the attack on the coffee shop had happened . . . and then unhappened.

"It is fortunate such a wide-spreading tree was planted here," Karl said.

"Yeah, it's been my lucky day all around," I said sourly. "Will it hide the car from the air?"

"I would think so," Karl said. "Though I do not think there is much to fear from the air while the rain persists. Perhaps by the time it clears we will have found a better place to conceal our vehicle."

We got out, Karl first retrieving the tire iron from the back seat. From underneath the oak, which sheltered us somewhat from the rain, we surveyed the resort. It had clearly been around a long time, and just as clearly wasn't thriving. There's a fine line between "rustic" and "run-down," and this place had crossed it at least a decade ago. The old sign had been absolutely accurate: the once-red cabins had faded to the same dusty pink as their images. The larger, longer central building, painted the same peeling brown as the fence, had a roof of green, slightly curly, and occasionally askew shingles. White Adirondack chairs dotted the veranda surrounding it. A shuttered window faced us, a bit of a shelf extending from its base: presumably the camp canteen. I wondered if, in summer, the owners of the resort put picnic tables beneath the tree above us, so families could enjoy ice cream from the canteen in its shade, and the minute I thought that, I knew it *had* to be true. I could see it as clearly in my mind's eye as I had pictured the resort before we arrived at it.

But I'd never been here before. How could I . . . ?

The thought died unformed as my stomach growled. I put a hand on it. "Let's explore," I said. "We're here until dark, right?"

"Yes," Karl said. "We will wait until two or three in the morning, when we are least likely to be observed, then carry on."

"Carry on *where*?"

"Later." He held up the tire iron. "Let us see what these buildings hold."

The door of the nearest cabin, though locked, proved no obstacle to Karl and the tire iron. He thrust the sharp end between the door and the jamb, and pulled hard. *Breaking and entering*, I thought as wood splintered, but couldn't muster any guilt. After all, if I had created . . . Shaped . . . this world, didn't *everything* in it belong to me?

We entered the dim interior. Nothing happened when I clicked the light switch by the door, but there was enough light to see two double beds with a table, bearing a lamp and an old-fashioned clock radio, between them, a small round table with two chairs in one corner, and a shelf with a clothes rod below it just outside a tiny bathroom. I made a beeline for the latter, and emerged a few moments later, feeling much relieved, drying my rain-soaked hair with a towel, to find Karl standing at the small window that faced the main cabin. He'd drawn the dusty pink curtains back, relieving the gloom a little. "If we are going to find food," he said, "it will be there."

"Let's find out," I said.

"In a moment." He disappeared into the bathroom. His going to relieve himself relieved me, too, as had his comment about food. Whatever else he was, he was human.

Or was he? The Adversary and the mysterious Ygrair were both aliens, he claimed. Was he one, too? Even aliens would have to pee and eat, wouldn't they? *The form is imposed by the planet* . . .

I kind of wished I hadn't remembered he'd said that.

When he emerged again, we crossed through the rain to the main building. Its door gave no more resistance than the cabin's. We stepped through into a kitchen. In the big room visible through an archway to our right stood half a dozen square tables, covered with plasticized red-and-white checkered tablecloths and surrounded by rickety-looking wooden chairs. A shelf just below the ceiling held exactly (again) the kind of knickknacks I'd expect this kind of resort to use for decoration: rusty kerosene lanterns, old crates with long-vanished trade names stenciled on their sides, a horse collar, and photographs of bearded men in dark suits and hats and women in long white dresses carrying parasols, standing on the lakeshore. Aside from the archway, a long counter separated the kitchen and the dining area, the space between it and the ceiling sealed with a fiberglass accordion-style curtain, in a rather unattractive shade of flyspecked yellow.

A big upright freezer and matching refrigerator, whose rounded corners marked them as dating back to the 1950s, stood like silent sentinels at the far end of the kitchen, beneath a long, narrow horizontal window just below the ceiling. In the middle of the kitchen, an island provided work space. The wall to our left held two giant sinks, beneath shuttered windows that, when open, would look out toward the cabins. The short counter to our left ran beneath the closed canteen window.

With the power off, I didn't expect to find anything edible in either the refrigerator or the freezer, and didn't—they were both empty and warm. But beneath the canteen counter, locked cabinets yielded (with the judicious application of the tire iron) chips and chocolate, jars of jerky, packs of peanuts, and scads of soft drinks. They were cheap brands I'd never heard of (Pepp's Ginger Ale, Rocky Cola, Eleven-Up), and of course they were warm, but beggars . . . oh, all right, *thieves* . . . can't be choosers.

We sat in the dim dining room and ate jerky, chips, and chocolate, washed down with sugar-laden pop, and if my teeth felt notably more corroded afterward than before, at least I felt a bit more energetic, and my headache lifted. Afterward, we explored the rest of the building. A room off the far end of the dining area turned out to be a staff locker room, and Karl ducked inside and finally got rid of his tights and doublet, emerging decked out in khakis and a dark-green golf shirt bearing the Candle Lake resort name. He even found a pair of hiking boots that fit, losing the ridiculously high riding boots, which had gone above his knees and been attached by garters to somewhere even higher up. He kept the cowboy hat and duster, and the dagger.

We walked back through diminishing rain to the cabin. Eating had helped my headache, but if anything, I felt even more exhausted. I'd been running on adrenaline since the coffee shop attack, and it was finally draining away. I lay down on one of the beds and closed my eyes, just for a minute. I heard Karl open the door and go out again.

*I shouldn't sleep*, I thought. *I'll be vulnerable if I fall asleep.* Karl could still be something other than what he claimed. If he were really, say, a deranged killer, having carefully arranged to be alone with him at a deserted resort was possibly not the wisest choice I'd ever made.

*He might not be a killer. Just a rapist.*

*Not helping*, I told my spinning brain.

And also, stupid. Because weird things had happened and he seemed to know about them. So far, everything he had told me had checked out. The simplest explanation was that he was telling the truth. Occam's Razor, and all that.

On the other hand, razors could produce painful nicks.

*I shouldn't sleep . . .*

But I did.

Karl walked through the rain from cabin to cabin, breaking into each to see if any held anything of value. He found nothing they had not found in the first cabin. When he reached the end of the line, he stared into the forest and wondered if he should just keep walking.

Shawna had power, more power than he had yet seen in a Shaper. Most, once they had Shaped their worlds, had very little ability left to continue to make changes to it, though they could usually at least Shape individuals as required. But Shawna . . . not only had she performed the amazing feat of resetting the clock three hours, she had twice now, he was certain, unconsciously Shaped the world on a much smaller, but still impressive, scale: first, the track into the woods to the old campsite (though that had not been as helpful as it had first seemed), and then this resort, complete with food conveniently left for them to find. He doubted either had existed until she had decided she needed them. It was no wonder she was exhausted: the wonder was she could function at all. That was certainly the kind of power a Shaper would need to do what Ygrair demanded. And yet . . .

She still had no memory of Ygrair, no memory of the training she had been given, no memory of her entry into the Labyrinth or her initial Shaping of this world. Karl had been in Ygrair's world when Shawna was in the school in the First World. He had never met her before she entered the Labyrinth, had known nothing about her until today. Clearly even Ygrair had not sensed her potential power, or she would have told him to seek her out.

The Adversary had recognized her—had called her by name—which meant they were contemporaries in Ygrair's school. Had she been one of those students Ygrair had hurled into the Labyrinth at the time of the attack? If so, that might explain her lack of memory . . . perhaps she had not been fully prepared . . .

Whatever the reason for her amnesia, if Shawna could not remember her past, *never* remembered it . . . would she ever truly believe him? As they journeyed through the Labyrinth, Shawna capturing the *hokhmah* of world after world with the goal of eventually delivering all that gathered knowledge to Ygrair, what if she began to doubt him? With her power, she could prove an even greater threat to the Labyrinth, to Ygrair, and to his own hopes, than the Adversary. She might even decide to become the Adversary's ally!

*No*, Karl thought, instantly rejecting the thought. *Not that. Not after she saw him kill her best friend.*

Still, even if that were a remote possibility, the other possibility, that she would reject Ygrair's mission and claim power for herself, remained.

The forest, dark and dripping, beckoned him seductively. If he left her here, sleeping in the cabin, the Adversary would eventually find her and kill her. Regrettable, but at least he would be free to find the place where he could open the next Portal, and flee to the next world. Perhaps its Shaper would be as powerful as Shawna, and unlike her, would remember—and thus feel loyalty—toward Ygrair.

Perhaps. But he would not be able to prevent the Adversary from passing through the next Portal, any more than he had been able to prevent him from passing through the last Portal into this world. Once the Adversary had finished with Shawna and consolidated his hold on her world, he would follow Karl into the next world . . . and the one after that . . . and the one after that. World after world would fall to him, inevitably, until Karl found another Shaper with enough power left to meet Ygrair's need . . .

. . . if such a one even existed. What if Shawna were the only one with that much power? Abandoning her would then mean his failure. The Labyrinth would be taken in full by the Adversary. He would leave the Portals open between the worlds he captured, drawing power from each, becoming unstoppable. Eventually he would reach Ygrair's world, claim it, and kill her, and then rule unopposed over all the Shaped worlds and all their myriad inhabitants.

Or so Karl assumed. He had to remind himself that the Adversary was not human, and his true goals and motivations might not be apparent. However, that was a somewhat uncomfortable thought, because Ygrair was not human either. Was he certain he understood her true goals and motivations?

*She has entrusted me with her world, and now with her life*, he thought. *I cannot start doubting her. Or the promise she has made to me . . .*

He returned his thoughts to the Adversary. If the Adversary succeeded, what would happen to Karl? He did not know, but he supposed it would not much matter. Whether he was hurled back into the First World, to try to piece together a life in a place now alien to him, or enslaved or executed somewhere in the Labyrinth, it would make no difference. If Ygrair died, the hope he had held on to all these decades, the promise that one day he, too, would be able to Shape a world to fulfill his deepest wishes . . . and one wish in particular . . . would die with her.

*I cannot abandon Shawna Keys*, he thought, staring into the sodden shadows of the trees. *She may well be my only hope of success. All I can do is stay close to her, do my best to instill in her the urgency of her mission . . . and try to keep her alive until she can fulfill it.*

He turned away from the woods, and walked back along the line of cabins to the one in which Shawna slept.

I awoke from a confused dream, which vanished the instant I opened my eyes and stared up at the strange ceiling. It was still light outside.

Karl sat in the chair in the corner, watching me, which was a little creepy. His black duster hung on the back of the chair, his cowboy hat rested on the table by his elbow. "Bad dream?" he said.

"Since this morning, everything has been a bad dream." I sat up. "How long was I asleep?"

"Three or four hours," Karl said. "I was about to wake you. We must discuss our next move."

I rubbed my head. I hated naps; as a rule, they left me feeling worse than before, and this one was no exception. My head felt full of damp cotton. I wished I had coffee. There *was* a coffee maker in the corner, on a small table under the clothes rod, but without power, there was no way to make use of it. I wasn't *quite* desperate enough to chew a coffee bag. "What we need," I said, as grumpily as I felt, "is for you to finally explain, in detail, what's going on."

"I have explained much . . ." Karl began.

"No," I said. "You haven't."

"Enough, at least, so that you understand that you are not safe, and that your world has changed."

"Yeah," I said. "That part I know. I still think there's some chance I'm hyped up on drugs and hallucinating all this from a hospital bed, but assuming I'm not, I admit recent events have made your insane claims about me being some kind of Almighty-God-like being *slightly* more believable."

"I have told you," Karl said, a hint of impatience in his voice, "several times, that you are not a god of any sort, and certainly not almighty. If you were, your world could not be changed by the Adversary."

"Start there," I said. "Start with the Adversary. You said he had his own world."

"Yes," Karl said. "And unlike you, he knew full well it was his to Shape. He made himself a kind of God-Emperor within it, exerting control over every aspect of it: nothing was beyond his ken, or purview."

"'Everything within the state, nothing outside the state, nothing against the state,'" I said.

Karl raised an eyebrow. "I am unfamiliar with that quote, but yes, that is very much the kind of world he Shaped. He saw it as a perfect world, one without disorder, crime, war, or poverty."

I had just quoted Mussolini at him, but suddenly I wondered if I had misjudged the Adversary's motives. "When you put it that way, it doesn't sound so bad."

"But in such a world," Karl said, "where there is only one way to think, ruthlessly imposed, there can be no freedom, no change, no creativity. All must be done as the Adversary orders it should be done. Worse, he Shaped his people—like the cadre of soldiers accompanying him from world to world—to obey his orders without question. He has stripped them of free will. He is the ultimate tyrant."

I grimaced. "Okay, I get it, bad Adversary. And that's what he intends to do to my world."

"Yours, and all others."

"If you think I can save other worlds . . . why can't I save mine?"

"It is too late. When he touched you . . . he already has this world's *hokhmah*. Only the fact you still live keeps him from imposing his complete will on it."

"But you want me to take the . . . *hokhmah* . . . of other worlds.

Just like he took mine. How will that work without me killing the Shapers?"

"The Adversary . . . stripped it from you. Stole it. He has technology, from his home world, that allows him to do this. But the transfer is not complete while you live. When *you* obtain the *hokhmah* from another Shaper, however, you will not steal it. It will be given to you willingly. And once given, it will be yours completely."

"How will that work, exactly? I don't have any special technology inside *me*."

"Do not be concerned about that. I will give it to you when the time is right."

I still felt exhausted, and my head still felt full of mush. What kind of Adversary-defeating heroine could I possibly be? "Why would another Shaper give up their power to me willingly?"

"Because unlike you, they will remember Ygrair and what they owe her."

"You expect them to be that loyal to her."

"I do."

"Sounds like wishful thinking to me. This Labyrinth of yours may be doomed. Did you ever think of that?"

"Of course I think of it!" Karl sounded as close to angry as I'd yet heard him. "I think of it every minute, every day, every week, every month, every year."

"Every *year*?" I stared at him. "Just how long have you been searching?"

A pause, as though he'd said more than he'd intended. "A long time," he said at last. "Although time is difficult to measure in the Labyrinth."

"And yet, other than the Adversary, I'm the first candidate to replace Ygrair you've found?"

"Yes," he said at last.

"How many worlds?"

Another pause. "I have not counted."

"A dozen? Dozens? Hundreds?"

He only shrugged.

"What if I say no? What if I refuse to go along with you on this quest of yours?"

"Then the Adversary will kill you," Karl said, voice flat. "As I have explained."

"But you say I still have power to Shape this world. I could create a hiding place . . ."

"It would be a prison," Karl said. "And it would not last long. The Adversary already has some of the authorities on his side, and I would imagine that every hour he is Shaping more of those in power to do his will. No matter what you do, if you stay in this world, he will eventually find you, and kill you or have you killed."

"But if I leave this world he'll turn it into a copy of his own!"

"Yes," Karl said. "But that will happen no matter what you do. Stay, and die, or leave, and live . . . either way, your world is lost. It has been lost from the moment the Adversary touched you in the coffee shop."

I tried to think. If Karl was telling me the truth—and again, Occam's Razor slashed a burning wound through my reasoning mind—I had absolutely no choice but to follow his orders, go where he told me to go, do what he wanted me to do. To do otherwise would be to countersign my own death warrant, already issued by the Adversary, and would not change the bleak future of my world one iota.

I was tired, and grief and possibly a full-blown blubbering breakdown were lurking just outside the crumbling walls of my self-composure. I wanted to go home. I wanted the life I had had the day before. I wanted to be sitting in the Human Bean with Aesha listening to the DNA Eruptions butcher a song. I wanted to be making love to Brent. I wanted to call my mom. I wanted to throw pots, fulfill the contracts I had, make new stock for my shelves. I wanted normality . . .

. . . and I could never, ever, *ever* have it again.

"So where do we go?" It took me a moment to recognize that tortured whisper as my own, to realize it had slipped out through the fear and sorrow that had my throat in a viselike grip. "How do we escape?"

Karl got up and sat on the bed beside me. His face, in the dimness of the shabby room, looked understanding, compassionate, caring . . . and every bit as exhausted as I felt, if not more so. He took my hands in his, his touch so warm and human and normal I almost started crying right then. "There's only one place we can go," he said.

I stared into his face. "Where?"

"A whole new world."

# SEVEN

"SUCHERL GEGNER" STOOD in the operations control room of the Montana headquarters of the National Bureau of Investigation, and listened to the chatter of the agents conducting a search for his missing quarry. The storm had dissipated, dwindling to an ordinary rainfall, taking with it the last of the creative energy that had flooded through the Portal from the last world. Without that, he could no longer sense the location of Shawna Keys—or of Karl Yatsar, his unwitting and unwilling accomplice, who had opened the Labyrinth to him and made possible the eventual execution of the arch-criminal Ygrair.

But though his Shaping ability was limited while Shawna lived, he did have the ability to alter the perceptions and beliefs of the Shaped denizens of this world, simply by speaking with them. He had first Shaped the Eagle River police chief. After that, it had been easy enough to gain access, either in person or over the phone, to increasingly more powerful people, including the Montana bureau chief of the NBI. The national director of that law enforcement agency was now on her way from Washington. Soon all of the United States' antiterrorism resources would be bent toward locating Shawna and Yatsar.

She *would* be found, but the Adversary did not expect to find Yatsar with her, ideal though that would be. Yatsar carried within his body Shurak nanomites, the technology that allowed him to open Portals. The Adversary intended to obtain those nanomites for himself. He did not even need Yatsar's entire body to do so—just a sufficiently large mass of tissue or blood.

The Adversary had known the moment Yatsar entered his world, because he, too, carried Shurak nanomites within his body, which had . . . resonated . . . with those in Yatsar's. Yatsar must have felt it, too, and realized his danger. He had eluded capture, and fled into the next world as soon as possible, no doubt thinking that once he closed the Portal behind him, the Adversary would again be trapped in a single world.

But he had been wrong. Ygrair's great crime had been the theft of the forbidden technology that gave access to the Labyrinth, making possible her escape from the Shurak home world in the ancient podship—a literal museum piece—in which she had eventually crashed on Earth. Before she left, she had attempted to destroy the sole, secret datastore that held the knowledge of that technology, but in her frantic haste she had been sloppy. The Elders had been able to re-create portions of the data, enough to design and implant in the Adversary the nanomites he now carried. He could not create a Portal, but he could find and open a closed one.

That ability had allowed him to follow and find Ygrair. Millennia ago, the ancient Shurak had discovered the Between (what Ygrair now called the Labyrinth), an interstitial space that could be accessed from, and provide access to, any world in the universe—provided that world had intelligent life.

Within every sentient race existed a few gifted individuals born with an innate connection to the Between: what Ygrair called Shapers. The Shurak had used their own Shapers to enter and travel the Between. They had invaded and conquered many worlds. At first, they had enslaved the Shapers they found among other races, forcing them to serve as pilots. Later they had learned how to strip the alien Shapers' power from them, what Ygrair called the *hokhmah*, and feed that power to their own Shapers, making them immensely strong. The universe had been at their mercy.

But that had been millennia ago. The Shurak Empire had fallen to revolution, its own people rebelling against their leaders' horrific, rapine abuse of other worlds. The Labyrinth had been closed, and access to it forbidden.

Ygrair had broken that law, and many others. The Portal she opened into the Between with her stolen technology, she had closed behind her—but with the nanomites the Elders had constructed teeming in his blood, the Adversary had been able to find that Portal, and open it. In a new podship, built from ancient specifications, he had entered the Between. It had been easy, then, to find the Portal to Earth—that one, she had not even closed.

On that primitive planet, wearing the human form it imposed on his more amorphous natural state, he had learned to fit in, and soon enough discovered Ygrair's "school." He of course had the Shaping ability she was cultivating among the humans (he could not have traveled the Between without it) and so he had infiltrated the school. The Elders had carefully crafted his nanomites so they would not resonate with the ones Ygrair carried. She took him for human, and began teaching him the "Lore of the Labyrinth," as she called it (while he also studied more mundane subjects like history, math, and science).

As soon as he could, he returned to his stealthed podship and sent a message into the Between.

He had been astounded to learn of the Shaped Worlds: so far as he knew, the Shurak Empire had never discovered that a Shaper could turn the quantum fog of the Between into a pocket universe of his or her own devising. But he had not seen the point of it, and he still did not understand why Ygrair had made it her life's work on Earth.

Several Earth years passed. Time in the Between was fluid, and so the Adversary was not surprised by the delay, since there was no way to be certain how long his message had taken to reach the Shurak home world, nor how long it would take a force to respond. In the interim, he let his human façade subsume his true nature. Shawna Keys did not remember him, for whatever reason, but he remembered her well. They had not been close, but they had socialized on occasion at school functions and with mutual friends. She had never struck him as special in any way, and it surprised him she was so powerful now.

The Elders' attack fell on the last day of term before the Christmas holiday. Only the Adversary and Shawna had been on the campus. The Adversary had nowhere else to go, and Shawna, he had noted before, never left for holidays, though he did not know why.

Ygrair somehow must have sensed the arrival of the podships the moment they exited the Between, high above the Earth. Perhaps the stealthing technology, which had worked so well when he had landed on Earth, failed this time; perhaps there were simply too many podships. However she detected the Shurak approach, she had acted quickly, first opening the Graduation Portal, through which students entered the Labyrinth to claim their worlds—and then doing something the Adversary had not known she *could* do. Without consultation, without consent, without even being in the same room, she had thrown the Adversary (and, it was now obvious, Shawna) through that Portal.

One moment he had been standing in his dorm room, looking out over the snow-filled yard toward the setting December sun, eagerly awaiting the impending attack and the summary execution of Ygrair for her unforgivable crimes. The next, he had been standing on a featureless black plain beneath a flat white sky: a blank world, ready for him to Shape.

He had been furious. He had tried to open a Portal, though he knew he did not have the ability; naturally, to no avail. After a period of useless flailing and fuming, and with no other choice, he had finally settled down to Shape the world he had been given.

He had begun by copying the First World closely, just as Shawna had: but then he had set to work to turn it into a human version of the perfect and orderly Shurak home world. He had taken some satisfaction in the process, but after ten years, he had begun to fear he was trapped there forever . . .

. . . and then Yatsar had arrived, opening a Portal, and unexpectedly offering him the hope of completing his mission, and finally rendering justice to Ygrair.

By now, Yatsar had to know what his fate, and the fate of the Labyrinth, would be if he were captured: another reason he would surely abandon Shawna if her apprehension seemed inevitable, and flee into the next world—thus opening the way for the Adversary. Yatsar had no choice: he could not risk capture, and even suicide would not destroy the Portal nanomites within his body, no matter what means he used, short of plunging into the heart of a star. The Adversary had heard a phrase, while he pretended to be a student in Ygrair's school: "Catch-22." It seemed to apply to Yatsar's predicament.

"We may have something, Mr. Gegner," a voice said deferentially to his right. He turned his head toward the man in the dark suit who stood there: Edwin Smoak, the Special Agent in Charge of the NBI's Montana field office. "A farmer spotted a car matching the description on a side road. The lead is several hours' old, but we'll dispatch helicopters to the area at first light, weather permitting, to conduct a thorough aerial search, as well as sending out ground forces. There are few roads in the area, so if they are still in the car, there aren't many places where they might have gone to ground."

"Excellent," said the Adversary. Neither Smoak nor anyone else now remembered that "Sucherl Gegner" had first presented himself as an ordinary citizen offering a helpful tip about suspicious activity. They all now believed—he had *made* them believe—that he was in fact a senior agent of GloPoSec, the Global Police and Security Initiative, which had a far better record of preventing terrorist attacks in this world than its counterparts in the First World—something Shawna had clearly desired, along with her own pottery shop, a boyfriend, lunar colonies, and, oddly enough, a professional lacrosse league.

GloPoSec outranked all local police forces, even the NBI, and so all deferred to the Adversary . . . which made his task easier. As did the fact that he could Shape others simply by conversing with them, which was why the national director of the NBI, with whom he had spoken briefly on the phone, was flying to Montana. He intended to use her, once she arrived, to put him in touch with even more exalted authorities. She, after all, had the ear of the President.

"It sounds like things are well in hand," he said to Smoak. "I believe I'll retire. You will of course wake me if anything turns up overnight."

"Of course, Mr. Gegner," said Smoak.

The Adversary left the control room and took the elevator to the third-floor quarters he had been provided. He was not human, and thus was not plagued by the human proclivity to lie awake worrying about unlikely eventualities. Two minutes after he undressed and lay down, he slept.

"A whole new world?" Visions of musical numbers atop flying carpets danced unhelpfully in my head, although certainly a blue wish-granting genie would have been most welcome at that moment. "But how?"

"I must open a new Portal."

I looked around the shabby cabin. "So . . . what are you waiting for?"

"It cannot be done here."

"Why not?"

"The Labyrinth will not allow it."

"You mean Ygrair won't allow it?"

Karl shook his head. "No. She did not invent the Labyrinth, she merely discovered its possibilities. It has . . . laws. As immutable as the natural laws of the First World. And one of those laws is that each Shaped World links to only two other worlds, and the Portals to those worlds can only be created where those worlds . . . touch. One of those locations will always be close to the Shaper, wherever he or she may be. The other is *not* close. It may well be on the other side of the world."

"It may well be? Don't you know?"

"No," Karl said. "Not yet."

I felt a flash of irritation. "You don't seem to know nearly as much as you should."

"I can sense it," Karl said. "I know it lies somewhere west of here. But that is all I know. As we get closer to it, I will sense it more clearly."

"So, to escape the Adversary, we have to somehow travel an unknown distance through a world increasingly turned against us and try not to get caught."

"Yes." He paused. "But that is the *second* thing we should do."

"The second . . ." I stared at him. "I would have thought escaping was Job One."

"Not quite. I think . . . I believe . . ." He stopped. "I am almost *certain*," he said, "that you have the power to enable me to do something else. I believe that, with your help, I can return to the Portal through which I and the Adversary entered this world, and destroy it forever."

"What good will that do?" I said, while part of my mind was turning over that unpleasant word "almost," spoken before the word "certain."

"It will keep him from returning to his own world. It will keep him from bringing reinforcements from that world. And it should weaken him."

"Should?"

"I believe that as long as the Portal remains open, he can draw additional energy through it from his own world, and the world he seized before entering this one. If we can close the Portal, we will sever him from that source of power."

I felt a sudden surge of hope. "And then we can get to the Portal into the next world, and destroy that one, too, and trap him here!"

"No," Karl said. "The Shaper of that world would have to work with me to seal it."

"So, if I get that Shaper's *hokhmah* . . . ?"

Karl opened his mouth, then closed it again. "I . . . do not know," he said. "Yes, you will have the ability to Shape that world, but you did not Shape it to begin with . . . I do not know."

"Why not?"

"I am not Ygrair. I have neither her knowledge or her power, and no way to contact her except to find my way back through the Labyrinth to her side."

"Find your way back . . ." I stared at him. "My God. You don't even have a map. You're going blind, world to world."

"The Labyrinth is large. It is not infinite," Karl said. "Ygrair promised that the Portal through which I exited her world would lead me through all the other Shaped Worlds before I passed through a Portal that would take me back to hers. Hers is the First

Shaped World—the keystone, again, or the clasp of a string of pearls." He paused suddenly. "A better metaphor than a Labyrinth, in truth," he said. "Each pearl a world, each touching two other pearls. We only have to carry on, world after world, and eventually, inevitably, we will enter Ygrair's."

"Who, I'm guessing, won't thank you if you come back without a Shaper full of *hokhmahs*, or with the Adversary in hot pursuit."

Karl didn't answer, instead standing abruptly and going to the window. He peered out through the curtains. "It's getting dark. If we were going to be found here today, we would have been by now. I think we can risk staying here tonight. We both need proper rest. And at least there is food . . . of a sort."

I yawned. Despite my nap, I still felt exhausted, more than ready to lie down again and sleep. But not yet. "If this Adversary is so powerful . . . can't he just figure out where I am? He found me easily enough in Eagle River."

"When he first entered your world, the energy pouring in from the last world helped him find you," Karl said. "But that energy dissipated with the storm. For now, he can find you no more easily than any other individual can be found by the ordinary efforts of law enforcement."

"No more easily than that."

"That's why I asked you if you had ever been here before," Karl said. "They will begin their search in such places."

A horrible thought struck me, a thought that should have struck me before. I sat up straight. "Mom! I've got to warn her!"

"No," Karl said. "That would only draw attention to her. It will take time for them to trace your connections."

"But I have to do something!"

"Where does she live?"

"Appleville, Oregon. More than seven hundred fifty miles from here."

"Then I would say that so far she has been left untroubled. The Adversary still hopes to capture you before you could possibly have traveled that far."

"So far" wasn't much comfort. I pictured NBI agents showing up at her door, demanding to know if she'd heard from me, or seen me. I felt sick. *I'm so sorry.* "But there must be something I can do."

"If you remembered your training . . ." He sighed. "But you do not. The best thing you can do now is rest. We do not know what challenges tomorrow may bring."

I stretched out on the bed, but despite my immense fatigue, I didn't sleep right away. I kept thinking about Mom. It wouldn't be hard for the authorities to trace me to her. She was listed as my next of kin in all sorts of documents, her phone number was written in the little personal directory I kept beside my bedroom phone, there were letters, emails . . .

*If only I could erase all of that,* I thought.

And then I thought, *I'm the Shaper. Maybe I can.*

The trouble was, I didn't know how to go about it. I could imagine it, I could almost see it, data, documents, everything that could link me to her, even Brent's memories, vanishing . . . but I didn't know how to make it happen.

I was still imagining it when I fell asleep. In my dreams, I kept seeing jumbled images of Mom, Brent, my shop, the police . . . but after a time, my dreams calmed. I dreamed I didn't need to worry about Mom anymore.

After that, I didn't dream at all.

I woke to the sound of a helicopter.

Normally I wake up slowly and gently, open my eyes, yawn, stretch, lie quietly for a while thinking about what I'm going to do that day, get up, have a shower, put on my dressing gown, have coffee while I sit and read a book, brush my teeth, get dressed, and only then feel I have come fully awake enough to cope with the day's exigencies.

This time I went from deep sleep to upright wakefulness, adrenaline rushing, heart pounding, in a time interval that felt too short to be measured. Karl stood by the window (had he even slept?), peering out through the curtains into the dim gray light of predawn morning. "It's a long way off, but I can just make out big white letters on it," he said. "NBI?"

"National Bureau of Investigation," I said. My heartbeat showed no sign of returning to normal, and my head ached . . . again. "They've found us!"

"I believe they are flying a search pattern," Karl said. "I do not think they have seen anything."

The sound of the rotors was already fading, but that didn't make me feel any better. "But the car. Even if they haven't seen it yet . . . their next pass may be closer and they will, even under the tree. Even if they don't, if they're searching this area, and we drive away in it, they'll catch us for sure."

"Probably." Karl let the drapes fall closed. "Therefore, we can no longer use the car, and we must ensure it cannot be seen."

"Did you see a shed big enough to hide it in?" I said. "I didn't."

"No," he said. "Not a shed." He crossed the room to the other window, whose curtains we hadn't yet drawn, and pulled them open. I got to my feet and looked past him, over a stand of low bushes, to the boathouse. Beyond it, mist wreathed the smooth gray surface of the lake.

"But . . ." My car, I wanted to say, but that was stupid, and I knew it. They knew my car. If there were helicopters searching the sky, there must also be patrols on the ground, cars on the roads.

All the same, I'd loved that car.

"If we can submerge it, it might buy us time," Karl said.

"But then we'll be on foot," I pointed out. "In the woods. With no food, no tent, and only the clothes on our back. That was a bad idea when we were in that clearing yesterday where I smashed my cellphone. Why is it any better an idea now? It's autumn. It probably frosted last night. How long will we last?"

"Long enough, I think," Karl said. "The Portal is not nearby, but it is not impossibly far away, either. It is in the mountains, but on this side of the first range of peaks."

"You can find it on foot?" I said doubtfully.

"I can feel it," he said. "Always. I am surprised you cannot."

I couldn't feel anything except for that nagging ache in my head. "So, the plan is, we sink my poor car in the lake, take a boat to the other side, and disappear into the woods, in the hope that we can walk through the wilderness to this Portal of yours before we die of exposure?"

He nodded. "Succinctly put."

I swung my feet over the edge of the bed. "Great. Wonderful way to start the day. Gets the blood pumping."

I went into the bathroom. When I came out Karl was gone, along with his hat and duster, but he hadn't gone far: as I stepped out through the cabin door I saw him entering the main building. I closed the door behind me to try to hide from casual observers—although if anyone happened by in the next few hours, they were unlikely to be *casual*—the fact we'd broken into the cabin, and then hurried to join him.

I found him in the employees' locker room. "There's a jacket in there," he said, pointing to an open locker. "You'll need an extra layer."

I nodded, and pulled on the lined red nylon jacket I found in the locker, while he opened a set of tall cabinets at the back, revealing about a dozen backpacks. "These are already packed with camping equipment," he said. He pulled out a bright green one and handed it to me, then took a blue one for himself.

I hefted the pack. It was heavy, but not unbearably so. I shrugged it on over the jacket. "How did you know . . . ?"

He smiled without answering and went back into the dining room. I followed, and found him standing in front of a bulletin board I'd largely ignored, pointing to a sign: "ENJOY THE GREAT OUTDOORS! Rent a SUPER LIGHT Backpacking Package! Only $163/night!" Beneath that were listed the contents of what I presumably now carried on my back (though I thought "super-light" was stretching it a bit): one ultralight two-person tent, one down-filled sleeping bag good to 15 degrees, one sleeping pad, one Rocketboil Flash Cooking System, one Finn Water Filtration System, one canteen, one flashlight, one compass, a butane lighter, waterproof matches, a hunting knife, a collapsible shovel, a tiny fold-up rainproof poncho, and a trowel.

"Only $163 a night," I said. "Sounds like a steal. In our case, literally."

I didn't even get a smile.

From the kitchen, we took as much food as we could, concentrating on granola, nuts, and chocolate, and forgoing the chips. We also filled our canteens.

Before we tried to deal with my car, we went down to the lake. In Karl's hands my tire iron did double duty as a burglar's tool once more, and we discovered that a) there was a motorboat inside the shed, hung on the wall, and b) there was no motor for it. "Out for winter maintenance," I guessed.

"No matter." Karl pulled a paddle from a blue plastic barrel full of them near the entrance, and handed it to me. "We will use a canoe."

"I don't canoe," I said.

"There are many things you have not previously done you will soon be called upon to do, I suspect."

Out into the frosty morning again. The sun still hadn't cleared the hills at the eastern end of the lake, but fiery orange lit the tips of the pine trees atop the much higher hills to the west, which blocked the view of the mountains we might otherwise have seen. The light crept downward. It wouldn't be long until we were in full sunlight—and easy to spot from the air if the helicopter returned. Karl walked to the end of the pier. I followed him cautiously, the boards swaying under my feet on tire-tube floats, and, like him, looked down. Rocks glimmered beneath crystal-clear water, stretching away into the lake, sloping very, very gently down.

Too gently: there was no way we could hide the car in the lake. We'd have to launch it from a ramp to get it far enough out for the water to even cover it, and the lake was so pristine that even then the car would surely be visible from the air. Even though I knew we *really* didn't want the car found, I still felt relieved my beloved Fjord would not come to such an ignominious end. I just hoped I wouldn't come to one instead.

"Unfortunate," Karl said, lifting his gaze from the water and turning to look back at the giant oak tree, whose golden top we could see clearly from the lakeshore, though not the trunk or the car nestled beside it. "At least the oak has not dropped its foliage yet."

He walked back along the pier to the boathouse and the stack of canoes beside it. Together we manhandled (personhandled?) the top one off the rack and lugged it to the water, pushing it down the sloping shingle beach until it floated next to the pier. Karl placed his paddle in the boat, then his backpack. *Ah*, I thought. *Good point. Wearing something that will drag you straight to the bottom . . . not a good idea in a boat.* I took off my pack and put it next to his, then steadied the canoe while he climbed carefully into the stern. Then it was his turn to steady it, holding on to the pier while I climbed in at the bow.

He looked up at the brightening sky. "We'll row close to the shore, as much beneath the trees as possible."

"Suits me," I said. "Preferably close enough I can wade if we capsize."

He frowned at me. "Can you not swim?"

"I can swim," I said defensively. "Well, sort of. A little." Not a lie: I could manage two lengths of the pool on a good day . . . but I'd never done it wearing a ski jacket.

"There are no lifejackets," Karl said. "Let us concentrate on not capsizing. Push the bow away from the pier."

I pushed, then took up my paddle and looked over my shoulder at Karl. He began paddling, switching sides like clockwork. "I will tell you which side to paddle on," he said. "Try not to catch a crab."

I blinked at that. "There are crabs?"

He actually laughed, for the first time since he had come so precipitously into my life the day before. It made him look years younger . . . not that I had the slightest idea how old he was. I'd originally guessed fifty, but it was impossible to tell for sure. If he really had been moving among multiple worlds for months or years, maybe his age was a meaningless number, anyway. "To catch a crab is to fail to clear the water with your paddle as you reach forward. The momentum of the canoe means you will suddenly encounter great resistance, with results that can be . . . disconcerting."

"Disconcerting," I said. "Wouldn't want anything 'disconcerting' to happen. Not on an otherwise perfectly normal day like today."

He laughed again, then stopped paddling for a moment, his paddle ready on the port side. (Port and starboard and bow and stern I knew: I'd never spent much time in a boat, but some of my favorite books as a kid had been the *Swallows and Amazons* series by Arthur Ransome, all about English kids having adventures in sailboats. In fact, now that I thought about it, I seemed to remember something in those books about "catching crabs" while rowing.

I was ashamed I had momentarily forgotten it.) "Face forward," he said.

I turned around, looking past the canoe's pointed prow into the tendrils of mist now beginning to lift from the water. At the western end of the lake, the sunshine was sliding down the slope, nearer and nearer to the shore.

"Paddle starboard," Karl said behind me.

I dipped my own paddle and pushed hard three or four times while he held his paddle still. The bow moved to port, so that in a moment we were pointing east, toward the dark trees atop the gray stone cliff at the lake's foot. The first blazing sliver of sun chose that moment to appear above their spiky tips.

"Alternate port and starboard," Karl said. "I'll look after steering."

We paddled away through the rising mist, the ripples of our passage spreading across the still water all the way to the far shore . . . a rather glaring betrayal of our presence, should anyone be looking. Fortunately, for the moment, at least, no one was.

I had never been much of a camper, and even on those rare occasions when I *had* camped, I was not one to rise with the sun (see my previous comment about liking to wake up slowly and luxuriantly), so I had seldom been up at dawn in countryside of any description, much less countryside as beautiful as that revealed by the growing light. Only a few birds were calling, of the lonesome-sound-of-wilderness variety (that was about the limit of my ornithological knowledge), and I felt a strange sense of peace and wonder rising in me as we slid silently through the water. *A girl could get used to this*, I thought. *Brent and I should . . .*

And then I remembered. Brent and I would never come to this lake, or any other. I would probably never see Brent again. Or my mom, or any of my friends. I would definitely never see Aesha again, shot down in cold blood by the same man who had sent men with helicopters and guns to find and possibly kill me.

The lake went from beautiful to frighteningly exposed in an instant. "Can't we paddle faster?" I said over my shoulder.

"This is a good pace," Karl replied. "You may need strength to run once we land."

"Need strength to run" implied he thought there was a good chance someone might be chasing us. More of the bloom faded from the wow-isn't-nature-beautiful rose.

It vanished completely when I heard the distant beat of helicopter rotors from the direction of the resort. I twisted around to look, but couldn't see anything. "Keep paddling," Karl said. "Starboard for a bit." We moved as close as we could get to the north shore, where gray rock now rose sheer from the water. I looked ahead. That stone cliff only grew taller, until it was twenty feet high in places. There was nowhere to land, all around the east end of the lake. Above the rock, the trees formed a protective wall against the sky. The cliff and the trees would hide us unless a helicopter came directly overhead, but they also ensured we were trapped on the water until we could get around to the south side, where the rock dwindled and we might find a place to clamber out.

I paddled and paddled, hoping against hope the approaching helicopter would just fly on past, like it had the last time. That would mean whoever was aboard it hadn't spotted the car, and we'd have a chance to . . .

The sound of the rotors changed, but the volume remained the same. The helicopter was hovering. And that probably meant . . .

"They've seen the car," Karl said grimly. "Paddle hard!"

A superfluous command: I was already driving the paddle back as hard and fast as I could, port, starboard, port, starboard, fatigue building fast in my shoulders and arms. The high rock wall crept by with agonizing slowness, but the helicopter still hadn't appeared over the lake. Maybe we had a chance . . .

The sound of the rotors changed again, roaring, then suddenly subsiding.

"They've landed," Karl said.

I nodded. I didn't have breath for anything else. Sweat, turned instantly icy by the near-freezing air, ran down my face. I couldn't tell if the shiver down my spine was from a drop that had found its way down my back or if I was just terrified.

Probably both.

*What are they doing?* I wondered as we finally turned south, though we were still at least ten minutes of paddling from anywhere I thought we might be able to climb out. Would it take them that long to check the car, confirm it was mine? What would they do then? Draw weapons, cautiously go cabin to cabin . . . ?

*No. They'll start with the main building. They'll see it was broken into. They'll find it empty. They'll come out. They'll look toward the lake. Will they notice a canoe is missing? If they do . . .*

I twisted around.

The pier was visible.

So was the man standing on it, staring at us with binoculars. He wore a bulletproof vest, emblazoned with NBI in white block letters, over a black uniform. He turned and ran up the bank and out of sight.

After that, the only thing that ran through my mind for a few minutes, in time with my pulling of the paddle, was *shit . . . shit . . . shit . . . shit . . . shit . . .*

"Stop," Karl said, backing water.

I obeyed, shoulders cramping, but twisted around to stare at him. "Stop? Are you nuts? They've seen us!"

I could hear the rotors spinning up again. In a minute, the helicopter would sweep over the lake. The NBI agents aboard it must have already radioed that they'd found us. They'd simply hover, keeping us in sight, until ground reinforcements arrived, probably with dogs. Even if we got in under the trees and out of sight of the helicopter, we couldn't escape for long. But it was our only chance. And Karl wanted us to stop?

I held my dripping paddle parallel to the water, and for a second toyed with the idea of hitting him with it.

"We cannot escape," Karl said. "Unless we change things."

"I'd love to change things," I snapped. "Lots of things. Like everything that's happened since yesterday morning."

"You cannot change things back to the way they were," Karl said. "You cannot even create the illusion of time skipping back anymore, not now that the *hokhmah* of this world is shared between you and the Adversary. But you can still change some things. More than he can, at least for now, since you Shaped this world first."

I lowered the paddle. "Are you saying I can just . . . wish the helicopter away?"

"Probably not," Karl said. "But you may be able to influence the men aboard it, convince them to help us instead of pursue us."

"But . . . how?" The helicopter roared. It was taking off.

"Imagine it," Karl said. "You Shaped this world to begin with. The men in the helicopter only exist here because you imagined them into existence, by copying so much of the original reality. If you imagine them to be a little different than they now are, it may become true."

I stared. "I can . . . do that?"

Karl hesitated. "You *should* be able to do that."

"*Should?*" I cried.

The helicopter burst into sight above the trees.

We were out of time.

# EIGHT

**THE HELICOPTER ROSE** above the trees beyond the pier, then turned toward us, cockpit glinting in the morning sun. It swept low over the lake, and hovered, the blast of the rotors sweeping a skiff of spray across the still water, which fractured into millions of tossing wavelets. The sound, so loud it felt like an assault all its own, echoed off the rock cliff to our right. With the sun shining on the cockpit, I couldn't see inside the helicopter, but whoever was in there could certainly see us.

"What if they have a machine gun aboard that thing?"

"They are police, not military. The helicopter is only a transportation device, not a flying weapon. They are simply watching you until reinforcements arrive."

"The men on board must have weapons."

"Indeed. So perhaps you would care to *hurry up*?"

I stared up at the hovering copter. Hurry up and do . . . what? *Imagine*, Karl said. The insipid tune of the pop song ran through my mind. I hoped I wouldn't have to sing it, because I'd always hated it. I much preferred "When You Wish Upon a Star," but the only star in sight was the sun, and it didn't look likely to grant me anything.

*Imagine.*

A game of make-believe, then. I closed my eyes, picturing the inside of the helicopter . . . an inside drawn from movies and TV shows, since I'd never been in a helicopter myself, but clear enough in my mind's eye. Two men, surely. A pilot, an observer. I imagined them staring down at me. I imagined them thinking, *We have to help her. The people chasing her are evil. We have to help her. We have to help her. The people chasing her are evil. We have to help her. We have to . . .*

My headache returned with a vengeance. At the same moment the helicopter slewed left, then right. It shot higher, spun in place, slewed again.

And then the passenger door opened, and something plummeted from it.

Even above the noise of the rotors I heard the scream of a falling man, a scream that ended abruptly as the plunging body hit the pier with the force of a bomb. Water and debris geysered. I found my hand clasped across my mouth, and lowered it, staring wide-eyed across the lake. *What have I done?*

The helicopter roared back over the lake, closer to us than before. The canoe rocked in the rotor-blast. An amplified voice boomed down. "You're safe now! I've called in, told them the sighting was a false alarm. No one else is coming. Return to the resort!" The aircraft roared away, and settled behind the trees to await our arrival.

Waves from the falling body hitting the pier still chased each other across the lake. I felt ill. I looked at Karl. "Is it a trick?"

"No," he said. "I would say you successfully Shaped the pilot, but not the observer. Some minds cling more tightly to their perceived reality than others. Unfortunately, his must have been one of them. The pilot had to . . . take action." He put his paddle back into the water, on the port side. "Paddle starboard. We're going back."

"Not . . . please, not to the pier," I said, thinking of the horrible sound the falling body had made as it struck the wood and water, imagining what might await us there . . .

Imagining. I'd just *killed* a man by imagining.

"Not to the pier," Karl agreed gently.

We paddled back, but landed on the shore a good hundred yards from the shattered pier and whatever horrors it hid, as soon as the gray rock wall permitted us to ground the canoe. We trudged through the underbrush. Emerging at the eastern end of the resort, we walked cautiously past the line of cabins toward the helicopter, which waited in the parking lot, its rotors still spinning lazily. The pilot door opened as we approached, and the same man I'd seen looking at us through binoculars from the pier, wearing black fatigues and a bulletproof vest emblazoned with NBI in white letters, clambered out. He raised a hand in greeting and came to meet us. "Special Agent Clarence McNally," he said. "Glad to see you're all right, ma'am . . . sir."

"Who was . . .?" My voice trailed off. *The dead man*, I wanted to say, but the words wouldn't come.

McNally looked grim. "Tom Reed, ma'am. He was one of *them*, would have turned you in, tried to call for reinforcements. I thought he was a friend, we've been partners for years, but when push came to shove . . . well. I shoved. Damn shame, but with the stakes what they are . . ."

I had to swallow hard to keep from throwing up. I'd just made this man murder his friend and partner in cold blood, had somehow altered his perception of reality so completely he thought Tom Reed was his enemy and I, whom he had never met, was so important he was willing to kill to keep me safe.

*With great power comes great responsibility . . .* The phrase ran unbidden through my mind.

*Shut up*, I snarled silently to myself. *This isn't a fucking comic book.*

"Thank you," Karl said; it must have been obvious I wasn't going to contribute anything more. "But now we need another favor."

McNally nodded. "A ride, I'll wager. Figured as much. Where to?"

He said the first part of that to Karl, but directed the second part to me—and I didn't have a clue. The Portal, presumably, but Karl hadn't told me where it was.

"The mountains," Karl said, drawing McNally's gaze back to him. He looked past McNally at the helicopter. "How much fuel do you have?"

"Flown a hundred miles since take off," McNally said. "Gives us maybe another two hundred fifty or so before we're nothing but a fancy rock. I'd strongly suggest being on the ground before then."

"I don't know the latitude and longitude," Karl said. "But I have a name. Snakebite Mine."

McNally's face lit up. "Oh, sure," he said. "I know that place. It's in Striper Valley. Plenty of fuel to get *there*."

"We cannot go right into the valley," Karl said. "Not by helicopter. The mine may be guarded. We will need to sneak up to it. Can you set us down somewhere else, far enough away from the mine nobody there will hear or see us?"

"Couple of valleys over, then," McNally said. He looked vaguely into space for a moment, then his face cleared. "Got it. There's an old logging camp high up, at the west end of Spukani Valley. It's abandoned, but there's room to set down there—it's a designated helicopter landing zone for firefighting."

"Monitored?" Karl said sharply.

McNally shook his head. "Maintenance crew goes up there a couple of times a summer, maybe, to keep the undergrowth cleared. Shouldn't be anyone there now, not when the snow could hit any day."

"How far from there to the mine?"

"Couple of days' hike, tops," McNally said. "You could do it in one in the summer, but not with the days growing short."

"That will do."

McNally gestured toward the helicopter. "Climb aboard, then."

The helicopter had two seats in front. McNally climbed into the one on the right. Karl handed me his backpack, then climbed into the one on the left. I glanced into the cockpit as I got into the back. It looked exactly like I had imagined it when I was in the canoe, before McNally . . .

I swallowed and hurried into the back. Here there were four seats, two facing forward, two facing back, upholstered in black leather and complete with cup holders, like the interior of a luxury car. I tossed our backpacks into two of the empty seats, then buckled myself into one of the forward-facing ones. I pulled on the waiting headphones just in time to hear, "N415AT, please report in. You're off radar. Have you landed? Over."

"N415AT, affirmative," McNally answered briskly. "We're at Candle Lake Resort. Wanted to be a hundred percent sure what we thought we saw wasn't anything to follow up on. We were right— false alarm. Just an old pickup that happened to be the same color as the suspects' car. Taking off again now." Even as he spoke, the rotors were spinning up. "Might be off radar for a while—gonna stay low," he continued. "Lots of places someone could hole up around here. Tom knows the area and wants us to check out some more campsites and resorts. Over."

"Roger," said the voice on the other end. "But don't miss another check-in, McNally. Over."

"I won't," McNally said. "Sorry again. N415AT, over and out." He twisted around in his seat. "That'll keep them off our tails for a while," he said with a grin. "Hopefully long enough, if I hug the treetops, to get us to Spukani Valley. And if they do catch us on radar and want to know what we're up to, my little story about Reed knowing the area and wanting to check out campsites should cover our asses. I'll just say we're playing a hunch."

"Well thought out," said Karl.

I didn't say anything. The mention of the man McNally had thrown out of the helicopter had hit me with renewed force. I stared out the window as the engine roared and the rotors began to spin faster and faster. In a few minutes, we were in the air and slipping across the forest, the tops of spruce passing alarmingly close beneath our skids. I hoped McNally's metaphorical "hugging" of the treetops didn't turn into a literal embrace.

I leaned the other way and looked forward, past McNally and Karl, over the high control console, with its bewildering conglomeration of dials and computer screens. I knew next to nothing about helicopters. So how could I really be the Shaper of this world?

*It's copied from the First World, Karl said. Real Reality, with a capital "R." All I've done is put my own twist on things . . . even if I don't remember doing it.*

And then I thought, *I must be a very boring person.* Because why would I create a world that was only slightly different? Why not create something more exotic, more exciting, a world of magic, or one where superheroes were real, or one where there really was a Time Lord in a blue police box who could take you anywhere and anywhen . . .

But as the mountains rose before us and the trees rolled away beneath us, I thought, *Exciting worlds are worlds where battles are fought and crimes committed and dark lords overthrown, and the death toll is enormous.* If I had Shaped such a world, could not *all* those deaths be laid at my feet? Just like the one I knew I'd already caused here?

Karl said the people of the Shaped worlds were real people, even if they were copies of people somewhere else. Didn't they deserve to live their lives free from the meddling of people like me?

I sighed. *But that's not really an option, is it? The Adversary is already meddling in this world, and he's clearly making it worse, not better.* Ignorant of who I was, I would have been more than happy to let everyone live their own lives if only I could have lived mine. But then the Adversary had found his way into my world. What had happened since—the attack on the coffee shop (which I had undone) Aesha's death (which I couldn't), and now McNally's murder of Tom Reed—it all began with the Adversary, not with me.

If there were any chance to undo what the Adversary had done, I would have taken it in an instant. But there wasn't.

Not, at least, if Karl were telling the truth.

I studied the back of his ponytailed head. What he had told me certainly seemed to explain the subsequent events, but that didn't mean he didn't have his own agenda. I frowned, struck by a horrible thought. What if what he said about the Adversary were true— *but he was himself the Adversary?* What if all of this were simply a ploy to get me somewhere he needed me to be, so he could eliminate me once and for all?

I shook my head. No, that was just paranoid. If Karl had wanted to kill me, he could have done it a dozen times by now, most recently just by pushing me out of the canoe, most easily by smothering me in my sleep the night before. He might not be telling the truth, and he might not really be on my side, but he definitely wasn't the Adversary.

That was some comfort, but not much.

"How long will it take us to get to this landing site?" Karl said.

"About half an hour," McNally said. He pointed to a beige leather pouch attached to the door on Karl's side. "Map's in there. You'll need it when you land."

Karl nodded and started rummaging around in the pouch.

"Then what will you do?" I said. "After you drop us off. After . . . what happened back there."

"My duty," McNally said. "I'll lead them on a wild goose chase."

"They'll arrest you," I said. *Or worse.*

"A small price to pay for your freedom, ma'am."

I closed my eyes. *What have I done?* I thought again.

Could I undo it? Could I Shape him again, back to the person he had been before he pushed his friend Tom Reed out of the helicopter?

Maybe. But it seemed a spectacularly bad idea. McNally would suddenly revert to being an NBI agent—an *armed* NBI agent—with orders to bring us in. Maybe Karl could fly a helicopter—although since he'd shown up wearing Shakespearean garb and didn't seem to know some of the basic facts about the world, it seemed unlikely—but I couldn't. If I played with reality up here, we might all go down in a flaming heap.

Perhaps it was selfish of me, but I didn't want that. What I *wanted*, the world the way it had been yesterday morning, I couldn't get. Those events had started a wild ride down a slippery slope to an uncertain landing. All I could do now was hold on. At least my headache was fading again.

Karl had found the map, and was studying it. There were occasional bursts of conversation over the headphones, other aircraft checking in, nothing to alarm us . . . until, just as we soared up a slope and into a long, narrow valley between two towering ranges, we heard, "Toma here. Got something. Candle Lake Resort. I think it's the car. Over."

"Damn," McNally muttered.

"Candle Lake?" said the voice from control. "McNally and Reed landed there, said it was just an old pickup. Over."

"Must be blind, then," Toma said. "We're hovering low in the parking lot, right where they would have had to land, and it's plain as day: late-model Fjord, as described. Over."

"Land and confirm," control said. "Over." A pause. "Control to Special Agents McNally and Reed. Where are you? Respond. Over."

"That tears it," McNally said. "They'll find Tom's body and put two and two together. But it sounds like we're not on radar—they've lost us." He pointed forward. "The old logging camp is right up there past the waterfall. I'll have you on the ground in ten minutes."

Control kept calling. McNally kept ignoring them. And then, just as we swept over the waterfall and we saw the clearing of the camp dead ahead, we heard, "Control, Toma here! Reed is dead! Repeat, Special Agent Tom Reed is dead. Shawna Keys was definitely here. McNally must be—"

McNally killed the radio. "That's that," he said. "But maybe we bought enough time and distance for the two of you to get away."

"And you?"

"I'll fly back down the valley, stay low, pop up fifty miles away and let them chase me," McNally said. "Don't worry about me. You just do what you have to do." He fell silent as he maneuvered the helicopter down into the clearing, a hurricane of dust and pine needles blasting away from it in all directions. As the rotors slowed, though, he twisted around to face me head on. "You hear me, ma'am?" he said. "Do what you have to. Save the world."

I wanted to. But if Karl was telling the truth, I couldn't: all I could do was escape it. Unable to speak, I nodded instead. Then I pulled off the headset, picked up our backpacks, opened the door, and stepped down into the dirt and scraggly weeds of the clearing. Karl followed, the map from the helicopter in hand. He took his pack from me, then pointed into the trees: McNally hadn't cut the engine entirely, and the noise was still enough to make it hard to talk. I nodded.

We shouldered our backpacks and headed into the woods. Among the trees, we turned and looked back at the helicopter as it roared to life again, raising our hands to shield our eyes from the blast of dust, twigs, and needles as it rose skyward. It thundered away from us, still frighteningly low to the tops of the trees, and out of sight.

"He's throwing away his career," I said miserably as we watched it go. "Maybe his life. He murdered his friend. All because of this power you say is a good thing."

"I do not believe that I ever said it is a good thing. All I said is that it is a thing. You can still choose not to use it. You can choose to surrender, now or later. You will not survive long after you do so, but it is a choice you can make."

"If I did?" I said, turning to him. "What would you do?"

"Leave," he said. "Move on to another world without you. Try to stay ahead of the Adversary. Hope that somewhere in the Labyrinth there is another Shaper with the power to do what Ygrair needs done." He pulled off his pack and put it on the ground. "McNally cannot buy us much time. He only has an hour or so of fuel left. Shortly after he lands they will know we are not with him. There are searchers on the ground who must have seen him. Which means they will soon realize he must have put us down somewhere in this area, and shortly after that, they will be looking for us up here." He had unzipped an outside pocket on his pack; now he pulled out a compass and stood up again, holding it in his right hand. "We have to move fast. We have to get to the mine. We have to get to the Portal and destroy it, to weaken the Adversary and cut him off from reinforcements. And then we have to find the place where I can make a new Portal that will take us out of this world and into the next."

I couldn't doubt him anymore, not after what had happened, not after what I had *made* happen.

We had to move. We had to get to the mine. We had to get to

the Portal. We had to destroy it. We had to open a new Portal and flee my world. I believed every word.

But at that moment, frozen in place by the weight of my own guilt, by the enormity of all that had happened and was still happening, I didn't think I would ever move again.

## NINE

"GOT IT," SAID the agent at the radar screen. The Adversary stood behind her, with Smoak, the Special Agent in Charge, at his right. "N415AT."

The Adversary leaned forward. "Where is that?"

"About a hundred and fifty miles northwest of Eagle River."

"Call him," said Smoak.

The agent obliged. "N415AT, this is Control. Respond. Over." She paused, then repeated the phrase, with no more success.

Smoak glanced at the time, displayed to the side of the radar screen. "He can't have much fuel left. He'll be looking for a place to land."

"He's found it," said the agent at the screen. "He's just set down at the old Greeley Lake AFB."

"Then we've got them," said Smoak.

The Adversary raised an eyebrow at him. "'Them'? Can we be certain that Keys and Yatsar are aboard? Could he not have set down and let them out while off radar?"

"Well, we'll know soon enough. Believe it or not, there's already a patrol waiting there. They'll nab them the minute they step off the aircraft. Pure luck."

"Luck indeed," said the Adversary. But he did not believe it was luck at all. Though Shawna still lived, and thus he did not have full control of this world, it did seem to him that it was beginning to accept him. For the moment, she could still do far more with it than he. Nevertheless, this bit of "luck" just might be evidence that his own power was growing. Perhaps soon he would be able to Shape more than just the weak minds of this world's denizens. "If all three are present, then even more luck," he continued to Smoak. "But if they are not . . . I will want to speak to this McNally personally." *To Shape him so that he answers questions*, he left unspoken.

"Of course," said Smoak.

"Very well, then." The Adversary gave him a pointed look. "Shouldn't you be taking charge of matters?"

Smoak hurried out. The Adversary took one more look at the radar screen. The blip of the helicopter had vanished once it landed. He nodded once, then followed Smoak.

Karl put the compass into the breast pocket of the black duster. Then he picked up his backpack and pulled it on. "Ready?" he said.

I didn't answer. I kept staring after the departed helicopter.

"Shawna," Karl said.

I still didn't move.

He stepped toward me, reached out a hand. "Shawna, did you hear what I said?"

Anger suddenly boiled up in me. I slapped his hand away and turned on him. "Yes, I heard!" I spat. "I've heard every word. Just give me a fucking minute."

Karl's mouth tightened. "We do not have a minute."

I folded my arms, glared at him. "Explain something to me. Eventually the Adversary is going to figure out we were let off up here. We're just a couple of valleys over from his precious Portal. Why won't he assume that's where we're going, and send this 'cadre' of his there to wait for us?"

"The Adversary does not know I can destroy the Portal, and he knows I know that he can reopen it if all I do is close it," Karl said. "He also knows it leads only back to the world we were in before. On that side, it is heavily guarded. If I were foolish enough to take you there, you would be instantly captured or killed. He has no reason to think, even if we are close to the Portal, that that is where we are headed."

"Are you saying it will be completely unprotected on this side?"

"There will be some sort of guard, but if we are fortunate, it will not be members of his cadre—there are only a few of them with him, and he does not like to divide them. Any guards will most likely be people of this world, and that means you can Shape them."

*Great.* Twist more minds, destroy more lives. I hated being a god: a Greek Olympian kind of god, toying with humans . . .

I changed tack. "What if you're wrong? What if he *has* left members of his cadre there?"

"Then we will change our plans," Karl said evenly. "As we have several times already. You must trust me."

"*Must?* I have to follow you. That doesn't mean I have to trust you. You could be lying to me. You could be as much of a threat to me as the Adversary. Why should I trust you?"

I suddenly realized I had shouted that last question, and pressed my lips together. My words didn't echo: they had fallen to instant silence on the floor of the forest, itself unnaturally quiet in the wake of the noisy departure of the helicopter, any birds or animals in earshot of that racket still cowering.

Karl looked at me coldly. "If you do not trust me, then you should not follow me. Abandon me now. Hike into the mountains, or down into the lowlands—it makes no difference to me. I will leave you, and make my way to where I can open a new Portal into the next world, where once again I will find the Shaper, and hope he or she has the power to do what Ygrair needs done. You will at least buy me time, since the Adversary must find and kill you before he can follow me to the next world. Perhaps, if you choose to stay and die, you will buy life for the next Shaper I find with sufficient power to fulfil my quest. But *choose*. Now. Will you trust me, and follow me, and do what we must do to escape, and defeat the Adversary, or will you try to run back to your old life, even though that life is gone forever and you go only to your death?"

I hated him at that moment. He had opened the Portal into my world. Had he never come, the Adversary wouldn't have either. My world—my life—would have continued, peacefully, just the way I liked it—just the way I had Shaped it.

But Karl *had* come to my world, and the Adversary had followed, and my old life was as dead as I would be if the Adversary caught up to me. Oh, Karl was right, I had a choice: I could leave him and take my chances. But even though I still didn't believe that everything he had told me was true, I did believe him when he said that without him, I was as good as dead.

"Fine," I said sullenly. "Let's go. I obviously have no choice."

"Not if you want to live," he said, voice still cold.

I spread my arms to take in the surrounding forest. "So, which way, exactly? I could die just as easily here in the forest as I would if the Adversary caught me. Do you know anything about wilderness camping and hiking? Because I don't."

"I have trekked through many woods in many worlds," Karl said. "I know the direction we must go, and as you saw, I have a compass." He took a deep breath, then actually smiled a little, as though consciously ridding himself of his anger of a moment before. "Although a . . . what are they called? . . . GPS unit would be more useful, had those who created these packs only thought to include one."

I took my own deep breath, used it to push down my own fury. "Well, it was a pretty low-rent resort."

His smile broadened a smidgen. I hated him a little less. But only a little. "First, we must get farther in among the trees," he said. "It is not impossible someone saw the helicopter and has a spyglass trained on us this very moment."

A *spyglass*? I shook my head and followed him deeper into the forest, which, as forests go, was rather scraggly. The thin undergrowth made getting in among the trees not a problem, but once we were out of sight of the clearing, I realized, looking around, just how much every tree looked like every other tree. Left on my own, I knew I would be lost in moments.

Karl opened the map he had taken from the helicopter and spread it on a handy bush. Not a breath of air moved through the trees to disturb it. Karl pointed. "This is our valley." He moved his finger a few inches south. "Here is the mine. As you can see, a road of sorts runs to it from the old logging camp where we landed." He lifted his pointing finger from the map and swung it toward the woods. "If we go that way perhaps two hundred yards, we should find it."

"A road," I said. "We're just going to walk along a nice, exposed road while the NBI, and probably state troopers, forest rangers, and maybe by this time the National Guard and the Boy Scouts, are all looking for us."

"No," Karl said. "We will parallel the road, in the forest, with great care."

"It would have been nice," I said, a little of my earlier anger bubbling up again, "if you'd had a better plan for escaping once you contacted me."

"It is impossible to plan," Karl retorted, "when the world can change around you without warning."

I didn't have an answer to that. After all, *my* original plan for today had been to make more mugs for the Human Bean.

We set off through the trees, and my confidence in Karl's non-GPS-reliant navigational abilities rose slightly when we found the road . . . well, track, really, rutted and so weed-grown it seemed clear no vehicles had been along it all summer . . . right where he said it should be. We set off parallel to it toward the south.

At first the going was fairly easy, the ground more-or-less level, the undergrowth sparse. But that changed as the track climbed the southern flank of the valley. My heart thudded in my chest, I was breathing way harder than I liked, and my legs ached so much I wished I'd never started using an electric pottery wheel. If I'd spent the last ten years kicking one to keep it spinning, I might be in better shape now.

At least throwing pots had given me strong hands, which would come in handy if I had to throttle anyone . . .

I stared at Karl, or at least the back of his blue backpack, all I could see of him as he toiled uphill ahead of me. I still knew next to nothing about him. Where—and when, exactly?—had Ygrair found him? He had to have parents, siblings, a hometown . . .

Or did he? Was he just another copy of someone from the First World, any memories of his family, of childhood, of adolescence, Shaped by Ygrair, his personal reality altered just as I had altered that of McNally?

Or maybe he had his own Shaped world somewhere, and even though he lacked the power to do what Ygrair needed done, had enough to undertake this quest of hers. He had evaded my question, when we first met, as to whether he, too, was a Shaper.

So many questions. I would have loved to have asked them of him as we hiked, if not for the fact I had no breath . . . and a strong suspicion he wouldn't answer them anyway.

About four hours after leaving the landing zone, as we continued to toil uphill, switchback by switchback, parallel to the road, I heard another helicopter, distant, behind us. We had hiked several miles, but as the crow—or helicopter—flies, we were probably no more than two or three from the clearing where we had disem-

barked, though we couldn't see it—or the approaching helicopter—
through the trees: a good thing, since otherwise whoever was
aboard it might be able to see *us*.

Karl stopped and turned his head toward the sound of the rotors. I gratefully plopped down on a fallen log, took off my pack,
and dug out my canteen. While I took a few good gulps, Karl placed
his pack beside mine, then picked his way through the trees to the
road. I saw him looking back down it the way we had come. He
ducked back into the forest almost immediately.

"I believe it has landed in the same clearing where McNally put
us down," he said as he rejoined me.

I felt a chill. "They got McNally."

"Perhaps. Or perhaps they saw us on radar after all. It does not
matter. What matters is that if anyone aboard that helicopter has
any tracking skill at all, it won't take them long to figure out which
way we went. About two minutes after that the helicopter will be
headed straight for us." He paused. "Unless you can stop them."

I lowered my canteen and shook my head. "No," I said sharply.
"I'm not doing that again. Someone died the last time I did that."

"It is unlikely you can Shape people at this distance. But you
might be able to do something else."

"Like what?" I demanded.

"It is your world, still, at least after a fashion," Karl said. "You
can still Shape it."

"What do you suggest?" I said, with less heat: I was genuinely
curious. If I could Shape the world without hurting anyone . . .

"Our trail needs to be hidden. So hide it. Or plant a false one."

My irritation returned. "Well, that's pretty much uselessly
vague. How, exactly?"

"You have to decide that," he said. "You have to imagine it. Believe it's true. You do not have to fill in *all* the details—the world will
do that for you, according to its natural laws. Just imagine, fully,

completely, that they cannot find our trail." He paused. "As you imagined the track that led us into the forest from the main road, and the resort."

I blinked. "Are you saying those weren't there until we needed them?"

"I cannot say for certain," Karl said, "but that is my belief."

"Then I did a piss-poor job of it. Or we'd have more to eat in our packs than trail mix."

"That's because you did it, more or less, by accident," Karl said. "You did not imagine it in detail. If you did it at all; admittedly, I may be seeing Shaping where there was none. But whether you created the clearing and the resort or not, I believe you still have power to effect some local change to the world to make it harder for our pursuers to track us."

Feeling like an idiot, but also feeling the urgency of doing *something* to keep us hidden from our pursuers, I closed my eyes. I imagined, as fiercely as I could, that we had left no trail in the woods, that we could not be tracked. I felt . . . something . . . a kind of unfurling of my subconscious. For a moment, I lost all sense of my body, as I went . . . elsewhere.

And then, with a shock like a rubber band breaking, I felt my body again. My cold, wet body.

*What the hell . . . ?*

I opened my eyes.

The sky had been clear and the air mountain-cool, but not cold, when I'd closed my eyes. Now clouds hung low above us, the temperature had dropped twenty degrees—and fat white snowflakes swirled among the trees, joining the six inches of snow already on the forest floor. No footsteps marred that white blanket, even though it must have snowed for hours to cover the ground that completely.

Except, of course, it hadn't.

I was shivering. I wrapped my arms around myself. I not only felt cold, I felt exhausted and headachy again, fatigued in a way completely different from the ordinary physical tiredness of climbing the hillside. I felt as though I'd used up a large portion of some store of energy within me I hadn't even known I'd had. I also, I suddenly realized, felt ravenous.

Karl frowned at me. "Crude," he said. "It will buy us time, yes, but such a large Shaping . . . the Adversary will almost certainly have sensed it. I did not expect . . ." His voice trailed off. "Perhaps I should have," he said after a moment. "After all, if you did not have unusual strength, I never would have approached you."

I reached for my pack, and unzipped it. "Yeah, and have I properly thanked you for that?" I said as I pulled out the thin flat rectangle of a poncho, hoping I'd put enough sarcasm in my voice to register even on Karl. I unfolded the poncho and put it on over my red nylon-shelled jacket. Though bright yellow and definitely not flattering, it at least provided an additional snow-deflecting layer. Then I started digging in the pack's outside pockets, trying to remember where I'd last put the trail mix.

"You can thank me later," Karl said absently, peering at me. Clearly I still needed to power up the sarcasm phasers a few clicks to penetrate his shields of obliviousness. "How do you feel?"

"Tired," I snapped. "Cranky. Cold." Where the *hell* was that trail mix?

"You have felt unusual fatigue before, in these past couple of days. And an occasional headache, too, I think?"

"Yeah," I said. "How do you know?"

"Every time you Shape, it takes energy. Just now, you expended a great deal of it. You should eat something. That will help with the physical fatigue."

I suddenly remembered I'd put the trail mix in my coat pocket, not a backpack pocket, the last time I'd eaten some. I fumbled underneath the poncho, found the jacket pocket, and pulled out the package. I upended the remaining contents into my mouth. "Gee, I never would have thought of that," I mumbled around a mouthful of nuts and berries.

Karl looked up at the clouds, which hid the peaks that had stood out clear in the sunshine just moments before. "Your Shaping will cover our tracks, true enough, but it will cause difficulties as we ascend, and we still have to get over the ridge into the next valley. And the Adversary now has a general idea where we are. He may even . . ." For a long moment, he just stared silently uphill into the snow.

I shoved the empty trail-mix package into one of the backpack's pockets. There were a couple of unopened packages in the main part of the pack, but I thought I'd survive for the moment. "You didn't finish your sentence."

He turned to me. "What?"

"'He may even . . .'" I prompted. "He may even what?"

"Remember," Karl said, "you are not the only one who can now Shape this world. We know for certain he has Shaped individuals, as you have also done, to serve his needs."

"I wish I hadn't," I muttered.

"Don't be foolish," Karl snapped. "If you had not Shaped the helicopter pilot, you would now be dead."

*Like Tom Reed*, I thought, but didn't say. "So, if I can do this," I gestured at the now-you-don't-see-it-now-you-do snowfall, "are you thinking he might be able to do something like it, too?"

"I do not think so . . . yet," Karl said slowly. "I think . . . I hope . . . that your . . . stamp, let us say . . . upon the world, the fact that all of it was originally Shaped to your desires, will prevent him from making changes on this scale, at least for a time. But the more he Shapes individuals, causing them in turn to alter this world in ways that serve him, the more he will weaken that connection to you. It may be that his power will grow. While yours . . ."

"While mine lessens," I finished for him.

"Possibly," he said. He paused. "Probably," he admitted.

"Great."

"All the more reason for us to do what we can to weaken his power by destroying the Portal, and then leave this world, as soon as possible," Karl said. He bent over, unzipped his own pack, and dug out his own poncho. "We should keep moving," he said as he pulled the poncho, bright pink, on over the black duster. He looked ridiculous, but he didn't seem to care. He took off his cowboy hat, slapped it on his thigh to dislodge the snow from its brim, then settled it back on his head. "Even though our tracks have been obliterated, the road we have been following will be an obvious route for them to send a patrol along. They have no vehicles, and we will be difficult to spot from the air in this," he gestured at the falling snow and low clouds, "so I would expect armed men on foot."

With resignation, I settled my backpack on my shoulders. "Fine. Let's go."

The earlier part of the hike had been tremendously tiring. Now it also became scarily slippery, cursedly cold, and wearingly wet—just all-around alliteratively annoying. The temperature, a handy thermometer built into one of the straps of Karl's backpack informed me, was twenty-six degrees, mild enough that climbing kept us warm (even a little *too* warm), but cold enough that I knew as soon as we stopped we'd feel the chill in a hurry. Even though I was about as far from an outdoorsy type as you could get, I liked to *read* about grand adventures, and thus knew all about hypothermia. (Also altitude sickness, malaria, trench foot, Ebola, and plague, and how unpleasant death by drowning is—all of which I *also* hoped to avoid experiencing firsthand.)

The slope only got steeper, and while the switchbacks of the road we followed mitigated the incline slightly, that's where "scarily slippery" came into play. My feet slid backward in the snow, until eventually I was climbing almost on all fours, like a singularly in- ept mountain goat, fingers freezing, snow finding its way inside both my poncho and my jacket and then down the back of my neck, icy water squelching in my shoes.

Just when I thought I couldn't go on any longer, we reached a plateau. Karl halted. "I can't . . . no more," I gasped out.

"We are at the top of the pass," Karl said. I noted with annoy- ance that he wasn't breathing nearly as hard as I was.

"How . . . do you . . . know?"

He pointed at something I'd taken to be a random pile of rocks, but saw now was too regular: it was a cairn, made of stones ce- mented together, capped with snow. Karl walked over to it, and I limped in his footsteps. He brushed off the snow, revealing a cir- cular plaque. "U.S. GEOLOGICAL SURVEY, COOPERATION WITH THE STATE," read capital letters curving around the top. Around the bottom ran the message, "250 DOLLARS FINE FOR DISTURBING THIS MARKER." In the middle was a pyramid with an eye in it, and the words "Elevation Above Sea 4,298 feet." Below that was a date, 1917, and what looked like someone's ini- tials, "A.C."

I stared at it. "This is what I don't get," I said.

"It's a survey marker," Karl said.

"I can see that. But I've never seen one before, I've never given them a second thought before, and I didn't know they're placed at the top of mountain passes, yet here this one is. According to the date, it's been here more than a century. It *looks* like it's been here more than a century. And yet you told me I made up this whole world just ten years ago. How could I make up something like that," I pointed at the marker, "when I've never known it existed?"

"As you would already know if your memory had not somehow gone awry," Karl said, "or if you had *listened* to me the other times I've tried to explain this, the bulk of this world—the bulk of *all* the

Shaped worlds—is copied from the Earth of the First World, from which you and all the other Shapers come. The Labyrinth is like . . . the clay you form into pots. All Shapers start with the same substance, but then make changes to it, so that each of you, like different potters starting with slabs of identical clay, ultimately creates something unique. Your world is close to the original." He tapped the survey marker. "No doubt in this valley in the First World, this same survey marker stands in this same pass."

"But not in the worlds some Shapers make?"

He nodded. "I have seen others that bear almost no resemblance to the original. Although even then . . . though this marker might not exist in another world, the stone and metal of which it is made are no doubt components of something else."

I found that vaguely annoying. I'd always thought of myself as an extremely creative person, and now Karl was telling me I'd only put a thin veneer of change on my world . . . a layer of ordinary brown glaze on a plain stoneware pot, as compared to the glistening metallic glaze other Shapers had lavished on extravagantly abstract ceramic sculptures. *Probably raku-fired, at that,* I thought sourly. *Show-offs.*

Then I shook my head. *I'm getting giddy.* Shivering shook me. *Not to mention cold.* In fact, the two things were almost certainly related. "We need shelter," I said, between teeth showing a definite inclination to chatter. "And heat."

"Agreed," Karl said. "It will be dark soon." He looked around, then pointed. "Over there."

I followed him to a small clearing among the trees. We each carried a two-person tent, but even without Karl saying anything I knew we'd have to share one, cuddling close for body heat purposes (but not for any others, thank you very much). I pulled the orange nylon bag containing the tent out of my pack.

A laminated sheet of instructions hung from the bag on a loop of fine chain. They weren't nearly as complicated as I'd feared: put down the "footprint," a sheet of waterproof fabric, set the tent on top of that, pull out the poles (which made a wire-frame dome onto which the tent itself was attached), spread and attach the water-impervious "rainfly" over top of the tent-proper's material (which was a fine mesh that would otherwise do nothing to keep out the snow), drive stakes into the ground at each corner, and "guy out" the tent with ropes to additional stakes a few feet away, in case the wind came up. It only took a few minutes, but I was wet and cold and miserable—I mean, wetter and colder and *more* miserable—by the time it was done.

We shoved our packs into the tent and crawled inside. We didn't dare make a fire with potential pursuers somewhere in the woods, and probably wouldn't have been able to find dry wood anyway, but we started up one of the little camp stoves to provide a little heat, then got out our sleeping bags and wrapped them around our shoulders. The packs included flashlights, but we left them off, sitting in the slight glow of the camp stove, munching trail mix by the handful.

We didn't talk. I was acutely aware I was sharing a tent with a strange man—a *very* strange man—in rather terrifying isolation in the middle of a forest, but at the same time, Karl had shown not the slightest indication he thought of me as an attractive woman. For all I knew he was gay. Or a robot. Or a zombie. Or, for that matter, a gay robot zombie.

In any event, climbing a snowy mountain is the best sleep aid ever invented. We turned off the camp stove, then lay down side by side in our sleeping bags. If Karl stayed awake or even lay there staring at me creepily, I never knew it: I fell asleep in seconds.

I jerked awake in the gray light of early morning to a weird coughing roar in the woods, gasped out, "What . . . ?"—and only then saw that Karl had vanished.

## TEN

**I TRIED TO** scramble to the door of the tent, but got tangled in my sleeping bag and instead flailed around uselessly for a few seconds. The roaring continued. In my half asleep state, I wondered if the Adversary had somehow managed to conjure a dragon out of thin air, then wondered whether if I started believing in dragons there really *would* be a dragon, and tried really hard to *stop* imagining a dragon, and then finally managed to get my head out through the tent flap.

A bear the size of an SUV stood at the edge of the clearing, glaring at Karl with its teeth bared, one giant paw pinning his pink poncho to the ground. It repeated the sound I'd heard. The fact it came from a giant bear and not a dragon was less reassuring than you might have thought. Karl held the pistol McNally had given him, but the bear was so huge that shooting it seemed more likely to enrage it than kill it, or even drive it away.

I'd frozen with only my head showing. I had a feeling attracting the bear's attention would be a really, really bad idea. But to my surprise, Karl spoke, his voice very calm. "Good morning, Shawna. I am not looking at the bear. You should not look at the bear either. Let us both remain very calm. I am going to back slowly toward you, while still not looking at the bear. You will come out of the tent and we will back up very slowly together, not looking at the bear. We are not threatening the bear. We are not looking at the bear. We have no food for the bear. The bear will go away." His voice was hypnotic. "If you could, however, perhaps find it within you to believe very, *very* strongly that the bear will go away, that might help, too."

It was *not* an easy thing to believe, with that mountain of brown-furred flesh glaring at us. *I'm not looking at it*, I reminded myself, and turned my head so that it was only a furry blur in my peripheral vision. The bear had stopped roaring, but clearly wasn't going anywhere right away. Leaving his poncho to the bear, Karl backed very slowly toward me while I, even more slowly, got out of the tent. "The bear is still there, Shawna," Karl said as he came even with me.

"'Lord, I believe, help thou mine unbelief,'" I muttered, the biblical cry of the father whose son had been possessed by an evil spirit surfacing in my mind from years of Sunday School. It was as close to a prayer as I had said in a long time. *Mom would be pleased*, I thought. Then I thought, again, *Is my mom in this world really my mom?* Then I thought, as the bear roared again, *This really isn't the time.*

I closed my eyes. This helped with the whole don't-look-at-the-bear thing, but it also meant I wouldn't be able to see the bear galumphing toward us with murder on its mind should it choose to do so. *Don't think about that.* Instead I imagined, as hard as I could, that the bear was no longer interested in us, that when I opened my eyes, it would have decided to go away and dig honey out of a tree or catch fish or eat berries or hibernate or whatever.

I felt . . . something. The huffing and roaring stopped. I opened my eyes cautiously. The bear, Karl's pink poncho hanging from its jaws, was calmly walking away from us, the hump on its shoulder rolling from side to side with each rocking step. In another minute, it had vanished from sight.

"Well done," Karl said. "You're getting better at this."

"Am I?" I stared in the direction the bear had taken, rubbing my right temple. Once again, Shaping had given me a slight headache.

"It wasn't struck by lightning or buried in a landslide, either of which might have been expected, based on your previous Shapings."

"Very funny."

"It wasn't meant to be."

I glanced at him. Sure enough, he looked as grim as always. "So why did it take your poncho?"

"I'm not sure. Although I am glad it took that and not the duster." He pointed to a bush, and I saw the black coat hung on its branches, along with his cowboy hat. "I left both there while I performed my morning exercises. The bright color of the poncho is probably what attracted the bear's attention in the first place. When you Shaped it not to be interested in us, perhaps you simply focused its interest more intently on the poncho."

"Uh, sure," I said, because that didn't sound any crazier than anything else that had happened or been said in my vicinity recently.

I discovered then that I was shaking. Also, cold. Also, in need of other relief, although going into the woods to do what bears do in the woods seemed like a really bad idea when said woods actually held a bear.

Karl continued to stare after said bear. "It is also possible our visitor may have been the Adversary's work. If the Adversary sensed your Shaping of the snowfall, he knows our general vicinity. Perhaps he decided to try to extend a little of his own power in our direction."

"You mean—he conjured that grizzly out of nothing?"

Karl shook his head. "He could not do that. The grizzly certainly already existed. But perhaps our pursuers spotted it from their helicopter, and thus the Adversary knew it was in our vicinity, and chose to make it more aggressive, so it would threaten any humans it found in its territory. To Shape a human, in this world he did not Shape and whose *hokhmah* he does not fully control, I believe the Adversary must speak to him or her directly. However, it is easier to Shape an animal, so the Adversary might have been able to do it from afar. Conjuring up bears out of nothing, though . . . no, he won't have that power yet. *You* might still be able to do it, but I wouldn't recommend it."

"Why not?" I said. "Not that I want to," I added hastily.

"The unintended consequences of making it snow pale in comparison to the potential unintended consequences of conjuring living things," Karl said. "There is a law. Call it the Law of the Conservation of Life. The Shaped Worlds are closed systems. There is only so much life force available within each, doled out by the Labyrinth according to rules we don't understand. Normal reproduction increases that life force, normal death decreases it. But if you conjure life out of *nothing*, its life force must be taken from somewhere else."

"So if I create a bear," I said, hoping I was misunderstanding him but very much afraid I wasn't, "something else dies?"

"Or multiple somethings," Karl said. "Creating a bear out of nothing might claim the lives of a flock of birds, a swamp's worth of mosquitoes . . . or three or four people."

That made me shiver in a way even the cold mountain air had not. "And there's no way to know which?"

He shook his head. "Not that I have discovered."

"Who created these diabolical rules?" I demanded. "Ygrair?"

"No," Karl said. "I told you, they are part of the Labyrinth."

"Can't they be changed?"

"No," Karl said.

"Maybe not by Ygrair," I persisted. "But if you're right, and I have the power to take her place, fresh and strong—"

"*They cannot be changed,*" Karl said, displaying a flash of fury so sudden and unexpected it left me shaken, like I'd touched a live wire.

Every time I thought I was beginning to feel like I was on solid ground once more, to accept the absurd situation in which I found myself, the earth shifted beneath my feet. Would my life ever be steady again?

*Careful,* I thought. *You could cause an earthquake.* I rubbed my temple again. "My head hurts," I complained.

If Karl heard me, he chose to ignore me. Instead, he turned slowly, surveying the woods. "It is of course possible he has also found *other* creatures to make more aggressive."

"Lions and tigers?" I said. "They traditionally go with bears."

Karl looked at me oddly. "Lions and tigers and bears? They don't go together. Not in North America."

"No lions and tigers and bears?" I said. "Oh, my."

I had already discovered while in Karl's company that escaping imminent death—and in this case, dismemberment, too!—made me giddy. It was just a shame so many of my jokes went right over his head.

Which was funny in its own right—funny odd, not funny ha-ha—when you thought about it, as I just had. *If every world starts as a copy of the world everyone came from originally, shouldn't some of these jokes work in lots of different worlds? After all, I wouldn't want to live in a world without* The Wonderful Wizard of Oz. *Surely others felt the same. So why doesn't Karl get them?* All the clues pointed to him having left the First World a very long time ago—far longer ago than his apparent age supported. But when, exactly? And how had he survived so long without aging?

Karl was still frowning at me. "Well, at least we're up," I said brightly. "Let's get packed up and moving." I hesitated. "I just need to, um . . . you know . . . and with a bear out there . . ."

Karl jerked his head toward a stand of bushes. "Over there. I'll turn my back. And keep an eye out for the bear."

I nodded, went and did what I *really* needed to do—an invigorating process in sub-freezing temperatures—washed my hands as best I could by rubbing snow between them, and then helped Karl take down and stow the tent in my backpack. Since it wasn't snowing anymore, I stowed my poncho, too. A cold breakfast of trail mix (I was getting heartily sick of trail mix) and chocolate alleviated both my hunger and my headache, and then we were on our way again, heading downhill now, which made things easier. Fog shrouded everything. The heavy mist seemed to absorb sound as well as light, so that we moved through the deepest silence I had ever heard (if that's not a contradiction in terms). At least we saw no bears (or lions or tigers), or, for that matter, dragons. Apparently, I *hadn't* accidentally conjured one—yay, me. But . . . could I have?

I asked Karl about that, too. "So . . . some worlds are more fantastical than others?" I said as we trudged through the snow, through a hush so deep I had to force myself not to whisper. "Not every Shaper copies the original world so closely?"

"No," he said.

"Give me an example," I said. "Are there worlds where dragons are real?"

He sighed. "Too many. I don't know what it is with Shapers and dragons. Also elves. They are always the same: pointy-eared, pale-skinned, inordinately fond of poetry and of hearing themselves sing."

"Tolkien," I said.

He shot me a look, frowning. "Who?" Then his expression cleared. "Oh, yes, the 'great writer of fantastic tales' you mentioned once before. He had dragons and elves in his stories?"

"Yes," I said. "Also orcs . . . um, goblins. And hobbits."

"Hobbits?"

"Very short people with big furry feet."

He sighed. "I ran into those once, too. This . . . Toll King, was it?"

"Tolkien."

"Tolkien. He has a lot to answer for."

Another thought struck me. "Does that mean *magic* is real in those worlds, too? Even though they're all copied from a real place where there *isn't* any magic?"

"You made it snow yesterday," Karl pointed out. Not that I needed reminding, since I was currently knee-deep in the product of my own Shaping. "You successfully wished a bear elsewhere this morning. Are you saying magic is not real in *this* world?"

That kept me silent for a few minutes, while we continued to trudge through the fog-shrouded forest. Then I said, "But I'm the Shaper. So it isn't magic. It's more like . . . a miracle. Like changing water into wine in the Bible."

"How many times do I have to tell you? You are not a god. Or the offspring of one."

*Well*, I thought. *Good to know he postdates the Bible, at least.* "Close enough. I guess I'm asking if there are worlds where people *other* than the Shaper have the ability to do things that appear magical."

It was Karl's turn to walk silently for a few moments. "I have seen a world like that," he said at last. "I did not stay long."

"Why?" I said.

"Because the Shaper had lost control," Karl said. "Whatever kind of world he thought he was making, by making magic real, he gave away too much power. His world was a place of warfare and terror and enslavement and death."

I stopped. "Wait," I said. "You're saying a Shaped world, *even if the Adversary doesn't show up*, can go . . . wrong?"

"Do you have crime in your city?" Karl said. "Are there wars?"

"Some," I said. "And sure, here and there. But they're contained . . ."

"Do you like wars and crime?"

"No, but there's nothing I can do to . . ." My voice trailed away.

"The Shaper," Karl said, "sets up the initial conditions of the world. How much power they have to continue to Shape the world varies with the Shaper. Some have none. Those Shapers, although they remember Shaping their worlds—unlike you—then simply live within them, unable to change them further. Problems may arise that they did not foresee, and are powerless to correct."

"So if the initial conditions have chaos built in . . ."

"Chaos will result."

"You said 'some' Shapers have no power left."

Karl nodded. "Other Shapers have a little power remaining, though if there are serious flaws baked into their worlds, they may not have enough ability to do more than protect themselves. It is very rare for a Shaper to keep as much power as you have kept. Which, of course, is what drew me to you." He sighed. "It would have been far more useful had you also retained your memories of who and what you are. Still, if we are fortunate . . ." He stopped suddenly. "Uh-oh."

If there's one thing you don't want to hear from the semimystical guide who is attempting to spirit you from one world to another without attracting the attention of a godlike murderous Adversary, it's, "Uh-oh."

"Uh-oh *what*?" I peered past him into the fog. "Another bear?"

"No," he said. "Another unintended consequence of the way you Shaped the world."

At first I couldn't figure out what he was talking about. Then I realized that the fog down the road from us displayed a certain . . . solidity. And then I realized it wasn't fog at all, but a wall of snow. As we moved closer, I saw toppled trees and shattered stone mixed in with it.

An avalanche.

"Heavy snow on warm ground, a layer of water forms, down it comes," Karl said, as if I hadn't figured that out myself.

"Can't we just . . . climb over it?"

"It might not be stable," Karl said. He looked up at the sky. "The fog is lifting. Let us wait until it clears a bit, and then decide how to proceed."

We sat on a rock, munching chips and (ugh) trail mix. The fog slipped slowly up the slopes, gradually revealing just how much of a problem the avalanche was going to be.

The answer turned out to be: not as much as it might have been. The slide had wiped away the road and splashed up the other side of the pass, but it looked like it shouldn't be too difficult to make our way around its tip, and presumably pick up the road again on the other side. The trees were thinner at this altitude, which helped. Once we could see where we were going, we began toiling up the eastern side of the pass, just beyond the farthest extent of the slide's tangled mass of snow, rock, and splintered pine.

There was, of course, a downside to thinner forest cover and lifting fog. About the time the sun began to break through the clouds, I heard a sound I was beginning to hate: the beat of a helicopter's rotors, rising up from the valley behind us. Clearly the chopper and its keepers had been waiting for just such a break to resume their aerial reconnaissance.

"Into the trees!" Karl ordered, and we both scrambled for the thin forest, but it didn't seem like nearly enough cover, even after we did our best to cover the brightly colored backpacks with leaves, and crouched behind some rocks ourselves. If the helicopter flew right over us . . .

. . . but it didn't. It came into sight, but hovered a considerable distance away, in the direction of our overnight campsite. Something moved in the woods. I caught a glimpse of pink . . .

Then I realized what I was looking at. It was our grizzly

morning visitor, still carrying Karl's poncho in its mouth. The bright splash of color must have attracted the attention of the observers aboard the aircraft. Not surprisingly, having a helicopter hovering over its head sent the bear hightailing downhill, back the way we'd come. The copter followed; maybe whoever was aboard thought the bear had raided our camp, and hoped it would lead them back to it. Maybe they just had a thing for bears. Maybe my Shaping was still helping to conceal us. Whatever the reason, the moment the helicopter was out of sight, we scrambled to our feet, grabbed our backpacks, and ran through the thin and spindly forest at the top of the pass to the much deeper, darker, and therefore more inviting forest down the other side.

We reached that thicker growth just as the sound of rotors waxed behind us once more, and crouched among heavy, snow-laden branches as the copter thundered by, somewhere off to our right. We couldn't see it, so I hoped no one aboard it could see us.

"They won't rely on the helicopter to find us," Karl said. "Now that they have seen the bear with the poncho, they're sure we came this way. Someone is almost certainly coming up the pass behind us on foot, and before long—if they are not already on their way—someone will be coming down the pass ahead of us. We must stay well clear of the road from here on."

He didn't suggest I Shape the world again. Looking back at the avalanche debris, I couldn't blame him. We could just as easily have been in its path.

"What about more bears?" I said.

"Grizzlies can have overlapping territories, so it's not impossible," Karl said, "but they need two hundred to five hundred square miles in total, so the odds are we will not see another one."

I stared at him. "You don't know *The Wizard of Oz* and you've never heard of J.R.R. Tolkien, but you know random facts about grizzly bears?"

"I know many random facts picked up during my journeys," he said. "Also, the wizard of what?"

I sighed. "Forget it."

"With pleasure," Karl said. He turned and pushed on through the trees, without looking back. He moved faster than me, too, so he was soon twenty or thirty yards ahead, his blue backpack my navigational beacon.

It occurred to me that I could easily step to the side and vanish from his sight, make my way back down into the forest, and . . .

. . . what? Find a secluded cabin, and try to hide out for the rest of my life? Survive on nuts and berries?

Nuts and berries was what trail mix was made out of. *Blecch.*

I kept following Karl.

As I had previously noted, all the trees looked the same, so I promptly lost any sense of direction, except for downhill: but since at times the slope petered out or reversed direction, even that would have done me little good if I were on my own. Instead, we navigated by Karl's compass. He would find south, and locate the farthest tree he could see in that direction. We'd walk to it, then he'd repeat the process. It wasn't fast, but it kept us more or less on the right course and, even more importantly, well hidden.

Late in the afternoon, we left behind the last vestiges of my Shaped snowfall, and just as the sun slipped behind the mountains at the head of the valley, plunging us into the shadows that would become our second night in the woods (though it was still a couple of hours until what would have been sunset on the prairie), we came out of the trees onto the banks of a stream, flowing swiftly toward the east, no doubt to join the river that gave my city its name. *If I had a boat*, I thought, *I could probably drift all the way home.*

Then I looked a little farther downstream, saw the foaming rapids, and amended that thought. *Well, my drowned body could drift all the way home.*

The stream was too broad and deep to ford even where we were. The aforementioned rapids offered little hope of an easier crossing downstream. That meant we'd have to head upstream—and that, of course, would eventually bring us back to the road, which presumably crossed the river on a bridge. *Which*, I thought, *would be a fine place for anyone chasing us to post a lookout.*

Karl clearly thought the same. He looked up at the sky. "We will rest here until dark," he said. "It appears it will be a clear evening. Moonlight and starlight should provide enough illumination for us to find our way upstream to a crossing."

I nodded and sat on a rock to dig out my . . . I sighed . . . trail mix. Water wasn't a problem, with the river right there, although Karl insisted we each drop a water-purification tablet into our canteens before we drank any of it. "Couldn't I just Shape any impurities out of it?" I asked, as I waited in the gathering dusk for the twenty minutes the tablet needed to do its magic.

"Possibly," Karl said. "But based on past experience, there is a better-than-average chance you would sterilize the entire stream."

I would have argued, except I thought he was probably right.

I had no idea when moonrise was (does anyone *ever* know off the top of their heads when moonrise will be?). It turned out to be about 8:45, or at least that was when the moon cleared the trees, and the moon turned out to be full. (Or had I made it full by wishing it would be full? Now *that* was a mind-boggling thought.) By its silvery glimmer we began to pick our way upstream, a slow, careful process, since the strange shadows cast by moonlight turned the gaps between the flat rocks covering the stream bank and the shadows under the trees as black as crude oil, which made the footing commensurately uncertain.

Ahead, moonlight glinted off of glass and metal. We stopped. "An SUV," I whispered to Karl. "It's the road." Then I saw a railing, and realized the vehicle was parked at the north end of a rudimentary bridge. If there was anyone actually *on* the bridge, I couldn't spot them in the uncertain light.

"We need that vehicle," Karl murmured.

I glanced at him. "Why?"

"On foot, we will be caught."

"In a stolen vehicle, we will *also* be caught."

"But it will not be stolen. It will be an official vehicle, on official business. It may get us inside the gate at Snakebite Mine, and thus closer to the Portal."

"You want me to Shape whoever's watching the bridge." I shook my head. "No. The last time I Shaped a human, someone died."

"So do it better this time," Karl said. "*Learn*. Shawna, we *must* get to the place where I can create a new Portal, and the sooner the better. But first we must destroy the Portal through which I and the Adversary entered your world. As I told you, I believe that will weaken the Adversary by severing his connection with the two worlds he already controls, and weakening the Adversary is crucial, because his power is waxing minute by minute, as his version of reality, imposed on those he Shapes, takes a firmer grip on this world. At some point, even if you remain at large, he may *exceed* you in power. But for now, you outmatch him. For as long as that is true, you *must* be willing to use your Shaping ability as necessary—and learn to use it *better* than you have so far. Or else the Adversary's men will catch us, and kill you. *Your world is already lost.* But if we beat him to the next, that world, and many worlds thereafter, may yet escape his corruption."

A part of me cried out silently, asking what I cared about other worlds. I cared only about my own. But Karl's grim words echoed in my mind: *Your world is already lost.* I thought again of my mom, and again pushed the thought away. It was too big and terrible to examine now. *If not now, when?* my mind demanded. But I left the question unanswered.

"So, what do you have in mind?" I said to Karl, though I admit I said it begrudgingly.

"There are probably two men, one on the bridge, one in the vehicle," Karl said. "Their orders are most likely to watch for us, call in if they see us, and apprehend us if they can. They are unlikely to have been directly Shaped by the Adversary: they are merely doing their duty. You need to Shape them so that they remember their orders differently; to wait for us, to give us their vehicle, uniforms, and identification, and then to head downstream, evading their own apprehension for as long as possible."

I blinked at him. The glitter of his eyes in the moonlight for a moment gave him a strangely inhuman look, as though he really *were* some kind of robot. "That all made sense except for the head downstream part."

"The longer they remain out of contact with their superiors, the more time our ruse will have to work."

I looked back at the bridge and the SUV. "And you trust me to try this?" I said. "After the snow and the avalanche and the dead man?" *Do I trust myself?* was the question I was really asking, but he couldn't answer that one.

He didn't exactly answer the question I'd asked *him*, either. "There is no other way," was all he said. "But think *carefully* this time."

I took a deep breath. "All right, I'll try." I closed my eyes. This was the fourth time I'd consciously Shaped. Undoing the attack on the Human Bean had been involuntary. The first time I'd *tried* to do it had been the helicopter crew, and I'd really only succeeded with one of them. The second time had been the "cover-our-tracks" attempt, which had worked . . . though it had also caused an avalanche that could easily have killed us if we'd happened to be in the wrong place at the wrong time. The third time had been convincing the bear that Karl's pink poncho was far more interesting than we were.

*Think carefully*, Karl had said. So I thought. I thought about what I'd felt, each of those other Shapings. The first time had been in a panic, but the other three . . .

Each time, I had felt . . . something. Something new: strange, yet familiar at the same time, like a muscle I'd never used before that I'd suddenly begun to flex. (Which might explain the recurring headaches: they were akin to the morning-after pain I felt whenever I resumed working out at the gym after a long hiatus.) Now I recalled that fledgling sensation, reached for it, drew on it. I pictured, as clearly and carefully as I could, what I wanted to be true when we approached the bridge. And somehow, even before I opened my eyes, I knew I had succeeded—and not just because of the headache and momentary fatigue.

Which didn't mean at all, of course, that there weren't going to be some unintended consequences. I was still new to this. I just hoped they weren't on the scale of the avalanche.

"All right," I said. "It's done."

Karl nodded. Together, we walked toward the bridge.

After about thirty yards I spotted the man stationed on the bridge, my eyes suddenly distinguishing his form from the misleading mottling of moon-cast shadows. He had his back to us, but he turned as the flat rocks of the stream bank shifted and clacked beneath our feet, announcing our approach. I tensed. If my sense of accomplishment had been misplaced, he would call for help—or draw a pistol and try to shoot us on sight—but instead, he waved what seemed a friendly greeting at us, then walked toward the SUV.

"So far, so good," I said to Karl.

He didn't reply.

We reached the bridge and scrambled up the bank to the road.

As we did so, I heard the SUV's door open and close. When we reached the top, both men were standing beside the black-and-white vehicle, which bore the word SHERIFF in capital letters on the door, with "Bear Valley County" in smaller letters underneath. "Glad you made it," said the one on the left, who was a bit taller and stockier than the one on the right—which was about all I could make out of either of them in the moonlight, other than the fact the man on the right was black. "We were beginning to worry."

"You have your orders?" Karl said.

The second man nodded. "Yes," he said. "Going to be a bit chilly, but . . ." He shrugged, and started taking off his clothes.

"You can have ours," I said, as he stripped off his jacket and shirt, his compatriot following suit. Boots came off next, then they unbuckled their gun belts, laid them on the hood of the SUV, and took off their pants. When they both reached for their boxers, though, I said quickly, "No need for that."

They stopped. "Are you sure, ma'am?"

I nodded vigorously. "Totally." Then I glanced at Karl. He'd obviously have to take the uniform from the larger of the two. "Give us a minute," I said. I took the uniform from the smaller of the two men and walked around to the far side of the SUV, where I quickly skinned out of my own clothes, shivering as I did so, and into the new ones. They fit perfectly—*part of the Shaping?*—even the boots. Then I rounded the SUV again and handed my jeans and flannel shirt to the smaller man, who pulled them on and replaced his boots with my shoes—good, practical sneakers, though I suspected even if I'd been wearing heels, he would have donned them if they fit. Which, I was convinced, considering how comfortable I was finding *his* clothes, they would have.

"Well then," said the larger of the two men, whose uniform had likewise fit Karl perfectly, and who now wore Karl's borrowed black duster and snakeskin-banded cowboy hat, "we'll head down the river. Good luck, ma'am. Sir. Hope your mission is a success."

"So do we," I said.

Without another word, they scrambled down the bank we had ascended, and began picking their way downstream, the clattering of the streamside rocks they disturbed soon lost in the rush of water.

I looked at Karl. "Now what?"

"We go to Snakebite Mine," he said. He'd put the pistol he'd gotten from the helicopter on the hood beside the sheriff's deputies' weapons. He left it there, picking up one of the gun belts instead and buckling it on. "With luck, our borrowed vehicle and uniforms gain us easy access. With your help, I destroy the Portal."

"'Drive up to the gate and see if they'll let us in' doesn't sound like much of a plan." I took the other gun belt, but didn't put it on. I'd only shot long guns growing up, never a pistol, and the weight would have been annoying. Instead I opened the SUV's door and tossed the belt into the back seat.

"I would be surprised if it did, since it isn't a plan," Karl said. He picked up the pistol from the helicopter and put it in the back seat, too. "It's simply all I have to offer. And in any event, as Helmuth von Moltke the Elder famously said, no battle plan survives contact with the enemy. Napoleon, I might add, said he *never* had a plan of operations. And yet he conquered most of Europe."

*Helmuth von* who? Perhaps I shouldn't be so uppity about the fact I knew cultural references he didn't. I sighed. "Will you drive, or shall I?"

"You," he said. "I do not have the skill."

"You've never learned to drive?"

"Not all worlds have vehicles of this type."

"But the First World does."

He nodded.

"Then . . ."

"I do not have the skill," he repeated. "The reasons do not matter. You drive."

Left wondering, yet again, who Karl Yatsar really was, and where (and when) he really came from, I climbed into the driver's seat of the SUV. Karl clambered in beside me. I started the engine and shifted into drive, and we rolled across the bridge and into the moonlit woods.

# ELEVEN

**JUST BEFORE WE** crested the final low rise that, Karl assured me, hid Snakebite Mine, I turned off the lights. We crept very slowly to the top of the hill, then eased a very few feet down the other side, just far enough to give us a clear view of the barbed-wire-topped chain-link fence surrounding the mine compound. For a place holding a mysterious gateway to another world, it looked remarkably mundane.

The road split perhaps thirty yards short of the fence. The main road turned left. A less-used branch turned right. And straight ahead, a narrow drive led to a gate, the chain and padlock securing it visible in the pool of illumination cast by flood lamps with wok-shaped shades atop each of the gate's metal poles. Aside from the gate, the lights lit nothing but scraggly grass.

Maybe seventy-five yards past the gate stood a small log cabin with a shingled roof. A yard light showed a big propane tank, a parked, rusty blue pickup, and steps up to the front door. There were no lights in the cabin itself. Farther back in the compound bulked the much larger shape of an old minehead. "Looks like a cakewalk," I said.

"Indeed," Karl said. "And if the only person guarding the mine site is the custodian who was here when I arrived, it will be. Even if he does not fully believe that we are the law enforcement officers we appear to be, you can Shape him to accept us and provide access to the mine itself, where the Portal is located."

"If?" I said. "You said 'if.'"

He looked at me. "It is still possible the Adversary has left additional guards on this Portal."

"So I'll Shape them, too."

"If you can," he said. "If he has left members of his cadre . . . you cannot. They are not from your world."

I frowned. "You told me, when I brought up the *exact same concern*, that you did not think he would divide his cadre like that."

"I did not think he would. I do not think he has," Karl said. "But I could be wrong, and so I am mentioning the possibility, so that we are prepared in the unlikely event that it is true."

*Maybe he was a lawyer,* I thought. *Or a particularly boring university professor.* "Would they recognize you?"

He nodded. "Without question."

"Would they recognize me?"

"If they were among those who attacked the coffee shop, yes. Though they may not be."

"But if they are, they'll shoot me on sight?"

"Most likely those are their orders."

I thought back to the attack that had launched me into this nightmare, and to the people who had died, who hadn't come back despite my massive reshaping of the world: to Aesha, whom no one else in this entire world even remembered. Some spark of fury I'd been carrying deep inside me, without even realizing it, suddenly kindled into a bonfire. "So we shoot them first," I snarled. "Hell, they're not even real in this world. *My* world. I didn't Shape the world to include killers like them. *They don't belong here.*"

Karl looked at me in silence for a long moment, his face impossible to read in the darkened cabin of the SUV, then turned his head toward the mine. "We do not know how many of them there may be. If we shoot anyone, it may only raise the alarm, and many more might appear. We might not escape."

I stared at him. "You brought me here," I said. "You said we have to destroy this Portal before we try to get to where you can open a new one. Now you're getting cold feet?"

"My feet are not cold."

"Is that a joke?"

He frowned at me. "What?"

"Never mind." I looked down toward the mining compound. "Do we try to get in there or not? Because if not, we should start this thing up and drive like hell while we've got the chance."

"If I did not think we should destroy this Portal, I would not have brought us here," Karl said. "I am merely trying to think through all the possible scenarios of our approach."

I pushed down my anger and frustration. If Karl wanted to play Spock I'd have to take on the role of Kirk. Or Dr. McCoy. *Dammit, Karl, I'm a potter, not a goddess.* "The original plan was to roll up to the gate and pretend to be the cops we appear to be," I said, trying hard to keep my voice calm and level.

He nodded.

"Which might work without any Shaping and will definitely work with it, provided someone from this world is guarding the compound," I continued. "However, that approach might get us killed if some of the Adversary's 'cadre' are there."

He nodded again.

"You say I can't Shape the Adversary's cadre." I chewed on my lip. "What if I tried to Shape some aspect of the mining compound instead? Maybe . . . create a new pathway to the Portal that opens from outside the compound?"

"No," Karl said sharply. "We're too close to the Portal. Your Shaping could literally backfire, reflecting off the Portal's energies in unpredictable fashion."

"Unpredictable?"

"Possibly lethal. To you."

"But presumably I'm going to use my Shaping ability to destroy it."

"Yes. Under my guidance, and while standing before it."

"Oh." I kept staring at the gate, at the bottom of the rather steep hill. "It's not a very strong chain on that gate," I said slowly.

Karl looked at it, then at me. "What are you thinking?"

"I'm thinking," I said, "that what we need is a diversion—something to bring the guards running, so we can see exactly who we're dealing with."

Twenty minutes later, I stood at the top of the hill alongside the SUV, which I'd moved a little farther downslope. I'd aimed the vehicle at the gate, pulled the emergency brake, put the transmission into neutral, and used my borrowed belt to lash the steering wheel so the SUV would (hopefully) roll straight when I released the brake. "This should work," I'd told Karl as I'd tied the belt in place. "*Mythbusters* even tested it once. The car went through the gate like it was made out of paper."

"*Mythbusters*?"

"Never mind."

After that, he'd melted into the darkness, to move as close to the fence as he could without revealing himself. I'd given him ten minutes to get into position. Now I took a deep breath, reached in through the open driver's door, released the parking brake, jerked my arm back, and slammed the door.

The SUV started to roll, slowly at first, then faster and faster. To my relief, it went straight, or at least straight enough that it hit the gate and not one of the gateposts. It wasn't moving nearly as fast as the car in the *Mythbusters* episode, though, so although it smashed the gate open, it didn't roll much farther, its momentum spent.

What it *did* do was make a most satisfyingly horrific noise.

Lights snapped on in the log cabin. A moment later a middle-aged man wearing only an undershirt and boxers—but carrying a shotgun—appeared in the doorway. I held my breath, hoping he was the only guard . . .

He wasn't. Two running, black-clad figures burst out of the darkness of the compound. I heard one shout something at the half-naked man, who promptly ducked back out of sight. Fury boiled up inside me. The killers from the coffee shop, or their brethren, at least.

One called to the other in a voice light and high-pitched. Brethren *and* sistren, apparently. The fact one of them was a woman didn't lessen my anger in the slightest.

They approached the SUV crouched, rifles ready. The woman held her weapon pointed at the cab while the man jerked the door open. Discovering the cab empty, he straightened, spun around, shouted something . . .

. . . and died, jerking back and falling out of my sight as the crack of Karl's pistol shot belatedly reached me.

The woman reacted with blinding speed, throwing herself to the ground and opening fire in the direction from which the shot had come, with a spray of bullets that could only have come from a fully automatic military weapon. The sound of it echoed back from distant cliffs for seconds after she quit firing and scrambled for the cover of the SUV.

She never made it. She jerked and quit moving as another pistol shot rang out.

I gasped air. I'd been holding my breath without realizing it.

The old man from the log cabin had not reappeared. I couldn't blame him.

I hurried down the slope, Karl emerging from the shadows to join me at the smashed gate. "Wait here," he said grimly. He strode over to the fallen man. I couldn't see the body clearly in the dark, but I could see the glistening spray of blood and . . . chunkier bits . . . splattered across the side of the SUV.

Karl moved on to the woman, bent over her. She moaned. He straightened, aimed his pistol at her head, and pulled the trigger.

I gasped. All my rage and hatred of a moment before evaporated. I turned, doubled over, and retched. I'd thought I'd wanted them dead for what they'd done . . . or at least for what their fellows had done . . . but it was one thing to think it, another to see them die so horribly, so close up: and worse, to see my own companion kill them without, so far as I could tell, the slightest compunction.

I spat, and wiped my mouth, and straightened. Karl came toward me, pistol loose in his hand. "All right?" he said.

*No*, I thought. "Yes," I said. I kept my eyes resolutely turned from the corpses. "Now what?"

"The house," Karl said. "Let us see if the guard will believe us to be policemen." He holstered the pistol. "Otherwise . . ."

I nodded. Otherwise, I would have to Shape his mind, already pried open and rearranged by the Adversary. *How much Shaping can the human mind take?* I wondered. *How much can you bend it before it shatters?*

As we approached the house, I pulled out the ID card that had come with the uniform. I hadn't looked at it before, and, rather too late to do anything about it, it occurred to me that the photo of the man who had worn the uniform before me definitely wouldn't look like . . .

Then the light from the house spilled across the plastic card, and I saw that not only did the photo look like me, it *was* me. And though the card had come from a man, the name on the card was "Elizabeth Norton."

I stared at the photo. I had no memory of it ever having been taken, which wasn't surprising, since in it I wore the very uniform I wore now, and obviously no one had had an opportunity to take my picture in the hour or so I'd been wearing it. Looking at that impossible photo, I felt reality shift around me, as though I stood on a beach, waves washing away the sand beneath my feet. How often had I unconsciously Shaped the world to meet my own ends, altering reality and the lives of those around me just so things would work out the way I wanted?

Aesha? Brent? Had I Shaped *them* so they'd befriend me . . . fall in love with me?

Was my mother just some random woman I had adopted as my parent, changing her so that she believed I was her child, so that she remembered raising me? Had I filled my own mind with pleasant lies so that I believed it, too?

Karl said I had really only existed here for a decade or so, that I was born in another world, the First World; that Ygrair had taught and trained me there, then placed me in this one because I had the . . . whatever it was that made me a Shaper. I couldn't remember any of that, though apparently I was supposed to be able to. But assuming it was true, then somewhere I had to have, or at least once had, *real* parents, a *real* life, *real* friends, everything I thought I'd had here . . . except everything I'd had here was, in one fashion or another, a lie.

Tears suddenly blinded me, so I could no longer see the ID badge at all: not tears of grief, but tears of anger, at Ygrair, at myself, at everything. I dashed them away with a sharp swipe of the back of my hand and followed Karl up the steps of the log cabin.

It took some cajoling and flashing of our stolen IDs, but eventually the custodian opened the door without forcing me to Shape him. Thankfully, he'd used the time to get dressed. His eyes, watery and red-rimmed, slipped past us toward the dark bundles lying motionless in the grass, visible in the spill of illumination from the gate and yard lights. "I don't understand. They were cops, too . . ." His gaze flicked back to me. "Weren't they?"

"Terrorists," I said, taking charge. Karl's strange, stilted way of talking—and complete lack of any understanding of any cultural references more recent then, as far as I could tell, the late nineteenth century—would probably not be reassuring. "We had a tip."

"Terrorists?" The custodian blinked. "Why aren't there more of you . . . ?"

"There will be," I said. "Lots more. On their way now. But we thought we were dealing with a hostage situation, so we had to move fast, before backup could arrive."

"Hostage? Oh, you mean me." He shook his head. "No," he said. "I believed them. Completely taken in." He hesitated. "Um . . . now what? Would you . . . like a drink? I'd like a drink."

*I'm not surprised*, I thought, and actually, yes, I *would* have liked a drink, but, "No, thank you," I said. "We're on duty. We need to see inside the mine."

The custodian frowned slightly. "Why? It's locked up. Nobody in there. A few yards of tunnels and a barred door."

"Please," Karl said.

The custodian's watery gaze flicked from side to side. "I'm really not supposed to let anyone in there . . ."

"We must insist," Karl said.

The custodian's shoulders sagged. "I'll get the keys." He disappeared back into the house.

I looked at Karl. "Why didn't he recognize you?" I whispered. "From when you came through the Portal."

"He did not see me then," Karl said in a low voice. "I left the compound without being spotted, having found a place I could climb over the fence."

"That duster and the cowboy hat . . ."

"Were his," Karl admitted. "But he never knew I stole them. It is perhaps fortunate I am not wearing them now, of course."

The custodian reappeared and stepped onto the porch, closing the door of the cabin behind him. "Got to keep the bugs out," he said. In his right hand he held an old-fashioned key ring, like a jailer's prop in a black-and-white Western, with five keys on it. They jingled faintly as he walked toward the back of the compound, where another dim light burned above what looked like the front end of a Quonset hut sticking out of the mountainside . . . probably because it *was* the front end of a Quonset hut sticking out of the mountainside, as I saw when we got closer.

When we were about forty yards away, the custodian stopped us. "You two wait here," he said, for no reason I could see. "I'll call you when I've got it open."

As we watched him approach the half-Quonset, Karl drew his pistol again. "That man is acting oddly," he said. "There may be more cadre inside."

I felt a chill, and wondered if I should have retrieved the other gun belt from the SUV. "Do you really think there are?"

"I have no idea." But he held the pistol in both hands, barrel pointing down, and waited.

The custodian reached the door of the half-Quonset and unlocked a padlock. He opened the door. "Just a second!" he called back to us, with a wave.

He stepped inside.

An instant later, flame and smoke erupted from the half-Quonset. The blast knocked me flat on my back, the impact with the ground driving the breath from me. I gaped up at the stars like a landed fish, trying desperately to pull a little air into my stunned lungs. It took agonizing minutes, during which I heard a deep rumble that literally shook the ground. When I could finally raise myself on my elbows, I stared toward the mine.

In the moonlight, it was hard to be sure of anything, but the shape of the mountainside above the mine entrance looked . . . different, as if it had subsided. The light that had illuminated the

Quonset hut no longer burned, but I could see well enough to know that the Quonset wasn't really there anymore, though a few brighter bits of debris might have been parts of it.

I suddenly realized one of the custodian's boots lay beside my head. A shattered bone, gleaming in the moonlight, stuck out of the top of it.

My stomach heaved, but there was nothing left in it to puke. "Karl?" I croaked out.

He was on his back, too, not far away. He groaned as he sat up. His face was just a pale smear in the moonlight. "He booby-trapped it."

"Who? The Adversary?"

"No," Karl said. He wiped his hand across his face, and I saw a smear of dark blood from his nose. "The caretaker."

"But . . . why?" I carefully did not look at the not-empty boot, tried not to notice other . . . things . . . I was beginning to make out in the grass around us. "He blew himself up!"

"Shaped," Karl said. "The Adversary Shaped him to protect the Portal at all costs. I doubt the Adversary expected him to do something like this, though. Even the cadre members may not have known about it."

"But he didn't protect the Portal," I protested, "he destroyed it!"

"Destroyed the Portal?" Karl said, refocusing on me. "Don't be ridiculous. Only we can do that . . . at least, I *hope* we can do it."

"But it's buried under tons of rock . . . it will take weeks to dig it out!"

"Not once the Adversary has control of this world. He can Shape it in a heartbeat. We must not give him that opportunity." Karl took a deep breath. "I think I can stand. Can you?"

"Maybe," I said, though I wasn't entirely sure.

In the end, we both managed it, though only by leaning heavily on each other.

"Now what?" I said.

"Now," Karl said. "You must Shape in a way you have not before." He pointed at the jumbled mass of stone and twisted metal. "Open a tunnel to the Portal."

"But how?" I stared at the wreckage. "I don't even know where it is!"

"Don't you?" Karl said. "Close your eyes. Concentrate. *Feel*. The Portal is a flaw in your world, a crack in its walls, a tear in its fabric. You can sense it if you try. *Try*."

"All right!" My ears were still ringing from the explosion, and my chest ached. But I closed my eyes and tried to push those sensations away, so I could concentrate on . . . whatever else I was supposed to be able to sense.

For a moment, all I could sense in addition to the aforementioned ringing ears and aching chest were the assorted other strains and bruises I'd picked up over our two-day hike. Oh, that and the lingering bitterness of bile in the back of my throat from when I'd thrown up just minutes before. Was there anything else? I reached deeper . . .

. . . and there it was. I might have put it down to . . . what were Scrooge's words? . . . "an undigested bit of beef, a blot of mustard, a crumb of cheese, a fragment of an underdone potato" . . . if not for the fact I'd had little else to eat but trail mix for the past couple of days and had just thrown up most of that.

Once I took note of it, I realized I had been feeling it for some time: a kind of . . . itch, or irritation, or disquietude, a feeling that there was something wrong with this particular place, that it wasn't quite . . . right. It was the feeling I'd had as a kid walking past an old house in our neighborhood we were sure was haunted, except, of course, that had been imaginary . . .

(My breath caught. Had my whole *childhood* been imaginary?)

. . . and this was real.

I opened my eyes. "That . . . wrongness? That's the Portal?"

"Wrongness?" Karl frowned, then his face cleared. "Ah. I suppose it would feel like that to a Shaper. I don't sense it like that. But you are attuned to this world, and the Portal is an opening into another world, Shaped by someone else, so of course it *would* seem wrong to you. Yes, that is the Portal." He pointed at the rubble. "Now imagine a path to it."

"I'll . . . try." I closed my eyes again and tried to empty my mind so I could flex that still-new Shaping "muscle." My mind had just seen three people killed violently (and I might have been killed along with the third if I'd been a little quicker following the mine's custodian), my ears still rang from the concussion, and one or two other disturbing things had happened in the recent past, so emptying it was easier said than done. But with less difficulty than I'd feared, my newfound power rose within me.

The Portal was . . . there. Annoying, disturbing. I wanted to be able to reach it, so I could remove the irritation. I imagined a tunnel, solid stone, well-lit, the Portal at its end. I released the image.

I instantly dropped to my knees, and then to all fours, all the aches and pains I'd pushed away suddenly rushing back to clobber me over the back of the head, along with a sudden wave of fatigue, as though I'd just completed an exhausting workout. "Ow," I said. Then I looked up, and saw the tunnel: white stone, like something out of a Grecian temple, torches burning in sconces every few feet, an arched ceiling, and, at the far end . . .

A rust-red door, bearing a white sign with KEEP OUT: DANGER written on it in faded red letters, completely out of character with the rest of the tunnel.

"Well done," said Karl.

"But I . . . didn't imagine white stone," I said, staring at the tunnel. "Or torches. Just a . . . generic tunnel. Well-lit."

"When you do not provide details, the world provides them for you," Karl said. "It drew some image from your mind, no doubt." He held out his hand. "Come."

"Easier said than done." What I really wanted to do was lie down. Right where I was. But I took his hand and, groaning, got to my feet.

Together, we walked to the tunnel I had just conjured out of . . . well, not of thin air, I guess, but out of thick rock. Although the tunnel was marble, and I was pretty sure the rock tumbled all around it was granite. "Ill-geological, Captain," I muttered, even though I knew Karl wouldn't get it. Sure enough, he cocked a quizzical eyebrow at me. Which was perfect, so I felt overall the quip had been successful, even if I was the only one who appreciated it.

We reached the Portal. That sense of wrongness was almost overwhelming. I wanted to . . . I didn't know. I reached for the rusty metal, then drew my hands back again. "We have to seal this," I said. "It's . . . disgusting."

"Is it?" Karl gave me another quizzical look. "Fascinating."

Despite everything, my mouth quirked.

He turned his attention back to the Portal. "Though this door is closed," he said, "the Portal is open. If I opened this door, you would see into the storeroom of a rather primitive inn. We might also find ourselves facing an unknown number of armed guards, however, so I do not recommend sightseeing." He put his hands on the door and blue light flickered over the surface, not all that bright, but somehow painful to my eyes all the same. He pushed . . . and the light steadied, flashed once, like a photoflash, and then vanished. "I have closed the Portal again," he said, "but the Adversary can still reopen it." He turned to me. "That's where you come in. I believe, with your power, we can destroy it permanently."

"How?" I stared at the hateful door. "Do I just . . . imagine it doesn't exist?"

"That won't work," Karl said. "The Portal is a place where two worlds touch. It is not yours to Shape. If the Shaper from the world on the other side were facing you across the Portal, and you both Shaped it at the same time . . . then, perhaps, you could make it disappear. But the Shaper of the world through this Portal has been the Adversary since he stole the *hokhmah* of that world from the original Shaper and then killed him."

"Then how do I do it?"

Karl looked at Shawna Keys' face, smeared with dirt, and hesitated, doubting his own resolve, wondering if he could even make happen what he thought could happen here. Once before, he had let a Shaper pour her power through his body. Ygrair, after placing within him the technology that enabled him to open Portals, had used her power and his combined to open up the Labyrinth, crafting what became known as the Graduation Portal, the gateway through which all the Shapers since had entered the Labyrinth to claim their worlds. And in the process . . . she had burned him out.

Shawna had asked him more than once if he was a Shaper, and he had never answered. But now, he thought, he must. "Through me," he said at last. "Just like the Adversary does, I carry within my body a . . . tool . . . from Ygrair's home world. He brought his with him, but Ygrair gave me mine. It is that tool, that technology, that gives me the ability to find, open, and close Portals. You have asked if I am myself a Shaper. Once, I was, or could have been. For now, I am not." *Though if I succeed in this quest, Ygrair has promised me that will change*, he thought, but did not say. "But the technology within me can channel *your* Shaping ability. With your power, I believe I can destroy this Portal."

"What do I have to do?" Shawna asked. Her eyes burned red in the light of the torches her mind had subconsciously Shaped to illuminate the marble tunnel.

"You must attempt to Shape me," Karl said. "It does not matter in what fashion. Try to turn me into a frog, or a pig, if that amuses you. Try to convince me to spin in circles and spout gibberish. Try to make me burst into flames. I cannot be Shaped by you, because I am not of your world. But I can take the power you hurl at me and turn it against the Portal."

Shawna's mouth quirked. "A frog?"

"If it amuses you," Karl said. He had offered the possibility because he knew the Shaper had a quirky sense of humor, even though he did not understand half of what she apparently thought were extremely funny witticisms. He did not care what she imagined him doing or becoming in her mind, as long as she fed him the power he needed.

He also very carefully did not tell her one other thing, something he knew from when Ygrair had channeled her power through him to open the Graduation Portal.

This was going to hurt him very badly indeed.

Despite the invitation, I did not attempt to Shape Karl into a frog. That seemed a bit harsh. Also, what if he was wrong, and the Shaping worked? A frog wasn't going to be able to get us to wherever we had to get to escape the Adversary, and who knew if I would be able to change him back? (Could I really turn human beings into other animals, or was that Karl's idea of a joke? It was hard to tell with him. Either way, I wasn't going to risk it.)

So instead I closed my eyes, reached for my Shaping ability—which was getting easier every time—and tried to do something very simple: give him a haircut. I've always hated graying ponytails on men: a little too Baby-Boomer-who-refused-to-grow-up for my taste (and trust me, around Montana, I'd seen my share of them). I imagined Karl with a trim business cut, and no mustache while I was at it.

I let my Shaping power flow toward him. Once again, I felt a sudden weakness, but only for an instant. Then my eyes snapped open as Karl did the last thing I expected: he screamed.

It wasn't a shout, or a yell. It was a scream, the kind of scream an animal makes when it is injured. I stared at him as he lurched away from me, still screaming, and slammed the palms of his hands against the old door. This time that strange, eye-searing-yet-not-quite-real blue illumination crawled over him, flickering and flashing as though he were being electrocuted—and from the agony he clearly felt, perhaps he was, in some fashion. Then it steadied. For a moment he glowed, as though he were an angel come to Earth, the contours of his body so light-filled I could see it through his clothes, so that it seemed he stood naked before me: and then all that light, all at once, slammed into the Portal, vanishing into it as though being sucked away into a black hole.

Karl was suddenly flung away from the door as though by an explosion, though I heard nothing. He landed on his rear end and skidded several feet across the smooth surface of the marble flooring of the tunnel I had Shaped. The red door swung open, and I tensed . . . but beyond it waited no guards, or new world. Instead, I saw only darkness, the torches of the marble tunnel picking up glints of damp rough stone and a rotted-looking wooden support beam.

I ran back to Karl, and knelt beside him as he struggled to a sitting position. His nose was bleeding again, scarlet dripping over his still-extant mustache. His ponytail likewise remained un-Shaped. He raised a shaking hand to pinch his nostrils, and said in a voice that, as a result, was a dead-ringer for Donald Duck's, "And that is that."

"I thought I'd killed you," I said.

"The . . . tool . . . within my body can use a Shaper's power," he said, still in that cartoon-duck voice, "but the power is . . . somewhat incompatible with my body itself." He waited a few more seconds, then cautiously removed his fingers from the bridge of his nose. The bleeding seemed to have stopped. He ran his hand across the lower part of his face, which just smeared the blood, giving him the alarming appearance of a vampire who had recently fed. "The Adversary will have felt that, for certain. He knows exactly where we are now. We must move fast."

"Suits me," I said. I helped him up, and together we limped back down the marble tunnel and out into the darkness of the main compound. "So the next step is to get to where you can create another Portal?"

He nodded.

"And where is that?"

He sighed. "The technology implanted in me only gives me a general sense of the direction in which it lies, at the moment," he said. "I will be able to locate it more precisely as we get nearer to it. I do not know exactly how far away it is, yet, but I can tell one thing . . . it is not close."

"How not close?" I asked.

"I do not know," Karl said. "It could literally be the other side of the world."

# TWELVE

**I TURNED MY** head to stare at him: since he still had his arm around my shoulders for support, his blood-smeared face was disconcertingly close. "The SUV," I pointed out, "is not going to get us to the other side of the world." I nodded in its direction. One headlight was smashed from its encounter with the fence, and its hood was slightly crumpled up, giving it a dishevelled air. Never mind the splatter of blood and brains on the driver's door, which would also seem likely to attract notice. "If it even runs."

"It will run if you believe it will run," Karl said.

I grimaced.

"But we cannot keep it long in any event," he continued. "An official law enforcement vehicle is not exactly inconspicuous even when it isn't damaged and blood-splattered. We must dispose of it, find different transportation, and try to escape further detection."

"Oh, is that all?"

Karl stopped then, and pulled his arm away. "Wait a moment," he said, and limped ahead of me to the SUV.

"Why . . . oh." I stayed where I was, wanting to look away but finding myself unable to, as he pulled the corpse of the man he had shot away from the SUV's splattered side. The blood on the white door and pooled on the ground looked inky black in the yard light's illumination. I swallowed, and only moved forward, gingerly, after Karl came around the front of the SUV and climbed into the passenger seat. I tried not to step in the blood and tried even harder not to touch the gore drying on the vehicle's side, and as a result got into the driver's seat very awkwardly. But at last I was in, though even there I had to view the world through red spatters on the driver's-side window. "You're right," I said, as I pressed the Start button. The engine roared to life at once; nothing mechanical had been mangled, at least. "We have to get rid of this thing."

Karl only nodded. He was digging in the glove compartment, and a moment later pulled out a plastic package of tissues and began using them to clean the blood from his face at last.

I backed up, turned the wheel to reorient us, and drove out through the shattered gate. At the intersection with the main road I turned left, certain without asking that deeper into the mountains, not down the valley toward the foothills and the city, was the only course open to us. "What will the Adversary do next?"

"I have no way of knowing." Karl wadded up the bloody tissues and stuffed them into a pocket in the door. "Except the broad strokes, which I saw in his own world and the last. He has already begun Shaping your world into a totalitarian one."

"With himself as the ruler?"

"With himself as God," Karl said. "He demands the Shaped beings of his world owe him absolute, unquestioning obedience."

The road was beginning to wind as it climbed up the head of the valley, but I shot him a quick glance. "God? Really?"

"Effectively," Karl said. "Humans seem to have an innate need for religious belief. Those who reject religion *per se* usually find something else in which to believe just as fervently, such as a political party, and often with as little—or far less—empirical evidence. The Adversary takes advantage of both those impulses. He Shapes humans' innate religious belief into a belief in him as a distant, unapproachable, but perfect Deity, and also Shapes that built-in human quality into a fervent belief in the absolute rightness of the system of laws he has imposed. The world then runs itself as he wishes it to, without him having to take a particularly active role. The Deists of the First World used to speak of God as a kind of master watchmaker, who set the universe in motion, then just let it run. The Adversary makes that view of God a reality.

"He is not human himself, remember, and he comes, in the First World, from an alien world which believes it is a utopia—but which in fact is a stagnant, totalitarian hellhole. His goal, so far as I can tell, is to impose versions of that alien 'utopia' on all the worlds of the Labyrinth. He objects to free will. He objects to individuality. He objects to anyone thinking things he does not want thought. He objects to anyone living in ways of which he does not approve. He objects to people saying things he does not want said. He objects to what he calls disorder. He objects to what he calls untidiness. He objects, in short, to human liberty."

I took a moment to digest what was, after all, one of the longest speeches Karl had ever given. "How do you know all that? You only met him two worlds ago." Which was one of the stranger sentences I'd ever spoken out loud, but I was becoming inured to such out-landishness.

"I know he comes, originally, from the world that Ygrair fled, and she told me what kind of world that was," Karl said. "I saw his ultimate vision of the perfect world when I stumbled upon his own. And I saw how he goes about altering another Shaper's world in the Shakespearean one I came to yours from. I have seen enough."

"All right," I said. "You also said he's out to get Ygrair. But they're both aliens from the same world. If Ygrair is also an alien . . . how do you know you can trust her?"

Karl said nothing for a long moment. We had reached the top of the hill we'd been climbing. The trees had closed around us again, pressing close like the bars of a wooden prison, and the road was now just a rutted track, so narrow that if we met anyone we'd have to drive half off of it to allow room for both vehicles to pass.

"Because," Karl said, as I slowed, "all those things he hates are the things that Ygrair holds dear. Her love for liberty is why she fled her own world, and she realized, when she discovered the Labyrinth, that the freedoms her world despises are the very freedoms the Labyrinth enables to thrive. Absolute freedom is what she offered the Shapers—like you—that she trained in the First World . . . like you. As you would know if not for your infuriating loss of memory." He sighed. "While I am sure you find all this fascinating . . . as you no doubt did the *first* time you were told, during the training you have forgotten . . . what matters in the here and now is that the Adversary is the Adversary, Ygrair is the one who gave you this world to Shape, the Adversary has stolen it from you, and now Ygrair needs you to save the worlds of other Shapers—and the Labyrinth itself—from falling under his sway."

After that, Karl was done talking, closing his eyes and reclining his seat. I wished I had the memories he had been so horrified to discover I did not. I might not have felt quite as much as though I were surfing a tsunami if I had my own experiences with the mysterious Ygrair to draw on. I wondered if I'd met Karl before, too. He hadn't said anything to indicate I had . . . so where had he been, while I was supposedly being trained by Ygrair in the First World?

Somewhere without *The Lord of the Rings*, *The Wizard of Oz*, or anything else that happened in the twentieth century, as far as I could tell. Which didn't sound like my idea of a wonderful world, but to each his or her own, I guess.

The road continued to narrow, to the point I began to worry it would simply peter out and we'd have to back out of what had become a trap . . . possibly right into the arms of whatever forces the Adversary might be rushing to his suddenly sealed Portal. I stopped. "Let's see that map."

"Hm?" Karl blinked and straightened. "What?"

"Map," I said. "Have a nice snooze?"

"I was not asleep," he said, "only thinking," which I didn't believe for a second. He reached into the back seat for his pack and dug the map out of it. I studied it by the glow of, appropriately enough, the map light. (Since I always used the map app on my phone for navigation, I'd never actually used a map light to read a map before. On the scale of the new experiences I'd had in the past couple of days, it ranked pretty low, but still.)

As I'd feared, the road wasn't *on* the map. As far as it was concerned, the road only went one way from the mine site, the other way, which we hadn't taken. That part of the road crossed over into the next valley, a much broader one, and there connected to a proper highway along which small towns were strung like beads a few miles apart.

I pointed this out to Karl. "Our best hope of finding new transportation might be one of those towns," I said. "If turn around . . ." I glanced at the dashboard clock: just after 1 a.m. "We could be in one of them before dawn."

"But we may run into pursuers," Karl said. "And even if we do not, if we abandon this vehicle in a town, it will be found sooner rather than later, which will help the Adversary track us. Better we take the road before us, and find a place to lose the SUV along the way."

"We'll take the road less traveled by, and that will make all the difference?"

Karl gave me a puzzled look. "What?"

I sighed. "Frost."

He frowned, leaning forward to look at the windshield. "I don't see any. Surely it is not that cold."

*Oh, right,* I thought. *Robert Frost wrote in the 1920s. Much too hip and up-to-date for Karl Yatsar.* "Never mind."

Karl leaned back. "So. We have a plan."

I folded up the map. "Your definition of plan, as noted before, is very different from mine."

"In what way?"

I shoved the map at him. "Plans involve careful . . ." I hesitated, but couldn't think of a different word . . . "planning," I finished lamely. "Not just, 'Oh, look, maybe that'll work, let's try that, and then we'll wing it from there.' That's not a plan. Also, I thought you didn't believe in plans."

"I did not say that. I said they do not survive contact with the enemy. Nor will this one, should our enemy find us. But as a plan for what to do next, it is acceptable." He shrugged. "Everything is in flux. And remember, 'The best laid schemes o' mice an' men gang aft agley.'" He glanced at me. "Robert Burns."

"I know," I said. *And so do you, which is interesting.* I tried to remember when Burns had lived. Early nineteenth century? No—earlier, late eighteenth.

"I am glad to hear it." He looked pointedly at the steering wheel. "Shouldn't we be moving?" He raised the back of his seat to emphasize the point.

I sighed, and put the vehicle into gear.

As I drove, I thought about the man and woman Karl had shot. (Since there was still blood on my window, I didn't have much choice.) I'd discovered something, watching the two members of the Adversary's cadre die, followed by the horrible death of the caretaker: I wasn't nearly as bloodthirsty as I'd thought I was. I'd actually *told* Karl to shoot the guards. I'd thought I wanted revenge for the attack on the Human Bean. I'd thought that desire for revenge had burned away any qualms I had about killing. I'd thought I wouldn't feel anything for those two black-clad guards, because they weren't even from my world, because they'd been brought into my world by the Adversary to help him seize control.

I'd thought all those things, and I had been wrong. Karl had told me that they were once just ordinary people. They hadn't *chosen* to serve the Adversary, they'd been *Shaped* to serve him—to practically *worship* him, if Karl told the truth. They were as much victims of his Shaping as the copilot of the helicopter had been of my own.

And this Ygrair, who supposedly valued human liberty, had put Shapers like me and him into the Labyrinth, where we had the power to bring into existence worlds filled with human beings—and then wipe away their free will. Freedom? For the Shapers, certainly. For those whom they Shaped . . . not so much.

Karl Yatsar wanted me to think Ygrair was the good gal in all this, valiantly striving to protect the Shaped Worlds from the depredations of the Adversary and the rest of her alien race. And maybe, relative to the Adversary, she *was* a little closer to the side of the angels. But she definitely wasn't one of them.

Whatever the dead man and woman had become, they were human beings. They had, somewhere, families, loved ones. They'd grown up . . . or at least had memories of growing up . . . and had had friends, and made mistakes, and done good things and bad things, made good choices and bad ones, laughed, and cried, and made love . . . had done all the things that every human being did.

And now they were dead.

Karl had killed them, not me, but I still blamed myself for their deaths. Which was stupid: the only way they might not have died would have been if *I* were already dead, because then Karl wouldn't have come to the mine to close the Portal.

*Or they might still be alive if I weren't a Shaper,* I thought, but if I weren't a Shaper, someone else would be sitting here now trying to escape . . . or else the Adversary would have already taken over, and I might already have been Shaped along with everyone else in this world. Like them, I would have been a helpless victim of powers not only beyond my control, but beyond my ken.

That, I decided, would have been far worse. I stiffened my spine, both figuratively and (because I was slouching and my back was getting sore) literally. I *was* a Shaper. I had power. And it was *way* better that I still be alive and those poor Shaped saps from the Adversary's original world be dead than the other way around. Selfish of me, perhaps, but there it was. And if someone else had to die . . .

*Maybe it won't come to that. Maybe we'll find this second Portal and escape this world, and I'll never have to worry about killing someone, or someone being killed on my behalf, ever again.*

It was a nice thought. But so was the thought that the next world might be a world of unicorns and rainbows. I didn't believe for a minute that it would be (although I supposed it wasn't *impossible* a particularly sappy Shaper had chosen to make it one), and I didn't believe for a minute that the violence that now seemed to follow me like a lost puppy had ended.

The moon-cast shadows of the trees were black as carbon. The road ahead, at the limits of the headlights, led only into darkness.

# THIRTEEN

**"THE ROAD AHEAD** led only into darkness" was such a nice metaphor for my state of mind that I was almost disappointed when a sign appeared a few minutes later, glowing bright green in our headlights. I slowed, and stopped a few yards short of it. There were two names and distances on it: MOOREVILLE 20, with an arrow pointing left, and BOW AND ARROW RANCH 32, with an arrow pointing straight up. "Mooreville is one of the towns on the map," I said. "Turn left?"

"What is Bow and Arrow Ranch?" he asked. "Have you heard of it?"

Oddly enough, I had: a friend of Brent's had spent a couple of weeks there during the summer, and had told us about his outdoor adventures in excruciating detail one night at the Human Bean, made bearable only by the beer and the fact that that night's otherwise execrable band (The Tosspot Turkeys) had been so loud I'd only heard one word in three. "It's a dude ranch."

He glanced at me, eyes glinting green in the spill of light reflecting from the sign. "A what?"

"You've never heard of a dude ranch? *Dude*, you showed up on my doorstep in a duster and cowboy hat!"

"They were not mine. Enlighten me."

"It's a ranch where dudes—city people—pretend to be cowboys," I said. "They ride horses and go camping and sleep on air mattresses in fancy tents and eat gourmet food prepared by a private chef—you know, just like cowboys do."

"Horses," he said. "Would there be horses there now?"

"Where else would they . . ." I realized what he was thinking. "Oh. I get it. We need to do something unexpected. Our pursuers will expect us to head to the towns. They won't expect us to head deeper into the mountains on horseback."

"Would you?" Karl said.

"Not if I knew one of the two people I was chasing was allergic to horses."

He frowned. "You are allergic to horses?"

"Yes."

"So much so you cannot ride them?"

I sighed. I was afraid he'd ask that. "No," I had to admit. "Just enough I'll be sniffling and sneezing and wiping my eyes the whole time."

I reached for the map. The road we had followed to this point might not be on it, but the road we had just intersected *was*. It showed that the road to Bow and Arrow Ranch wound through a series of canyons. Just like the road we'd taken into Candle Lake Resort, this was clearly a back road: the main access marked on the map was from the Interstate we were trying so studiously to avoid.

I took a closer look at the terrain. We still needed to lose the SUV. If the road through the canyons ran close to a big enough body of water . . . nothing showed on the map, but maybe, I thought, that doesn't matter. I closed my eyes. I pictured a deep lake . . . no, an old quarry. Steep sides, full of water. Drop the SUV in there and it might never be found . . . I reached for my Shaping ability.

I Shaped.

Pain exploded behind my eyes and I jerked back, gasping, my head slamming hard against the headrest. "Ungh," I said. Then, for good measure, "Ohhhh . . ."

"What did you just do?" Karl said sharply.

I licked my lips, unable to speak for a moment. Then I took a deep breath, the ache in my head subsiding, and brought my head forward to look at the map again. "There," I said, pointing a shaking finger at a small blue rectangle. "That's an old quarry, full of water now. The road runs right by the other end. We can dump the SUV there."

"That was foolish," Karl snapped.

"Why?" I asked, and winced. My own voice seemed to be hurting my head for the moment.

"It was another major Shaping. Though it did not involve the Portal, it may have been sensed by the Adversary."

"Can he pinpoint it?" I said.

"Probably not. But—"

"He already knows we're in this area. Losing the SUV should be worth the risk."

"Even if that is true," Karl said, "such a major Shaping after the power expended back at the mine . . . it hurt you, did it not? And fatigued you?"

I couldn't deny that: he'd seen how I reacted. "Yes," I said reluctantly.

"You have enormous power. As I have told you many times. But you have also used it—a lot of it—over the past few days. It is not unlimited. It will regenerate, with time, but we do not know how often we will absolutely need it, or for how long, before we can open a new Portal and escape. The pain and fatigue are warnings. Do not Shape on a whim."

"It wasn't a whim," I said stubbornly. "We need to lose the SUV."

"But there might well be a natural place where we could hide the SUV, without you having to Shape anything," Karl said. "Or a less major Shaping might have done the trick. Creating an entire quarry . . ." He shook his head. "Impressive. But a terrible waste of energy."

"Impressive. Powerful." Anger swelled in me. "You're right. I'm damned impressive, and damned powerful. I made time jump back three hours, made it snow, made that tunnel, gave you power to seal the Portal, conjured a quarry. So why am I running? Why am I only trying to hide from the Adversary and not trying to attack him directly? We sealed the Portal to weaken him. Shouldn't I take advantage of that? If I defeated him . . . *killed* him . . . I'd have the *hokhmah* of my world all to myself again. I could undo everything he's done." I glared at Karl. "If you think I'm strong enough to save the Labyrinth, why do you think I'm too weak to save my own world? Let me go after him. If I can kill him, we could stay here while you teach me whatever it is I've apparently forgotten, train me. When I'm ready, *then* we could enter the next world, and . . ."

But Karl was already shaking his head. "No, Shawna," he said, the sorrow in his voice genuine and unmistakable. "It's too late. Though you are indeed strong, so is the Adversary: strong enough that when I entered his world, I hoped *he* might be the one to do what Ygrair needs done, before I realized the magnitude of my mistake. And in addition to strength, he *also* has immense experience and knowledge. He remembers *his* training. He has already Shaped two worlds to his will, and even with his currently limited ability, has begun the process of Shaping this one—and the more he Shapes it, the stronger his ability to do so will grow. You would be killed, by police, or military, or some random stranger, before you could get anywhere close to the Adversary in this world. And even if you faced him—then what? You cannot Shape him, or his cadre. It is impossible."

"Forever? My power and knowledge will grow—"

"*If* you and I escape this world, *if* we can stay ahead of the

Adversary long enough, *if* you can save enough worlds, *if* you deliver the *hokhmah* of as many worlds as possible to Ygrair . . . then *she* will deal with the Adversary."

"Fine," I said angrily. "And once she's done that—will I be able to rescue *my* world? Return it to the way it was?"

Karl didn't answer for a long moment. "Maybe," he said.

*"Maybe?"*

Karl sighed. "In truth, I do not know."

I tamped down the rage that flooded into me then, or tried to. After all, I'd just conjured a giant hole in solid rock and filled it with water. Who knew what damage I might do if I lost my temper? *Don't make me angry. You won't like me when I'm angry.*

And then I thought, *And before you get too full of yourself, maybe you'd better be sure you actually* did *just conjure a quarry out of thin air. Because objectively, all you've really conjured is a small square of blue ink on a map.* That thought made me smile, and my anger ebbed. I reached for the gearshift. "Bow and Arrow Ranch it is," I said, and we rolled down a slight incline onto the new road, just enough wider and less-rutted than the one we'd left, apparently, to rate it representation on the map.

Unless . . . unless that road *should* be on the map, *had* been on the map, but I had needed it to *not* be on the map to help hide our trails, and so it had vanished from, not only our map, but *all* maps . . .

*How do true gods keep it all straight?* I wondered.

Then I snorted. *They have staff. I wonder where I could hire a few angels, cheap?*

A few minutes later we crested another hill, and there it was: a huge, water-filled, abandoned quarry, exactly as I had pictured it my head. Its appearance awed me all over again. I'd done *that*?

Its appearance also meant it was time to say good-bye to our purloined, smashed-up, bloodstained ride. Since the road, as I'd specified, made a sharp left-hand curve at the bottom of the hill, to run alongside the quarry, and (as I'd also specified) there was no guard rail at the bottom of the hill, we simply parked uphill from the quarry and reenacted our attack on the mine gate, after removing our backpacks, the extra gun belt, and the pistol from the helicopter from the back seat. I put on the parking brake and shifted the transmission into neutral, rolled down all the windows, and then got out into the chill night air. The moon beamed down at us from above, and its perfect reflection in the mirror-still water of the quarry beamed up at us from below. The sky blazed with stars: I'd forgotten how many more stars you could see when you weren't in the city. A satellite sparkled, arrowing across the sky—one of the big space hotels, probably. I'd always wanted to go to one. I'd planned to reward myself with a space trip once the shop was established and successful.

Now I never would.

I reached in through the driver's-side window and disengaged the parking break. I withdrew my arm as the SUV started to roll.

It didn't pick up a lot of speed before it reached the end of the road, but it didn't need a lot. It rolled off the edge, slid into the water, and vanished with very little fuss at all, although a few bubbles surfaced and big, slow ripples rolled out across the still water, disrupting the moon's reflection.

I shouldered my pack, which I'd set on the ground; Karl already wore his. He'd tucked the spare pistol into his pack. For the first time, I buckled on the gun belt that had come with my sheriff's deputy uniform. Then I looked ahead to where the road, after running alongside the quarry, turned and climbed the hill beyond. It looked like a very big hill, on foot, and there were still a couple of miles to go beyond it before we reached the dude ranch and the sneeze-inducing means of transportation we hoped to find there.

Karl set off without a word. As I followed him, a thought percolated up. "If I can Shape people," I said to the back of his head, "why can't I Shape myself, make it so I'm not allergic to these horses we hope to find?"

"Because you can only Shape things that are part of this world," Karl said, without looking around.

"But surely I'm part of this world."

"No, you are not. You are from the First World. You cannot Shape the Adversary's minions either, remember. Or the Adversary. Nor could you Shape me, which is why I was able to funnel your power rather than turning into a frog, or whatever else you had planned."

"Doesn't seem fair," I muttered.

"Fairness has nothing to do with it. If you drop something heavy on your foot and break a toe, that is neither fair nor unfair. Gravity just *is*. Shaped by God, if you believe in God. The laws of the Labyrinth are just as immutable."

"Also Shaped by God?"

"A question for theologians," Karl said, "should one of them ever find out the Labyrinth exists."

I quit talking after that, as the slope steepened and I discovered I needed all my breath, and it had just been established I couldn't Shape myself into a much fitter person. But I still had enough oxygen to think—barely—and once we were heading downhill into the next, shallower, valley, I said, "But from what you've said, there are worlds where natural laws are very different. Like, when I was handed this world," *man, these conversations are getting weird*, "I *could* have Shaped it so that, say, superheroes exist . . . couldn't I?"

"I am not certain what you mean by 'superheroes,'" Karl said.

"People with extraordinary powers. People who can fly, or bend steel bars, or lift giant boulders."

"Like Hercules."

"More or less, but without the demigod backstory."

"Yes," Karl said. "You could."

"So, in a world like *that*, could I have made *myself* a superhero?"

Karl sighed. "No. Again, because you cannot Shape yourself. These 'superheroes' you speak of aren't possible in the First World. Things from the First World, such as yourself, are *real*, in a way the things in the Labyrinth are not. You have no control over anything from the First World, including yourself."

"So if we do finally get into another world," I said, "even if it's a world with dragons and unicorns and wizards, where magic is real, the Shaper will be as ordinary as I am?"

"You just made a quarry appear out of nowhere," Karl said. "That is hardly ordinary."

"You know what I mean. Even if a Shaper Shaped a world where sorcery is real, she wouldn't be a sorceress herself."

"That is correct."

"And a lot of Shapers have very little power left after they've Shaped their worlds."

"Also correct."

"I see." I fell silent, thinking about how vulnerable those Shapers would be to the Adversary: they might have crafted the world in which they lived, but if they'd used up all their power, they could be as easily slain as the most ordinary of their world's denizens. As I would have been if I had not managed to make time skip a beat during the attack on the Human Bean, despite knowing nothing of what I truly was.

We were climbing again, so I focused on heavy breathing for the next few minutes. Once the slope eased, as we neared its crest, I panted, "How many?"

"What?" Karl said.

"How many worlds have you already passed through? You wouldn't answer me the last time I asked."

Karl stopped and turned to look at me, his face pale in the moonlight, his eyes shadowed by his brows. "I have passed through twenty-nine worlds, counting this one. In none of them did I find anyone with the power you displayed in the Human Bean. I closed the Portals behind me, but I could not seal them. I am in many ways relieved the Adversary chose to pursue me instead of simply going back through all those worlds and claiming them as his own. One reason I wanted so badly to destroy the Portal at the mine was to protect those worlds from him."

"Twenty-nine?" I stared at him. "But how many are there?"

"According to Ygrair, eight hundred and twenty-four Shapers have entered the Labyrinth since we . . . since *she* opened it to the First World. Some of those Shapers may have died, of course."

"Does that destroy their worlds?"

"Ygrair is uncertain," Karl said, "and therefore so am I. What is certain is that, if a Shaper dies, his or her world can no longer be entered. It is possible the world continues, but is rendered inaccessible. Since it is inaccessible, there is no way for us to know."

"And you intend to take me to *all* the worlds that are still accessible?"

"I intend to take you to as many as is necessary for you to do what Ygrair needs done," Karl said.

"And how will you know when that is?" I pressed.

"I will know." He turned away. "Now save your breath. I believe we will find this 'dude' ranch on the other side of this ridge."

I shut up, but I wasn't through with questions. Not by a long shot.

A new valley opened up below us as we topped the ridge. A river wound through it, glinting here and there in the moonlight, clearly visible because, although more dark woods rose on the far side, on this side of the stream a large swathe of land had been cleared, the resulting fields enclosed by split rail fences. At the south end of the cleared land clustered several buildings: a three-story log house, four long, low log structures that had the look of sleeping quarters, about a dozen individual cabins, three small sheds, and a giant red-and-white barn. Yard lights burned throughout the compound, but no light showed in the big house or any of the other buildings, which wasn't too surprising at . . . I checked my watch . . . three-thirty in the morning. When I saw the time, my lurking fatigue hit me over the head like a rubber mallet. I yawned hugely, but there was no prospect of sleep anytime soon.

There had to be people down there to maintain the buildings and look after the horses, but if we were lucky, Bow and Arrow Ranch, like Candle Lake Resort, was closed for the season, and there would be no tourists in those cabins. The single car in sight, parked up against the house, made that seem likely.

"It may look like we're in the middle of nowhere, but horses are valuable," I pointed out to Karl. "There's going to be security of some kind. Motion sensors. Lights. Alarms."

Karl raised a Spockian eyebrow at me.

I groaned. "But I don't know what I'm doing! When I hid our tracks, it caused a snowstorm and an avalanche. If I try to cut the power I'm likely to start a fire or something."

"You do not need to cut the power," Karl said. "You're right, tampering with things like that is fraught with potential dangers. That is because it is not so much that you Shape the world to your desires, as that the world Shapes itself to meet your desires."

"Very nice," I said. "I think I read that on a motivational poster once."

Karl ignored that: no doubt it had gone over his head. "The world changes itself according to the rules that govern it, to achieve the end you as its Shaper desire. I did not see what happened when you made that quarry, but I would guess that some deep subterranean cavern is no longer there, that the rock that vanished from the quarry filled it. A lake nearby is probably much diminished, to provide the water. And so on."

"And all this helps me deactivate whatever security is in place down at Bow and Arrow Ranch . . . how?"

"It doesn't. I'm telling you why you should *not* deactivate the security. There are too many variables, and it will waste more of your great, but not unlimited, power. Stick to what you know, what you have already proved will work. Rather than deactivate the security, deactivate the security guard, or guards. Shape him, or them, so they assume any alarms we trigger are nothing, in fact, to be alarmed about."

"But I have to see them to do that," I said.

"Don't you think triggering an alarm will make them appear?"

I sighed. "So, in order to get by the security system, we first have to *trigger* the security system?"

He nodded.

"What if I fail?"

"I still have a weapon."

I stiffened. "No! No killing. These are people of my world. I'm responsible for them. I've already gotten two killed. I won't have any others killed."

"Then Shape carefully," Karl said.

"'Shape carefully,' he says," I muttered to myself a few minutes later, as I crouched in the bushes just outside the split rail fence nearest the house. "Like I'm an expert now." I turned my head toward the barn. Karl must be about to make his move. He intended to break into the barn, snapping off the padlock on the barn door using a shovel we'd found leaning up against an outbuilding.

*Maybe we're wrong*, I thought as I waited for something to happen. *Maybe there isn't any security after—*

Lights flashed on all over the ranch, and a raucous jangling sounded inside the house. In the sudden flood of illumination, I saw Karl, still ten feet from the barn, shovel in hand: there were motion sensors on the outside of the buildings as well as on the inside, apparently.

More lights snapped on inside the house. I saw a silhouette against a venetian blind, moving toward the front door. It swung open, and a burly, bearded man in dark-blue pajamas stepped out onto the porch, a shotgun clenched in his hands. He turned toward the barn and saw Karl, and the shotgun snapped up. "Hold it right there!" he bellowed. "Move a muscle and you'll be picking buckshot out of your ass for a year." He took the steps down from the porch two at a time, landing on the grass in his bare feet . . .

I reached out with my Shaping ability, trying to tell him Karl was a friend, this was all just a misunderstanding, there was no need to be upset, he'd known Karl was coming, he'd just forgotten, he'd promised Karl two horses . . .

The man blinked and lowered the shotgun. "Wait a minute . . . Karl, you old sidewinder, is that you?"

I relaxed. Best of all, I'd felt only a twinge of a headache.

And then the second man came out, younger, wearing only boxers, a rifle in his hands. He caught me by surprise. Before I could gather my wits, he shouted, "Fucking horse thief!" at Karl, and raised his rifle . . .

. . . and the first man, roaring, spun and fired his shotgun into the younger man's face. His head exploded in a spray of brains and bone, and his body fell limply backward, thudded against the wall, and slid lifeless to the porch beneath the Rorschach splatter of his own blood on the front door.

I heard screaming, then realized it was my own. The shotgun swung toward me, and I suddenly remembered I had done nothing about Shaping the bearded man to not see *me* as a threat. "Bitch!" he bellowed at me. "You killed Johnny!" The shotgun came up—

—and another gun fired from my right.

The bearded man twisted his head to look down at the hole in his left side. Then, as blood started to pour from it, he dropped the shotgun. He fell to his knees, one hand going to the wound, and then toppled facedown and motionless into the grass.

I had almost nothing in my stomach. I dropped onto my hands and knees and retched anyway, bringing up mucus and bitter bile. *Not again!* The thought ran over and over in my head. *Not again!*

Karl came over to me. He waited until I was done gagging, then held out his hand to help me to my feet. "I did it again," I said as he pulled me upright. My heart pounded and the taste in my mouth was as foul as my humor. "Two men dead, because I tried to Shape them . . ." I suddenly turned and shoved him away from me so hard he staggered back and almost fell. "You knew that would happen!"

Karl straightened, wincing. "I did not. The first Shaping went well. He would have simply given us the horses. It was the unexpected appearance of the second man that brought about catastrophe."

"No," I said. "*I* brought about catastrophe. This fucking ability you value so much . . . it's not a gift, it's a curse. It destroys people."

"Your clumsiness destroys people." Karl's voice, cold and remorseless, felt like a slap across my face. "The fact you have forgotten everything Ygrair taught you destroys people. You must learn—relearn, since you once had it—better control. You must think through *all* possibilities before you Shape. You should have been prepared for the possibility of more than one man in the house. You should have been prepared to Shape any other man who appeared as you did the first. Because you failed to think ahead, your Shaping of the first man caused him to see his friend as an enemy, someone who was going to harm me, who you had so successfully convinced him was someone he had to help at all costs. When you suddenly drew attention to yourself by screaming, the cognitive dissonance you had set up in his brain twisted his perception. Unable to accept that he had just killed his friend, he transferred that guilt to you. In that instant, he believed he had just witnessed *you* killing Johnny. He would have killed you next if I had not taken action."

I clenched my shaking hands into fists and took deep breaths, trying to regain some semblance of calm. "You could have warned me. You could have helped me figure out what to do, how to plan for contingencies."

"You are the Shaper, not I," Karl said. "The quickest way for you to learn is by mistakes such as these. You will not make the same mistake again."

"No," I said. "I'll make a new one. And maybe more people will die. Maybe me." I glared at him, and spat the next words. "Maybe *you*."

"If it is me," Karl said, "it will be you, as well, because without me you cannot leave this world, and the Adversary will kill you soon enough. And if it is you and *not* me, I will grieve, but then I will simply renew my search. Somewhere, in some other world, there may yet be another Shaper with your power, someone else who can fulfill Ygrair's task."

Well, that was even more chilling than the combination of freezing mountain air and the shock of two violent deaths. *I'm expendable*, I thought, staring at Karl, who looked back steadily, face calm, jaw set, not a hint of doubt in his expression. In a way, I already knew it, from things he'd said earlier, but he had never put it quite so baldly before, so that it felt like a dash of ice water in my face. *Valuable, but not invaluable. If it comes down to letting me die, or him escaping into the next world in the Labyrinth . . . he'll let me die.*

"Let's get those fucking horses," I said, and since Karl didn't react to my use of obscenity any more than he had to my last use of it a minute earlier, he clearly didn't know just how angry and upset I had to be to use it . . . which meant he didn't really know me well at all.

Any more than I, apparently, knew him.

# FOURTEEN

**DESPITE MY DRAMATIC** and profane commitment to the procurement of mounts, the first thing we did wasn't "get those fucking horses" but get some new non cop clothes, although that involved going into the house, which involved going past the horror on the front step. I closed my eyes and held my breath and dashed past while Karl held open the door.

The house was homey in a very masculine sort of way: lots of leather and antlers and dirty dishes. One again, we found clothes that fit us perfectly, I in the room I presumed had belonged to the dead man on the porch, Karl in the room of the man who had shot him. Dressed in jeans, a red flannel shirt, hiking boots, and a warm sheepskin coat, and leaving the gun belt I'd never wanted in the first place on the dead man's bed, I joined Karl outside again, though I left through the back door and not the front. He was dressed almost identically to me, except his coat was black leather, like the duster he'd worn when I first saw him, but shorter and scruffier. He'd discarded his gun belt, too, but he had a pistol in each pocket, the one from the helicopter and the one from the sheriff's deputy. "Not a coincidence the clothes fit so perfectly, is it?" I said rather sourly to him

"No," he said. "A Shaping, though an unconscious one, on your part."

We walked over to where we had left our packs behind a bush, and pulled them on. "Now," Karl said, as he adjusted the straps to

fit better over the leather jacket, "we will 'get those fucking horses.'"
He turned and walked away before I could see if he was smiling
or not.

Could he be *joking*? It *sounded* like a joke . . .

I followed him back toward the barn, still wondering.

The last (and first) horse I had ridden, on an "equestrian adventure" at a dude ranch not unlike this one, had clearly carried one
too many touristy sack-of-potatoes tenderfoot along the same trail
one too many times, because it had spent the entire ninety minutes
trying to scrape me off against every handy fence post and tree
trunk along the well-worn path. Since I had been sneezing and
sniffling and watery-eyed the entire ride (for it was then that I discovered my allergy to all things equine), it had not been a fun time
for either me or, I suspect, the horse, who against all odds had
failed to dislodge me.

I had high hopes the animal Karl led, saddled and bridled, from
the barn (where I dared not venture if I wanted to keep breathing)
would be different, since I could Shape the beast to be docile and
obedient—even if I couldn't Shape it to be non-allergenic.

Or could I? Karl had discouraged it, but maybe . . .

I focused on the horse at Karl's side, reached out, and imagined
*very hard* that this horse would no longer produce the allergens to
which I responded so strongly.

To my horror, the horse stumbled, dropped to its knees, and fell
onto its side, its final breath whooshing out in a long sigh. Karl
jumped back as it collapsed, stared at it, then turned and glared at
me. "What did you do?"

"I thought . . . I know you said I couldn't Shape myself so I'm not
allergic . . . but I thought maybe I could Shape *it* so I wasn't allergic
to it . . ." My head hurt again, but that wasn't why I felt awful. "I
didn't mean to kill it!"

"I never realized how much of a menace an untrained Shaper

could be," Karl muttered. He bent over the horse's corpse and began stripping it of saddle and bridle. "Whatever substance within the horse's body makes you allergic to it was clearly necessary for the horse's continued survival. Your attempt to make the horse into something to which you are not allergic removed that substance, and killed the beast."

"Proteins," I muttered. "Allergens are typically proteins."

"I have heard that word but am unclear as to its meaning," Karl said. He had pulled off the horse's bridle and set it aside. "Help me with this saddle."

I went to him and together we tugged it out from under the animal's dead weight. Morbidly, I noted I wasn't tearing up despite standing right next to a dead horse. *So the Shaping succeeded*, I thought. *Kind of.*

"I'm surprised you know the word 'allergy,'" I said. "You're a lot older than you look, aren't you?"

"Subjectively, I am the age I appear to be," Karl said. "But time has little meaning in the Labyrinth, and does not flow the same from world to world. As to my vocabulary, I have learned many words I did not know when I was younger. Haven't you?" He took another look at the dead horse. "You *must* learn to fully consider the possible consequences of your Shaping," he said. Again. With a sigh, he hefted the saddle and bridle and trudged back toward the barn.

The dead horse, which I had killed with a thought, bore mute witness to the fairness of his reprimand. At least this time my attempt at Shaping had only killed a horse, and not a human being. I felt almost as guilty about it, though. The helicopter copilot would have captured me, the young man from the house might well have shot me or Karl. This horse had done nothing to threaten me. Making me sneeze shouldn't have been a death sentence. *Human beings turn to gods to assuage their guilt and find forgiveness*, I thought. *To whom do gods turn?*

But then, as Karl kept telling me, I wasn't a god, despite the powers I had in this world given me by the mysterious and alien Ygrair. It sounded like she was far closer to a god, or goddess—and she had her Adversary, her Lucifer, trying to overthrow everything she had created . . . although, come to think of it, she had apparently stumbled on the world-making possibilities of the Labyrinth by accident, which raised the uncomfortable notion that she might not have any better idea of what she was doing than I did, and like me, was just making it up as she went along.

*Well,* I thought then, *to be fair, making it up as you go along, trying to do the right thing, and failing as often as not pretty much describes human existence.* That was the path we followed, whether we believed in a god or gods or not, or, apparently, were the next thing to one.

Karl seemed to be taking a long time to bring out another horse. I looked nervously over my shoulder at the trail we had followed into Bow and Arrow ranch, then looked past the house to where a large gate beneath an arching sign marked the main entrance. The well-lit drive to that gate, and what I could see of the road beyond it, was paved. Just past the gate the road crossed the river on a low bridge, streetlights at each end, and then disappeared into the dark forest, presumably on its way to the highway. If the Adversary had figured out where we'd gone, he and his unShapeable minions could show up from either direction at any time.

I listened hard. No helicopters, at least.

Karl finally emerged from the barn leading another horse, a chestnut mare who shied when she saw her dead stablemate. Karl calmed her—apparently, he had a good rapport with horses *without* resorting to Shaping—and led her to me. The mare rolled her eyes at me, clearly distrustful: I reached out (very cautiously this time) to Shape her into being calm and trusting and eager to carry me wherever I wanted to go. After that, she didn't flinch even when

I sneezed three times in quick succession, the nasal explosions not doing my headache any good. I sniffed and wiped my suddenly streaming eyes, while Karl returned to the barn for a mount for himself.

He emerged leading a big black gelding, whose reins he looped around a handy fence post before helping me climb up onto my mare. "I thought you said you had ridden before?" he grumbled as I awkwardly clambered into the saddle, with way too much grabbing of the horn and a considerable amount of unladylike grunting, the weight of the backpack making the whole thing even more difficult than it would have been anyway.

Though the mare was much smaller than his horse, I still found her girth uncomfortably broad. I remembered that feeling from my lone trail ride all those years before. I also remembered how sore my muscles had been . . . and how chafed my inner thighs had been . . . by the time even that short ride was finished. And then, of course, there had been the . . .

"Ah . . . CHOOO!" I wiped my nose, blinked my watering eyes, and stared owlishly down at Karl. "I *have* ridden before," I said haughtily. My voice had that odd trapped-in-a-barrel sound you get when every available empty space in your skull is filled with snot. "But only once." I sneezed again. "For obvious reasons."

"Oh, this should be enjoyable," Karl muttered. He unhitched his gelding, swung into the saddle with practiced ease, then tugged the reins to turn the horse toward the far end of the ranch. "Follow me."

I pulled at my own reins, expecting my mount to fight me like that long-ago jaded trail-ride steed, but my Shaping, for once, seemed to have worked perfectly: the mare turned almost eagerly, and together we rode after Karl toward the pine trees that rose beyond the paddock.

"So . . . where are we going, exactly?" I called to the horse's ass in front of me (and Karl, too).

"The goal remains the same," Karl said over his shoulder. "To keep the Adversary, his cadre, or those of this world who now consciously or unconsciously are carrying out his orders, from capturing us before we can reach the place where I can open the second Portal. Riding on horseback into the wilderness for a time seems like a good way to complicate pursuit . . . although," he added sourly, "leaving behind two dead men and one dead horse rather undercuts my hoped-for element of stealth."

"Then we shouldn't ride very far before we change modes of transportation again," I said, hopefully.

"Agreed," Karl said. "But we will want to give the *impression* we have ridden much farther than we actually have." He patted the breast of the leather jacket, which I guessed meant he'd put the map in an inside pocket. "This hiking trail intersects a paved road a few miles west of here. We will dismount on that road, then you will Shape the horses to continue along the trail, which continues on the far side of the road. Walking on the pavement, we will leave no tracks, while with luck, the horses will lead any pursuers several miles astray. We will hike along the paved road until another means of transportation presents itself."

"What about food? And . . ." A yawn gripped me, followed by another sneeze. I wiped the back of my hand across my nose. "Sleep?"

*You could have gotten food from the house*, my brain pointed out.

*Not after what I saw on the porch*, I snapped back.

"After we have released the horses . . . perhaps," Karl said.

*Perhaps?* I didn't like the sound of that. What with hunger, exhaustion, and that slow-fading headache that took on fresh life every time I Shaped anything, I was getting very, very close to needing a "for sure" when it came to food and sleep. Aspirin wouldn't hurt, either. (It would be counterproductive if it did.) What time was it, anyway?

I glanced at my watch. 3:47 a.m. Splendid. What better time for a nice horseback . . .

"Ah-CHOOO!"

I wiped my nose again, massaged my temples with my left hand, sighed, and let my horse follow Karl's horse without any more talking, unless sneezes, coughs, wheezes, and sniffs counted as communication.

A short distance past the fence we clattered across the river on a wooden bridge, then plunged into the forest. I might have fallen asleep as we plodded through the dark woods, if not for the aforementioned sneezing, coughing, wheezing, and sniffing. Plus that damnable headache. Instead I simply hung on, sunk in misery.

We finally reached the promised road at . . . I checked my watch through bleary eyes . . . 4:38 a.m. This late in the year, sunrise wouldn't be for almost three hours: we still had lots of darkness.

The road was paved, all right, but barely: its asphalt, cracked and potholed, clearly hadn't been properly maintained for years. Still, it wouldn't show our footprints, and that was the main thing. Karl jumped lightly down from his towering gelding, then helped me get down from my much shorter mare, not-so-lightly and with a lot more groaning (and, of course, another sneeze).

"Now," Karl said. "Carefully—*carefully!*—Shape the horses so they continue to follow the trail. According to the map, it ends at a campground, where they will surely be found and cared for, so you needn't worry about their welfare."

"As long as I don't screw something up and kill them both on the spot," I muttered, but the instructions seemed simple enough. I was almost too tired to think straight, but I concentrated, and after a moment both horses neighed and trotted across the road and into the woods on the other side.

After that Shaping, of course, I was even more exhausted, and my headache had gotten worse again. At least I still had a little water and a bit of (gag) trail mix in my backpack; I finished off both. Karl also ate and drank. My nose cleared rapidly with the horses gone, although one more sneeze shook me as I shoved the canteen and trail-mix package, both now empty, back into my pack. I sighed, wiped my nose and eyes with my sleeve, and then said, wearily, "Which way?"

"Right," Karl said. "Left would lead us to the main road we went to the ranch to avoid."

"And right takes us . . . ?"

"According to the map, in about seven miles it leads to the small community of Elkjaw."

"Seven miles." I shook my head. "I won't make seven miles."

"We will camp as soon as we are far enough from here to make it unlikely anyone following the horses will find us. Perhaps a mile or two."

"A mile or two." I took a deep breath, and exhaled it in something that wasn't quite a groan, but only thanks to extraordinary self-control on my part. "Wonderful."

A mile isn't really that far to walk. Or even two. But my butt hurt, my head throbbed, my legs ached, my thighs stung, and I'd been sneezing for two hours, all thanks to the horse; I had assorted aches and pains from a long day of hiking, followed by a short bout of being almost blown up; I was cold; our last camp, the one where the bear found us, had been a *very* long time ago, and . . .

Well, that night, a mile was a very, very long way to walk.

So, of course, we went two.

It was after five-thirty when Karl finally led the way off the road along a streambed, a trickle of water running musically through ranks of rounded rocks. Even if someone followed the road, searching for signs of our leaving it, the streambed would defeat them. I applauded Karl's foresight. I applauded even more the fact that at last we were going to *stop*.

We didn't bother setting up a tent. The night was clear, not to mention almost over, and the sleeping bags warm. We spread them out on a grassy patch next to the streambed, I crawled into mine, and within seconds I was dead to the world.

I woke to bright light, blue sky, and nose-nipping cold. In my sleep, I had pulled most of my head into the bag, but I blinked over the edge of its mouth, then hauled my arm out and looked at my watch: 9:26, which meant I'd slept less than four hours. Not enough—not *nearly* enough—but better than no sleep at all. Barely.

Now if only we could do something about food . . .

I sat up. In the shade, frost glistened on the grass and weeds of our clearing. Karl wasn't in his sleeping bag, which wasn't too surprising, since it was rolled up tight. I took advantage of his presumably momentary absence to find a privacy bush, shivering as I squatted. Then I went down to the little stream to wash my hands—a rather numbing experience—and refill my canteen, dropping in another of the water-purifying tablets.

Karl appeared from the direction of the road. "I watched for half an hour and did not see a single vehicle," he said. "Nor have I heard or seen aircraft. If anyone is searching for us in this area, they are not being obvious about it. I think we can press on."

"We'd better," I said. "I'm out of trail mix."

"As am I," said Karl.

We packed up our sleeping bags, pulled on our packs, and headed back up the streambed to the road. Just as the little bridge— really just a culvert—came into sight, a bright-red car rumbled over it, heading toward Elkjaw. I froze, but the car was only visible for a second or two, and the driver didn't even glance in our direction. I heaved a sigh of relief.

"Just a random traveler," Karl said. "Probably." He looked up at the sky. "Perhaps, though, we should now parallel the road under the cover of the trees, rather than walking on it or on its shoulder."

"Couldn't I Shape a passing driver?" I said. "Get him to pull over and give us a lift?"

"Alter the mind of someone driving sixty miles an hour along a winding mountain road?" Karl said. "Splendid idea. What could possibly go wrong?"

"Nobody likes a sarcastic mystical guide," I muttered.

The day hadn't warmed much yet: our breath came in clouds, which caught the morning sun as it finally cleared the mountains. Only once did we hear another car approaching, and we tucked ourselves deep into the shadows of the forest until it had trundled past.

I was wondering exactly how we were supposed to "obtain transportation," when, unexpectedly, the opportunity presented itself, in the form of a dark-green car parked in one of those "scenic turnouts" that feature a wooden railing, a garbage bin, and a sign identifying whatever scenery it is you are supposed to be admiring. (Sometimes, if you're really lucky, there's an outhouse.) In this case, the scenic object in question was Fortress Mountain, a lonely peak whose side facing us featured sheer, red cliffs and upthrust spires that resembled (if you squinted just right) the walls and turrets of a medieval castle. The road had been climbing steadily since we'd started along it (a fact to which my aching calves could certainly attest), while a valley opened to our right, so the scenic turnout gave an unobstructed view out over several miles of forest to the picturesque pile of rock.

On the other side of the fifteen-year-old Chevre sedan that had pulled into the turnout, steam rising from its tailpipe as it idled away in an environmentally unfriendly manner, stood a big, black-bearded man in a leather coat, holding a camera that sported the longest telephoto lens I'd ever seen anyone try to use without a monopod. Though the sun, just peeking up from behind Fortress Mountain, cast the distinctive cliffs into shadow, it also created a striking silhouette, which he was apparently trying to capture.

"There's our ride," Karl said.

"We're just going to jump in and steal it?" I said.

"No," Karl said. "That would raise flags. You need to Shape him, just a little. He needs to think the car is ours, we drove him out here so he could take some pictures, and his plan is to walk into town once he's done. Can you manage that without also convincing him he needs to jump over the railing or gouge his eyes out?"

"I've spoken to you before about your sarcasm," I said. But I felt nervous all the same as I reached for my power. I very carefully formulated what I wanted the man to believe, as if I were crafting one of the short stories I had been (slightly) famous for in high school. I reached out and touched the man's mind. A few hours' sleep seemed to have helped replenish my power a little; I didn't feel any pain or sudden surge of exhaustion, just a slight . . . pressure . . . inside my skull, as though I were mentally pushing through some kind of thin, stretchy barrier. The man took another photo, then turned and waved at us. "I'm good!" he called. "Thanks for the ride! I'll probably be out here a couple of hours before I walk into town for lunch."

"Have a great time!" Karl said. He walked over to the door and graciously opened the driver's door for me.

"Thank you," I said, wondering why he was being so gentlemanly. I paused before climbing in, looking over the car roof at the photographer. "Can't wait to see your pictures!" I called.

"Sure!" said the man. "Next time we . . ." He blinked. "Um . . ."

"Let's go," Karl said sharply. He put his hand on my shoulder to force me down into the driver seat—definitely *not* the act of a gentleman—then hurried around to the passenger side, threw his backpack into the back seat, and got in. I put the car into gear. As we drove onto the road, I glanced into the rearview mirror and saw our provider-of-transportation staring after us . . . but my last glimpse of him showed him turning his camera once more toward the view.

I rolled the shoulder by which Karl had painfully pushed me into the seat. "What was that all about?" I said irritably.

"Every detail matters," he said. "You Shaped him to believe a very simple narrative, but it had holes in it because it *was* so simple. He has no memories of spending time with us, of making friends with us, of ever knowing us before this moment. If he thinks too hard, he will remember owning this car. As it is, he will be horribly confused when he gets to town and the narrative you imposed runs out. But your unnecessary comment to him almost brought him to that point of cognitive dissonance right then and there . . . which would have resulted in an ugly scene, and would also have ensured he reported us for stealing his car, which would immediately point the Adversary once more in our direction."

"It would help," I grumbled, "If Shapers were given an instruction manual."

"They are," Karl said. "You *were*. Several years of training. All wasted, since you do not remember any of it."

"I didn't forget on purpose."

"How do you know, since you cannot remember?" he said.

A perfectly logical question, and I didn't have a good answer for it, which annoyed me no end. I drove in silence for a minute or two. "Can we get food in Elkjaw?" I said at last.

"Better not," Karl said. "Someone might recognize the car and wonder why *we* are driving it. We'll go on." He pulled the road map out of his coat pocket again, and opened it up. "This road takes us to the Interstate," he said after studying it a moment. "Much too dangerous. But look here."

He pointed. I shot a quick look at the map, but couldn't decipher it from that angle. "What is it?"

"A small airport."

"How does that help?" I said. "I can't fly a plane. Can you?"

He shook his head. "No. But if we can find someone who *can* . . .

we could transport ourselves far out of the area where the Adversary's efforts are likely to be concentrated. The bigger the area he has to search, the less likely he is to find us."

A thought struck me. "We could fly directly to where you can make a new Portal!" I said excitedly.

"Possibly," Karl said. "Though I cannot tell yet. I only know it is west of here. How far, I do not know."

My momentary excitement died. "Too far west, and we hit the Pacific Ocean. What if it's underwater?"

"It won't be," Karl said. "It will be on dry ground. It always is. But it *could* be on an island, which we might not be able to land a plane on even if we find a pilot to take us however far it is. And if it proved to be out of range of the aircraft, we would have to return to the mainland. By that time, the Adversary might be waiting for us."

"If it's offshore, and we can't fly, we'll need a boat," I said. "I can't drive one of those, either."

"I can," Karl said. "Or sail one, at least." He nodded down the road ahead of us. "We are nearing the town."

I slowed to a sedate twenty miles per hour as I drove through the little community of Elkjaw. All of its businesses . . . a couple of restaurants, a gas station, three bars, a small grocery store, a few others . . . were strung along the road, with houses mostly perched on the hillside to our left, since to our right the ground fell away sharply. Fortress Mountain rose in the distance, angled now so that its distinctive cliff faces weren't as visible, which must have been why our photographer friend had headed out of town to take pictures of it.

It suddenly struck me he might not live here, that he might be a tourist. What if his luggage was in the trunk, and we'd just stranded him with nothing but the clothes on his back?

I'd liked my world better before I knew I could Shape it.

If the photographer *was* from the town, and if anyone recognized the car and the fact there were strangers in it, they didn't react visibly—as far as I could tell, none of the handful of people on the streets gave us a second look. But that didn't mean someone behind one of those shop windows wasn't calling the sheriff right that minute.

No sirens pursued us in town or out of town, though, and we drove on in serene isolation for another twenty minutes before we saw a sign, with a small graphic of an airplane on it, pointing right down a side road, indicating that Marshall Field was two miles thataway.

"Marshall Field?" I muttered as I turned. "Really?"

Karl glanced at me.

"Famous Chicago department store," I said. "I never noticed before just how many puns there are on road signs."

"Based on what I have noted of your sense of humor," Karl said dryly, "I rather suspect that is a side effect of your initial shaping of the world."

"You mean I'm the one who named this Marshall Field?"

"In a manner of speaking," Karl said. "Your personality seeped into the Shaping, which means lot of what you wrought was purely subconscious. Anything that is in this world that isn't in the original reality is indeed something you Shaped, but that does not necessarily mean you did it deliberately."

"I'm going to have to have a talk with my subconscious."

The road took us through the woods to a big, airfield-sized clearing. There was only one (grass) runway, half a dozen small hangars, and a two-story building with glass windows on the second floor that hardly qualified as a "tower." A tiny community field like that could very well have been deserted at that time of the day—or pretty much any time of the day—but either we were in luck, or the world was still ordering itself to help me out, even when I wasn't conscious of it: someone was fueling a small plane from a big aboveground tank, located well away from the hangars. I turned off the road into the field, and we bumped across the grass until we were maybe twenty yards from the plane.

"Keep it simple," Karl said quietly to me. "No need for him to change his destination. He has offered us a ride, that's all. Suggest that he forget all about us after we land. That should mean no trail for anyone to follow. And no chance of bad consequences . . . for him, or for us."

I nodded, and we got out of the car, Karl trailing me by a few feet. The man watched us warily. "That's close enough!" he called when we were about ten yards away. "Who are you and what do you want?"

I took a deep breath, and once more reached for my Shaping ability. Every time it became easier. I crafted this Shaping with even greater care than the last, released it, feeling that strange pressure in my head, but again escaping a headache, then took a deep, shaking breath. The pilot's hostile expression blanked for a moment, a disconcerting sight, as though he had literally lost his mind. Then he smiled with genuine warmth. "Great to see you! Beautiful day for a flight, isn't it?"

I didn't say anything, afraid I'd confuse this . . . "victim" was such an unpleasant word, but it was the one that came to mind all the same . . . the way I had the photographer.

"It is," Karl said. "Can we put the car in your hangar for safe-keeping before we take off?"

"Sure," said the pilot. He pointed at the row of hangars. "The blue one. Here." He reached into his pocket, pulled out a key hanging from a rabbit's-foot fob (although no rabbit that ever lived had had fur that particular shade of fuchsia), and tossed it to me.

I nodded, still not speaking, got back into the car, and drove it to the hangar. The key opened the padlock on the sliding double doors; I pulled them open, drove into the hangar, got out, tossed the car keys into the driver's seat, went back out, closed and locked the hangar doors, and then trudged back to the waiting airplane.

The pilot was already inside; Karl and I climbed in together, him in the front, me in the back. The pilot started the engine, the propeller whirled fiercely, and a few bumpy minutes later we lifted off from the grass runway into the blue late-morning sky.

I didn't have a clue where we were headed, and didn't dare ask the pilot, in case I triggered more "cognitive dissonance," which seemed like it would be an even worse thing in someone flying an airplane than in someone driving a car.

Especially when I was in the airplane.

Karl didn't ask, either. Nor did he make small talk. The pilot seemed almost to have forgotten we were there. He hummed to himself as we winged our way westward, avoiding the highest peaks to fly along the valley and over the passes the Interstate traveled: I could see it far below, a string of cars, windows reflecting the sun.

Fortunately, the pilot had to check in with air traffic control along the way, which was how I found out we were headed to somewhere in Oregon. Air traffic control was in Portland, but our destination was—my breath caught—Wing and a Prayer Field.

*Wing and a Prayer?* That meant . . .

I glanced at Karl. *Not yet. After we've landed.*

My stomach growled as we flew, though I was the only one who could possibly have known over the buzz of the engine. The food situation was getting critical. I had a little cash, so we could buy something if we ever got to a store or restaurant—using plastic was obviously out of the question—but so far, the only places we'd seen had been in Elkjaw, where we hadn't dared to stop.

Since no one on the airplane was offering me lunch (or even a diminutive bag of pretzels and a tiny glass of pop), I rested my slightly aching head against the window, stared down at the valley and up at the snowy peaks, and wondered what the Adversary was doing. By now he must know what had happened at Snakebite Mine, that two of his cadre members and the caretaker were dead, and that his Portal had been destroyed. The two sheriff's deputies whose SUV we'd taken had probably been picked up by now, too.

We'd disposed of the SUV in the quarry I had Shaped, but that bit of cleverness, Karl had said, had probably been sensed by the Adversary, and in any event had been thoroughly negated by the disaster at the horse ranch. There we'd left two dead men, bringing our Bonnie-and-Clyde-like total to six, in what had turned into a bloody rampage across the state. I winced at that thought, but I could not deny it. Karl had shot three: in self-defense, you could argue, but he had shot them, nonetheless. The other three . . . I had not killed them in cold blood, but their deaths were my fault, all the same. As, too, if I were honest, was that of the third man Karl had shot, at the ranch, since my bungled Shaping had led to that disaster.

I tried to put that out of my mind and concentrate on how the Adversary would view things. At the ranch, it would be obvious one man had shot the other, but then had been shot by someone else, no longer to be found. One dead horse, cause of death unknown. Two horses missing (if there were records our pursuers could check, which there must be). They would follow the horses: a dead end, but how much time would it buy us? Once the horses turned up they'd understand what we'd done, and then they'd be searching and questioning everyone along the road we had taken, in both directions from where the horse trail crossed it.

It all hinged on the photographer. How well had I Shaped him? Would he eventually report his car stolen? Someone would remember us driving through town. But no one had seen us turn down to the airstrip, and the car was hidden in a locked hangar.

There, if nowhere else, we might have shaken any pursuit. For the moment.

The trouble was, the Adversary was Shaping people, too, at much higher levels than I was. Our pictures . . . or mine, anyway; Karl had not existed in my world until a few days ago . . . must be plastered everywhere by now, in every police database. Every branch of law enforcement must be looking for me.

The view through the airplane window was breathtaking, but in reality, this whole beautiful world, the world that had once been my own, the world I had loved, and had a place in, and in which I had expected to live out my quiet, settled life, was no longer safe. Was no longer *home*.

I knew that. After all that had happened, denial no longer had the slightest bit of wiggle room in my mind. But if we really were landing at Wing and a Prayer Field, there was one more place I had to go before I left this world forever.

The day slipped away. The sun crossed over our heads and began to sink in front of us, lower and lower as the hours droned past. My stomach kept growling. "Getting close," the pilot said at last, although it seemed as much to himself as to us.

I leaned over a little so I could look between him and Karl and out through the whirling propeller. In the far distance, I glimpsed the flat expanse of the ocean, glittering in the lowering sun. Just as I saw it, we banked right. I glanced at my watch: a little after four o'clock.

Karl spoke for the first time in hours, twisting in his seat to look at me. "It's out there somewhere," he said. "West, over the water. I'm sure of it. Can you feel anything?"

I looked out over that immense body of water, endless and

empty. "No," I said, although that wasn't quite true. I could feel one thing very, very well: hunger.

The ocean wasn't the only thing that was empty. The sooner we were on the ground, the better. And then, *I* would be choosing our next destination—not Karl Yatsar.

# FIFTEEN

**THE ADVERSARY STARED** out the rain-spattered window of his NBI-issued room at a wet, windswept parking lot, bordered by tossing trees. Two cadre members were dead, as well as the mine caretaker, who had, most unexpectedly, blown himself up—apparently the man had been some kind of explosive expert during past military service, which was why he had interpreted "protect" to mean "booby-trap."

His death had accomplished nothing. The Adversary had wakened in the night to a feeling akin to amputation, as his connections to his own Shaped world, and the Shakespearean world he had Shaped next, were severed. The Adversary had known instantly that he would not be able to restore them. Had Yatsar merely closed the Portal, he would still have been able to sense it through the nanomites in his body, the same technology that allowed him to force a closed Portal open. But the Portal through which he had entered Shawna Keys' world had not merely been closed: it had ceased to exist. Unless Yatsar created a new one—which he certainly would not—there would be no returning to the Shakespearean world, or his own.

That meant he could summon no replacements for the two cadre members slain at the mine, a married pair. That left him with only ten of his elite, superloyal followers. At least their weapons had been copied from the First World, and thus ammunition was readily available here.

From the mine, it seemed clear Yatsar and Keys had fled in a stolen sheriff's SUV. Two deputies had been discovered making their way downstream from a bridge not far from the mine. They had tried to evade their own colleagues, but had been captured. Then, early this morning, two bodies had been found at a place called Bow and Arrow Ranch. There'd been no sign of the SUV, but horses were missing. Investigators were following the horse trail. Others were spreading out from the ranch, questioning everyone they could find.

One thing was clear, from the cases of the helicopter pilot and his deceased partner, the wandering deputies, and the bodies at the ranch: Shawna Keys had begun Shaping humans to her own ends (or really, Karl Yatsar's ends), just as the Adversary was Shaping them to his.

The destruction of the Portal had also clearly been accomplished with her power, though undoubtedly fed through the Shurak technology in Yatsar's body. And there had been other powerful Shapings by her. The time displacement after he stole her *hokhmah* had been the most astonishing and impressive, but several times he had sensed the world shifting. Some of those Shapings on her part must be deliberate; others might not have been. He could not pinpoint their location, but he had a general sense of where they had happened. She seemed to be heading west.

He had to find her: find her, and kill her. Not Yatsar, of course: he needed Yatsar alive. The blood-borne nanomites that gave Yatsar the ability to open Portals would cease to function if Yatsar were killed. But if he could capture Yatsar, or get a large enough sample of his blood or tissue while he still lived, he could claim those nanomites for himself. Then he could open Portals as he wished, and in short order, he would find Ygrair and make her pay for her crimes.

It was *possible* he could recover the nanomites even from

Yatsar's corpse, examine them, reverse-engineer them, and make them work within himself, but that would take a great deal of time: years, even decades, perhaps, depending on the technological capability of the world in which found himself—and during those years, Ygrair would have time to pursue her own ends, replacing Yatsar with a new envoy, seeking out a new Shaper powerful enough to hold the *hokhmah* of multiple worlds and deliver that knowledge to Ygrair, enhancing her power and putting those worlds out of his reach.

The destruction of the Portal through which he had come was almost certainly a one-off, possible only because Shawna Keys was such a powerful Shaper. Only the Shaper of a world could possibly provide the specialized energy necessary to destroy a Portal into that world. He did not believe she could do it in any world she had not Shaped. And if he were wrong . . . well, she certainly wouldn't be able to do it in any world she had not Shaped if he killed her in this one.

A knock. "Mr. Gegner, sir?" a woman's voice called through the door from the hallway. "The car is here to take you to the airport."

"Coming." He turned his back on the window. Law enforcement had disseminated photos of Keys, and a description of Yatsar, far and wide. The remaining members of his cadre, except for two serving as his personal bodyguards, were operating independently, conducting their own search and tracking efforts, their orders specific: shoot Keys, take Yatsar alive.

Yatsar was clever, and with Keys now actively Shaping those they met, the duo might yet slip through the fingers of the local law. Which meant it was time to up the ante. He still could not effect change globally with the ease he would be able to once Keys was dead. But he would Shape what he could. The meeting in Washington, D.C. he had arranged for that afternoon, through judicious Shaping of the people he had been able to meet or talk to in his guise as Gegner, would make it much, much harder for Yatsar and Keys to escape apprehension for very much longer.

He opened the door and smiled at the young NBI agent waiting nervously outside. "We'd best be off," he said to the woman. "Mustn't keep the President waiting."

Shaping a world, I'd already decided, was a lot like writing a story. This world of mine . . . or at least which *had* been mine . . . reflected my personality in a lot of ways, as Karl had made clear. Perhaps that was why, whenever I had some deep and meaningful insight, or thought of a nice metaphor, or a clever turn of phrase went through my mind, the world had a way of promptly turning it on its side and throwing it in my face, like a pulp author trying to make every chapter end in a cliff-hanger.

*The sooner we're on the ground the better*, I'd thought, and okay, that's not exactly a *clever* turn of phrase, just a rather clichéd way of saying something needed to happen soon. But not two minutes later the pilot straightened in his seat. "Say again?"

He listened, one hand on his right earpiece, and then said, "Roger." He glanced at Karl. "I've been denied permission to land at Wing and a Prayer. I'm instructed to land at Cross Wind instead."

"Did they say why?" Karl said.

The pilot shook his head.

"What's the difference between the two fields?"

"Cross Wind is on the outskirts of small city," the pilot said. "Wing and a Prayer is rural—nothing there really. The closest town is five miles away, and it's a speck of a place."

"So why are you going there?" Karl said.

"Camping," the pilot said cheerfully. His face fell. "I'll never get there in time to hike up to the lake and camp tonight if I have to land at Cross Wind."

Karl glanced at me. "They're checking aircraft," he said. "They will be waiting for us at Cross Wind."

"But if they know we're up here, why not just send men to Wing and a Prayer?"

"I don't think they know for certain."

"It's not just me," the pilot said. He tapped his headset. "Everyone is being diverted to a few larger fields. Everyone's pissed off about it, too."

"See?" Karl said to me.

I didn't argue. I reached out to the pilot, very, very carefully, since my previous concerns about Shaping someone responsible for keeping us several thousand feet in the air remained fully operative. I introduced the idea that we were going to land at Wing and a Prayer Field no matter what air traffic control said.

I risked it not only because Karl wanted me to, but for my own reasons . . . which I suspected he wouldn't be happy about when he found out, but, hey. Life's like that sometimes.

I opened my eyes. "To hell with that," the pilot muttered. He banked right. He must have gotten an earful from air traffic control a few minutes later, because he jerked off his headset and let it hang loose around his neck. Since presumably that meant he had also cut himself off from any warnings about other aircraft in the vicinity, I developed a whole new interest in staring out the window.

Bit by bit we slipped down toward the broad valley below, mountains to the right, mountains to the left. Ahead I could see the little V-shape of the runways at Wing and a Prayer Field, and beyond it, the "speck of a town" the pilot had mentioned, with its tiny downtown and a few surrounding blocks of houses.

My heart skipped a beat.

With a deft hand on the controls, the pilot dropped us neatly, with barely a bump, onto the end of one of the two runways. We rolled to a halt outside one of three hangars, all closed. The only official building was a small square structure with an antenna on top, also closed: even less of a tower than Marshall Field had had, although at least this field had two runways and both were paved.

Clearly no one was expecting us.

"Not a very busy airport," Karl observed.

"Barely used," the pilot said. "Privately owned by a couple of aircraft owners in town, rich enough to keep it in operating condition. I'm friends with one of them, so I get to use it, too." A look of confusion crossed his face. "But I was supposed to land at Cross Wind. I'll be in trouble . . ."

"No, you won't," I said, with a hint of Shaping, and his expression cleared again. I resisted the urge to add, "These aren't the droids you're looking for."

An instant after that came the guilt. I was playing with the poor man's mind, and he *would* be in trouble with the authorities. "Forget you ever saw us," I added then. "We're already gone."

His face blanked, then cleared. He turned and, whistling, made his way to the square building, fishing keys out of his pocket as he went. He didn't look back.

"That won't necessarily protect him," Karl said, watching the pilot go.

"It might protect *us*," I said shortly.

My guilt returned full-force. *Did Obi-Wan feel guilty for clouding the minds of the Imperial Stormtroopers?* part of me demanded.

*That's just a movie*, the guilty part rejoined. *This is reality.*

*Is it?* the other part asked.

*Shut up*, I told both parts. Out loud, I said, "We need to keep moving."

"I agree." Karl turned back to the plane and hauled our packs out of the back seat. He handed mine to me, then pulled on his own. With a sigh, I hefted the heavy thing up on my shoulders again. I was getting heartily sick of it.

The pilot had disappeared into the control . . . hut. I wondered if he would see us again for the first time if he came out before we were gone. I didn't want to find out.

"That way," I said, pointing to a fence off to our left. "We can get into the woods again."

Karl nodded, and we jogged through the long grass growing alongside the runway, climbed carefully over the low barbed-wire fence, and plunged into the autumnal forest, the red and gold of deciduous trees contrasting sharply with the brooding green of the conifers. It was warmer here than it had been at Marshall Field outside Elkjaw, both because we were much closer to sea level and because we were closer to the ocean. The forest smelled alive in a way the frostier woods of the mountain heights had not.

I led the way without talking, but that couldn't last. "You walk," Karl finally said from behind me, as we followed a barely there track through the woods, "as though you know where we are going."

"Just trying to get us to this Portal-making place of yours," I said.

"Which is out to sea somewhere, or on the other side of it. And since, as I keep reminding you, you are neither a god nor the off-spring of one, walking will take us no farther than the shore." He quickened his pace, and came up beside me. "Where does this track lead?"

"Somewhere," I said evasively.

"The 'Portal-making place,' as you call it, lies to our west. We are not walking west."

"We're walking northwest. Close enough. Besides, it's faster walking on the track than off of it." I slowed. "And look, here's a road."

We had indeed come out of the woods alongside a road, paved though potholed, its center stripe badly faded and its crumbling shoulders ranging from narrow to nonexistent. It stretched to our left and right a good two or three miles each way before curving out of sight. No cars moved along it, and I couldn't hear any, either.

Which wasn't too surprising, given how small the town about five miles down the road to our right was, and given that this road didn't really go anywhere in particular except to a few resort properties, mainly used on weekends by folks who drove out from Portland to get away from it all.

I set off to the right. Karl trailed me again. "We need to get to the coast," he said. "We need a boat. We are not headed to the coast. We are now headed due north."

"There's a town up here, remember?" I said. "Another chance to find transportation." My stomach growled and cramped. "And food."

"Another chance to be reported to authorities, who may very well then descend on us with guns blazing," Karl said. "Air traffic control will know that our pilot ignored instructions and instead landed at his original destination. There may be law enforcement officials on their way."

I kept walking.

"Shawna," Karl said.

I ignored him.

After that he gave up, following a few feet behind as we trudged along the road. Only once did we have to move into the woods at the sound of an approaching vehicle, and it proved to be nothing but a beat-up blue half-ton flatbed with a hole in its muffler hauling a load of bricks, which passed us in the direction of the town. The blue smoke of its exhaust lingered long after the echoes of its raucous passage had died away.

Karl coughed as we stepped back onto the road. "I confess," he said, "there are times I prefer the worlds Shaped into a preindustrial state."

I didn't reply. Up ahead, the road crested a small hill. A

distinctive tree grew to the left of the road, a giant spruce that had been damaged in a windstorm at some point in its growth, and as a result had split maybe fifteen feet up its trunk, two fully formed crowns spreading out from that point and fighting for dominance over the decades since. My heart thudded in my chest, more than the exertion of walking could account for. I walked faster.

Karl jogged to catch up, and then walked beside me, matching my rapid stride. His eyes searched my face in profile. "What have you not told me, Shawna?"

I ignored him. I looked both ways, then crossed the road, so that we came alongside the forked spruce as we reached the top of the hill.

A white picket fence began just past the spruce, enclosing an acre of green grass, carefully mowed. A white, wooden, two-story house occupied the center of the acreage, well back from the highway. The gate in the fence was marked by a silver mailbox with an American flag attached to it and some low rosebushes on either side, barren of blooms this late in the year. A driveway, bordered by ground-hugging evergreen shrubs, curved up to the front of the house, where a classic silver Roosevelt town car from the 1970s, roughly the size of RMS *Titanic*, stretched out in the afternoon sun like a giant cat.

The house had green shutters and a green roof and a red tiled porch with white pillars on either side. To the left of the house was a detached two-car garage, to which the Roosevelt would be retired once the snow started, but which now would hold the everyday car, a blue Fjord electric, on one side, and, on the other, a small outboard motorboat and other odds and ends, including a sparkly girls' bicycle, with pink and white vinyl tassels trailing from its handlebars.

A woman came around the side of the house, carrying a rake. She wore a big straw hat with a yellow flower on it, green overalls, white gardening gloves, and yellow rubber boots. She vanished from my sight even before she entered the house through the front door, because my eyes filled instantly with tears.

Karl noticed, of course. And also, of course, put two and two together. "Shawna, why are we here?" he said, but as if he already knew the answer.

"It's my home," I said. "It's the house where I grew up." I took a deep, shuddering breath. "That woman is my mother."

# SIXTEEN

**I HAD SEEN** Karl slightly irritated, coldly murderous, infuriatingly calm, and even (rarely) joking, but until that moment, I had never seen him truly furious, except for that one flash of rage when I had asked if the laws of the Labyrinth could be changed. "You sentimental fool! She is *not* your mother. She is at best a copy. More likely she is a complete fabrication, Shaped to be the mother you wished you'd had, rather than the one who gave you birth!"

I slapped him. I didn't think about it, I just did it. The sound of my hand against his cheek was so loud I half-expected Mom to come back out of the house. Then I glared at him. "Even if that's true," I said, each word cold and sharp as a sliver of ice, "I love her, and nothing you can say will change that. And because I love her, I had to come here. My world understands that, even if you don't. I didn't consciously Shape our destination, but the pilot we 'lucked' into finding was already headed to the airfield a couple of miles from my house!"

Karl might have been carved from stone if not for the angry red imprint of my hand on his face. "I do not question your love," he said, and his words were every bit as icy as mine. "Or the strength of your Shaping ability, conscious or unconscious. I do, however, question your sanity." He pointed at the house. "This house is almost certainly under surveillance. We may already have been seen. Or, the Adversary may have simply Shaped her to report you if she sees you. Or worse, to kill you on sight."

That word-dagger slipped through my guard and slid into my heart so suddenly I gasped. I hadn't thought of that possibility. Could it be true?

Of course it could. If Karl had thought of it, the Adversary might have, too.

But he might not have, either. That night at the resort, before I really knew how to Shape (not that I knew much more now) I had tried so hard to imagine any information connecting Mom to me vanishing. Then, in my dreams, it had seemed that I had succeeded. I remembered the feeling of relief before I woke, the certainty that I didn't need to worry anymore.

Just a dream? Maybe. Or maybe not. Maybe I really had succeeded, my subconscious doing the Shaping while I slept. After all, Karl thought the whole resort might have been a Shaping I had done subconsciously. Our arrival at Wing and a Prayer Field had to have been done subconsciously. (Maybe that was why my hunger had seemed so acute on the plane—I'd used even more Shaping energy than I'd known.) Surely a little erasing of records wasn't too much to ask . . .

Either way, I was here. I was willing to take the chance Karl was right. But I forced myself to think, as well as speak, coldly. "You're still armed," I said. "If my mother threatens me, do what you have to."

I said it, and I meant it, but I could not begin to imagine what it would do to *me* if he shot the woman I remembered as my mother on the steps of what my heart insisted was my childhood home. Then again, what was it going to do to me to do what *I* intended to do, the thing I had not shared with Karl, could barely share with myself?

I couldn't talk anymore. I turned away from Karl, climbed over the fence, and set off across the yard toward the house.

*My* house.

My room was on the second floor at the back, overlooking the forest. I remembered countless mornings waking up and peering out into the trees. Many times I'd seen deer feeding in the morning mist, just outside the picket fence. Once a bear had wandered by, stopping to sharpen its claws on a fallen pine. I remembered the smell of bacon downstairs as Mom readied breakfast, which I would scarf down just in time to run out to the curb to catch the school bus.

Dad had died when I was a baby. I didn't remember him at all. Didn't that put the lie to Karl's suggestion I'd made a fake mom when I Shaped the world? Because I would have loved to have had a dad, and I hadn't. All I'd had was Mom.

But if I *hadn't* made this all up, if I'd just copied it, did that mean that in the First World I had grown up in a house just like this one? Was my mom there, my real mom, still alive, wondering where I'd gone? And if so . . . *why had I left her*?

Ten years had passed in the First World, Karl said. Had I just vanished mysteriously? There would have been police searches, news stories, but nothing ever found . . .

Unless I did something, this mom, in this world, would experience something just as horrifying. I would vanish if we succeeded, or die if we didn't. In this world, I was already a wanted terrorist. Would Mom believe it? Would she be *forced* to believe it? Or would she believe me innocent, but still have to live with the heartbreaking fact of my disappearance or death?

I swallowed hard, my stomach churning, as I reached the porch. I climbed the four steps between the white pillars. I reached for the door handle without thinking—it was my home!—then stopped my hand, and instead pressed the doorbell button with a trembling finger.

The familiar chimes echoed inside. I heard footsteps approaching, and clenched my hands into fists to stop them from shaking.

The door opened, and there was Mom, eyes widening as she saw me.

I'd been home just a couple of months ago, and she hadn't changed a bit since then. Her hair was drawn back in a practical ponytail, and her face was still largely unlined, and those things combined to make her look only a little older than I was, instead of in her mid-50s. My heart pounded in my chest as I waited for her reaction.

"Shawna!" she said, and her face broke into a huge smile. "Sweetheart, what a wonderful surprise! What are you doing here?"

Something broke inside me. I burst into tears and flung my arms around her.

She held me tightly. She smelled like *Mom*, the slightly spicy, slightly floral scent of her favorite perfume, lightly applied, taking me back to my childhood in an instant, to all the other times Mom had held me and made whatever trauma had ruined my world go away. "Honey, what's wrong?" The she saw Karl. "Who's that?"

I took a deep breath, released her, and wiped my eyes. I tried to smile, but knew I was largely unsuccessful; my lip was trembling too much. I turned. Karl stood at the bottom of the steps. His hand was in his coat pocket. I knew why.

"He's . . . a friend," I said. "We came out here to . . . do some camping." We were both wearing backpacks, so it seemed as good an excuse as any. "I wanted him to meet you."

"Really?" Mom frowned. "What about Brent?"

"We . . . broke up. And Karl isn't . . . he's just a friend." *Is he?* I wondered.

"Oh, honey, I'm so sorry." Mom hugged me again. "It will get better," she whispered in my ear. "I promise."

*She thinks I'm upset because of Brent*, I thought, holding on to her for another long moment—though it could never again be long enough. And in a way, I was. Upset about losing Brent, and Aesha, and everything else I loved. Soon I would lose my whole world . . . or if things went really badly, my whole life.

But first . . . another loss.

I pulled free. "Mom, could you leave us . . . just for a minute?"

She blinked. "What?"

"I need to talk to Karl. Alone." That sounded awkward and awful, and I could tell Mom was puzzled, but all she said was, "Of course, dear. Come in when you're ready. I'll make some tea." She went in and closed the door behind her.

"Shawna," Karl said. "This is still—"

"Shut up," I said, and rather to my surprise, he did.

I turned back to the house. I closed my eyes. I reached for my Shaping ability. I took a deep breath.

I Shaped.

No mere pressure this time. It *hurt*, a stab of agony like an icepick between my eyes. I had to reach out a shaking hand and lean against the doorjamb for support. I breathed deep until the pain receded enough I thought I could speak. Then I rang the doorbell again.

Footsteps. Mom opened the door. "Yes?" she said, looking at me with no recognition at all. Her eyes flicked to Karl. She frowned. "Can I help you?"

"I'm sorry to bother you, ma'am," I said, though it was hard to speak through my constricted throat. "I think we've taken a wrong turn. Which way is the Lake Tanim trailhead?"

Mom's face cleared. She gave me a sunny smile. "Oh, you're not too far away," she said. She pointed down the road, in the direction of town. "Just around the next bend, there's a parking lot and a sign. I'm surprised you missed it."

"Me, too," I said. I gave Karl a look. "I told you that was it."

"Sorry," he said. He still had his hand in his pocket.

"Thank you, ma'am," I said to Mom.

"Can I offer you a cup of tea?" she said. "I'm just making some for . . ." She blinked. "For some reason."

"No, thank you," I said. "Thanks again."

"You're welcome." She looked up at the sky. Clouds were beginning to drift across it from the west. "Not sure it's going to be a very nice afternoon for a hike, though. Could rain."

"We like rain," I said. I tried to smile. My lips curled up, but the expression felt like a dead thing stapled to my face. "Thank you again. Good-bye."

"Bye," Mom said.

I turned and descended the steps. I heard the door of the house I had grown up in close behind me with a finality that made my knees go weak, so suddenly I stumbled. Karl caught me.

"Why?" he said. "Why risk this?"

I straightened and pushed him away. "Because now she won't hurt when I disappear, or die, or when she hears about some woman who happens to share her last name being called a terrorist."

"She will hear her own name mentioned in news reports as your mother."

"I am the Shaper of this world," I said. "No, she won't." I said it with as much conviction as I could. I thought I had already done that, but I had made it certain with this Shaping, just as I had made certain my beloved room on the second floor, and every other nook and cranny of the house, no longer bore any trace of me, or any other child.

"It was a foolish risk," he said. "A risk for us, and a risk for her. If she had been Shaped by the Adversary to kill you, I would have been forced to shoot her in front of you."

"It was a risk worth taking," I said.

He shook his head stubbornly. "I disagree. The fate of the whole of the Labyrinth, an unknown number of Shaped worlds, may well depend on you. Why risk all that for one woman?"

I stared at him, at the pale blue eyes in the dark, mustached face, and wondered, not for the first time, what Karl Yatsar had become over his long years of life. "Because of love," I said. "Something I'm guessing you know nothing about."

I pushed past him, striding down the driveway of my childhood home. My eyes blurred again with unshed tears, but I didn't look back.

# SEVENTEEN

**WE WALKED ALONG** the road in rather surly silence, Karl following several steps behind me, clearly no more interested in talking to me than I was in talking to him. The promised sign for the trailhead for Lake Tanim came into sight, the turnoff into the parking lot opening on our left. I came even with it, and kept walking.

That finally brought a comment from Karl. "Aren't we taking the trail?"

"No," I said, and kept walking.

After a few more feet, I heard him quicken his pace. He came up beside me. "Why did you ask where it was, then?"

"To make sure Mom had been . . ." My throat constricted; I had to swallow hard to resume talking. "Shaped."

"It goes in the right direction. West. Why *not* take it?"

"Because it's a dead end," I said. "It leads up to the lake, but the only way down again is along the same trail. If we took it, we'd be trapped."

"Then why choose it for your . . . examination question?"

"So that if someone on our trail asks Mom if she's seen us, she'll tell them we were headed to Lake Tanim. It's a half-day hike. It buys us time."

Karl didn't say anything for a moment. "Logical," he finally commented.

"Thank you, Mr. Spock," I said sourly.

Another moment of silence. "I apologize for my anger," he said next, surprising me. "Passing through so many worlds, I have become focused on my goal, which at times has seemed impossibly out of reach, to the exclusion of all other considerations. It has made me selfish. It was kind of you to think of trying to protect a woman you love from the pain this changing world will bring her."

Some of my own simmering anger cooled at that. "Thank you," I said. "Apology accepted."

We trudged on a few more yards.

"Who is Mr. Spock?" he said at last.

That made me laugh, which felt good. "He's a half-Vulcan," I said. "An alien." *Like Ygrair, I guess*, which was a seriously weird thought. "Pointy ears. Emotionless. Logical."

"I am only one of those things," Karl said. "I am logical, or try to be. But I am not emotionless. Nor do I have pointy ears. And I am human."

"One out of five is close enough."

Another moment of silence.

"So where are we going?" he said then.

"The trail we really want, the one that takes us west, begins on the other side of town," I said. "It's called the Sky-to-Sea. It crosses those mountains in the west, then leads all the way down to the coast—a two-day hike from here. Probably two nights' camping, considering how late it's getting." I glanced at my watch. Well after five o'clock. "It will be dark almost as soon we are on it."

"Two more days on foot," Karl said. "We'll be vulnerable."

"Appleville is even smaller than Elkjaw. Too small to risk taking someone's car," I said. "Even if I Shaped someone to give it to us, somebody would notice strangers were driving it. Or worse, would recognize me." Recognize me. I suddenly realized that even though I'd Shaped my mom to forget me, there were dozens of people in Appleville who knew me—people I'd gone to school with, business owners, friends of my mother's. They'd talk to my mom. She'd be confused . . .

. . . unless my Shaping had covered even that? Again, I remembered how relieved I had been after my dream at the resort.

*I hope*, I thought. *Oh, I hope.*

"Horses?" Karl said, oblivious to my sudden internal turmoil.

"Same problem. Also, I prefer breathing."

We walked on.

"Perhaps we need a stealthier option," Karl said after a few more steps. "Does anyone travel regularly from . . . what is the name of the town, again?"

"Appleville," I said.

"Appleville?" He looked around at the valley. At that very moment, we were passing between giant orchards; in the distance, several people on ladders were picking fruit. "Not very original."

"Don't blame me, I didn't . . ." My voice trailed off. "Or maybe I did?"

He shrugged. "You would know better than I if there is a town named Appleville in Oregon in the First World."

I sighed. "I really hope there is," I said, "because I'd hate to think I was that lacking in creativity."

Karl actually smiled. "I think it is safe to say," he said, "that there is no such thing as a Shaper lacking in creativity. Creativity is pretty much the primary distinguishing characteristic of such individuals."

I let myself smile back. "You didn't finish your question."

"Does anyone . . . or anything . . . travel regularly from Appleville to the coast?"

"Why?" I said, and then suddenly understood. "Yes!" I said in sudden excitement. "Apple trucks! It's right in the middle of the harvest. There'll be trucks driving west every day—there's a big processing plant on the coast. I should have thought of that!"

"That's our ride, then," Karl said.

"I love apples," I said, mouth watering . . . which, come to think of it, probably wasn't surprising, since I'd chosen to Shape my world so my hometown was, literally, Appleville, USA.

By the time we reached town it was past five-thirty. If we had really been going to set off west on foot, it would have been dark almost before we began the journey. But now we had a different plan. Now darkness would serve us.

Whether I had really grown up in Appleville or conjured it entirely out of thin air, I knew every inch of the town. The local apple growers had banded together to form the Appleville Growers' Cooperative. All of the AGC's fruit went to the Pacific Breeze Fruit Company, which maintained a state-of-the-art processing facility on the coast, convenient to rail lines and the Interstate for shipping around the country, and with its own harbor for overseas shipping. Some apples went out in bulk, while others were sliced, diced, mashed, or juiced.

I would have loved to have gone into the tiny downtown and bought a hamburger at either Burger Baron or Sandwich Sultan, two locally owned restaurants which had been locked in friendly rivalry my whole life. But since I couldn't be certain I wouldn't be recognized, I didn't dare.

Instead we lurked in a copse of trees within sight of the AGC warehouse, waiting for the sun to go down and the traffic—such as it was—to lessen. I was so hungry I actually wished we still had trail mix.

A little after six o'clock, a guard appeared at the gate in the chain-link fence surrounding the warehouse, a hundred-year-old wooden rectangular structure two stories high, with big windows on all sides and skylights in the ceiling. It was in dire need of painting, but the faded logo of a stylized apple, with a banner floating in front of it bearing the co-op's name in old-fashioned letters, could still be made out in the fading light.

The guard stepped out through the gate, swung it closed behind him, locked it with a padlock on a chain, and walked down the street, whistling.

Except I was *quite certain* the padlock had failed to latch properly. Which meant, of course, it was true.

I'd been leery of even that much Shaping, after the agony of my effort to protect Mom, but it didn't hurt, although it did seem to take more effort than I thought it should. *Well*, I thought, *that last Shaping was a doozy.*

We waited another hour, while the sun vanished and darkness gathered, hastened by the thickening cloud Mom had noted rolling in from the west. The warehouse stood on the very edge of town, so the nearest houses were a couple of blocks away. There were no motion sensors or security cameras—it was, after all, just a big building filled with apples—and once it seemed clear no one remained in the compound, we went to the gate, swung it open, and walked in.

I closed the gate behind us and made sure that this time the padlock really *did* lock, with a loud click. Then we hurried out of the pool of illumination cast by a light near the gate and into the concealing shadows.

There were six loading docks, three marked Receiving, three marked Shipping. Semitrailers were parked at two of the latter. One, we saw when we opened it up, was packed solid with flats of apples. The other, though, was only half full. It was easy enough to rearrange things so that there was empty space at the front, with a wall of fruit behind it to conceal us.

The workers wouldn't notice that anything had been moved. I was sure of it.

We took our sleeping bags from our packs and made ourselves as comfortable as we could on the wooden floor. I sat in the darkness, munching an apple. It was a Red Delicious, the most popular variety grown in the state. I'd never cared for the variety myself, but that night, I thought it was the most wonderful thing I'd ever tasted.

I guess I could have tried to Shape it into a Honeycrisp—my personal favorite—but it didn't seem worth the effort. And it was an effort: I'd done so much Shaping today that the last couple of times I'd consciously Shaped something—like the padlock—I'd I had to . . . I guess "push" is the word . . . harder than I had before. Though it least it hadn't hurt like my erasure of Mom's memory . . .

My apple suddenly tasted like sawdust. I had to wait a moment before I could continue eating, but I *did* keep eating: I'd barely made a dent in my hunger. I finished the first apple, put it aside, and grabbed another.

*A steak would be better*, I thought as I bit into it, and despite my concern a moment before about wasting energy, was suddenly sorely tempted to try to Shape one into existence, right there in the dark, medium rare, maybe with blue cheese or mushrooms . . .

. . . and then thought better of it, remembering how badly things had gone when I got a Shaping wrong. Unintended consequences could be disastrous, and if I couldn't quite figure out why conjuring up a nice steak would be disastrous, that probably only meant, Karl's reassurance to the contrary, that I lacked imagination.

*I'd probably end up with a whole cow*, I thought. *And there's barely room enough in here for both of us.*

I thought about asking Karl what he thought, but then I heard his breathing, slow and steady, and realized he'd already fallen asleep.

I put my second apple core to one side and stretched out in my own sleeping bag, using the backpack as a lumpy but better-than-nothing pillow. I felt utterly exhausted, mentally and physically, but my mind kept racing.

I thought about Aesha.

I thought about Brent.

I thought about Mom.

I thought about everything I'd thought I'd had, and would never have again.

And finally, for the first time in a long time, I cried myself to sleep.

I woke with a start to the crash of the trailer doors being flung open. Gray light and cold air flooded around us, filtered through the pallets of apples. Male voices joked and laughed and cursed. The trailer shifted, and shadows moved over the slits of light as workers continued the loading, half-completed the day before.

"They'll block us in completely if we're not careful," Karl whispered.

"No, they won't," I whispered back, because I'd thought of that and made sure it wouldn't happen. A night's sleep had rejuvenated me somewhat: the minor Shaping hardly fazed me.

Just a few minutes after the loading began, someone called, "That's it! Close her up!" The doors slammed shut, plunging us into darkness. I heard the door of the cab open. The truck swayed as someone climbed aboard. The cab door slammed shut. The engine started. Gears clunked.

We began to roll.

Relief flooded me. We'd done it! Nobody could possibly know we were aboard this truck. Our trail was as dead as a doornail. (Whatever that means. I've never understood why a doornail should be considered deader than any other kind of nail. Or any other inanimate object, for that matter.) I took a deep, apple-scented breath, and celebrated by grabbing another Red Delicious from the nearest pallet and biting into it.

Beside me, I heard Karl's teeth crunching into an apple of his own. "How long?" he said after a moment to chew and swallow.

"A couple of hours to the coast road," I said. "Another hour north along it to the processing facility."

"Will the truck stop before it reaches the processing facility?"

"How should I know?"

"Let me rephrase that," he said. "We *need* the truck to stop before that, as soon as we have reached the coast, in fact. We will need a boat, and it should be easier to obtain one unobtrusively in a small town than a city."

I sighed. "Yay. A boat. That's worse than a horse."

"You cannot be allergic to boats."

"Of course not," I said. "Seasickness isn't an allergy."

Karl sighed in turn.

"Also," I said, "I don' know nothin' 'bout berthin' no boats."

The joke, proud though I was of it, was of course wasted on Karl. "We don't want to berth it," he said. I couldn't see him, but I knew he was frowning at me again. "We want to sail it away from its berth."

"Well," I said, "as I told you once before, I don't know nothin' 'bout sailin' one, neither."

"And as I told you," he said, "I do." He paused. "Provided, of course, it is an actual sailboat. I am less experienced with motorized vessels."

Just thinking about setting blindly out to sea in an unfamiliar boat was beginning to make me feel a little seasick already. "Just how far do you think we'll have to sail to find this . . . weak spot between the worlds?"

"I still cannot tell," Karl said.

"That's the Pacific Ocean over there to the west. You do realize it goes on a very, very long way."

"I am aware of that."

"Could this Portal-making place be as far away as Japan, or China?"

"Yes."

"So, you're proposing that, if necessary, we will sail across the Pacific Ocean in a small stolen sailboat."

"It would make us difficult to trace," he pointed out.

"It would make us dead," I pointedly pointed back.

"I have sailed the Pacific, or versions of it, on other worlds. On one watery world, I sailed an ocean that makes the Pacific look like a duck pond. In any event, we have no choice."

"Better steal some Dramamine along with the boat," I muttered.

For the next several minutes we rode in silence, the pallets of apples swaying and creaking in the darkness around us. Then Karl said, "You said the truck will turn north when it reaches the road along the coast, to head toward the processing plant?"

"Yes."

"We should feel it, when that happens. That is when we'll want the driver to stop."

"Sure," I said. I knew he was right. We had to stop the truck, and that meant I would have to Shape the driver. And for once, Karl didn't even say anything about unintended consequences.

He should have.

Almost exactly two hours after we started to roll, the truck slowed—but it didn't stop. It swung sharply right—north—and then accelerated.

I thrust my thoughts at the driver, pushing hard, harder than I should have had to, I thought again. *Stop. The truck needs to stop. You need to stop.*

I guess I thought he would pull over, in a rest stop, maybe, or at least on a wide part of the shoulder. But once again, my Shaping went awry.

He stopped, all right. Suddenly, by slamming on the brakes. Tires squealed. Pallets of apples overbalanced, pelting us with fruit. The trailer fishtailed violently. It tilted, teetered . . .

. . . and fell over.

# EIGHTEEN

**HAVING ALREADY MET** the President once, the Adversary no longer had to wait to see her. He walked into the Oval Office, and she rose to greet him. "All federal law enforcement agencies, and the armed forces, are on high alert, Mr. Gegner," she said. "What else can I do?"

"I need to start talking to other world leaders," the Adversary said. "Can you arrange that?"

"Of course, Mr. Gegner," the President said. "I'm the President of the United States. Which ones do you need to talk to?"

"All of them, eventually," the Adversary said. "But let's start with the major ones and work our way down."

The President nodded. "Very well. Where would you like to make the calls?"

The Adversary looked around the office. For some reason, in Shawna Keys' world the President lived in pale-green mansion called the Emerald Palace, rather than a White House, but the Oval Office looked much the same as it had in pictures of it he had seen in the First World. "This will do nicely. If you don't mind."

She didn't, of course.

Two hours later, the Adversary said, "Thank you, Prime Minister," to the Canadian leader, and hung up the phone. There were still many world leaders to Shape, and of course different leaders had different measures of effective control over their countries—

one of the annoying things about this world being so close to First World—but nevertheless each call made it that much more difficult for the Enemy and the Shaper to move around the planet undetected.

Ultimately, of course, all this unruly nationalism, independence, dissent, and diversity of thought and governance would vanish. It would not take long, once the Shaper was dead, and her world was solely his, to make it perfectly ordered, peaceful, and submissive, like both the world he had Shaped and the Shurak home world. But for now, this would have to do.

The trail had gone cold in Oregon. Members of his cadre, monitoring law enforcement efforts, had noted that a private plane had refused instructions to land at a designated airstrip. It seemed likely Yatsar and Keys had been on that plane, but they'd been unable to track them past that point. Yatsar and Keys had been trending generally west, but of course they could have turned north toward Canada (where the Canadian Security Intelligence Service and the Royal Canadian Mounted Police were on high alert, as Prime Minister Sawyer had just assured him). They might have turned south toward Mexico, though that was much farther away. They could have doubled back east. They might be headed for the coast, which was why the Coast Guard was now heavily patrolling the Oregon and Washington shorelines.

Wherever they were, he was slowly tightening the noose, drawing more and more resources into the search for them. It was only a matter of time.

He stretched. The intercom buzzed; he pressed a button.

"Mr. Gegner, the President of Ukraine is on the line," said a disembodied male voice.

"Thank you," he said. He picked up the phone. "Mr. President. Thank you for taking my call . . ."

Karl slammed into me so hard it drove the breath from my lungs, but even as I lay there, gasping for air, the thought crossed my mind that the fact we'd managed to capsize a truck on dry land did not bode well for our upcoming ocean voyage, if we ever reached the water.

Karl groaned and rolled off of me, but I was still half-buried in apples. Light had flooded the trailer: the crash had jolted open the doors. When I could breathe, I struggled through the welter of fruit and broken pallets, dragging my backpack behind me, and a moment later tumbled out into long weedy grass. Sore, and still a little breathless, I struggled to my feet and stared around.

At some point we had crossed the Interstate, but fortunately we hadn't turned onto it. As I had expected, we were in fact on a much narrower, more rural road, the old highway that ran along the coast west of the Interstate. That made sense: fruit from Appleville had been shipped to the Pacific Breeze Fruit Company plant for decades, since long before there was an Interstate . . .

*Since long before this world existed.* I shoved that always-unsettling thought aside.

Good thing: if the driver had slammed on his brakes on the Interstate, he would have caused a multicar pile-up . . .

The driver. I hadn't thought of him until then. While Karl crawled out of the truck behind me, I limped around to the front, hoping I hadn't just killed another man.

I was relieved to see him sitting on the grass at the front of the truck, knees pulled up, massaging the back of his neck. He had his back to me, and I didn't see any point in introducing myself. *Hi, my name's Shawna, and I used to run this world. I just made you crash by making you think you absolutely* had *to stop. No need to thank me.*

No need at all. I hurried back to Karl. "He doesn't know we were on the truck," I said. "And nobody else has come along. If we move fast . . ."

"I am not entirely sure I can," Karl said, but he picked up his pack, and I shouldered mine, and together we limped into the nearby woods. We had just entered the cool shadows of the trees when a helicopter pounded overhead, so low the wash of its rotors showered us with pine needles.

I tensed, expecting the helicopter to land to investigate the toppled truck, but it roared away without slowing or hovering. "Nothing to do with us, maybe?" I said to Karl.

"Maybe," he said, but not as if he believed it.

We'd only gone another hundred yards or so when another aircraft streaked overhead: not a helicopter this time, but a fighter jet. A second followed. Then a third.

We were out of sight of the road, but still far too near for comfort, so we redoubled our efforts to lose ourselves in the woods—which wasn't hard, since we didn't have a clue where we were or where we were going, except, of course, west.

The forest wasn't wilderness; definitely second or even third growth, perhaps reclaiming former farmland. I knew we weren't far from the coast. The old highway was now a designated scenic route, for those more interested in seeing assorted oceanic vistas than getting quickly from A to B. The fact no one had come by in all the time that had passed between the toppling of the trailer and our escaping into the forest was mostly a function of the season: there weren't that many tourists around this late in the fall, and the local residents had seen all they needed to of the sea and sky and forest. When you're local, getting where you want to go as quickly as possible is your definition of a good time on the road.

Once we had climbed almost to the top of the next hill, we discovered we could see the Interstate behind us, over a lower ridge to the east. Though the cars on it were little more than glittering specks, I could clearly make out the lights of police cars, weaving through the traffic. "What's going on?" I said. "Helicopters? Jets? Multiple police cars? Are they all looking for *us*?"

"No way to be certain," Karl said. He turned the other way. "Will we see the ocean once we are over this hill?"

"Probably," I said. Suddenly feeling very exposed, I turned and hurried up to the windswept, rocky, barren hilltop.

Not only did I see the ocean when I reached the crest, I almost fell into it: the other side of the hill ended in an abrupt precipice. Maybe a hundred feet below, the ocean surged.

Karl came up beside me. "The Pacific Ocean," he said, entirely unnecessarily. "A formidable barrier. It is too bad you decided to keep it."

"Sorry. I'll remember for next time."

Karl stared north and south along the coast. "Now we must find a boat."

Even as he said it, one came nosing around the headland to our left: a big one, white, with a prominent bow and a much lower stern, gunwales encircled by a bright-red bumper. Antennae bristled above a glassed-in bridge, and a very large and serious-looking machine gun poked up in the bow. Four men in orange lifejackets stood in the stern behind a metal rail, from which hung a bright red life preserver, above the words painted on the hull: U.S. COAST GUARD.

Two of the men scanned the shore with binoculars; the others stared just as intently. I hastily grabbed Karl's arm and pulled him back over the crest of the hill. "If they're looking for us," I said to Karl, "and it sure looks like they are, then why are they looking for us *here*? The Adversary can't possibly know we got on an apple truck headed for the coast!"

Karl looked troubled. "I think it means the Adversary's claws have sunk far deeper into this world far faster than I hoped."

"You think *all* this activity is related to us?"

He nodded.

"Even the fighter jets? Isn't that overkill?"

"They might just be a side effect of whatever Shaping the Adversary has done to make it likelier we will be caught," Karl said. "Not tasked *specifically* with finding us. Though I am glad we are no longer in the air."

"But how could the Adversary muster that much firepower?" I protested. "He hasn't even been in my world for a week!"

"All he has to do is Shape people," Karl said. "The right people. One after the other. Each leads him to someone with greater authority still. How many such steps would he have to take before he was within Shaping distance of the highest authority of all?"

*Six degrees of separation*, I thought. *But the target isn't Kevin Bacon.* Who totally existed in my world, because I clearly hadn't been *that* stupid. "The President?" I said. "You think he's Shaped the President?"

"You've kept the President? Then yes."

"But why would she even talk to the Adversary?"

"He planted the idea with regional law enforcement officials that you are a terrorist," Karl said. "National security issues get elevated quickly within governments of *any* kind. Does it really seem so impossible that he might have reached the highest levels of your government with his concerns in just a couple of days? Especially when he can Shape everyone along the way to facilitate it?"

"I guess not," I said slowly, my heart sinking. I'd thought once we were well away from my old haunts, we could simply vanish. But now the whole country might be looking for us. *Good thing we're leaving the country, then, isn't it?* I thought. *That's why we're on the coast.*

But . . . fighter jets. Helicopters. Coast Guard boats with radar . . . not to mention machine guns. Trying to escape out to sea might only get us caught quicker.

The rumble of the Coast Guard vessel's engine had died away. I clambered back up to the cliff top and took a look. "All clear," I said. "No ships in sight. At sea, or handily waiting for us to grab them."

"Stealing a vessel may be more fraught with risk than I anticipated," Karl said.

"You think?" I said. "The Coast Guard is going to be checking every small craft they find."

"The key, then, will be to remain undetected."

"Good luck with that," I said. "Ever heard of radar?" Karl being Karl, I wasn't entirely sure he would have, but he nodded.

"Of course. But I do not mean that the boat we are on must remain undetected, I mean that we must remain undetected on the boat."

"Stow away? Like we did on the truck?"

He nodded. "Precisely."

"Which capsized."

"We will endeavor not to repeat that aspect of our previous journey," he said.

I looked out at the ocean. It seemed pacific enough today to live up to its name—not exactly glassy smooth, but not storm-tossed, either. But there was no guarantee that would continue, and while I'd been on a few boats on a few lakes, I'd never been to sea. Yet it seemed, as with so much else that had happened in such an extraordinarily short amount of time, I had no choice. Apparently, the only place Karl could make the Portal that offered my only hope of escape from certain death at the hands of the Adversary lay out across the water somewhere, and so out across the water we would go.

"So where do we look for this boat?" I said. "North or south along the coast?"

"The processing plant is to the north? And presumably a sizable town as well?"

I nodded.

"Then south," Karl said. "We want a very small town or private marina, where we will be far less likely to attract attention. The amount of control the Adversary now has in your world suggests he will also have access to surveillance devices. Those are most likely to be found in population centers, as are law-enforcement forces, of course."

"South," I said. I looked down the slope toward the coastline. "There's a trail of some sort down there," I said, pointing. "A hiking trail, maybe. Looks like it goes the way we want it to."

"I am not surprised," Karl said. "Let's go, then." He set off along the cliff top.

"I didn't Shape it," I said to his back. Which was true as far as I knew. And I didn't feel any strange fatigue or headache to make me think perhaps I had Shaped it unconsciously. On the other hand, if there was one thing I'd begun to realize as these preposterous adventures unfolded, it was that nothing in this world was as real and solid as I had always believed it to be.

We set off in search of a boat.

And hopefully, I thought uneasily, imagining tossing on the blue water stretching out to the horizon, Dramamine.

# NINETEEN

**THE HIKING TRAIL,** whether or not it had been there before we needed it, led us down to the beach. We hadn't gone far along it before we saw a boat.

"How about that one?" I said, pointing out to sea. A giant cruise ship, her bow improbably marked with giant mascaraed eyes and luscious hot-pink lips (*how embarrassing for her,* I thought) was steaming . . . dieseling? . . . steadily north. "Those things have stabilizers. I might not get sick."

"My nautical abilities do not extend to either steering or navigating something the size of an island," Karl said dryly. "Also, were such a ship to go off course, it would attract a great deal of unwanted attention. *Also,* how do you propose we get to it. Swim?"

"You need to learn to tell when I'm joking," I said.

"You were joking?"

"Of course I was joking."

"I was under the impression," Karl said, "that things which are jokes are funny."

"Hey!" I paused. "Wait, was that a joke?"

Karl only smiled slightly in response.

The sun hung low over the ocean, and I had eaten the last of the apples I had stuffed in my backpack the night before (and was almost as sick of apples as trail mix, much as I liked them) when we crested a small hill and at last saw a few boats of more appropriate size: eight, to be specific, bobbing alongside two piers.

The piers stretched out from a dock, which ran alongside a long, low building. The dock seemed to double as a deck, since close to the building, like a troop of mushrooms, sprouted white-and-red umbrellas bearing the familiar logo of Rebellion Ale. No one sat at the tables beneath them, though.

The big parking lot inland of the building had spots for maybe forty cars. Only five were occupied, by the kinds of cars I'd never be able to afford, including a bright-red Peneveloce and a silver Limburger Countessa, which I'd only ever seen in movies: the giant rear wing was unmistakable.

Canvas covered all but one of the berthed boats, an alarmingly small sailing vessel with a single mast. Someone moved in the cockpit, man or woman, I couldn't tell at that distance: he or she disappeared belowdecks almost the moment I noticed him/her.

"That," Karl said, pointing at it, "I can sail."

I looked out to sea, toward the setting sun, now slipping behind a long, low bank of clouds, limning the leading edge bright orange. "In the dark?"

"A boat sails the same in the dark as in the light," Karl said.

"Unless it runs into something," I pointed.

"What is there to run into in the middle of the ocean?"

"Other boats. Buoys. Gulls. Buoys and gulls together. Rocks. I don't know, I'm a landlubber."

"The risk is not great," Karl said. "And darkness is better than light if we wish to remain undetected."

"Doesn't stop radar."

"We are not going to find a better option," Karl said stubbornly.

I sighed, but I couldn't deny it. The hiking trail ran past a wooden staircase leading down into the parking lot; as we approached the top landing, we finally saw a sign: SEABREEZE YACHT CLUB. PRIVATE PROPERTY. NO TRESPASSING.

I blinked at it, then started down the stairs. "If this is really my world," I said, "it's not really trespassing, is it?"

"An intriguing legal question whose answer would be of absolutely no practical use," he said. "I suggest you instead focus on how you are going to Shape the owner of that yacht."

"Um . . . I thought just . . . you know . . . sail out to sea, don't tell anyone we're on board?"

"If we are stopped, the skipper will need to have a reason in mind as to why he is sailing straight out to sea. A destination. Where might a small boat sail from here?"

"How should I know?" I said.

"Exactly. We must figure that out before we approach the boat." We reached the parking lot and set out across it. The encroaching clouds had swallowed the sun, and the breeze that had been blowing all day from the sea had died away to almost nothing. Lights had sprung to life inside the yacht club, shining through the big glass windows, revealing an elegant dining room, but no one sat at any of the white-clothed tables or sipped wine from the glittering glassware. I tried to think what day it was. Tuesday had been the attack on the Human Bean, and that night we'd been in the resort. Wednesday we'd commandeered a helicopter. That night we'd camped. Thursday, we'd been visited by a grizzly, reached the mine, destroyed the Portal, driven off, ridden horses, finally camped. Friday we'd seen Mom. We'd spent last night in the apple truck. Which made this Saturday.

Saturday. So why wasn't anyone using this fancy yacht club's dining room? The club looked like a place that would ordinarily be busy every night . . . the kind of establishment you'd pay big bucks to join, and so would want to get more use out of than just as a place to berth your boat.

I wondered if the strange emptiness had anything to do with all the helicopters and police cars and fighter jets. If the Adversary really had gotten to the President . . . what if the whole country was under martial law?

Or just scared?

And all because of me. It was horrifying—no, infuriating—to think that the world I had thought was *the* world, the only one there was, might soon turn into some kind of authoritarian dystopia, like North Korea had been before reunification ten years ago . . .

My mind stumbled over that thought. Karl said I'd really only been in this world about ten years. The Koreas had unified ten years ago. Peace in the Middle East had followed in short order. The world wasn't a paradise, but it was far better than it had been when I was a kid . . . had I done all that? Had that been part of my Shaping of the world?

*Whoa.*

And then the fury rose up again. The Adversary was going to undo it all, was *already* undoing it. He would abolish freedom, individuality, the rough-and-tumble interaction among individuals that, yes, produced conflict, but also inspired creativity, innovation, and diversity of thought. He would destroy my world and plunge everyone in it into slavery.

I stopped dead in the middle of the parking lot. Karl took two more steps, realized I wasn't following, and turned to face me.

"How can I do this?" I said to him. "How can I just let the Adversary take my world? Why should I? If he can Shape the President, so can I. We could fight back."

Karl opened his mouth, but I rushed on.

"I know you told me he's too experienced, too knowledgeable about Shaping. But I've done a lot of Shaping myself since then. I'm learning fast. And he doesn't expect me to fight back. He'll think I *can't* fight back. Just like you do." A bloodthirsty thought once more reared up in my mind, like a movie monster rising from the grave. "If I could take him by surprise, kill him . . ."

"If you could do that—I do not believe such an attempt could possibly succeed, but assuming it did—this world would remain yours, yes," Karl said. He stepped closer, his eyes locked on mine. "But think what that would really mean. He has Shaped the President, it seems clear. That means he has had access to other world leaders. Perhaps you could reach some of them, turn them back to your side. But not fast enough to prevent open conflict. War would be inevitable. Millions might die, and the world be devastated."

"I'd Shape it. I'd fix it."

"You already know your power is not unlimited. You would have to husband it, let it regenerate . . . if it can: many Shapers, if they completely deplete their power, never regain it to the same degree. It would take a very long time to repair the damage—and even then, the millions who died would still be dead, just as your friend Aesha is still dead.

"And that is the *best*-case scenario—if, somehow, you managed to kill the Adversary. But if you failed . . . and you would . . . then you would be dead, and not only would your world be his, but potentially every remaining world in the Labyrinth, because although I will continue my quest, there is no guarantee that I will find anyone more capable than you, or even *as* capable as you, of capturing the *hokhmah* of all the worlds for Ygrair. I understand your anger and your desire to fight for your creation. But it is misplaced and ultimately selfish."

My nails were digging into the palms of my clenched fists, my body shaking. I wanted to Shape *him*, right then, into something small and slimy that I could crush underfoot. But he was immune to my power, and remained unchanged, and my own anger and desire for revenge and destruction shocked me.

I forced myself to step back from the precipice of my rage and try to think dispassionately. And dispassionately . . . he was right. God help me, he was right. If I tried to fight the Adversary, the world . . . my world . . . and its people would suffer. Including my friends . . . Brent, Policeman Phil, so many others. Whereas if I fled, followed Karl out of the world . . . well, their new lives would not be their old lives, but they wouldn't remember their old lives, would they? At least they'd *be* alive.

They wouldn't remember me, either, I suspected; the Adversary would surely blot all traces of me from the world, just as I had blotted all traces of me from my mother's memory, and all connections linking me to her, erasing myself from her life. They would not know that there could be, that there *had* been, a better world.

Unless, some day, I returned.

I swore there and then, silently, that once I became strong enough and knowledgeable enough, I *would* return to this world, *my* world, and make right everything the Adversary was making wrong. It might not be an oath I could fulfill. But I would keep it close to my heart through whatever might still be to come.

I took a deep breath. I unclenched my fists. "Fine," I growled. "Then let's find a fucking chart and steal this fucking boat and get the hell out of this fucking world."

Karl gave me a narrow look. "That is an unusual amount of profanity, for you."

"I'm feeling unusually fucking profane." I brushed past him.

He followed me across the parking lot and up the steps of the yacht club. Neither of us was dressed well enough to even pretend to belong to such an establishment, but no one seemed to notice we had entered. I heard the muffled sound of a television in some back room, the kitchen, maybe. I wondered if everyone were glued to the news, trying to make sense of whatever lies the Adversary was using to begin the process of overwriting their reality.

I looked around. We were in a lobby of sorts, dark wood, green carpet. Ahead of us were open doors leading into the brightly lit, but empty, dining room. A corridor went left; another went right. "Where would we find a chart?"

Karl stepped over to the wall on our right, where, between two photos of racing yachts at full sail, a framed map of the building hung. He pointed to it. "How about the Chart Room?"

I looked: sure enough, there was a room down the corridor to our right, at the north end of the building, labeled "Chart Room."

"It's a long shot, but okay," I said.

We found the Chart Room exactly where advertised, four doors down on the right, just before the door at the end of the corridor labeled, "Emergency Exit Only: Alarm Will Sound." Inside the Chart Room we found a dark wood table surrounded by chairs, shelves on two walls laden with books, a big window looking out over the marina, a door next to it opening onto the deck (this one without any warnings about sounding alarms), and, on the fourth wall, a giant flat-screen monitor, a wireless keyboard waiting in a niche just below it. Below the shelves of books, wide, flat, narrow slots held (I guessed) charts. "Now what?" I said.

"The destination you will implant in our yacht skipper's mind needs to be a reasonable distance away, something he . . ."

". . . or she," I noted.

"Or she," Karl granted, "could reach in a day or two." He bent over to scan the embossed labels beneath each of the chart slots. "Ah." He pulled out a stack of paper from the second from the top. I leaned over to see the label: ONE- TO TWO-DAY TRIPS.

Karl spread the charts, four in all, across the table's shining brown wood. They didn't look anything like the road maps I was used to: although the land portion wasn't too dissimilar, the water part was white, not blue, and covered with dotted lines and small numbers. "Depths?" I guessed.

Karl nodded. He pointed to a blob of land about . . . I glanced at the scale . . . a hundred nautical miles off the coast. "We need a closer look at this." He bent over it. "'Dead Seal Island.'"

"Lovely name." I looked at the ranks of books on the shelf, and didn't know where to start; then I remembered the monitor and the keyboard. A remote control rested beside the keyboard. I turned on the monitor, and as I'd hoped, it lit not with, say, the Bargain Channel, but the familiar Goggle search engine screen. I pulled the keyboard from the niche, swung one of the chairs around to face the monitor, sat down, typed in, "Dead Seal Island," and clicked SEARCH.

It turned out there were two islands by that unappetizing name: a bunch of rocks somewhere off of Antarctica, and the one we were interested in, which didn't look much more promising. "Nobody lives there," I said to Karl, "but it does have an unimproved camp- ground, an old lighthouse—automated, these days—and a place to tie up boats."

"That sounds ideal," Karl said. "That is where you will tell the skipper he . . . or she . . . is going."

"Dead Seal Island," I said. I looked at the barren bit of land in the photo on the screen. "You don't suppose that's the spot where you can create the Portal?"

Karl didn't bother looking at the photo: he stared at the chart. "No," he said at last. "It is not in quite the right direction, and far too close. No, we will be going farther afield than that, I fear."

"I wish it *was* a field," I muttered. "Instead of the fricking Pacific Ocean." I stood up and shoved the keyboard back into its place. "All right, then. Let's—"

"Who are you?" said a voice from the doorway. "And what are you doing in the Chart Room?"

It's amazing how an unexpected voice can set your heart racing. Not to mention trying to jump up your throat to flop wetly around on top of the chart table. I gulped to push it back into its place, and turned toward the hallway.

The owner of the voice proved to be a pimply faced youth in an ill-fitting waiter's uniform (white shirt, black vest, bow tie, black pants), who looked like he *might* graduate from high school in a year or two if he were lucky: not exactly a threatening presence, but I still felt like I'd been caught doing something illegal, immoral, or both.

"We are meeting our friend out on the slip," Karl said smoothly, "and were asked to check some depth soundings on the charts."

"You can't take them out of the room, you know," the boy said severely. "If you need a chart you have to ask for a copy in advance, and it gets charged to your membership account. Or Julia's account, I guess." He scratched behind his ear. "She's a friend of yours?"

*Ha!* I thought. *The yacht skipper* is *a she.* "From college," I said, and then realized that for all I knew Julia was seventy years old, but the kid either figured everyone older than twenty was equally ancient, or I'd lucked out on our relative ages, because he didn't even blink.

"You know your way out to her boat?"

"Of course," Karl said.

"Okay, then," he said. "Be sure to put the chart back in its drawer before you go." He went back into the hallway, closing the door behind him.

"Didn't even have to Shape him," I said.

"Not the curious type," Karl said. "Fortunately." He nodded at the door onto the deck. "Perhaps we should go join our 'friend.'"

I took a deep breath. "Right." Feeling guilty, because, after all, we'd just been told we couldn't do it, I rolled up the chart showing Dead Seal Island, then pushed open the door.

We stepped out onto the planking. It had grown quite dark

while we were in the clubhouse, and a cool wind now blew from the land out to sea. "A good wind for sailing," Karl said.

"If you say so."

Pole lights illuminated the piers every few yards. Of the eight docked boats, only Julia's yacht showed lights: one at the mast, a green one on the side facing us, and a cozy glow through the portholes. "Her running lights are lit," Karl said. "That means she is close to sailing. We must hurry."

Even as he said it, I heard the putt-putt-putt of an inboard engine starting up. Julia (presumably) emerged from the cockpit and stepped onto the pier. Silhouetted against the light at pier's end, she bent over to lift a loop of rope from the short, thick wooden post to which the yacht's stern was tethered . . . a bollard, my mind supplied, again from my childhood reading.

Karl broke into a trot, and I followed a second later. The sound of our footsteps on the planks of the pier made Julia look up from the second bollard to which the boat was tied, at the bow. "Who's there?" she called, voice tense.

Karl slowed. "Sorry to alarm you," he said. "We're friends of yours."

"What? I'm not expecting anybody. Who are you?" She stepped closer, peering through the darkness. "I've never seen you before in my life!"

Karl shot me a look, and I nodded. I closed my eyes. I Shaped. *Friends . . . night sail to Dead Seal Island . . .* It was harder than it should have been; again, I felt a strange resistance I had to push my way through.

But it worked. "Glad you could make it!" Julia said, her voice now infused with delight. "I was getting worried."

"Held up by traffic," I said. "A truck had turned over on the highway."

Karl gave me another look, of mild disapproval, this time, but I didn't care, because, once I'd overcome the resistance, I'd felt a rush of . . . "pleasure," was the only word that seemed to fit . . . as I once again used the power I hadn't known I'd had until a few days ago.

*Whoa*, I thought. *That's new. I like it.*

And then I thought, *That could be dangerous.* But that second thought seemed unimportant. "Hi, Julia," I said.

Now that we were standing right in front of her, I could finally make out her features. A short, wiry black woman with short curly hair, Julia wore blue jeans, sneakers, and a white windbreaker beneath a bright-orange lifejacket. She grinned at me. "Hi . . ." she began. Then she faltered. A look of confusion flitted across her face.

"Shawna," I said, with just a *soupçon* of Shaping thrown in. "And Karl." *You've always known that.*

She blinked, then laughed. "Good grief, couldn't think of your name for a second. Weird, since we've known each other forever." She turned her smile on Karl. "I'd never forget you, of course."

"Of course," Karl said. "Nor I you."

"Well," Julia said, indicating the bollard, "as you can see, I'm all set to pull away. Clamber aboard! Lifejackets in the locker under the stairs. You can put your stuff in the forward cabin. I like the aft berth so I'm handy for the cockpit. Not that I'll be sleeping while we sail out to Dead Seal Island."

"And you're okay with that?"

She shrugged. "I like sailing at night. And I like sailing solo. And *Amazon* is a sweet vessel."

"*Amazon*?" I looked at her, eyes wide in sudden delight. "From the Arthur Ransome books?" The very books from which my knowledge of things like port and starboard and bow and stern and bollards had been obtained!

Her grin grew even wider. "I forgot you loved those, too!"

"Why not *Swallow*?"

"Nancy Blackett, of course," Julia said. "Shiver my timbers, you galloping galoot!"

I laughed—but an instant later the laugh died on my lips, and all the joy I'd felt from Shaping drained from me like beer from the bunghole of an upside-down barrel. *We could have been friends for real. But I forced her to be my friend. She's not really a friend at all.*

*Or is she? It's real for her, isn't it? She'll never know it* wasn't *real, unless I Shape her again.*

I felt a little sick. All this manipulating of people. It had already led to deaths, and even something like this . . . wasn't it wrong?

Sunday School lessons floated up in my memory again. God gave people free will. I used to wonder why, considering what abysmal use they made of it, in biblical times as in the present. But now I thought I understood. *He wouldn't have been able to live with Himself if He hadn't.*

Karl looked from one to the other of us as though we'd lost our minds . . . and *Swallows and Amazons* was a cultural reference from almost a century ago, although admittedly a somewhat obscure one.

I tossed my backpack onto the boat, then followed it aboard. The yacht shifted under my feet, a little preview of things to come. And we hadn't found a source of Dramamine.

I climbed down into the . . . let's call it "snug," instead of "claustrophobic," shall we? . . . interior. To port, an open door revealed a tiny cabin, almost completely filled by a narrow bunk. To starboard was a closed door, next to a tiny table, lit from above, on which was spread a chart. I glanced at it. It showed the coastline to our south. I pulled the chart we'd taken from the yacht club from my backpack, unrolled, and placed it over the one on the table, pinning its curling edges in place with a couple of anchor-shaped lead paperweights. Then I moved forward, past a sink and a tiny toilet . . . no, on a boat, it was called the head, wasn't it? (although that hadn't been in Arthur Ransome's books, where no one ever went to the bathroom) . . . and through a small central mid-ship space, with padded benches along each wall, to the forward cabin. Like the stern cabin, it was mostly bed, though in this case, a double one.

Which Karl and I were supposed to share.

Oops. Just what had I Shaped Julia into believing about us? I remembered something Karl had said about any particular individual's mind shaping its existing reality around the new, hard, immutable "facts" my Shaping introduced into his or her world. *Like an oyster forming a pearl around piece of grit*, I thought. This particular pearl appeared to have made Karl and me a couple.

Well, it wasn't worth arguing about. I wasn't some Victorian maiden whose reputation would be ruined if word got around I had slept in the same bed with a man who wasn't my husband. Anyway, we'd already shared a tent. It wasn't like we were going to do anything except sleep.

Don't get me wrong: Karl was not unhandsome, but there was absolutely zero sexual attraction between us that *I* could detect. And if he felt anything like that toward me, he hid it so well that even if it existed, it might as well not have.

*For something that doesn't matter, you're thinking an awful lot about it*, that annoying second- or third-thoughts part of my brain murmured.

*Shut up*, I told it, and tossed my backpack on the bed.

I turned around to find Karl right behind me, and Julia, back by the cockpit steps, looking at the chart I had placed on the table just seconds before. *Whew*, I thought. "Sorry," I said out loud to Karl, and stepped to one side.

"For what?" he said. He tossed his backpack onto the bed next to mine, and if *he* had any second, or even first, thoughts about the sleeping arrangements, he kept them to himself. He turned and led the way aft, as Julia, her navigational questions apparently answered, climbed back up into the cockpit. Karl found the promised locker under the cockpit steps and pulled out a bright-orange lifejacket for each of us. I noticed they each had a waterproof flashlight attached by a carabiner on the right side, and a multi-tool on the left, which worried me a little: why would we need *those*?

As I struggled with the buckles, I heard a whirring, splashing noise from the bow, and the boat shifted beneath us. I glanced up at Julia, though all I could see were her feet and the bottom half of her legs.

"It is perhaps just as well that we did not steal this vessel," Karl said, glancing in the direction of the sound. "The boats I have sailed have been considerably less technologically advanced. I believe she just used some kind of automated mechanism to push the bow of the *Amazon* away from the pier. A water jet, I would surmise. I would not know how to operate such a thing."

"Then how do you even know that's what it is?" I said.

"I have been in many worlds," Karl said. "I have seen many technological wonders. That does not mean I have learned how to use them."

I filed that away in my why-is-Karl-so-weird mental folder, just as the engine noise changed. We were definitely moving now, the sway of the boat slight but unmistakable. Lifejacket finally snugly secured, I stuck my head up through the cockpit hatch. Julia smiled down at me from the wheel. "On our way," she said.

I climbed out. The cockpit had benches on three sides: I sat in the starboard one, and looked astern at the pier, slipping away behind us into the night, devolving into nothing but anonymous lights. Above us, stars blazed, but I remembered the clouds that had been rising in the west. No lingering light remained there, but peering forward, past the swaying mast and over the bobbing bow,

I realized I could still make out those clouds in the starlight, as a silvery edge with nothing but darkness beneath it, now covering about a third of the sky.

Then, beneath the silver lining of that rising cloud, lightning flickered.

*Uh-oh.* "Is that a storm?" I did my best to keep my voice in its accustomed range.

"Forecast was for some light thundershowers," Julia said. "Shouldn't trouble us."

"Won't it get . . . choppy?"

"Might," she said cheerfully. "That's when it's fun."

I was beginning to doubt that un-Shaped Julia and I could ever have been friends, *Swallows and Amazons* notwithstanding. We clearly weren't cut from the same cloth, sailing-wise. "Remember what Mrs. Walker told the kids when they were allowed to camp on Wild Cat Island?" I said. "No night sailing? Think she had a point?"

"Absolutely," Julia said. "But I'm not twelve years old, and *my* mother gave me permission."

I smiled, a little weakly, and then grabbed the edge . . . the coaming . . . of the cockpit as the boat lurched a little more.

"Almost out of the cove," Julia said. "Not enough wind to sail. We'll keep putt-putting along with," she flashed me another grin, "'the little donkey' for the time being. Even without Roger to keep it oiled."

I nodded and smiled at the additional Ransome references. But I didn't let go of the coaming.

Karl came out of the cabin and settled in on the port bench. Completely relaxed, he leaned back and looked up at the mast. "I could help you make sail when the time comes."

"No need," Julia said. She pointed to a row of buttons on a pedestal to her left, each covered by a hinged, plastic guard. "All I have to do is push a button and the mainsail hoists itself. Another button for the jib. The others control the mainsheet. I can even reef if I have to, without ever leaving the wheel."

Karl looked almost . . . offended. "You might as well have a powerboat."

"*Amazon is* a powerboat at the moment," Julia pointed out. "No wind." But then she grinned. "I don't *have* to use the hydraulics. Sometimes I deal with the sails myself. But at night or in bad weather, I'm glad to have them. I'm out here to have fun, not to prove how tough I am."

"Fun," I said. I swallowed. We'd apparently entered the open ocean. The swell had increased, and my stomach was already rebelling.

Julia glanced at me, looking slightly confused; then her expression cleared. "Oh, right, you get a little seasick, don't you? Don't know why I didn't remember that. Dramamine in the first aid kit in the locker under the sink. And then you might be happier lying down. Nothing much to see at sea at night anyway, and we won't raise Dead Seal Island until sometime tomorrow morning."

I swallowed again, and decided she was right. "Thanks," I muttered, and ducked into the cabin. I found the first aid kit where she'd promised it would be, found the blessed Dramamine, took two, and then made my way to the bed in the bow, turning off the light in the little dining area as I went, and then the one over the bed itself, so that I lay in semidarkness, the only illumination coming from over the sink. My nausea faded quickly, whether from being horizontal or from the drug I couldn't tell. Exhaustion flooded in to take its place. It had been a long day, and I'd Shaped Julia not that long ago. That Shaping had, unusually, felt pleasurable . . . but it had still taken energy to push through that troubling new sense of resistance.

I hadn't taken off my lifejacket—and wasn't about to—but despite its bulk around my body, my eyes closed and I half-dozed.

I came alert again as our engine stopped. Things whirred and thudded on the deck above my head. The boat heeled to starboard. I heard water rushing along the hull, close to my head. The swaying of the boat no longer bothered me. In fact, it seemed pleasant, rocking me to . . . to . . .

I snapped instantly awake from a deep sleep, without a clue as to how much time had passed. A new sound, deep and throbbing, vibrated the hull. Then bright light flashed through the porthole over my head, and a man's amplified voice boomed, "Sailing vessel *Amazon*! This is Coast Guard Vessel RB-M 45602. Maintain your course and speed. We're coming aboard."

I jerked upright, to see Karl at the door to the cabin. "We're in trouble," he said. "How did you Shape Julia?"

My brain was fuzzed from interrupted sleep and the Dramamine, and for a second his question made no sense. "What?"

"How did you Shape Julia?" he said again, more urgently. "Will she let them board?"

"I . . . I didn't . . . I never thought about it," I stammered. "I just wanted her to accept us and sail us out to island. But even if I had . . . how can she stop the freaking *Coast Guard*? They've got guns. If they want to board, they'll board." I took a deep breath, trying to calm my racing heart. it didn't work.

"Hey, you two!" Julia called. All I could see of her from the front cabin was her feet. "We're going to have visitors. Make yourselves decent."

The bright light returned, shining through the portholes, casting sharp-edged circles of light on the starboard side of the cabin. Karl took a quick look through the nearest porthole, then ducked down again. "I believe it is the vessel we saw nosing along the coast.

It is hard to see much with the spotlight shining on us, but it appears they are preparing to launch a smaller boat, no doubt to come alongside." He looked at me. "You must stop them."

"How?" I said. "That boat we saw had a freaking machine gun in the bow, remember? And you can bet those men coming over here are armed, too."

"Shape them."

"To do *what*? Just not notice we're here? Will that work?"

Karl frowned. "No," he said. "You cannot make us invisible. Not reliably." He took another look. "Two men getting in the boat. How many crew on a vessel that size?"

"I don't know anything about Coast Guard boats," I said.

"They cannot be allowed to find us," Karl said.

"Why not?" I said, inspiration striking. "Why not let them take us aboard their boat? I could Shape the crew once we're over there. It'd be like the helicopter and the SUV. We'd be using one of the vehicles sent out to capture us. Perfect disguise."

But Karl shook his head. "Too dangerous now," he said. "The Adversary has had much more time to work. Law enforcement and the military may well have orders to shoot you on sight. At the least, they will have been ordered to incapacitate you. The Adversary knows you can Shape others just as he can. He will have made provisions for that ability to be taken from you in some fashion."

"Then what?" I said, beginning to feel desperate. *End of the line. All of our effort for nothing . . .*

"Shape something else," Karl said. "We need to lose them."

Lose them. At sea . . .

The *Swallows and Amazons* books came back to me, boats in fog, trying to find each other . . .

Karl was at the porthole. "They're casting off."

*Fog.*

I closed my eyes, reached out to the sea all around us, imagined . . . *believed* . . . it was not a clear night, that there was a thick, thick fog, too thick for the Coast Guard boat to find us . . . especially since their radar didn't work . . .

The Shaping didn't come easy. In fact, it felt like trying to lift an enormous weight. I could feel a strange tearing sensation in my mind, not pain, exactly, but disquieting, disturbing. But I didn't stop.

*Fog. Miles of it. Covering the ocean. Hiding us. Faulty radar.*

"What the hell?" The shout came from Julia.

I opened my eyes. All I could see of the world outside was a little bit of the cockpit, where Julia stood at the wheel, but even that was enough to show me that thick fog shrouded the boat. The bright light of the spotlight had become a diffuse glow.

"Sailing vessel *Amazon*!" the Coast Guard vessel boomed. "Heave to!"

I closed my eyes again, reached out to Julia. *We have to get out of here.* I pushed the idea into her head. It wasn't pleasurable this time. It felt like trying to push a car uphill, singlehandedly. It hurt. *We can't let the Coast Guard catch us. We have to get out of here.*

Over our heads, a creaking sound. The boat had been heeling to port, now she heeled to starboard. There was a jerk. "Changing course," Karl said. "Leaving the Coast Guard behind."

I scrambled off the bed and headed aft. Julia looked down at me, face pale in the fog. "Close call," she said. "They almost caught us." She glanced astern. Light flashed there, diffused by the fog. Confusion flitted across her face again as she turned to face me once more. "Wait. I'm running from the Coast Guard. Why am I running from the Coast Guard? That's crazy. And useless. They have radar."

"Their radar doesn't work," I said. *I hope.* I climbed into the cockpit beside her. "And you didn't have any choice. Remember?"

Her expression cleared. "You're right," she said. "We've got to get you two to Dead Seal Island." She laughed. "I always enjoyed spy novels, but I never thought I'd be caught in one. I'm glad you trusted me."

I wondered what story her mind had crafted to explain all this. I didn't ask. Instead, I settled myself on the starboard bench once more. Karl climbed up and sat on the port one.

We sailed on. Five minutes. Ten. Fifteen. The motion of the boat increased, each swell bigger than the last. My nausea remained under control, though. I actually started to relax a little.

But only for a moment. The fog suddenly lit with bright white light again, but this time it didn't come from the Coast Guard, but from the sky, and the crack of thunder followed hard on its heels.

Thirty seconds later, the waves hit.

## TWENTY

**THE ADVERSARY SAT** alone in his private Situation Room in the
Emerald Palace. Unlike the President's Situation Room, there were
no giant video screens, no ranks of people at laptops, no crackling
radio transmissions, and no advisors. Just him, in a chair, at a desk,
with a phone, waiting.

He had the security apparatus of almost the entire world at his
disposal now, searching diligently for Shawna and Yatsar. He had
only to wait. Their discovery was inevitable. Any force amenable to
such orders had been ordered by its commanders to shoot Shawna
on sight. Those whose codes of conduct or terms of engagement
prevented such orders (and whose commanders were in some fashion constrained from changing those codes and terms) had strict
orders to incapacitate her: render her unconscious, in whatever
fashion they could, before she could act against them.

Karl Yatsar was not included in the shoot-to-kill orders. He was
to be captured alive.

And then, as he sat there, the world . . . shifted. He felt it. A
Shaping, and on a scale greater than any Shawna had attempted
since that in extremis time-skip in the coffee shop: greater even
than the snowfall that had hidden her and Yatsar's tracks in the
mountains.

He waited impatiently for the news he knew would come.
Twenty minutes later the phone finally rang. He pressed the
speaker button. "Yes?"

"We have an anomaly, Mr. Gegner," a woman's voice said. "In line with what you told us to watch for."

"Tell me."

"A Coast Guard boat was about to send a boarding party to a small sailing yacht off the coast of Oregon when the weather . . . changed," the woman said.

"Changed how?"

"A thick fog came up out of nowhere," she said. "So thick, and so sudden, they instantly lost sight of the yacht. Their radar malfunctioned at the same time."

"How long ago did this happen?" the Adversary asked, though he was certain he already knew.

"Twenty minutes," said the woman, confirming his supposition.

"Are there other vessels with radar in the vicinity?"

"Yes, sir. But they are also unable to track the sailing yacht at the moment."

The Adversary frowned. "Why?"

"They are currently fighting to stay afloat in a Force 10 gale," the woman said. "Wave heights are such that radar is useless."

"I take it this storm is also . . . anomalous?"

"Extremely so, sir. The storm followed the fog within minutes. Meteorology predicted neither. A line of squalls was moving through the area, but that was all. Satellites now show what looks like a typhoon. Meteorology says it can't possibly be there."

"I see," said the Adversary, his frustration mingled with admiration: frustration because Shawna and Yatsar had to have been aboard that sailing yacht, but had now slipped out of his reach again; admiration because Shaping on that scale, of the ocean itself, was impressive, especially after all the Shaping she had already done in her attempts to evade him, and with him now sharing her *hokhmah*. It was no wonder Yatsar had decided she might be the one who could fulfill his quixotic quest . . .

Yatsar. If the boat went down, and Yatsar with it . . . this might be the last world he would ever enter. With the Portal back to the Shakespearean world and his own closed, and lacking Yatsar's nanomites, he would find himself once more trapped, unable to continue his own quest to find and eliminate Ygrair.

"If we have any vessels strong enough to risk those seas, get them out there," he said into the phone. "Planes, too. I want that yacht found, but *do not board it*. Track it. I want to know where it makes landfall. And I want a team prepared to move in the moment it does."

"Yes, sir," the woman said. "We'll do our best."

"Do that."

The Adversary pressed the button to end the call, and then stared at the map that graced one wall of the room. This world, like the original, was mostly water. If Shawna and Yatsar had risked a small boat in that vast expanse of blue to the west of North America, the location for the next Portal had to be out there somewhere. Capturing Shawna and Yatsar at this point would be counterproductive. The best course of action was to let Yatsar think he was safe, so he would open the next Portal—and then move in and capture him, and kill Shawna, before he could pass through it.

If the storm Shawna had somehow Shaped ended up killing both her and Yatsar, the irony would be . . . painful.

I had never imagined anything like the towering wall of water that appeared out of nowhere, invisible until the terrifying moment it raced out of the fog into the feeble illumination of our running lights. *Amazon* rode it up and up, as though climbing a mountain; teetered at the top; and then went racing down the other side, a heart-stopping descent into a watery canyon. At the bottom, *Amazon's*

bow plunged into a new wall of water rising after the first, and water and spray raced backward over the deck and crashed into us, leaving me soaked and spluttering, but at least not seasick—apparently, complete and total terror was a cure for me.

Frankly, I preferred nausea.

Julia looked as terrified as I felt, which was saying something. She punched buttons, and the sail began shrinking, to a quarter of its former self. I found out why as we reached the top of the next wave, and the wind hit us, a blast of air that felt as solid as the water had, and just about as wet, since it carried spray ripped from the surface. Bizarrely, the fog remained, though it swirled over the boat in tatters that slithered snakelike through the illumination of our lights. Lightning flashed, lighting the fog and the few yards of water we could see a ghastly camera-flash blue.

Under shortened canvas, we raced down another watery slope, battered the bow into the next wave, labored under the weight of water, rose again. Water poured around my feet, and looking down from the cockpit, I saw the floor of the cabin awash, stray objects floating in the foam. Julia pointed at the hatch. "Close that!" she cried. She pushed another button, and I heard the sound of pumps starting, before their rhythmic thump was lost in the shriek of the wind as we rose again to the crest of a wave.

I dropped to my knees in the water in the floor of the cockpit, and reached for the hatch. Karl knelt beside me. "Don't start thinking we're sinking," he yelled urgently to me above the roar of the storm. "Concentrate on us not sinking! This boat cannot sink. Think it. Shape it. Make it true!"

"Did I do this?" I cried, finally getting a handle on the handle and hauling the hatch down: it was a complicated folding assembly but it slipped into place without difficulty, just before another dollop of water crashed over our heads and into the cockpit, where it ran out through openings I hadn't noticed until then, kneeling next to them.

"Shaping the fog," Karl shouted. "Unintended consequences. Enormous transfer of energy. Transformed that line of thunderstorms into . . ."

Into what, I didn't hear, but then, I hardly needed to: the wind shrieking through the rigging as we crested another wave both drowned him out and finished—and put an exclamation point—on his sentence.

*Metaphorically* drowned him out. A literal drowning might still follow.

I crawled back to my place, held on, and set myself to believing, as fiercely as I could, that we weren't going to sink, that *Amazon* could weather any storm . . .

A wave slammed over the coaming, hurled me sprawling to the bottom of the cockpit, water swirling around me. Julia shouted something. I couldn't hear her, but Karl nodded and knelt beside me, opening a locker under the seats. "Tethers!" he yelled into my ear. "One end to the lifejacket, one end to the jackline."

"The what?"

He snapped one end of the tether he had handed me to my vest, and another tether to his own, then snapped the far end of his tether to one of the lines I'd previously hardly registered, running along the boat's gunwales from bow to stem. Julia had already tethered herself by the time I managed to get back into my seat and clip mine into place—just in time, as we plunged down the back side of another wave and buried the bow in the next one, the water pouring over us with so much force that, even holding on with all my might, I was almost swept up and out of the cockpit.

If that happened, would the tether hold me to the boat? Would I be able to pull myself aboard?

I resolved not to find out.

"Go below!" Julia shouted at me. "You can't help! Karl knows how to sail—if anything breaks loose forward he'll have to go fix it. You'd be better off in the cabin!"

I thought of locking myself in there, thrown from side to side, unable to see what was happening, water sloshing around my feet, rising—and shook my head violently. "No!" I shouted back. "I'll stay here!" *And concentrate really, really hard on my firm, total, rock-solid belief that* Amazon *will not sink.*

Thinking about *Amazon* sinking conjured images of her sinking, and even thinking about that seemed to my panicked mind to make the boat wallow more heavily and recover more slowly. I closed my eyes. I focused fiercely on images of *Amazon* sailing triumphantly through the storm. I kept my eyes closed. I wouldn't look at the waves . . . *oof!* One crashed into my face like a punch from a cold, wet boxing glove . . . I wouldn't listen to the storm . . . *What was that crashing sound below? . . .* I'd just think, long and hard, about how solid and stable *Amazon* was, how *nothing* could sink her.

I visualized *Amazon* triumphant, the waves subsiding. I visualized us safe from, and undetected by . . . no, *undetectable* by . . . any pursuers, and as I did so, as I focused with all my might on safety and stability . . . something happened.

The storm still raged. The boat still tossed and wallowed and rolled almost onto her beam-ends—but as I dove deeper and deeper into the internal ocean of my mind, the outside ocean faded from my senses.

Karl hung grimly on to the coaming of the cockpit and watched Shawna Keys. Her eyes had closed, but her body had not relaxed into sleep: instead, she sat as tensely as he. She just wasn't . . . present . . . any longer.

Another wave roared across the deck from bow to stern. He ducked his head as it washed over him, then looked at Shawna again. She remained unmoved, apparently unaware of the weather raging around them . . . the weather she had Shaped.

He still could not believe the power she had wielded. Raising a fog, and in the process, however unintended, a typhoon? After all she had Shaped in the past few days? He had never seen another Shaper who retained that much power after Shaping his or her world, or one who seemed able to recover from Shaping as quickly as she. *But there is a limit*, he thought, staring at her. *And whatever she is doing now to keep us safe may be driving her close to it.*

If that were the case, then just when . . . *if* . . . they got to where they were going, and really, *really* needed her Shaping ability . . . she might not have it.

But he dared not stop her. He had sailed in many oceans on many worlds, and this storm, he knew, could kill them at any moment.

He held on, and watched Shawna, and waited to see what would happen.

Some unknowable time later I returned, slowly and uncomfortably, to an awareness of my body, feeling first cold, then cold *and* wet, and finally cold, wet, and aching, every muscle strained or cramping. The vision I had held on to for so long slipped away, but not like a dream, disappearing in an instant: rather, it faded slowly, the colors leaching, the images thinning, becoming translucent, blurred, foggy . . . gone.

Something else slipped away from me, too, something I didn't have a word for. I felt . . . empty, lost, in a way I never had before.

Something that had always been a part of me suddenly wasn't part of me any longer: or maybe something I had been connected to, I suddenly wasn't connected to any longer. I didn't have words for it.

I didn't have words for anything. I opened my eyes, blinked up the swaying mast, felt hands prying my fingers from the coaming. Then everything faded away: not like the images from my vision, but in the old, familiar way of passing out.

Though it was very, very early in the morning in Washington, D.C., the Adversary remained awake in his palatial room in the Emerald Palace, reserved for private guests of the First Family. He sat at an antique desk, looking at a computer monitor showing a satellite image of the storm that still raged off the coast of Oregon, its hurricane winds too much for even a Coast Guard cutter, far too much for helicopters and jets, all of which had been forced back to base. No empirical evidence existed to suggest where *Amazon*, the boat Yatsar and Shawna had commandeered, might be beneath that enormous swirling mass of cloud and rain and wind.

Yet the Adversary knew they were there; and knew, too (much to his relief) that *Amazon* was in no danger. Once more, he had felt a Shaping, even greater than the Shaping that had created the fog (and triggered the storm): an outpouring of energy he might have been able to match in his own world, but could not come close to mustering in this one, which he still, infuriatingly, shared with Shawna Keys.

So powerful was the Shaping that he did not even have to guess what she had done, the thrust of it communicated to him through the *hokhmah* they shared. He knew she had protected *Amazon* from the storm's fury, changing the natural flow of wind and water, cloud and lightning. This Shaping was greater than the conjuring of a fog because it *continued*: he could *still* feel it, hours after he had first detected it.

Powerful indeed. But unless he missed his guess, once this Shaping ended, it would be a very long time before she could match it. Shaping took its toll, and Shawna Keys, he was almost certain, was burning herself out.

If this world were still solely hers, powerful as she was, she might have regained her ability quickly. But this world was no longer just hers. They were sharing its *hokhmah*, and that would interfere with her regaining her strength. It would take her a long time: with luck (his luck), more time than she had, for either he would catch her at last, and she would die, or Yatsar would escape with her through a new Portal. Either way, she would never Shape this world again.

All very encouraging. Less encouraging was the fact she and Yatsar had managed to vanish again. At sea, yes, and presumably somewhere under that swirl of white battering the coast. But where?

And where were they headed? Where was the second Portal to be opened?

All he could do was wait for the storm to clear, so that the forces he had committed to the search could resume their work.

He frowned. Or was it?

If Shawna's ability to Shape this world waned as she exhausted herself, perhaps his would wax. Perhaps it already had. He knew he did not have *full* control, and thus could not change the things he really wanted to change—but could he perhaps move a little bit beyond merely Shaping the minds of people and animals?

He looked around the room for something small, something whose Shaping would not cause unforeseen consequences, and his gaze fell on the pillows on the bed. Filled with a light foam substance, they were firmer than he liked.

He looked at them, then closed his eyes. After five minutes, his eyes flew open again. He put a hand to his right temple, and muttered a curse. Then he got up and punched his fist into one of the pillows.

It remained, stubbornly, foam; and Shawna Keys remained, even more stubbornly, far more powerful than he—and also remained in Yatsar's hands.

The Adversary had never seriously entertained the thought that Yatsar's quest could succeed—until now. He lay down on the bed, rested his head on the disappointingly still-firm pillows, and, for the first time in a long time, lay awake worrying.

## TWENTY-ONE

**I WOKE IN** the bed in the cabin in the bow, pale gray light streaming through the portholes, the boat swaying easily along through waves that, though I couldn't see them, I could tell were mere ripples compared to the mountainous seas of the night before. I stared up at the pale wood of the ceiling for a long moment, then sat up . . . or tried to; my muscles didn't want to obey me.

With an unladylike amount of groaning and grunting, I succeeded on my second attempt, and with an additional effort (and a couple of choice swear words), managed to haul myself fully upright on the third attempt. I walked/staggered to the head, emerged much relieved, and continued my unsteady advance until I reached the steps up into the cockpit. A glance into the aft berth showed a stationary lump under a red blanket. *Karl or Julia?* I wondered, then glimpsed a dark-skinned hand lying limp on the mattress. *Julia.*

That hopefully meant Karl was at the wheel, and not that he had been washed overboard and the boat was lolloping along on autopilot. Which, as high-tech as *Amazon* seemed to be, she probably had.

The companionway hatch remained closed, but after a moment's fumbling I figured out the knack of it and swung it up and back out of my way.

Karl indeed stood at the wheel, pale and haggard beneath a thickly overcast, but non-threatening, sky. Scraggly whiskers had joined his neat mustache over the course of our adventures. *Give him an eye patch, a headscarf, and a green parrot to squawk on his shoulder, and he'd make a fair pirate*, I thought.

So, of course, I greeted him with, "Arrrr, matey."

He blinked blearily. "I beg your pardon?"

I sighed. "Never mind. We survived, I take it."

He nodded. "Thanks to you."

"Me?" I blinked. "I passed out."

"You did," Karl said. "But do you remember what you did before that?"

I frowned at him. "I remember the storm hitting. I remember us putting on the tethers. I remember . . . holding on . . ." My voice trailed away. There was a . . . hole. A gap in my memory. Now that I'd cast my mind back, I could sense it, feel the shape of it, like the hole left by a pulled tooth, but I couldn't seem to fill it, no matter how much I prodded it with my mind's tongue (to carry on the rather disgusting dental metaphor). "I don't remember anything else."

"You Shaped us out of danger," Karl said. "*Most* impressive. Despite the storm raging around us, the rain, the wind, the constant battering by the waves, and the violent motion of the boat, you plunged deep into your mind and held an image of the boat at peace. You were all but catatonic for two hours. And during that time . . . the storm calmed. Not everywhere, just in a bubble around us. Even the clouds opened directly above us, so the stars shone down. I could see the waves, as tall as ever, rushing by not fifty yards away in every direction. But they could not penetrate the bubble of safety you had Shaped for us, a bubble that remained even after you woke from your trance—after which you promptly passed out again. We sailed calmly on and emerged from under the storm just before dawn." He gestured behind him. "It is still raging back there, somewhere. But we, I think, are clear of it."

I stared at him. "I don't remember doing any of that. It's a blank."

"I am not surprised," Karl said. "And I fear . . ." He let his voice trail away. "Well, time enough to test that later. Right now . . . do you think you can take the wheel?"

"What?" I stared at him. "I've never driven . . . steered . . . helmed? . . . a boat in my life. Seasickness, remember . . . ?" My own voice trailed away. I didn't feel the slightest bit seasick, though the boat was swaying far more than when we had first cleared the headlands sheltering the yacht club. Had I really been cured by terror? *Try our terror-cured bacon. It's delicious.*

"Over it, are you?" Karl said, though he probably didn't *intend* to sound like Yoda. "It sometimes happens like that. You have your sea legs, as the saying goes."

"I hope I keep them," I said.

"You might . . . but you might not," Karl said. "Some sailors get sick every time they go to sea."

I sighed. "I hope I'm not one of them." *In fact,* I thought, *I hope this is the last time I ever find myself in a boat on the ocean, on this or any other world, so it never, ever matters.*

"Come around behind the wheel," Karl said. "Fasten your tether first. The seas have lessened, but better safe than sorry."

I nodded, and clipped the end of the tether, still dangling from my lifejacket, to the jack line. Then I eased around to beside Karl. "All right," he said. "Take the wheel."

Gingerly, I did so. *Amazon* suddenly felt like a living thing, in a way she hadn't a moment before. The sails were no longer reefed, and I could feel *Amazon* tugging, eager to obey the pressure of the wind and swing much farther around than she was currently heading.

Atop the upright post supporting the wheel, a compass glimmered beneath a transparent dome. It showed our heading as a bit south of west. Karl pointed to it. "Keep this heading. West by south. That is all you have to do . . . well, that, and awaken me in two hours."

"Are you sure this is a good idea?" I said nervously, staring down at the compass. It kept swinging back and forth around the heading Karl had indicated, never quite settling on it precisely or steadily.

"There is nothing you can hit out here," Karl said. He looked around. "Probably," he amended. "But keep a weather eye out, just the same. If you do see anything, roust me with a shout."

Was it just me, or was he even talking a bit like a pirate? "Aye, aye, sir," I said. Then, "Julia's sound asleep."

"As she should be," Karl said. "She is an excellent seaman . . . woman." He yawned and stretched. "When I wake up, we will see about something to eat." He turned to go below.

"Wait!" I said.

He glanced back, eyebrow raised. "Now what?"

"Where's Dead Seal Island?"

"No doubt we blew past it in the storm. It must be miles astern by now."

"But that's where we were going to leave Julia."

"Yes . . . but circumstances, obviously, have changed. In any event, she is likely to sleep for hours now that the danger has passed." He yawned again. "As I wish I could. But two hours, no more."

I nodded, and he went below at last, leaving me at the wheel of a sailboat out on the Pacific Ocean (perhaps the most unlikely place I could ever have imagined finding myself), alone with my thoughts—and the gaping hole in my memory.

I'd created a "bubble," Karl had said, a bit of stability in the howling storm I'd inadvertently formed by calling up fog to hide us from the Coast Guard. Once again, the unintended consequences of my Shaping of the world had almost killed us.

It suddenly occurred to me, like a blow to the stomach, that it might have really killed others, who had been sailing blithely through a lovely night, expecting nothing worse than a squall or two from the line of thunderstorms we had seen in the distance.

Thinking that, I would have wished I'd never met Karl—if not for two facts: first, if I hadn't, the Adversary would have killed me by now; and second, wishing seemed a really dangerous thing for me to do.

Keeping my eyes on the compass, I tried to call up my Shaping ability, to see if it felt different after the previous night . . .

. . . tried, and failed.

I knew I had done it before, but I couldn't do it now. In fact, I could barely *imagine* doing it. It was as though some other person entirely had done the things I knew I had done: altered minds, erased my mother's memory, conjured a quarry, demolished a Portal, killed a horse, summoned a snowfall, formed a fog (which transformed into a typhoon), and delivered us from drowning.

The hole in my memory wasn't the only hole inside me, I realized. My Shaping ability had vanished.

I had a sudden sinking feeling, not a pleasant thing to have on a boat. I thought about calling Karl, but bit my lip and carried on steering, too far one way, then too far the other, but generally keeping the course he had set, though I didn't know why he had set it. The time slipped away. I saw nothing except water, heard nothing but the rush of it along the boat's hull, miscellaneous creaks and groans, the slapping of a rope against the mast.

My watch still worked, apparently as waterproof as it claimed to be. As the two hours Karl had specified ticked to their end . . . about 10:30 in the morning, unless we'd traveled far enough west to change time zones . . . I leaned down to call into the cabin, only to pull up short as Julia appeared in the shadows at the bottom of the companionway steps. "Where are we?" she said sharply, without so much as a good morning. She climbed up into the cockpit

"I haven't got a clue," I said honestly. "Karl told me to keep sailing . . . um, west by south . . . and wake him in two hours. Which are just about up."

Julia leaned down into the cabin. "Karl!" she shouted. "Get up!" Then she turned back to me. "Give me the wheel," she snapped. "You're yawing all over the place."

Feeling a little miffed, even though I hadn't really wanted to steer in the first place, I surrendered the helm to her. She was, after all, both skipper and owner of *Amazon*.

"What the hell's going on, Shawna?" she said, sounding a little less angry with the wheel in her hands. "First the Coast Guard, then the fog, then the storm . . ."

I didn't answer.

She shook her head, leaned over, and looked at the compass. "I've got a GPS navigation/sonar system on order. Always resisted getting one. Don't know why. Seemed like cheating. Wish I had one now. Then we'd know where we are." She raised her head again. "Don't want to radio, not with the Coast Guard looking for us . . . for you." She blinked. "What the hell, Shawna?" she said again. "After all we've . . ." Confusion drifted across her face. "I mean, I've known you since . . ."

*Uh-oh*, I thought. "Since grade school," I said, trying to put conviction into it, to Shape her as I had before, but she only looked more confused.

"No," she said. "Why would you say that? You didn't go to school with me. Neither did Karl . . ." The confusion grew. "We met . . . last night . . . on the pier . . . that was the first time." Her eyes went wide. "I don't know you at all! Who are you? What did you do to me?"

"Julia . . ." I tried again, but I had nothing, no Shaping ability left. It was as though I'd used myself up completely quieting the storm.

Maybe I had. Maybe I wasn't a Shaper anymore. Hadn't Karl said that happened sometimes?

Maybe if that was the case, the Adversary wouldn't want me dead. I could go back to my old life . . .

Except Aesha was dead.

Except my mother no longer remembered me.

Except the Adversary would reshape the world into a close approximation of how North Korea used to be, if Karl were telling the truth.

As if on cue, he appeared. "Julia," he said.

"Who the hell are you?" she snarled at him. "Why did I let you on my boat? And where have you taken her?"

Karl looked at me. "Shawna?"

I shook my head. "I've . . . lost it," I said. "I can't do anything."

"Lost it?" Julia stared at me. "Lost what? Your mind?" She snorted. "That's what I lost, letting you on, letting you convince me we knew each . . ." Her voice faded away. "But we do. Don't we? I have memories . . . but I have other memories . . . they're different . . ."

"Julia," Karl said. "It's all right. You're just exhausted. Your mind's playing tricks. You should go back to bed."

"No," Julia said, fire returning to her voice. "*Amazon* is mine, and I'll damn well stay at the wheel." She glared at him. "Why are we sailing south by west? Why aren't we heading back to port?"

"Heading back to port would take us through whatever's left of that storm," Karl said. "At the least, we need to recuperate."

"But we're heading farther and farther out to sea."

Karl hesitated. "There's a . . . place . . . I need to get to. This course will get us there."

"When?"

"Eventually."

Julia gave him a scornful look. "Eventually? This course will also take us to *Asia* 'eventually.' But we don't have the provisions or nearly enough fresh water. And another storm could put us under." She shook her head. "We're going back." She started to turn the wheel.

Karl put his hand on it. "No," he said.

I gaped at him. Julia glared at him. "I'm skipper of this boat!"

Karl released the wheel. "So you are," he said. He turned and went back down into the cabin.

"We're heading back to the coast," Julia said. She looked at the compass again, then glanced up at the sails. "We'll have to tack . . ."

"I'm very sorry," Karl said, emerging from the cabin again. He held a pistol in his hand, either the one from the helicopter or one of those belonging to the sheriff's deputies; I couldn't tell. He pointed it at Julia. "Please release the wheel. Shawna, take it."

Julia looked furious. "This is piracy!"

*Arrrr*, I thought irreverently. I should have been shocked . . . but I wasn't. Karl had already shown he'd do whatever he had to do to get us where we needed to get. There were already dead people in our wake. Some were my fault, but some were his.

"Do what he says, Julia," I said. "He's . . . we're . . . serious about this."

"*Dead* serious," Karl said quietly.

"But you're my . . ." Her worldviews must have been colliding in her head with as much force as the storm we'd fled. "I thought . . . no, we've never . . ."

"Julia," Karl said, almost gently now. He kept the pistol aimed at her with his right hand, but held out his left. "Come below."

Her fingers tightened on the wheel for a moment—I saw them turn white—but then the fight went out of her. Whether due to the confusion I'd engendered in her through my Shaping or the exhaustion she had to be feeling after a night's hard sailing, or both, her shoulders slumped, and she let Karl take her hand and lead her into the cabin.

She'd only turned us a little more south; I steered us back onto our previous course and waited for Karl to emerge again, which he did minutes later. "I locked her in her cabin," he said. He'd shoved the pistol into his pocket; the grip was just visible below his life-jacket.

"Would you really have shot her if she hadn't given up the wheel?" I said.

"I have killed many people in many Shaped worlds," Karl said flatly. "Reluctantly, but when necessary. They're not . . ." His voice cut off. After a pause, he said, "I do not enjoy it. And fortunately, it was not necessary this time."

"They're not what?" I said. "Real?"

"I will take the wheel," he said, instead of answering me. "Go below. Get something to eat." He came around the wheel, almost shouldering me out of the way. I let him have the helm, but I didn't go below right away. Instead I sat down in my accustomed spot to starboard. Karl didn't look at me: his eyes were on the horizon. Mist was gathering again beneath the low overcast—whether my doing, left over from my previous Shapings intended to conceal us, or natural, I couldn't tell.

Had that really been what he'd been about to say? *They're not real?* Was that how he saw everyone in the worlds he visited, except for the Shapers?

My blood ran a little cold at that thought. If he considered the citizens of the many Shaped worlds as little more than characters in a video game . . . what atrocities would he be willing to commit, so long as they moved him closer to his ultimate goal?

But I didn't confront him about it then. After all, he hadn't shot Julia out of hand. He had to have *some* compunction about how he treated the people of the worlds he traversed. "What went wrong with her?" I said instead. "With Julia. She'd been completely convinced we were friends and she had to help us . . ."

"Once again, your Shaping of her was incomplete," Karl said. "Again, because you have forgotten your training, no doubt. She is suffering from an internal conflict. Her new reality is at war with her old reality. She will not help us willingly again. She thinks we have fooled her somehow, though she does not understand how we did it."

"We have," I pointed out.

"We had no choice."

I felt anger then, an unfocused anger, partly directed at Karl for criticizing me, partly directed at Julia for failing to accept the reality I'd Shaped for her, partly directed at myself for having lost my ability to Shape her again, and *this* time get it right. "Okay, then, what's gone wrong with *me*? Why couldn't I Shape her again?"

"I think," Karl said slowly, "that you have burned out."

My anger fizzled away into dismay. "Burned out?"

Karl nodded. "The amount of creative energy you had to expend to create our bubble of safety within the storm was . . . immense. You have at last reached the limit of your power to Shape, great though it is—at least, with the Adversary sharing your *hokhmah*. As a result, you can no longer access your ability."

"Forever?" The word burst out of me with more terror behind it than I would have expected. Wasn't that what I'd wanted? To be a normal woman again?

*Not anymore! Not in a world the Adversary is taking over piece by piece!*

"No," Karl said. "Only for now. If you remain in this world long enough, your ability will return. But I sincerely hope we will have left this world before that happens, because it may take several days."

I felt relief . . . then worry. "So, whatever we have to do now, we have to do it without my being able to Shape. We're defenseless."

"It won't matter as long as we do not let the Adversary find us." Karl looked up at the overcast sky. "The gathering mist, and that low layer of cloud, I believe are still part of your original Shaping to hide us from the Coast Guard. Aerial searches will achieve nothing. I would not be surprised if you have somehow made this boat invisible to radar, as well. Even if you have not, she has a very small radar footprint, and the ocean is very big. I believe we have some breathing room."

"We also have the skipper of this boat locked in her cabin. Are we just going to keep her prisoner?"

"It's either that," Karl said, "or we put her in the dinghy and set her adrift. She *might* survive."

I sighed. "No. We can't do that."

"We will not harm her."

"More than we already have, you mean. She may survive, but she'll never have her old life back."

"No one in this world will have their old lives for much longer," Karl said grimly. "The Adversary will see to that. But at least she will have her boat back once we reach . . . wherever we're going. Though she will not enjoy it for long. Those who live in the world the Adversary Shaped for himself, as I saw firsthand, do not have much time for frivolous pleasures, and their personal belongings are rigorously limited. I suspect *Amazon* will end up in government service. As will Julia. But she won't mind, because once this world is Shaped, she will forget she ever owned a boat called *Amazon*, or sailed her freely wherever she wished."

"But the Adversary can't rewrite time. You said even what I did in the coffee shop after the attack was only an illusion of time winding back."

"He will not be rewriting time. He will merely be rewriting people's memories. The past will still be the past, but no one will remember it."

"And the dead will still be dead." *Aesha*, I thought.

Karl inclined his head. "Yes. Death is forever. Even for the Shaped beings inhabiting the worlds of the Labyrinth."

Again, I wondered if he even saw those people, dead or alive, as real. *It doesn't matter how* he *sees them,* I thought fiercely. *They're real to* me. *Aesha. Brent. Mom. Julia . . .*

A thought struck me. "We could take her with us!"

"Who?"

"Julia," I said impatiently. "Into the next world. She's clearly a highly competent woman, and not just at sailing. She could be useful."

Karl shook his head. "No," he said. "It's impossible."

"Why?" I demanded.

"Because it would kill her," Karl snapped. "As you would know if you hadn't managed to discard all memories of your education. She was Shaped into existence when you Shaped this world into existence. She exists only in this world. She *can* exist only in this world. She could not pass through the Portal into another world. She would be . . . unmade."

"The Adversary's cadre passes through Portals," I pointed out.

"The Adversary . . . has achieved a number of things I thought impossible," Karl said. "I cannot explain it. All I know is that *you* cannot take a person Shaped in this world into the next."

I subsided, but still felt awful, thinking about Julia. *Another life screwed up by Shawna, the Great and Powerful.*

I'd always thought individuals mattered, that anyone could change their life and their future through hard work and hard choices. But day by day I seemed to be losing control, not gaining it, all my work wasted, all my decisions disastrous, the consequences of all my choices either bad, or worse.

I had to follow Karl. That had not changed. I had to get out of this world, the world I had Shaped to be my own, or the Adversary would kill me. And then, apparently, I had to somehow save a whole bunch of other worlds, and deliver myself to Ygrair so she could use the knowledge I had gathered to . . . save the Labyrinth.

That was the impossible future stretching out in front of me. I had no choice but to accept it.

I snorted. Not quite true. I still had *one* other choice: I could die. *Nope. Still doesn't appeal to me.*

"Fine," I said. "So how much farther do we have to sail to reach the place where you can make a Portal?"

Karl looked away from me again, over the bow to the endless tossing sea, gray beneath the gloomy sky. "I wish I knew," he said. "I really wish I knew."

## TWENTY-TWO

**THE ADVERSARY, AT** the President's insistence, had moved his operations into the official Emerald Palace Situation Room, which was long and narrow, dominated by a conference table surrounded by black leather chairs, with video monitors, it seemed, everywhere: some built into the walls, others freestanding on the table.

A flood of information poured from those screens. The Adversary had now spoken to enough world leaders that the world was reshaping itself: in nation after nation, there had been mass arrests of dissidents, crackdowns on protests, confiscation of property . . . a start toward a more orderly world, though the messy implementation was not ideal: a function of the regrettable fact he still shared the world's *hokhmah* with Shawna Keys and thus could not Shape it directly.

The President, at the Adversary's insistence, had absented herself from the Situation Room. He could now issue whatever directives he needed to in the President's name, so her presence was only a distraction. She would not hold office much longer, in any event: he had chosen an otherwise obscure (though remarkably ruthless) prime minister from a failing African state as the person he would elevate to Supreme Leader of the entire world, once he could Shape things properly.

A goal which continued to elude him, because Shawna and Yatsar continued to elude him, despite his having almost the entire law enforcement and military apparatus of the United States and other countries at his disposal. The missing sailboat *Amazon* had not gone down: he could be certain of that since he would know instantly if Shawna died. He suspected, though he was less certain of it, that he would also sense Yatsar's death.

Therefore, the boat had to be somewhere beneath the extensive layer of low gray cloud that was all that remained of the now-dissipated storm, which showed no sign at all of lifting. More of Shawna's work, no doubt. Radar showed nothing beneath that cloud, even though wave heights were now too low to block the yacht's reflection: Shawna might have arranged that, as well. The ceiling was so low aerial searches were all but useless. Visibility at sea level was limited to less than a mile in heavy mist. Spotting a small vessel under those conditions would be a miracle, and as long as Keys lived, the Adversary couldn't quite manage one.

Of course, by now *Amazon* might have turned back toward shore, or turned due north or south, the straight-out-to-sea episode nothing but a red herring to keep him looking one way while Yatsar took Shawna in an entirely different direction, to wherever he would open the next Portal.

The Adversary poured another cup of coffee from the carafe the attentive Emerald Palace staff had provided, sat back in the black office chair, and sipped the bitter liquid. The multiple monitors showed multiple feeds from multiple vessels and multiple aircraft, but in all of them, he saw only multiple versions of the same dull, blank grayness.

He had sent all of the remaining members of his cadre except for his two-man bodyguard to the USS *Bonhomme Richard*, a *Wasp*-class amphibious assault ship involved in the search. If . . . when . . . *Amazon* was sighted, its crew would be flown to the vessel, where his cadre would kill Shawna and secure Yatsar until the Adversary could join them.

The Adversary had done all he could do. For amusement, he

turned his attention to a video feed showing protestors being tear-gassed on Canada's Parliament Hill and settled in to wait.

We sailed all day across gray seas beneath gray skies. The waves would have seemed monstrous to me two days before; after the storm, they seemed next door to a dead calm. The motion didn't upset my stomach at all, and I gladly ate a hot breakfast of scrambled eggs and bacon, which seemed like the first really good meal I'd had in days . . . probably, I realized upon reflection, because it *was* the first really good meal I'd had in days.

I filled a plate for Julia, and took it to the door of her cabin. Karl had said he'd locked it, but of course it only locked from the inside. What he'd actually done was tie the sliding door closed with a piece of rope, which ran through its handle and was knotted around a stanchion supporting the companionway steps. I put the plate on one of the steps, untied the door, then knocked. "Julia."

"Go to hell," Julia said. "Whoever you are."

"I have food," I said. "Bacon and eggs. The door's open, if you want it."

A pause. Then the door slid open. Julia sat on the edge of the bed—there was barely space between it and the door to accommodate her feet, so all she'd had to do to reach the door was lean forward. I held out the plate, and she took it hungrily. I sat on the steps and watched her as she ate.

When she'd finished, she handed me the plate. I put it on the step beside me. "Where are you taking me?" she demanded then. The light spilling down from the cockpit lit her face enough that I could see her eyes were red and watery.

"I don't know," I said. "I don't know where we're going."

"Does he?" She jerked her head toward the cockpit.

I glanced up at Karl. I didn't know if he could hear us or not; he was just a few feet away, but the sound of wind and water might be drowning us out. I looked back at Julia. "Sort of," I said.

"Shawna, you have to listen to me," Julia said urgently. "I told you earlier, we're not outfitted for a long ocean voyage. We'll run out of water in three days, food in a week. And the pumps are still working off and on. That means water's getting in. I think we've strained the hull. If we hit another storm . . ."

*We won't*, I wanted to say with absurd confidence . . . but I couldn't guarantee it. Nor could I do anything about it. I just shrugged.

"What are you running from?" Julia demanded then. "What kind of trouble are you in that you'd risk *this*? Why did the Coast Guard want you?" She shook her head. "And why the hell did I think I needed to protect you? Did you drug me? Hypnotize me?"

"No," I said. "Not exactly."

"Then what, exactly?"

I shrugged helplessly. What could I say to her? *Hi, I created this whole world out of primordial nothingness ten years ago. You didn't exist until then, and sometime soon your whole reality is going to be rewritten so thoroughly that you won't remember this conversation, your old life, or even the fact you owned a yacht.*

What I actually said to her was, "There's another piece of bacon, if you want it."

"Too crispy for my taste," she said.

"Sorry," I said. "I'm not much of a cook."

"The eggs were proof of that." She suddenly smiled. "Remember that time when you . . ." The smile faded. "No. That never happened. I . . ." Her voice trailed off. "It's so weird," she said after a moment. "I have memories of you, but I have other memories that contradict those memories." Her voice rose in pitch and volume as she spoke. "I remember doing things with you, but I also remember doing them with someone else. I remember going to Niagara Falls with you on a high school choir trip. But that wasn't you, it was Marilee, my best friend back then. I remember that, too. They're the same memories, but with different people in them. Am I going crazy?" And then, again, the sixty-four-dollar question. "*What have you done to me?*"

"You should get some rest," I said. "And I'm sorry, but I need to lock . . . tie . . . you in again."

Julia's lips tightened. "You better hope I don't get out. Both of you." She pulled her feet back. I slid the door to the cabin shut, and secured it with the rope. I put the dirty plate on top of mine in the tiny sink, but I didn't wash either, Julia's warning about how little fresh water we had lingering in my mind. I'd swish them over the side later.

I climbed back up the steps to Karl. "Julia is . . . badly confused," I said.

"She would be." He didn't look at me.

"She said we don't have enough water or food for a long voyage."

"We won't need it," Karl said. He sounded a little strange, and I took a closer look at him. He was staring out to sea, but his eyes looked almost unfocused. "We are far closer than I had reason to hope." He turned the wheel to the left; the boom swung a few degrees, the mainsheet (clearly also automated) tightened, and then we were sailing . . . I half-stood so I could crane my head to see the compass . . . due southwest.

I looked down the length of the boat, past the billowing jib, but saw nothing but the same thing I saw in every other direction: white-flecked gray waves, fading in the indeterminate distance into gray mist beneath a gray sky. "Are you sure?"

"Very," Karl said. "If you were not . . . exhausted, by now you would be feeling it yourself." He cocked his head. "We are getting closer every minute." He frowned. "Although, there is something odd . . . something I have never felt in any of the other worlds

I've . . ." He paused. When he spoke again, his voice was sharp. "Keep a sharp lookout."

In books, characters aboard boats are always saying things like that, but it's harder than it sounds when everything looks the same and mist has erased the horizon. I stared into gray nothingness until my eyes ached, but saw nothing. Not in the first hour, nor the second, nor the third.

Noon came and went. I went below and made ham and cheese sandwiches. I handed a plate up the companionway to Karl, then knocked on Julia's door. She didn't respond, and a quick look inside showed her asleep, one arm thrown over her head. I hesitated, then shrugged, closed the door, and tied it up again. I wrapped her sandwich in plastic wrap and put it in the tiny refrigerator, then took my own up into the cockpit, where I resumed staring into the mist while I chewed and swallowed, seeing nothing more than the nothing I'd seen all morning.

As the afternoon wore on, it seemed to me the mist might have lifted a little; though it still shrouded the horizon, I could see a wider expanse of water. I took the wheel for a while to give Karl a break, but he seemed restless; he went below long enough to use the head, and to temporarily let Julia out to do the same. He also gave her the sandwich I'd made for her. I heard her yelling at him, and his monosyllabic replies, though I couldn't make out any of the words. He shut Julia back into her cabin and climbed up again to take the wheel.

"We must be practically on top of it," he growled, sounding frustrated. It would be suppertime in a couple of hours. I was thinking about what other supplies I'd seen in the cabinets below, and wondering if I dared use enough water to boil pasta. "Where the blazes is it?"

"Who says 'blazes'?" I said. "Honestly, you talk like you came from a Dickens novel sometimes."

"Thank you," he said. "He was a favorite of mine. His reading of *A Christmas Carol* was . . ." His voice trailed off even as I shot him a startled look. His eyes had narrowed, and he was staring intently ahead. "There's something in the . . ."

He never finished his sentence. With a horrible crunching noise, *Amazon* ran aground.

# TWENTY-THREE

**KARL HAD TOLD** me, during that long day, that we were sailing at about seven "knots," which he had translated, at my insistence, to "about eight miles an hour." If you're in your car and you run into something at eight miles an hour, you'll get a horrible jolt. If you're really unlucky, you might get whiplash. But if you're smart enough (or at least law-abiding enough) to be wearing your seatbelt, it won't seem that bad.

We weren't wearing seatbelts. And the tethers we *were* wearing were only designed to keep us from separating from the boat if we fell overboard. They did nothing to stop us from being hurled forward as the boat came to a sudden halt in the middle of what had looked like open ocean. I was thrown hard into the bulkhead next to the companionway hatch. Karl bounced off the wheel and went down behind it, groaning. Below, things crashed.

And then Julia screamed, "There's water coming in!"

Dazed, I rolled over and stuck my head into the companionway.

Water was bubbling up through the carpet in the bottom of the boat . . . and Julia was trapped in her cabin.

Adrenaline surged through me, clearing my mind like a bucket of ice dumped over my head. I scrambled to my feet and down the stairs, stepping off into water already ankle-deep, and rising fast. I fumbled with the rope holding Julia's cabin door closed, managed to undo it as the water reached my knees, slid it open. Julie, eyes wide and white in her dark face, held out her hand. I grabbed it and pulled her out of the cabin. She'd taken off her lifejacket at some point, but she snatched it from the bed, then followed me up the steps.

Karl had a nasty bruise on his forehead, but was conscious and getting to his feet. "Rocks," he said, unnecessarily, I thought, unless we'd hit a submarine. Then he jerked his head forward. "Island."

"That's impossible," Julia said, as she struggled into her life-jacket. "There are no islands for hundreds of miles along the course we've been sailing . . ." She followed his gaze, and her protest died away. "Oh."

The mist had lifted some more. Maybe five hundred yards away, wet black stone rose precipitously from the ocean, festooned with pine trees growing on preposterously small ledges or, in some cases, emerging from what seemed to be nothing more than cracks in the rock.

"We have to abandon ship," Julia said, and I could hear the pain in her voice even through the practical-minded sailor's advice. She fastened the latches on her lifejacket, pulled the tabs tight. "If she slips off this rock and goes under, she'll drag us with her even if we're trying to swim away."

"Dinghy?" Karl said.

Julia shook her head. "It's an inflatable, and its stowed . . ." she pointed into the cabin, now awash all the way to the portholes.

"Then we swim," Karl said, and started forward. Julia followed, and I brought up the rear. The boat seemed strangely solid now, where before it . . . she . . . had bobbed and swayed. Before she had been alive; now, stuck on the rock that had ripped open her belly, she was dead, or at least dying: another death to add to the list of those I'd caused or abetted.

"You said you can swim?" Karl said to me. He didn't ask Julia, presumably assuming anyone who owned and skippered her own boat could swim . . . or maybe he didn't really care. My previous thoughts about whether he even considered her a real person bubbled up again like indigestion.

"I did," I said. He didn't know I'd qualified it to myself with "sort of," and the distance to the island was a lot more than a couple of pool lengths, but at least I'd be wearing a lifejacket.

*Amazon* suddenly shifted under us, groaning. The sail, which had gone flat, filled as a gust blew across the water. The boom swung sharply out . . . and slammed into me.

I felt the blow, felt myself flying through the air, felt myself hit the water. Dazed, I would have drowned there and then if not for the lifejacket: maybe even with it if not for the hand that grabbed me and guided me to the surface. It was Karl's, of course, who must have jumped in after me. Now, treading water, he looked at me with worry-filled eyes as I coughed and spluttered. "Are you all right?"

From the pain in my side, I thought I might have cracked a rib, but there was nothing to be done about that. I nodded.

Julia splashed into the water behind Karl. "We have to get away from her!" she cried.

"Come on," Karl said to me, and struck out toward the island, which somehow looked much farther away from down there in the water than it had from the listing deck of *Amazon*. I swam after him, every stroke stabbing my flank with pain, kicking as best I could. My strokes were clumsy and splashy, but I didn't really need good form with the lifejacket keeping my head above water: at least I was moving.

Julia moved a lot faster, leaving me behind, and soon catching up to Karl. I persevered womanfully, and a few minutes later crawled up onto a narrow bit of rocky beach beneath the black cliff, where I promptly got to my hands and knees and retched up a stomach's worth of salt water, along with some partly digested ham sandwich, every heave tearing at my bruised side. When nothing else came up, I crawled away from the mess and flopped over onto my back, staring up at the trees clinging to the cliff. "Oof," I said. I thought for a moment, then added, "Ugh."

Karl appeared in my vision, carrying his lifejacket loosely in one hand. He still had the pistol stuck in his pocket; I wondered if it would fire after being submerged in salt water. "All right?" he said, looking down at me.

"No," I said. "But alive." I sat up, wincing. "I think the boom may have cracked a rib."

"You were lucky it did not hit you in the head," Karl said. "And maybe lucky the lifejacket cushioned the blow a bit."

"Maybe," I said. "Where's Julia?" I looked around, and spotted her a little ways off, still wearing her lifejacket, sitting on a rock, with her arms wrapped around her chest. She was rocking back and forth, weeping, as she stared out at *Amazon*, now heeled over so far that her keel was exposed, awash in the surf. "Oh," I said in small voice. "I feel so guilty . . ."

"Both guilt and remorse are a waste of mental energy in this circumstance," Karl said. "You are almost done with this world." He stared up at the cliff. "Somewhere on this island we will find the place to open a Portal. I can feel it, but there is still something . . . strange . . ." He closed his eyes but kept his head tilted back. "Up," he whispered. "It is above us. And inland." He opened his eyes again, and pointed at the cliff. "Up above that, somewhere."

"Oh, good," I said. "Rock climbing. Ranks right up there with swimming and sailing and horseback riding on the list of things I'm no good at."

"We cannot climb this cliff," Karl said. "We must find another way inland." He looked both ways along the beach, then pointed past Julia. "Over there is a gentler slope. We will start there." He put his lifejacket on the ground and knelt beside it, disconnecting the flashlight and the multi-tool. "These may prove useful." He stood again, attaching the flashlight to his belt and pushing the multi-tool into his left-hand pants pocket—the pistol still bulged in the other—and then walked toward Julia.

I got up, took the flashlight and multi-tool off my own lifejacket, dumped the lifejacket itself on the ground, and then limped after him. Karl strode by Julia without a glance, but I stopped. Guilt and remorse might be a waste of energy, as Karl had said, but I felt them nonetheless. I put my hand on Julia's shoulder. "Julia." She didn't move. "Julia," I said again. "We're going inland. The place we're looking for . . . it's somewhere on this island."

"The thing I loved most in this world is being torn apart by the sea, thanks to you," she replied, her voice as gray and flat as the sky.

"I'm so sorry," I said. "We were going to let you have *Amazon* back as soon as we'd landed. We didn't know about the rocks."

"How could you?" she said dully. "They don't exist."

I blinked at her. "What?"

She turned red-rimmed eyes toward me. "There is no island here. It does not exist on any chart. It's not real."

"It was real enough to wreck your boat," I said. The words came out more harshly than I'd intended, and I immediately wished I could call them back.

Julia turned away again, to look back toward the hidden rock that had killed her beloved yacht. "I don't think you're real, either. I don't think I am where I seem to be, I don't think *Amazon* is really stuck on a rock, I don't think there was a storm. I think I'm hallucinating all of this, both of you, the rocks that wrecked *Amazon*, this island. I think I was in some kind of accident and I'm drugged up and lying in the hospital. And eventually I'll wake up, and everything will return to normal."

I'd thought the same at one point. Sometimes I still wondered. But the cool damp air in my face, the smell of seaweed, the pain in my side . . . no. This was real. For me, and for Julia. "Julia . . ." I began.

Julia cut me off. "It would be interesting if a figment of my imagination were able to convince me it was real, but you do not have that power."

I felt . . . stung. Angry, in fact. *I* wasn't real? I was the Shaper. If anything, *she* wasn't real. She was literally a figment of *my* imagination. No, not even that—she was a mere copy of someone in the First World, a doppelgänger the Labyrinth had created to populate the world I had Shaped for myself.

If I had my Shaping power, I'd *show* her who was real, and who wasn't. I'd . . .

The anger faded, so suddenly it left me shaken, wondering where it had come from. Tales of vengeful Greek gods ran through my mind. Was that what they had felt, fury that mere humans had dared to defy them, or failed to appease them, or fallen afoul of some arbitrary law? Was that what I was going to become: another Hera?

I swallowed. "I hope you're right," I said. "I hope you're right, and you wake up soon, and find everything has gone back to normal."

"I'm not listening to you anymore," she said. They were the last words I heard from any of the people who inhabited the world I had Shaped: an appropriate farewell, I suppose.

I strode past her to where Karl awaited me, and then together we moved inland to find the place where Karl could form a Portal, and I could leave my world forever. After all I had done to it, and the people within it, I was beginning to think it would be better off with the Adversary.

Another day had passed in Washington, D.C. without a hint as to the location of *Amazon*, another day with no break in the strange mist and cloud hampering the search efforts. Strange to the meteorologists, at least; not so strange to the Adversary, still monitoring the situation in the Emerald Palace Situation Room, who knew the clouds and mist had been Shaped by Shawna Keys. He remained impressed once again by her power, but also more certain than ever that she had put so much effort into protecting *Amazon* during the storm that she had temporarily exhausted her Shaping ability. She had rendered herself defenseless. All he had to do was find her. But so far . . .

The Adversary sighed and rose from the Situation Room table. He was expected at a private dinner, arranged by the President, with the justices of the Supreme Court. But as he turned toward the door, one of the three other people in the Situation Room, monitoring the many streams of information pouring into it, jumped to his feet. "Mr. Gegner!" the young man called.

The Adversary glanced at him. "What is it?"

"A signal, sir. From *Amazon*'s EPIRB."

The acronym meant nothing to the Adversary. "Explain."

"An EPIRB is an Emergency Position Indicator Radio Beacon," the young man said. "They're automated devices that send out a signal pinpointing . . . well, within two nautical miles . . . a vessel's location if it gets into dire trouble."

"How dire?"

"Typically, sunk or in the process of sinking. The EPIRB triggers automatically when it's submerged in salt water."

Neither Shawna nor Yatsar had died; of that, the Adversary was certain. But if *Amazon* had foundered, perhaps damaged past the point of seaworthiness by the storm despite Shawna's best efforts, they might have abandoned her. Which meant they would now be in a small open boat, and could not have traveled far from the sinking yacht. "Show me the location." He turned toward the nearest monitor, in the wall to his left. "Here."

"Yes, sir."

A moment later the screen lit with a chart of the Pacific Ocean off the coast of Oregon. A red dot blinked.

"Any land nearby?"

"No, sir," the young man replied.

"How far by helicopter from the *Bonhomme Richard*?"

A green dot appeared on the map, fifty miles from the red. "That far, sir."

"Excellent. Contact the *Bonhomme Richard*'s captain and provide the coordinates. My cadre will, of course, be in charge of the operation."

"Yes, sir." The young man sat down. As he pulled on a headset and began to speak into its microphone, the Adversary donned the headset from in front of his own chair and touched the button he had programmed to connect him directly to Captain Arneson, his cadre leader.

"Arneson here," said a deep voice.

"We've received a signal from the boat," the Adversary said. "Your ship's captain has the coordinates. Take two helicopters— only your men, except for the pilots. I expect you'll find Shawna Keys and Yatsar in a small boat on the open sea. You know your orders."

"Kill the woman, take Yatsar alive. Yes, sir."

"Don't worry about the reaction of your pilots to whatever actions you might take," the Adversary advised. "Once Keys is dead, it won't matter."

"Of course, sir."

"As soon as you can arrange it, Arneson."

"Yes, sir."

The Adversary ended the call, and rather than continuing to the dinner with the Justices, sat down in his chair at the end of the table and poured another cup of coffee. "Once the mission commences, display all available video feeds," the Adversary said.

"Yes, sir," said the young man who had first brought the signal to his attention.

The Adversary sipped his coffee and waited for the end.

# TWENTY-FOUR

**WE HEARD THE** beat of the helicopter rotors just as we began our third attempt to scale the sodden slopes of the improbably tall mountain at the center of The Mysterious Island.

"The Mysterious Island," caps and all, was what I'd started calling it to myself since I'd left Julia behind and joined Karl, and we'd made our first attempt to make our way inland toward the precise location where the "thin spot" between the worlds existed. *The Mysterious Island* had been my favorite of Jules Verne's books as a kid: for years, I'd had vivid adventure dreams in which I explored just such a place. The idea of an island nobody knew existed, with a secret at its core, had struck a chord. Even though I doubted we would find Captain Nemo and the *Nautilus* waiting for us when we reached the center of *this* island—if we ever did—the general description fit the circumstances.

I'd wondered, though, as our second attempt to find a path up the mountain had ended in a sheer rock wall and we'd had to backtrack yet again (the mist, which had conveniently saved us from aerial discovery, thickened as we ascended, most *inconveniently* making it impossible to see far enough ahead to spot even obvious barriers like cliffs until we were faced with them), whether there might be a world where Captain Nemo *did* exist, along with the *Nautilus*; another where the Wizard presided over Emerald City; one where King Arthur and the Knights of the Round Table held court in Camelot. Karl had as much as said there were worlds where elves still sang in Rivendell and hobbits dwelt in the Shire.

It was both an exciting thought and a disturbing one. Exciting, because what reader wouldn't love to find herself in a world she had previously only visited in her imagination, and disturbing, because some of those worlds were definitely places you might want to visit, but would never want to live.

It was also disturbing because, as I'd thought before, the fact I'd chosen to Shape such a close replica of the original world seemed to say disappointing things about me. In the First World, had I really been such a boring person, with such boring dreams? I mean, a pottery shop? Really? When I could have made myself Queen of the World?

Back on the beach, we slogged along for another quarter mile or so, until we found a place where the forest thinned and the slope was relatively gentle, at least as far up as we could see. But we'd taken only a few steps uphill before the sound of choppers cut through the mist.

Karl stopped and stared in the direction of that distant thunder. "The Adversary has found us."

"How?" I demanded.

"Luck. Some technological device we do not know about. It doesn't matter." He glanced at me. "The real question is, who is aboard those helicopters? Are they people from your world, or members of the Adversary's cadre?"

"What difference does it make?" I said. "I'm burned out, you said. I can't Shape them either way."

"Probably not," Karl said. "Though in extremis, you should at least make the attempt. But that is not the only reason I would like to know. The Adversary's cadre will undoubtedly have orders to kill you on sight. Law enforcement or military types . . . maybe not."

I shivered. "That *would* be a very good thing to know," I admitted. "But wouldn't it be even better to never find out?"

A brief smile flicked across his face. "An excellent point." He turned back to the slope. "They will have a very difficult time tracking or seeing us in this fog. With luck, perhaps we can avoid them until we reach the place inland where I can form the Portal."

With luck, perhaps we could, but it wasn't going to be easy. Our third climb ended, like the first two, in a sheer cliff. I was uneasily aware that we only had a couple of hours of daylight left, no food, no water, and no camping equipment. In fact, I was beginning to wonder if there *was* a way to the top. I said as much to Karl.

"There has to be," he said, without explaining why that was more than just wishful thinking.

To be sure, wishful thinking had worked out rather well for me recently, but I still had no Shaping power that I could sense. We had no choice but to descend, to continue working our way around the base of the mountain.

The sound of the helicopters had died away shortly after we'd first heard them: now, as we neared the beach once more, we heard them again. I tried to picture what they might have done. Landed, probably, and disgorged armed men to search for us on foot. They were presumably looking for our tracks, which they would most certainly find, since despite my love of Tolkien I was neither hobbit nor elf. The mist would help conceal us, but for how long?

Now, it sounded like the helicopters had taken off again. Why? Returning to wherever they'd come from, for reinforcements or fuel? Giving up? (That was *definitely* wishful thinking.) Or . . .

"Do military helicopters have sensors that can penetrate fog?" I said. The unpleasant thought had just occurred to me. The helicopters were distant, and their sound waxed and waned, but it never died away completely—which meant they must be searching the island.

"I am unfamiliar with the technology available on military helicopters in your world," Karl said.

"Well, do they have them in the . . . um, First World?"

"I am equally unfamiliar with the technology available on military helicopters in the First World," he said.

The sound of the helicopters no longer waxed and waned: now, it just waxed. They were headed our way.

"We should get under cover," I said; but we were traversing a barren stretch of shale, remnants of some long-ago fall from the cliff face. None of the rocks were big enough to hide behind, and the nearest tree, a dim ghost in the mist, was likewise too skinny to be of any use. "Up the slope!" I cried. If the helicopters did have some kind of fog-penetrating radar, surely it only showed outlines. If we were pressed up against the cliff, we might look like nothing more than oddly shaped protuberances. But out here in the open, we'd show up like sore thumbs.

Karl didn't argue. We stumbled up the slope through rocks that shifted treacherously beneath our feet, threatening sprained ankles or worse. The pain in my side had eased—which probably meant a bruise rather than a cracked rib—but I still felt like I was being poked with a sharp stick at regular intervals.

We reached the cliff. It had a kink in it, a deep fold, and down at the bottom the rock was blacker than . . . no. Wait.

That wasn't black rock. It was a hole.

A cave!

I pointed it out to Karl, and he scrambled down to it and into it, with me close behind, shale skittering in my wake.

Just in time. As I plunged into the darkness, the roar of the helicopter became earsplitting. Even if it didn't have fog-penetrating sensors, those aboard would surely have seen us if not for the cave: the helicopter practically exploded out of the fog, terrifyingly close.

It wasn't a Coast Guard chopper but a full-on military model, gray and bristling. It hovered, visible through the mouth of the cave, for a terrifyingly long time before finally swinging away to our left and sweeping on around the mountain.

I released a breath I hadn't realized I was holding. "I don't think they saw us."

"They may not have seen us," Karl said grimly, "but I am certain they saw the cave. Ground troops will undoubtedly be sent to investigate. We must keep moving."

I sighed. "Well, if you'll give me a boost, I can probably get back up the . . ."

"Not out there," Karl said.

I turned around, and saw that he wasn't facing me, but staring into the darkness at the back of the cave. I took a step toward him, and saw what he saw: the cave not only continued, it sloped up, toward the center of the mountain . . . and the center of the island.

At least it's not the first step of a *Journey to the Center of the Earth*, I thought, and suddenly wondered if this island were my doing, if I had Shaped it, my own Mysterious Island, my own endless caverns—but no, this island didn't exist in my world. Julia had said so.

Did that mean it had somehow . . . leaked . . . from the new world we were trying to get to? Was *it* a Vernesian world? Or something similarly steampunky? Karl had kept saying he sensed something odd . . . was that it?

Karl took the flashlight he'd rescued from his life jacket off of his belt. I reached for mine, but he stopped me with a hand on my wrist. "Let us limit ourselves to one at a time," he said. "We do not know how long they will last, and we do not know how far we will have to follow this tunnel."

I nodded. *Makes sense.* "Lead on," I said. But before I followed him into the darkness I took a look back at the entrance, hoping for a convenient boulder we could roll across it, trying to believe with all my heart that such a thing existed.

Nothing changed.

I hadn't known I was a Shaper until three days ago. Now I felt like a part of me was missing.

The cave appeared to have started life as a natural crack in the massive upthrust stones of the mountain, which flowing water had widened and smoothed over millennia. (On an island that Karl insisted was really no more than ten years old, but never mind that.) It started out high enough to walk through, but soon it narrowed, until eventually we were crawling on our hands and knees. The rock beneath my palms was moist and slimy, and all the time I was uneasily aware of the tons of stone above me and surrounding me. A slight shrug of the Earth would reduce us to smears of paste.

But the Earth did not shrug, and after a few dozen uncomfortable yards, the tunnel opened out again, allowing us to stand upright. Unfortunately, it also got a lot steeper, so that in places we were climbing near-vertical walls, moving from handhold to handhold in the dim light of Karl's flashlight, attached to his belt again so it mostly illuminated his knees and feet, with occasional blinding flashes into my eyes.

I had gone through a brief climbing-wall phase at my local gym. I'd like to say that experience went a long way toward increasing my confidence as I tried to make my way up the middle of a mountain in the dark, but that would be lying. My heart pounded, my breath rasped, and my fingers and calves and arms and shoulders burned. I tried really hard not to think about the sheer drop beneath me, with little success.

At least, I *thought* my heart was pounding—until I heard voices echoing behind us. Then I discovered it had barely been beating at all.

I started to say something to Karl, but snapped my mouth shut just in time. *If we can hear them, they can hear us.*

Clearly Karl's pessimistic prediction had proved prescient: the helicopter crew *had* seen something and had called in the Marines. Possibly literally. At this point, that was the *best*-case scenario. Soldiers from my world were less likely to shoot me on sight, unless they'd been directly Shaped by the Adversary, and he couldn't have Shaped *every* individual involved in the search for us.

If, on the other hand, those now pursuing us up the tunnel were members of the Adversary's cadre . . . well, best not to be seen anywhere within rifle shot.

In fact, best not be seen at all.

The slope abruptly flattened. I scrambled onto level ground and stayed on my hands and knees for a minute, panting. Karl had already moved farther down the tunnel, but now he paused. He unhooked the flashlight from his belt and shone it on something I couldn't see.

I got to my feet, joined him, and blinked at what he had found.

The cave we'd been struggling through had been formed by natural forces. The continuation of it had not: not unless natural forces had somehow formed a perfect stone staircase, lined the tunnel with brick, and installed iron brackets, each containing an unlit torch, every twenty feet or so. "Who would have made this?" I whispered to Karl, still fiercely aware we had company some unknown distance back, though I'd heard nothing since that first burst of voices. That might mean that our pursuers had turned back rather than climb after us, but it could just as easily mean that some commander had told whomever had been talking to STFU, and they were still hurrying upward through the dark.

"I have no idea," Karl whispered back. He glanced at me. "Does it look familiar?"

"Nothing I've seen outside of TV shows, movies, computer games, and the occasional nightmare."

"Nightmare," he repeated. He looked forward again. "I wonder . . ."

"We're being followed," I said then, just in case Karl was deaf or had suddenly been struck dumb, in the stupid, not speechless, sense of the word.

"I know." He quit musing and resumed moving, climbing the stairs, the flashlight casting a circle of illumination on the floor ahead of him.

I followed, trailing one hand along the damp bricks as we ascended, wondering who had gone to all the trouble of lining the tunnel with them—and why. Why cover what must already be walls of solid rock with brick? Sure, it was more aesthetic, but who would see? What I'd said to Karl was absolutely true: there was something . . . fake . . . about all this, as though it were just a set for an old episode of *Doctor Who*—a program that had always loved tunnels—or one of those original-series *Star Trek* episodes where the gang found itself in a quasi-medieval castle that was really a projection of some powerful alien intelligence.

It also reminded me of the overblown tunnel I had Shaped to give Karl access to the Portal at Snakebite Mine. But I hadn't Shaped this. Had I?

The steps climbed straight ahead, never deviating left or right. Every thirty feet or so there was a landing, a flat spot, where we could catch our breath before continuing the climb. At the third such landing we encountered something new: a statue, of the heroic male nude variety, a variation on Michelangelo's *David*, perhaps, although this "David" had the head of a ram, and held a sword in one hand and a decapitated human head in the other. Also, unlike David, this nude male was . . . aroused. Impressively so.

"Um," I said, looking at the statue with disquiet. "What is *that*?"

"No idea," Karl said. "Not from your world?"

"Nothing I've ever seen," I said. "Although parts of it are famil-iar." I winced in the dark. Considering what the most immediately noticeable part of the statue was, that hadn't come out at all the way I'd meant it to sound.

"Parts of it." Karl said thoughtfully. "Then I think know what it is. It's a chimera. In fact," he looked around at the brick walls, "I think this whole island is a chimera."

"A chimera," I protested, "is a fire-breathing female monster from Greek mythology." I tried to remember pictures I'd seen of them. "Um . . . I think they usually have a lion's head, a goat's body, and a serpent's tail." I nodded at the priapic statue. "That has none of those things and is most *definitely* not female."

"Chimera in the generic, rather than the mythological, sense," Karl said. "Something formed from bits of one thing, bits of an-other. In this case, elements from the world we are about to enter, combined with elements from your world. It is my hypothesis that this island is, in a sense, a world of its own: Shaped, not consciously but subconsciously, by both you and the Shaper of the next world over. I believe this island exists in both worlds, but is not fully of either."

"So, this statue could be Michelangelo's *David*," I said slowly, "with bits from the next Shaper's imagination grafted onto it." *His rather* disturbing *imagination.*

"Or simply bits of his or her world," Karl said. "Or bits from your subconscious . . . which, based on your own comments, and that tunnel you Shaped at the mine, may be where this endless staircase came from, as well." He turned away from the disquieting sculpture and resumed climbing.

It was perhaps slightly reassuring that whatever that statue represented was unlikely to be part of the world we hoped to enter. On the other hand, if that thing properly represented the mini-world of the island, which we were penetrating more and more deeply, it wasn't reassuring at all.

It was even less reassuring when we reached the next landing, and the next after that, and the next after that. Each had similar statues: a nude winged woman with pendulous breasts, the feet of a hawk, bat wings, and the head of a fly, holding a squalling baby by one heel. A slim preteen boy with snakes for arms and a mouth in his stomach, and below that . . .

Well, never mind. I quit looking at them in detail after that one. If any of that had come from *my* subconscious, I was one sick puppy.

At about the seventh landing, where there were two nightmar-ish statues either engaged in an extremely deviant sexual act or devouring each other alive (or both), the tunnel split into three. One branch continued up, one went left, and the one to our right went a short distance and ended in a wooden door, reinforced and barred with rusted iron. From the other side of that door came the sound of scratching: long, slow, grating noises, like giant claws be-ing drawn through the wood. Karl looked at it thoughtfully. "Inter-esting."

"I think you mean terrifying." I started up the next set of steps, but he put a hand on my arm.

"No," he said.

"No?" I looked over my shoulder. We had heard nothing from below us since that initial burst of voices, but surely our pursuers were almost to the brick-lined stairs by now, if not already on them and climbing toward us. "We—*you*—need to get that Portal open."

"You hardly have to tell me that," he said. "However, that way," he nodded up the stairs, "is not the most direct route to where I can perform that task." He nodded at the barred door. "That way is."

I stared at the door. "But . . . there's something monstrous on the other side of it."

"Is there?"

"Can't you hear it?"

"I hear a scratching noise," Karl said. "But I cannot be certain what is causing it."

At that precise moment, a howl echoed from the corridor to our left, a long, moaning wail that sent shivers down my spine, as though the mostly wolflike contours of the sound had been mixed with a good dollop of fingernails on a blackboard. My heart skipped a beat. "We've got to get out of here! Up is the only safe way."

"Up *seems* to be the only safe way. Just because we cannot hear anything coming from that tunnel does not mean it is safe. But in any event, it may not lead where we need to go. Whereas I am certain that this closed door *does*. Here, hold this." He handed me his flashlight, then pulled the pistol from his pocket, popped out the clip with practiced ease, took a quick look, and snapped it back into place. "Two shots left." He looked down the steps, keeping the pistol loose in his right hand. "Not enough for who's following us." He nodded at the closed door. "But it might be enough for whatever's behind that."

The howl sounded again, closer, and then I heard something from somewhere down the long staircase . . . a muffled curse, it had sounded like. Our pursuers were getting close. I groaned. "What's the plan?"

"You open the door, I shoot whatever is behind it if I must, we go through the door, we close the door, we continue, and we hope that our human pursuers make the same unwarranted assumption you did about the best route, and continue climbing."

I swallowed. It did nothing to slow my racing heart. "Fine." I switched the flashlight to my left hand, took a deep breath, and then strode toward the door. I touched the iron of the bar securing it, and found it so cold the sweat on my hands froze to it, stinging my skin. I took another deep breath, and then lifted the bar.

The scratching paused, then redoubled.

The door had a griplike handle, the kind with a thumb plate you push down to release the latch. It had a keyhole, too. Could it be locked as well as barred? The continuing scratching almost made me hope so.

I touched the handle. It, too was colder than ice.

I pushed my thumb down. The latch clicked.

The scratching stopped.

I took a deep breath, trying to prepare myself for whatever might be on the other side of the door, ready to leap back as whatever it was came roaring out . . . then pulled the door open.

There was nothing on the other side of it at all: just another dark tunnel.

Karl raised an eyebrow. "Anticlimactic," he said. "But not entirely unexpected."

I felt both relieved and cheated. "What the hell?" I shone the flashlight through the door.

Another tunnel, another set of steps leading up, a few feet beyond the door, at right angles to the ones we had been climbing. No decorative brick adorned the stone walls, but a thin layer of glistening mud covered the floor between the door and the stairs. Nothing marred its smooth surface: no footprints, no animal tracks. Whatever had made the scratching noise had left no sign of its presence. Had it been imaginary?

The howl sounded behind us, very close now. Maybe whatever was making that sound was imaginary, too—but maybe not.

The howling drove us through the door. I turned at once and pulled it shut behind us. To my delight, on this side of the door a key rested in the keyhole. I locked the door, then pocketed the key. It was only then that I saw the deep scars in the door, four parallel marks, clawed through the wood, over and over again. I looked at the ground. The only marks there were from our feet.

"Perhaps we should keep climbing?" Karl said.

I heard muffled voices outside the door. The howl sounded again. Shouts and curses rang out—and then gunfire, shockingly loud even through the thick wood—which might not be thick enough to stop a bullet, come to think of it. I turned away and hurried toward the stairs. "Absolutely!"

We started up. As before, there were landings every twenty steps or so, but these (thankfully) had no statues. At the third landing, the steps turned left, so we were climbing once more in the same direction as before, toward the island's interior.

I had little breath for talking and my legs and side ached, but I was also sorely puzzled. "So, you think we . . . me and the Shaper in the next world over . . . created this island jointly, but not consciously?"

"That is my belief," Karl said. To my annoyance, he didn't sound out of breath at all. "I think it was Shaped by your subconscious: the things you fear, without reason; the things you think, without regard for propriety or rationality; the . . ."

"'The Monsters from the Id.'"

"Id?"

"Um . . . Sigmund Freud? By way of *Forbidden Planet*?" But that, of course, just earned me a blank look. *Of course*, I thought. Freud was early twentieth century, like *The Wizard of Oz*. Too late for our Mr. Yatsar. And that curious comment earlier about Charles Dickens' live performance of *A Christmas Carol* . . . clearly, Karl had left the First World sometime in the late nineteenth century. Which made him well over a century old. Which was . . . puzzling. Or disturbing. Or both.

*Not the time*, I thought. *Back to the terror at hand.* "So, whatever made the scratching sounds wasn't real." I frowned. "Except it was, because it left marks on the door." I frowned harder. "But no footprints."

"Rationality has no place in a place created without rationality," Karl said, which had the sound of an aphorism. I could almost see it on a (rather lame) motivational poster. I wondered how many worlds *he* had entered in which rationality had no place . . . and how many I would have to visit, too. Based on this island, such worlds might not be very pleasant.

"Whoever is chasing us shot at something," I said, the next time we paused at a landing for breath. "It was real to them."

"Perhaps. Or maybe they shot at shadows, at what they feared or imagined was there, rather than anything with corporeal reality."

I looked down the stairs. "I didn't hear the door open behind us. Do you think they've gone up the central stairs?"

"Possibly," Karl said. "Or possibly they are extremely skilled at keeping quiet as they climb." He gave me a pointed look. "Unlike us." He took a long, slow breath, as though perhaps, just perhaps, he was willing to admit to being ever-so-slightly fatigued, and resumed climbing.

I took a few deep, ragged breaths (because I had admitted I was more than slightly fatigued at roughly the third landing of the first set of stairs) and followed him.

The end came abruptly. What looked like just another landing ahead of us carried on into the darkness, a long, flat tunnel. And at the end of it that tunnel . . .

. . . a light.

*Talk about a cliché*, I thought.

"We're very close," Karl said. He looked behind us. "I think we may have evaded them."

"Then let's hurry!" I strode forward.

"Wait!" Karl cried, but too late.

Between the light of the flashlight and the light ahead, I couldn't see the floor of the tunnel.

The other reason I couldn't see the floor of the tunnel was that it wasn't there. I took a long step . . . and tumbled forward into darkness.

## TWENTY-FIVE

**THE ADVERSARY STARED** at the young man standing nervously before him. "I beg your pardon?"

"The island. Where they found the boat. It doesn't exist."

"Explain yourself. Clearly it exists, or they wouldn't have found it."

"Sorry, Mr. Gegner. I don't mean it isn't physically there, because of course it is. What I mean is, it's not on our charts. Or any other charts. Or any satellite images."

The Adversary had no interest in the peculiarities of the Shaping of this world, or any other, except in so far as it served his interests. Still, this was . . . unexpected. "But it registers to the senses?"

"Yes, sir."

The Adversary looked pointedly at the screens that were supposed to be showing him video feeds from the many cameras carried by his cadre, and the naval personnel accompanying them. "Then why is not visible to me?"

"I don't know, Mr. Gegner," the man said. "Everything seems to be working, but . . . no images are getting through. We can hear them, but we can't see them."

"Curious," the Adversary said. "And annoying. Very well. What are they telling us?"

"They found the owner of *Amazon*, the wrecked sailboat," the young man said. "She told them the other two had gone inland.

Helicopters circumnavigated the island using fog-penetrating radar, but didn't spot them. However, they *did* find an opening into an extensive network of caves. It seems clear Yatsar and Keys entered them. Your . . . um . . ."

"Cadre," the Adversary supplied.

"Yes, sir. Your cadre entered the cave, with two Marines. The rest of the ground force is working its way around the island in both directions. The helicopters are standing by."

"And what do the forces inside the mountain report?"

"Nothing, sir. No contact since they entered. Too much stone for a signal to penetrate."

"I see. Very well, then, how fast could I be transported to this island?"

The young man blinked. "Sir?"

"You heard me."

"You want to go in person?"

"I believe I just indicated that."

"Well . . . several hours, sir. I can't be more precise off the top of my head."

"Make the arrangements."

"Uh . . . yes, sir."

The young man scurried off. The Adversary looked at the still-blank screens. The mysterious island was clearly the location for the next Portal. Either Yatsar had already opened it, or he would soon.

Whatever would happen on the island would certainly have happened before the Adversary could get there. But a new Portal would mean a new world to conquer, as soon as this one was fully under his control—as it would be very soon. Either Shawna Keys would die, or she would escape into a new world, and he could Shape this as he pleased. While her escape would pose new challenges, the setback would only be temporary.

Wherever Karl Yatsar and Shawna Keys traveled in the Labyrinth, the Adversary would follow.

I fell, and kept falling, screaming as I plummeted through darkness. I only stopped screaming because I ran out of air, and when I did, I heard Karl shout, "Shawna! Open your eyes!"

How could he still be so close? I was still falling. Worse, I was still *accelerating*.

I had gone skydiving once. The adrenaline rush had been amazing. Back on the ground, I had chattered about it for hours. But the thing about skydiving is that once you've reached terminal velocity, you stop accelerating. You're still falling, but you don't *feel* like you're falling. As they say, it's not the falling that kills you, it's the sudden deceleration at the bottom.

But now . . . I could still feel that sensation of falling, that initial terrifying plunge. The sensation wasn't stopping, not at all, but I'd been falling for seconds . . .

I was facing down into darkness, but I still held the flashlight, gripped so tightly in my hand my knuckles ached. Karl's voice had come from behind me, and not very far behind me, at that. I twisted my head to the left, and pointed the flashlight in that direction—and saw a wall of stone, which wasn't moving. I twisted around further, my body rotating as I did so, and saw Karl not six feet above me, standing on the edge of the precipice from which I had fallen . . . was *still* falling, for even though I could see I wasn't really falling, the sensation was still there, making my heart race, my body sweat. It was all I could do not to scream again.

"What's happening?" I cried. Oh, all right, *squeaked*.

"Hang on," Karl said. He paused. "Perhaps not the best choice of words," he added apologetically. Then he disappeared.

By twisting around to look at him, I'd started a rotation I couldn't stop. I kept spinning, slowly, like a rotisserie chicken, and tried to control my panic at the endless . . . endless . . . endless . . . falling.

*It's a nightmare*, I realized suddenly. *Falling forever . . . it's a classic nightmare.*

But terrifying though it was, it wasn't one of *my* nightmares. Was this something else that had leaked into the island from the world we were trying to get to?

I took a shuddering breath as I rotated again and continued, in my head at least, to fall. *Maybe this didn't* used *to be one of my recurring nightmares. After this, I'm pretty sure it will be.*

Karl reappeared sometime between when I turned facedown and when I turned faceup again. He now lay flat on his stomach. He had removed his leather jacket (which was much the worse for wear after a thorough saltwater soaking aboard *Amazon*). Holding on to one end of one sleeve with both hands, he reached down as far as he could, so the end of the other sleeve dangled just above me. "Grab it."

I did, gratefully, as it came into reach. My rotation stopped with a jerk as the jacket tightened, but I kept falling.

Maybe just a *little* scream . . . ?

I clenched my jaw shut.

Karl pulled. I rose effortlessly, as though I were a helium-filled balloon, for about five of the six feet . . . and then suddenly my weight returned. I gasped, and swung forward against the wall of the pit with a bone-jarring impact. But now I could get an elbow over the lip of the precipice, and with Karl's help, added a leg to that. A second later I rolled onto my back on the solid rock, panting, drenched in sweat. "What a nightmare!"

"Why were you screaming?" Karl said. "You only fell a few feet. After that, you hung suspended."

I explained. He looked thoughtful. "So it was *literally* a nightmare. But not yours."

"It is now," I muttered.

"You are a very powerful Shaper," Karl said. "As you know. But I am beginning to believe that whoever has Shaped the world we will be entering next must be almost as powerful as you. That is the only way I can imagine your subconscious minds Shaping this island in this fashion. It is most interesting . . . I wonder if Ygrair is familiar with the phenomenon, and if we might encounter it elsewhere?"

"Interesting?" I said. "I think you mean terrifying."

"That too, no doubt. Though, obviously, more so for you than for me." Karl looked over his shoulder in the direction we had come. "Your screams were . . . piercing. We may have revealed our location to our pursuers. We should keep moving."

"How?" I demanded. "That pit blocks the way forward."

"Not quite," Karl said. "There is a thin ledge. Over there." He pointed to the right. I aimed the flashlight in that direction. Sure enough, there was a ledge, though even calling it "thin" seemed a little too gracious.

"I think we should both have flashlights from here on," I said. I handed him his.

"I agree. It appears there may be an end to the tunnel in sight, in any event."

I was taking my flashlight from my belt, with a hand still inclined to tremble, when I heard the distant sound of breaking wood from the direction we had come . . . a sound like someone had just taken an ax to the door we had locked, at the bottom of the stairs.

"Time to go?" I said flashlight in my hand.

"Indubitably," Karl said.

We eased along the narrow ledge. Even knowing that falling into the pit wasn't falling to my death—unless my heart gave out—I didn't want to repeat the experience. Also, floating helplessly in a nightmare pit didn't seem like a good place to be when those chasing us, who we had every reason to believe would shoot me on sight, caught up.

On the far side of the pit, I flashed my light at the floor, the walls, and the ceiling. I didn't see any more traps. That didn't, of course, mean they didn't exist.

Ahead of us the gray light gleamed. The tunnel curved just enough that we couldn't see where it was coming from. But there was a sound, too, a rushing sound . . . the sound of falling water.

We hurried along the tunnel. The gray light grew closer with unnatural reluctance, as though the tunnel were lengthening almost as fast as we rushed along it . . . which it might very well be. Running along a tunnel you could never get to the end of, pursued by something or someone murderous—that *was* one of my recurring nightmares.

Shouts behind us. An instant later Karl tackled me, so that we slammed to the floor together. A deafening bang, a spray of rock from the ceiling . . . someone had fired at us. "Turn off your light!" Karl cried, suiting actions to words. "Roll!"

I didn't argue. Flicking off my flashlight, plunging us into darkness again—the gray light around the bend still an unknown and completely unreasonable distance in front of us—I rolled hard to the left, just in time, as another shot hit the floor where I'd been an instant earlier.

More shouts. I looked back. Lights bobbed on the helmets of six dark figures. I hoped they didn't have night-vision goggles, but even if they didn't, we were pinned down. If we stood up we'd silhouette ourselves against the light at the end of the tunnel. If we stayed where we were, they'd soon be even with us . . . or they'd just hose us down with bullets.

"What do we do?" I whispered to Karl.

He didn't say anything for a second. Then, "What is your worst nightmare?"

"You mean besides having people who want to kill me chasing me down a dark tunnel that never seems to get any shorter?"

"Yes," he said. "Besides that."

"Why?"

"Because I think you can Shape it into reality."

"I'm burned out. No Shaping ability. You know that."

"In *your* world. But this is not, or at least not entirely, your world, is it? It is partially yours, and partially someone else's. There is creative energy bound within it, holding it in place. You should be able to access that energy."

"But why would I use it to Shape a nightmare?"

"I think that's all you *can* Shape in here," Karl said. "Things that are buried in your subconscious, things that aren't real, the things that go bump in the night."

I looked back. The dark figures were at the edge of the pit I had fallen into. They'd soon find the ledge we had followed and come after us.

"My worst nightmare," I said, "is being buried alive."

"Make it theirs," Karl said softly.

I swallowed. The armed men . . . and at least two women, it looked like . . . had found the ledge. They were moving toward it.

I reached for my Shaping ability. To my surprise, I found it, but it felt . . . different. Tainted. Odd. Twisted. Uncomfortable.

I didn't want to bury anyone alive. I certainly didn't want to bury *us* alive. But if I could bring down the tunnel between us and them, buy us time, enough time to escape . . .

I imagined the ceiling of the section of tunnel we had just passed weakening, cracking, the weight of the rock suddenly too much to be supported. I *believed* it. But even as I did so, I felt something else mixed in with my belief, something that came from outside, something I didn't put there.

The ground shook. There was a series of earsplitting cracks. And then something massive and made of stone dropped from the ceiling . . .

. . . but it wasn't just a falling rock. It had a shape, a humanoid shape. It hit the floor with a grinding thud, and then roared with a voice like an avalanche thundering down a mountainside.

"What did you do?" Karl cried.

"I don't know," I shouted back above the cacophony. "I thought I was shaping a rock fall, not a . . ." I suddenly realized I knew *exactly* what the thing was. "Not a troll!"

"A troll?"

"I think so." Which had to have come from the Shaper of the next world. Just what kind of world *was* it?

We weren't buried alive and neither were our pursuers, but perhaps that was the next step: the troll reached up and tore pieces of rock from the ceiling as if they were chunks of bread from a fresh loaf and then hurled them down the tunnel. Away from us, for the moment, but I didn't believe for a second that the troll would spare us if it saw us. I had Shaped the stone, but someone else had Shaped whatever spirit animated it. It was, literally, a creature from someone *else*'s nightmare.

Still, it had the killers chasing us occupied, and so we took our chance and scrambled up and ran.

Maybe my Shaping gone wrong had accomplished one other thing: the tunnel suddenly seemed just an ordinary tunnel, no longer stretching interminably out in front of us. We reached the bend just as the troll roared again. I wondered if it had seen us, but only for a second, because all doubt was removed when a boulder half the size of the SUV we'd sunk in the quarry crashed into the floor at our heels, the shock knocking me to my knees. I stumbled up. The next one would crush us . . .

But no more boulders came our way. Weapons fired in the tunnel behind us, flashes of light silhouetting the monstrous form of the troll, which presumably therefore had other things to attend to.

The sound of falling water surrounded us now, and I saw that the gray light that had guided us along the tunnel streamed in through a waterfall, a liquid curtain across the cave mouth, thick enough to hide whatever lay beyond it. It might fall a thousand feet, and we would step through it to our deaths. Or something even worse might await us.

But we couldn't wait where we were. Behind us, the rifle fire stopped. The troll roared defiance.

And then, a second later, came the explosion.

Clearly the forces trailing us had more than small arms at their disposal: at a guess, they'd been carrying a rocket launcher. The shockwave from whatever they'd fired knocked me to my knees. The head of the troll, a crude approximation of a human's, slammed against the end of the tunnel, and rolled to within a foot of me. Blank, black obsidian eyes gleamed blindly up at my face.

Karl staggered, but remained standing. He pulled me upright. "Come on," he said, and plunged through the curtain of water.

We didn't fall to our deaths. Instead, we emerged into an amphitheater. The water flowed out of the rock fifty feet up a granite cliff and dropped smoothly into a narrow trench, draining away as fast as it entered. Around us rose ranks of benches, carved into the stone of what looked to be a natural bowl-shaped depression in the top of the mountain, so many rows of them that the topmost seats faded into the thick, dripping fog that still hung over everything.

At the center of the amphitheater's smooth granite floor stood a massive block of black stone, steps leading up to its top on two sides. On top of that pedestal stood . . . was that an altar? Also black, of course.

"This," I said, "makes no sense. No one lives on this nonexistent island. So who uses this place?"

"Think dreams and nightmares again," Karl said.

"This isn't my dream or my nightmare."

"Are you sure?" he said. "Do you remember all of them?"

That stopped me, because of course I didn't: no one remembers *all* of their dreams. I looked around uneasily. Had this . . . sacrificial stadium . . . come from some deeply buried part of my subconscious?

It was not a comfortable thought.

"Our friends may be joining us at any moment," Karl said then. Yet he did not move from where he stood. "Can you feel it? The thin place between the worlds, where I will open the Portal? Can you see it?"

"Where?"

"Up there." He pointed to the top of the stone block.

At first, all I saw above the altar was the cloudy sky, darkening now as twilight neared. But then something else registered . . . a kind of shimmer, like you see over a blacktop road on a hot summer's day, although there was nothing hot or summery about where we stood. As soon as I saw it, I didn't understand how I *hadn't* been able to see it a moment before . . . and I hated it; hated it, because that shimmer looked *wrong*. Not evil, like the altar, but . . . out of place.

Which I supposed it was, if it was a spot where elements of another world were leaking into mine. It really *was* out of place. Out of its own world.

And we were going to try to tear it wide open.

Or Karl was, at least. Only he could do it.

"We need to get right up to it," he said. "We have to move."

We started across the granite floor. As we got closer to the black block I saw that it had channels carved in its sides, running down from the top to rusty metal grates in the granite floor. I didn't think for a moment they were meant to convey water.

"If even half this stuff is coming from the next world over," I said as we approached that towering pedestal, our footsteps echoing back from the terraced stone benches, "are you *sure* we want to go there? This looks very tear-the-heart-out-of-a-human-sacrificey to me. What if it's a Mayan world, or a Conan the Barbarian one? Or someone with a Lovecraft fetish?"

"We have no choice," Karl said. "The worlds touch the worlds they touch."

I looked at that forbidding block of stone, looming above us now. If any inanimate object could look evil, it did. The stone wasn't just ordinary black stone, like that of the cliffs that had thwarted our first attempts to reach the island's interior: up close, they had been speckled with shining bits of other minerals. *This* rock was so black it seemed almost to glow, a kind of *negative* glow, as though it were actively sucking light from its surroundings. And I really, really *hoped* that it had come from someone else's subconscious, because if it was from mine . . .

I shot another look over my shoulder at the screen of water. "Do you think the tunnel was blocked behind us when the troll was destroyed?"

"Possibly," Karl said. "But there are multiple ways into this amphitheater."

I looked around. Off to our left, a pillared portico extended from an ornate archway. I could see bricks lining the tunnel inside. Would those central stairs have brought us to it if we had continued climbing them?

At the far end of the amphitheater were two plain-looking wooden doors, one toward the left, one toward the right, far too flimsy to pose much of an obstacle to our pursuers if they came that way.

"No matter what, we have little time," Karl said. He started up the steps.

Reluctantly, I followed. Even through the soles of my boots, the black stone seemed . . . unclean . . . as if it were covered with a thin layer of tar. "Why build an amphitheater if there are no people to sit in the seats and watch the . . . show?" I wondered out loud. The stadium seemed to grow larger as we climbed, as more seats materialized in the fog hiding the upper reaches.

"Perhaps something other than people comes to watch," Karl said.

"More monsters?"

He shrugged.

*If you build it, they will come*, I thought, and wished I hadn't.

We reached the top of the black block of stone. It seemed taller than it had from below, as if it had grown as we climbed: in fact, we now seemed to be almost level with the topmost seats in the amphitheater. *Like the tunnel*, I thought. *Like a nightmare*. For the first time, I saw that flags flew all around the stadium's rim, red flags, the color of clotted blood. The drop to the stone floor below was now terrifying in its own right.

That strange, disquieting shimmer hung in the air above the altar. It set my teeth on edge. "How do you do this?" I said. "How do you open a Portal between worlds?"

"I have told you," Karl said. "I have been given a . . . tool . . . which makes it possible."

"And only someone with that tool can do it?"

Karl hesitated. "I am not certain. It is possible Ygrair can open Portals solely through the force of her Shaping ability . . . or could, at the peak of her strength, before she was injured."

"Then is it something *I* can learn to do?"

"I do not yet know *what* you can learn to do," Karl said. "And unless you escape the Adversary, neither you nor I nor Ygrair will ever find out." He stepped forward, so that his thighs pressed against the altar. Roughly the size of a dining room table, the stone slab might have passed for one if not for the openings cut in its surface, which led to the gutters I had noted running down the block's side: those, and the exceedingly unappetizing carvings around the slab's base. I didn't examine them in detail, but they seemed closely related to the monstrous statues we had seen in the tunnel.

Karl reached out into the air, into that shimmer. As his hand entered it, it grew indistinct—ghostly. He closed his eyes, and cocked his head to one side, concentrating: then he moved his hand up, as high as he could reach, over to the right a few inches, down, left, down, then up again, repeating the pattern over and over, faster each time.

And as he did so, the shimmer strengthened, and began to glow—not some kind of mystical glow, but the glow of sunlight, bright sunlight, streaming out of midair into the gray fog of my world. At first that light poured through a tiny opening, maybe the size of a teacup, but with each pass of Karl's hand, the opening grew. To the size of notebook. The size of a microwave. And, eventually . . . the size of a door.

I could see through it, as though I was looking through a pane of rippled glass. Blue above, green below. No details, like an Impressionist painting. No sound. "Is it open?" I breathed.

"No," Karl said. He pulled his hand back, stared at it. "Something is keeping it from opening all the way. It's as though . . ." He blinked, looked down at the altar, then looked up again. "Oh," he said.

"Oh?"

"I think—"

But what he thought he didn't say, because at that moment four black-clad armed figures burst through the wall of water onto the granite floor of the amphitheater, far below us.

Except suddenly they *weren't* far below. As they came into sight, perspectives altered. The black block of stone on which we stood suddenly seemed to shrink, back to the same size it had appeared when I first saw it. The stone benches of the amphitheater rose high all around us, once more vanishing into the mist, which hid the flags I had seen seconds below.

And every seat in the amphitheater was filled.

## TWENTY-SIX

SHADOWY, INDISTINCT SHAPES now occupied the terraced ranks of stone benches. I thought I could make out heads and faces and arms and legs, but the spectators' forms kept changing. One moment they looked like a modern-day lacrosse crowd, the next like ancient Romans in togas, the next like Victorian ladies and gentlemen. They roared their approval as our pursuers advanced cautiously across the floor of the amphitheater.

I froze, expecting them to see us and open fire on us. There was nowhere to take shelter, nowhere to run . . .

But the four black-clad figures, all members of the Adversary's cadre, I was certain, spread out across the granite floor as though oblivious to our presence atop the stone block, blind to the light pouring through the Portal from the next world, and unable to see the shadowy watchers in the stone seats.

"What's going on?" I said to Karl, whispering in case they could hear us, even though they apparently couldn't see us.

"I'm not sure," Karl said.

"Can we go through the Portal?"

"No. It is not fully open."

"So how do we open it?"

"Something else I am not sure about," Karl said. "I have not encountered a situation like this before."

*Well, that's just great*, I thought. *So much for my omniscient guide to the multiverse.* "They don't seem to be able to see us."

"Apparently not."

"But why?"

"I have no idea."

The screen of falling water suddenly stopped, and a metal portcullis clanked and rattled into place where it had been, sealing off the tunnel through which we and our pursuers had come. A moment later similar iron gates closed off every other exit from the amphitheater.

Our pursuers spun around, weapons raised, but there was nothing to shoot at. Except us, but, fortunately, we still seemed to be invisible to them. Nor did they seem aware of the strange observers in the amphitheater's seats, who at the moment looked like extras from a zombie movie.

A voice spoke out of midair, a heavy, booming, male voice, like Darth Vader with the bass cranked up to eleven. "You have come to the Place Between. Blood must spill."

The fighters below heard *that*. They looked around, weapons swinging. "Who's speaking?" shouted one of the men. He was huge, broad-shouldered, black-skinned, and easily six and a half feet tall. In fact, his voice boomed almost as deep and loud as that of the hidden announcer.

"Blood must spill," Darth Vader on steroids repeated. "You are the leader. You must fight."

"Fight *who*?" the man shouted, but suddenly he wasn't standing where he was. He was standing on the other side of us, and he was naked. His three companions rushed to him, but came up comically short, bouncing off of what was clearly a barrier of some kind, though there was nothing to be seen.

"Choose your champion," the voice said, but now it was softer, closer, as though the owner of the voice stood on the platform with us and was speaking just loud enough for the two of us to hear.

"We have to fight *that* guy?" I was staring down at the man who had spoken. Even unclothed, maybe *especially* unclothed, which showed off his muscles (and other attributes) to great effect, he looked like he could break the back of either of us like a twig. "Naked?" (I'm not ashamed to admit my voice squeaked a little on that last word.)

"They are limited to their own devices," Karl said. "We are not."

I stared at him. "What does that mean?"

"Remember the troll."

"*I* didn't form that thing," I said. "I was just trying to collapse the tunnel."

"The effect was the same," Karl said. "Try. Shape something to defeat him, using the power this island has provided you."

I looked down at the naked giant, who was feeling out the dimensions of the mysterious barrier. It seemed to be about fifteen yards on a side. The guy was seriously built, and I was reminded again of Michelangelo's *David* . . .

And suddenly, there he was. Michelangelo's *David*, in all his nude white marble glory, but animated and alive. He stood almost three times as tall as the man, who stared up at the statue in sudden slack-jawed astonishment.

David bent over and smashed him to the granite floor, like someone slamming his fist down on an overripe watermelon, with much the same squirting, splattering effect.

The moving statue vanished again in the next instant, but the mess of shattered bone and pulped organs on the smooth stone remained. The crowd roared approval. They seemed more solid than a moment before, and even more ghoulish.

My gorge rose. I swallowed hard to keep from throwing up. "I didn't mean . . ."

"'Blood must spill,'" Karl shouted, not to me, but to the air. "Our champion is victorious. Open the way!"

"Your champion has earned you the *right* to open the path

between the worlds," the voice said. "But blood spilled below counts for naught. Blood must spill *on the altar.* Make the sacrifice, or the way will be barred forever."

"I don't understand," I said, still feeling sick. One of the man's comrades, the only woman, was kneeling beside his broken body, weeping. The two remaining men stood guard, their eyes flicking around the amphitheater, but never looking up at us. "Who's talking? Who made these rules?"

"I have never seen anything like this." Karl sounded grim. "But I think . . . I think this island, Shaped subconsciously both by you and by the Shaper of the world on the other side of this Portal, has developed its own reality. The figures in the stands, and the man who speaks to us, are its residents. Ghosts would be as good a word as any, or spirits: insubstantial, but powerful within their own realm." He turned to look at the Portal, the sunlight from the next world lighting his face. "Powerful enough to keep this Portal closed to me unless we meet their arbitrary rules."

"Blood must spill . . . on the altar, he means."

He nodded.

"*Human* blood?"

He nodded again. Then he pulled out his knife, and before I could say anything else, sliced his palm open with a single swipe. Grimacing, he held his hand out over the altar. Blood dripped from the wound onto the black stone.

I stared at the Portal. It didn't change. The world beyond remained blurred and indistinct.

"Blood cannot be freely given," the voice said. It sounded . . . amused. "It must be taken."

I gulped. Then I held out my hand. "If you cut me—"

"Blood cannot be freely given," the voice repeated.

"Clearly that will not work, either," Karl said. "You cannot volunteer your blood." He clenched his hand, scarlet seeping between his fingers. He looked down at the fighters below. "It will have to be one of them."

"If we go down there, they'll kill us."

"I do not believe they will kill me," Karl said.

"What?" I stared at him. "How can you be sure?"

"I am not sure," he said. "I said I do not *believe* they will kill me. That belief could be in error. But I think it highly unlikely. The Adversary cannot open a Portal. He wants to capture me. He needs the tool, the technology I carry within me. He will have issued commands to his cadre accordingly." He stared down at the fighters again. "Stay where you are. Once they see me, they will follow me. I will lead them up here. And then . . . blood must spill."

I swallowed. "You want me to . . ."

"No, *I* will do what must be done. You stand ready to pass through the Portal." He put a hand on the altar. "Climb up here."

"Uh . . . all right. Be careful."

He gave me what I think is usually called a withering look, then started down the steps.

Following orders, I climbed up onto the altar. As I did so, I inadvertently put my hand in Karl's blood, thickly splattered across the black table. I felt a jolt, as though I'd touched a live wire, and then a burning sensation. I hurriedly wiped my hand on my jeans, but my gore-stained fingers still tingled strangely as I reached out tentatively toward that astonishing doorway in the air.

An invisible barrier stopped me. It felt like . . . vibrating glass. My fingers tingled even more as I pulled them back, and I wiped them again, to no avail.

I turned my back to the Portal, and peered down. Karl had just stepped onto the amphitheater's polished granite floor, out of sight of the three remaining fighters on the other side of the stone block.

Only three. There had been six in the hallway where the troll had appeared; I suspected there'd been more than that when they'd first entered the cavern. I wondered what had happened to the others. Nothing good, I was willing to bet, though not quite willing to hope. I didn't wish death on any of them; I regretted the death of the man below. I just wished to avoid my own.

Karl rounded the corner of the stone block. "Are you looking for me?" he called. Three heads jerked around, three rifles came up, and then the remaining fighters exploded into motion, one man running toward him, one man running the other way, presumably to stop Karl should he try to dash around to the other side of the block. The woman who had been kneeling by their dead companion stayed where she was, but on her feet now, weapon ready, her gaze and aim flicking around the arena, alert for any new threats. At one point she looked up, but she still didn't seem to see me or the incipient Portal.

A good thing: she probably would have shot me.

Karl came pounding back up the steps toward me. The man who had run straight toward him started up after him. The second man, rounding the corner of the stone block, skidded to a halt. He looked around in bewilderment, but even though he stared up at the block, he was clearly unable to see the rest of us.

Karl leaped up the last two steps onto the top of the block, then turned to face his pursuer, but the man had caught up and charged into him. Karl fell backward and slammed to the stone, and I suddenly saw the weakness in our plan.

Karl was tough and tall and wiry, but the man who had chased him up the steps, though not as big as the naked behemoth David had crushed, was tougher, and taller, and must have outweighed him by forty pounds. He held Karl in place by the simple expedient of sitting on him, rifle pressed hard against Karl's chest with both hands. "Where is she?" the man shouted. And then he blinked, as though he had just registered the sunshine from the next world illuminating Karl.

He looked up . . .

. . . and, finally, saw me.

He lifted and shifted his grip on the rifle in an instant. The barrel swung toward me, but Karl, his arms now free, straight-armed the weapon. It flew up and out of the man's grasp, hit the edge of the stone block, and plunged out of sight.

The man backhanded Karl across the face, then jumped up and kicked him in the ribs, sending Karl rolling toward the edge. But he didn't follow up the attack: instead, he jerked a knife from his belt, spun toward me, and leaped up onto the altar beside me. I tried to shove him off, but he ducked under my arms and came up, knife in hand, to drive it into my—

From behind, Karl grabbed his ankles and pulled.

The man slammed belly-down onto the altar and released the knife, which skittered away across the black stone table. Karl scrambled up onto the altar as my assailant, half-winded, got to his hands and knees. Both reached for the knife. Both had it. They struggled. "Stay where you are! Be ready!" Karl shouted at me.

Somehow, the fighter heaved his body upright, dragging Karl with him. Both on their feet, they faced each other, locked in an intimate embrace. Karl had the knife, but his opponent had his wrist. He squeezed. Karl's hand opened.

Ignoring Karl's orders, I threw myself forward, grabbed the knife as it hit the top of the altar, raised it—and drove it with all my strength into the top of the fighter's booted foot. He yelled in mingled pain and fury, and as blood from the wound poured onto the altar, kicked me hard in the side, the knife dislodging and vanishing from my sight as he did so.

My breath whooshed out. I felt myself lifting, flying backward. The air seemed to thicken around me, buzzing like a swarm of bees. My skin vibrated. Inside my head, I felt something tear loose, as though a deeply embedded gland had been excised with one brutal slash of a scalpel.

For an instant, I seemed to be in two places. Hot sunshine warmed my skin at the same time as cold fog chilled it. A crowd roared, while birds sang. A man shouted, while wind sighed quietly through leaves.

My world, the world I had Shaped, the world I'd once thought was the only world there was, faded from my senses. The last I saw of it was Karl rolling away from me, falling from the altar onto the stone block. The man I had stabbed reached for me . . . but his fingers bounced off of empty air, off the same barrier that had stopped my hand earlier.

*One sacrifice per customer*, I thought.

And then the Portal, and my world, vanished.

I lay flat on my back on green grass, my side hurting where I'd been kicked, my right hand still tingling from touching Karl's blood on the altar, staring up at a blue sky studded with fluffy white clouds. Air, warm and sweet and still, enveloped me. The birds had fallen silent, but slowly their song resumed, liquid, trilling.

I was in a new world.

I was hurting.

And I was alone.

# TWENTY-SEVEN

**KARL CAUGHT HIMSELF** at the edge of the stone, just before he would have plummeted to a neck-breaking impact on the granite far below . . . exactly how far below, it was hard to tell, with the variable size of everything in this strange realm. He felt the Portal close: not just close, but disappear, taking even the possibility of its existence with it.

Shawna Keys had left her world without him. She would be trapped in the next world, alone, unprepared for what she might find there, until he could join her—and to do that, he would have to travel again, an unknown distance, to wherever the two worlds were touching now that this connection had been broken.

He felt a tremor in the stone. He thought he knew what it meant, and knew he had little time.

The knife Shawna had stabbed into his attacker's foot had fallen from the altar when the man kicked her. Karl rolled over and, on his hands and knees, scurried for it, seized it. The wounded fighter, befuddled and infuriated by the loss of his prey through the now-vanished Portal, turned and saw him moving, roared, and jumped down—but his wounded foot gave way, throwing him off balance, and in that moment, Karl drove the knife into the man's stomach and pulled it upward, ripping him open. Guts and gore poured from the wound, and the fighter fell backward, and off the block of stone, hitting the floor a moment later with a wet, crunching thud.

The stone block shuddered again. Karl, covered in blood, his ears ringing and side aching from his attacker's earlier blows, crawled to the edge and looked down. His two remaining adversaries stood staring down at the body of their fellow: just as well, since, with blood spilled on the altar and the Portal gone, he doubted he was still invisible to them.

An instant later their attention was seized by the sudden appearance, out of thin air, of the Adversary. Karl gasped, and rolled to the base of the altar, out of sight of the floor below.

The Adversary, 30,000 feet in the air aboard a military transport, felt the Portal open . . . and felt the moment when Shawna Keys passed out of her world. He sucked in a deep, shuddering breath as at last the *hokhmah* of her world became solely his, and an enormous surge of power flooded into him, going some way—though not nearly far enough—toward replacing what he had lost with the destruction of the Portal leading back to the Shakespearean world he had stolen, and to his own Shaped world beyond.

Then he gathered his wits and his new power, and completed his journey to the Portal in an instant: under most circumstances a waste of Shaping energy which, even now, was not unlimited, but in this case, he thought, warranted.

He stood in an amphitheater, empty and crumbling, its granite floor worn and chipped, its stone seats losing form, beginning to slump into rubble. At the center of the arena stood a massive block of black stone: what purpose it served, he could not tell.

Two members of his cadre, man and woman, stood beside the crumpled remains of another. Farther back, a smear of blood and bone and skin and internal organs must be all that remained of a fourth. Only these two, and the two he had left aboard the transport, remained of the twelve loyal, trained fighters who had accompanied him from his home world, empowered by the links he had forged to each of them through his Shaping power and the nanomites within his blood to survive, alone among all Shaped beings, the transition to worlds not their own. He would have to take the time to prepare more, in this world, before he went to the next . . .

If he could get there. This was where the Portal had opened, but it wasn't open now. Nor was it simply closed, like the ones he had reopened after Karl Yatsar had sealed them behind himself. Like the one through which he had entered this world, the Portal that had opened here was not just closed, but gone. Vanished as though it had never been.

Along with Shawna Keys. And Karl Yatsar . . . ?

He strode to the two remaining cadre members. The granite beneath his feet felt very odd, quaking and somehow porous, as if it were metamorphosing into volcanic tuff. "Report."

Tersely and efficiently, the remaining man did so. The eight members of his cadre had landed with two Marines and followed Yatsar and Keys into a cave. They had lost a Marine when they were attacked by a giant furred monster with wolflike characteristics. With two possible routes to follow, they had split, six cadre members taking one path, the remaining Marine and two cadre taking the other. The six had seen and fired at Shawna and Yatsar, but had then been attacked by a humanoid made of stone. Two more cadre members had been killed before they destroyed the creature with a shoulder-mounted rocket launcher one of the dead had been carrying. The remaining four members of the cadre had entered the amphitheater. The three who had taken the alternate route had never appeared.

He heard about the voice, the sudden appearance and disappearance of a giant white statue, and the death of Captain Arneson, crushed to the floor of the arena. He heard how Karl Yatsar had appeared at the base of the block of stone, and how he had been pursued by the second man who lay dead, both of them vanishing from the others' sight. And he heard how, somehow, bright sunlight had flashed out over the amphitheater for a moment, though the fog had never lifted—and then of the fall of the second dead man from the block of stone.

The Adversary looked up. He could not see the top of the block. "Climb up there," he ordered. "See if anyone is hiding on top."

But even as he ordered it, the island shook again, and with a sound like a thunderclap, a crack ripped across the arena floor. The Adversary and his cadre members staggered. The stone block began to sink into the ground with a grinding noise. The arena floor, now two separate plates of stone, tipped toward it. In a moment both the Adversary and his followers would slide helplessly into the abyss he could see opening.

He reached out with his Shaping power to stop whatever was happening, but the power rebounded. Somehow, this island was not something he could Shape: he had no connection to it, though he had seized the *hokhmah* of the rest of this world. He did not know how that could be, but it left him with no choice.

As suddenly as he had arrived, he departed, taking his followers with him.

Karl clung to the crumbling block of black stone. Behind him, the altar split in two with a sound like a rifle shot, and then shattered into shards and dust. Below him, the Adversary vanished, along with his two followers. Unless Karl missed his guess, the entire island would soon follow.

He had to get off of it.

A worthy and necessary goal. How he could achieve it, however, remained unclear. *Amazon*, the boat on which they had arrived, had, the last time he saw her, been aground on a rock . . .

*Hmm.* That rock was part of this island, which clearly was rapidly losing its independent existence, now that the place where the worlds touched had relocated, and one of the Shapers whose subconscious had created it had left this world entirely. Which might . . . just *might* . . . mean that *Amazon*, if not too badly damaged, would come afloat once that rock vanished.

A thin strand of hope to cling to, perhaps, but the only one at hand.

As the black stone block sank lower, it tilted. In a moment Karl would fall.

Instead, he jumped.

He landed with a bone-jarring thud on the tilting granite, an impact that surely would have broken bones if not for the fact that the "granite" was now so soft his feet and knees left divots in it as he hit it and toppled forward. He scrabbled up the slope before the incline grew so great it would send him sliding into the seething, grinding maelstrom of earth and dirt into which the entire island seemed to be devolving, collapsing from this pinnacle down to the sea. A ring of flat flooring still existed just beneath the cracking walls of the amphitheater. He paused there, panting, to take stock and to strip off the useless and heavy leather jacket.

The iron gratings sealing the exits from the amphitheater had melted away, along with all the doors. The openings remained, though, including the one that had been sheltered by a pillared portico, the one he'd assumed led to the stairs they had not climbed, which should be the most direct route to the beach. He ran for it. The remaining bit of floor disintegrated beneath him as he leaped into the brick-lined tunnel. The stairs stretched down before him into darkness, but he still had his flashlight. He flicked it on and dashed down.

The stone of the stairs became softer and softer beneath his feet, until he was leaving footprints in it. The evil statues decorating each landing now looked like unformed clay from Shawna's pottery workshop. He ran faster, risking a broken leg or worse, as a thunderous rumbling behind him spoke of collapsing ceilings and walls.

One landing was smeared with blood and bone, strings of intestine, and dark-red lumps of tissue, scraps of cloth and leather and chunks of twisted metal scattered in the gore. All, presumably, that remained of the missing members of the group that had come in pursuit of them. He could not imagine what had so . . . enthusiastically . . . destroyed them, but was more than pleased that with the island's dissolution it was not waiting for him, too.

He reached the landing where he and Shawna had taken the door through which they had heard scratching. The door no longer existed, and the corridor beyond it had collapsed. He ran on. Somewhere ahead, the stairs ended, and he would have to pick his way down the raw stone face of the natural cavern . . . if it had not collapsed already.

But when he reached the end of the steps, he saw light to his right, a rift in the mountain slope that had not been there before. Rather than plunge farther down into darkness, he turned and clambered up the gentle slope to that opening. As he hauled himself out into the open air, a rumble behind him spoke to the wisdom of that decision. He clung to the ground as it shook, and then, with a great heave, like a bedspread flicked by some celestial giant, the entire mountain burst outward. Karl felt himself flung up, and out, and waited for the killing impact against the stones below, or the stones all around him, but suddenly there *were* no stones below or surrounding him, nothing but wisps of gray dust, vanishing even as he fell.

He plunged deep into seawater, black as soot, but softer than rock, and fought his way to the surface. Immediately he struck out, fearing a vast undertow as the island subsided, but instead, the water smoothed, the black muck within it vanished, and within seconds, he found himself swimming in the open ocean, as calm and unsullied as though the island had never existed . . . which, in a fashion, might well have been the case.

He trod water, and looked around. A white speck perhaps half a mile away beckoned. He could swim that far.

He *had* to swim that far.

His clothes dragged at him, but he had always been a strong swimmer, and he had had occasion to practice the skill more than once in the worlds through which he had journeyed in his service to Ygrair. A little more than half an hour, he judged, from when he set out, he reached the white speck: *Amazon*, listing and low in the water, but not beneath it. He hauled himself aboard and lay for a long moment panting, staring up at the blue sky. His hand stung: he lifted it, and saw the gash across the palm he had inflicted on himself in his first attempt to open the Portal, still oozing blood. Then he rolled over, pulled himself upright, and began assessing *Amazon*'s condition.

Twenty minutes later he knew: it wasn't good, and if he ran into more bad weather, he might not survive, but he could salvage her. What had seemed a killing gash in her hull was not as bad as it had seemed. While he could not stop it from leaking, he was able to slow the intake of water using the tools, waterproof glue, and fiberglass sheeting he found in one of *Amazon*'s lockers. He silently thanked the absent Julia for her care in stocking her precious vessel. He wondered what had happened to her.

*Amazon*'s rigging remained intact, her mast upright. Her pumps still worked. How long her batteries would continue to provide power he did not know, but there were strange panels on her deck that he believed made electricity from the sun—he had seen such things in other worlds—and a mechanism beneath her hull (discovered as he swam beneath her as part of his inspection) which, he believed, must generate electricity from the flow of water. With luck, there would be power enough to keep ahead of the leak.

He could not sail her across the Pacific. The best he could do was to sail back to the mainland. Then he could begin the long journey to where he could make a Portal . . . for he could already feel that the connection now lay east and south of his present location. He desperately needed to get to Shawna, but it would be days or weeks before he could join her, assuming she still lived.

And if she did not . . . ? He did not like to consider it, but he already knew, from the existence of the strange island, that the next world's Shaper was also remarkably powerful. If Shawna Keys were lost to him, perhaps that Shaper—who, at least, *would* surely remember Ygrair, and the training she had provided—would be strong enough to do what must be done . . . even, perhaps, strong enough to destroy the new Portal he would create before the Adversary could come through. The Adversary had taken *this* world, but if Karl could ensure he went no farther into the Labyrinth, he was more than welcome to it.

Karl lived. Therefore the quest lived. As he had through all the long decades since he had met her, as he would to his last breath, he would serve Ygrair, in the certain hope of the reward she had promised him.

With stars blazing above him, Karl Yatsar sailed into the night.

The Adversary stood beneath those same stars on the deck of the USS *Bonhomme Richard*. No one had returned from the island except for him and the man and woman of his cadre whom he had spirited away as it collapsed. Shawna had escaped from the world . . . but Karl Yatsar had not. He still lived within it, somewhere. The Shurak nanomites within the Adversary's blood knew it, and therefore, so did he.

He did not understand why the Portal had vanished after Shawna passed through it. He did not know how Yatsar had escaped the island. But no matter. Yatsar had to go after Shawna, which meant he would have to open a new Portal. With the disappearance of the strange island, the location where this world and the next intersected had no doubt shifted. Yatsar would have to travel to wherever that interface now existed. The Adversary would try to capture him before he got there, of course, but even if Yatsar succeeded in opening a new Portal, he could not keep the Adversary from following him unless he could find the Shaper of the world into which it opened and convince that Shaper to help him destroy the Portal, as he had enlisted Shawna to destroy the Portal from the last world . . . and even then, only if the new Shaper were as powerful as Shawna, which seemed unlikely.

In any event, he would not have enough time. With full control of this world now his, the Adversary would know the moment the new Portal opened. He would enter the new world hard on Yatsar's heels, capture him, and claim the nanomites within Yatsar's body for his own. Then *he* would be able to open Portals at will, and the Labyrinth would fall, world by world, until the Adversary faced and defeated Ygrair, finally meting out to her the punishment she so richly deserved for her blasphemous actions of so long ago.

The Adversary could have Shaped himself back to the Emerald Palace, instead of lingering on the *Bonhomme Richard*, but it seemed a waste of energy. In the morning, he would have himself flown back to the mainland, and there begin Shaping this world in earnest, into a copy of his own, a human version of the orderly Shurak utopia. He would reconstitute his cadre, if he had time before Yatsar opened a new Portal. However many cadre members he had when that Portal opened, he would take them with him into the next world.

Of course, he would continue to bend all of this world's available resources to the capture of Yatsar, but even if Yatsar could not be apprehended, his quixotic quest was ultimately doomed to failure: if not in this world, then in the next . . . or the next.

The Adversary looked up at the blazing stars. In this world, he knew, they were mere lights, a painted backdrop; but in Reality, one of them lit his home world. He wondered which one it was, and if he would ever return to it.

Then he turned and went belowdecks.

I sat up, wincing, pressed my hand to my bruised flank, took a somewhat painful breath, and stared around.

I was still on an island, but rather than cold gray mist and rising ranks of stone seats surrounding me, I saw green and gently waving grass sloping down to a dark pine forest, over whose crowns I saw the blue and sparkling sea. I looked over my shoulder, and there saw more pines, climbing up steep slopes to an upthrust fang of bare white stone.

A stone's throw to my left, a stream gurgled along a reedy streambed. Bobbing on a tall cattail in the cool breeze, a bird sang a trilling waterfall of melody.

I stared around. Apart from the bird, I seemed completely alone. "Karl?" I called.

My voice seemed to travel no distance at all. But it caused the birdsong to pause, and in that pause, two things happened: the island shook, the ground heaving like a seasick sailor—and I heard a strange sound behind me, a throbbing, thrumming sound, like and yet unlike the helicopters whose thunder I'd come to hate so much.

I looked around again, then scrambled to my feet as the white peak suddenly shattered, rock showering down from all sides into the forest as the thunder of its destruction reached me. Swinging around that crumbling peak came the largest flying machine I had ever seen, an airborne improbability that looked like a ship's hull held aloft by a veritable forest of masts, each topped by two whirling rotors. Two propellers, fore and aft, drove the impossible monstrosity through the air.

The ground again heaved beneath me. Trees writhed and toppled in the forest. The bird vanished in mid-trill, like a popping soap bubble. The stream stopped gurgling, the water audibly slurped down into the ground, which suddenly felt spongy beneath my feet.

The flying machine descended toward me, the thunder of its propellers shaking the air. Rope ladders appeared over the side, and figures began to descend them.

The grass withered away, leaving bare dirt, now so soft I began to sink into it. I reached desperately up toward the flying machine as it hovered above me, the wash of its rotors tearing at my clothes.

The hillside had become quicksand. I was up to my knees, up to my waist, up to my . . .

The nearest descending figure, a man in an old-fashioned sailor's uniform, was suddenly right above me, one hand gripping a rope rung, the other reaching down. He clasped my wrist and pulled me up onto the bottom of the ladder as, with a roar, the island simply fell away beneath me, collapsing into the sea, turning to dust as it fell, vanishing entirely before it hit the water.

As I was lifted up and up from the suddenly empty ocean below, for the first time I saw the giant flag in the bow of the flying machine, flapping furiously in the wash of the giant rotors: a standard black as pitch, bearing a golden sun.

I recognized it.

*Toto*, my mind whispered, *I've a feeling we're not in Kansas anymore.*